Praise for Lia Matera and
STAR WITNESS

"Lia Matera writes brilliantly."

—Cleveland *Plain Dealer*

"Matera offers a fast-paced narrative stuffed with incident and characters. . . . Informative and funny. . . ."

—*Library Journal*

"Santa Cruz writer Lia Matera has proved more than once that she is the master when it comes to dabbling in Northern California flakiness for her mystery plots. . . . She cleverly walks the line here between milking the material for humor and taking it . . . seriously. She teases. . . . Mystery fans . . . can't fail to be entertained. . . ."

—*San Jose Mercury News* (CA)

"I'm in love with Willa!"

—John Leonard of *Fresh Air*

"Say this for Willa Jansson: She doesn't shrink from the big cases."

—*Kirkus Reviews*

LAST CHANTS

Featuring super-sleuth Willa Jansson

"It's a treat to watch the normally levelheaded Willa crawling around in the woods, searching for naked gods."
—Marilyn Stasio, *The New York Times Book Review*

"The real pleasure is Willa, who alternates between humor and annoyance at her predicament—and whose love-hate relationship with men strikes a chord with many female fans."

—*Entertainment Weekly*

"Learning to tell the difference between the evil killers and the good weirdos is half the fun of this . . . enchanted mystery."

—Patricia Holt, *San Francisco Chronicle*

"Readers will find *Last Chants* an unexpected gift that will stay with them a long time after they finish reading it."
—Harriet Klausner, *Ed's Internet Book Review*

"An intriguing plot, well developed with interesting characters in a picturesque location. *Last Chants* rewards a read."
—Judith Kreiner, *Washington Times*

"Fortunately, Willa is back in fine form in her fifth adventure. . . . Matera has produced a first-rate mystery, exhibiting her usual hallmarks of excellent plotting, solid characterizations, and brisk pacing. A sure thing for fans and a great way to introduce new readers to an outstanding mystery series."

—*Booklist*

"Few writers possess Lia Matera's wry humor, especially when it comes to putting down lawyers. . . ."
—*San Jose Mercury News* (CA)

And Praise for Lia Matera and
DESIGNER CRIMES
Featuring detective Laura Di Palma

"Tantalizing . . . sizzling. . . . Designer crimes—now there is an idea that could power a series on its own."

—Pat Dowell, *The Washington Post*

"Di Palma is one of the smartest, most open-minded sleuths in the lawyering trade. . . . [Matera] writes with intelligence and feelings about issues that still hurt and people who still care."

—Marilyn Stasio, *The New York Times Book Review*

"This is a winner."

—Patricia Holt, *San Francisco Chronicle*

"Resonant with dark and cynical undertones, this novel also shines with a fresh plot premise, strong action scenes, and entirely credible characters."

—Mary C. Trone, Minneapolis *Star Tribune*

"Two knotty cases, some fine detection, a satisfying explosion when Laura puts all the pieces together, and an unusually honest meditation on going home again. Laura's fifth appearance may be her best one yet."

—*Kirkus Reviews*

"Matera's skill and literary flair are everywhere on display. . . . Every word counts, and the pieces of the puzzle fit together with exhilarating precision. Not until the last five pages does the entire picture come together in a final undulation that seems both inevitable and perfectly unexpected."

—Paul Reidinger, *ABA Journal*

"With this fifth installment in the Di Palma series, Matera once again demonstrates her mastery of characterization, plotting, and pacing. . . . Matera is too good to miss."

—*Booklist*

Books by Lia Matera

Star Witness*
Last Chants*
Designer Crimes
Face Value
A Hard Bargain
Prior Convictions*
The Good Fight
Hidden Agenda*
The Smart Money
A Radical Departure*
Where Lawyers Fear to Tread*

A Willa Jansson Mystery

LIA MATERA

STAR WITNESS

POCKET **STAR** BOOKS
New York   London   Toronto   Sydney   Tokyo   Singapore

This book is a work of fiction. Names, characters, places and incidents
are products of the author's imagination or are used fictiously. Any
resemblance to actual events or locales or persons, living or dead, is
entirely coincidental.

 A Pocket Star Book published by
POCKET BOOKS, a division of Simon & Schuster Inc.
1230 Avenue of the Americas, New York, NY 10020

Copyright © 1997 By Lia Matera

Originally published in hardcover in 1997 by Simon & Schuster Inc.

ISBN: 0-671-00420-4

First Pocket Books printing June 1998

10 9 8 7 6 5 4 3 2 1

POCKET STAR BOOKS and colophon are registered
trademarks of Simon & Schuster Inc.

Cover art by Alexa Garbarino

Printed in the U.S.A.

foreword

Much of *Star Witness* is set in Davenport, California, which is a real town. But there is no San Vittorio Road there, and as far as I know, no strange sightings have been reported. Santa Cruz, California, is real, too, though no description could quite do justice to this flaky, funky, gorgeous place. I've included various of its buildings and landmarks in my story, but no characters are modeled after actual residents. No locals were harmed in the writing of this book.

In particular, my descriptions of the District Attorney's Office and its lawyers, and the Sheriff's Department and its deputies, are fictitious. Anyone coming to Santa Cruz for fun might recognize the town from my book, but anyone getting arrested here will be on unfamiliar turf.

Speaking of unfamiliar turf, I did not invent the UFO theories discussed in *Star Witness*. I concocted the UFO-logists but not their positions or assertions. Whether one "believes in" UFOs or not, the sheer number of reported sightings and abductions makes alien contact our fastest-growing oral tradition. In and of itself, that's a fascinating comment on life on Earth.

For interested readers, I have included a bibliography and video list at the end of the book. More material is available in my Web site, http://www.scruz.net/~lmatera/liamatera.html.

Foreword

Many of us are natural skeptics, and skeptics often conclude in advance that UFO evidence is faked. But take a look before writing it all off. Skepticism should be at least as much trouble as gullibility.

To Anna Matera,
Lillian Rehon, and Pete Rehon, Sr.,
with love and thanks

It's the cursor of God's reality processor. When you see the blinking light in the sky, it means there's about to be a text insertion or deletion.

TERENCE MCKENNA

prologue

The ambulance slammed to a stop, lights swirling and siren blaring. Up ahead, backlit by searchlights, two cars were stacked like blocks. The top one, a small sports car, had flattened the roof of the big American car beneath. Both windshields had burst into hundreds of beads of safety glass, littering the lonely stretch of coastal highway.

Paramedic John Bivens glanced at his partner and said, "Wow!" Then he jumped out of the unit, hurrying toward waiting firemen.

Between the ambulance and the lime green engine of Davenport Fire & Rescue, damp road and chrome reflected strobing red and blue lights. Broken glass glinted like strewn gems.

Amped on adrenaline, his steel-shanked boots crunching over glass, John realized he'd have hated to miss this call. He'd have been jealous of any medic who got it instead of him, though he hadn't thought so when the radio jolted him out of a sound sleep at two-thirty in the morning.

He approached the two cars as Fire gave him a quick report: "We can see the guy inside the bottom car breathing, so we know he's alive. We can't get a response out of him —hasn't opened his eyes or moved or said anything. We're thinking if we cut away the back door and part of his seat, we can maybe get him out that way."

The top car, a Fiat, was wedged into the old Buick, its front end torpedoed into the passenger compartment so that the grille rested on the Buick's dash. The Buick's roof was squashed beneath it, with the rear bumpers piggybacked. The Buick's lights were off and the Fiat's were a mere flicker.

"Highway Patrol called it in," Fire continued. "But he didn't see it happen, so we don't know how long ago. He's off looking for the owner of the Fiat."

John's partner, Barry, was standing beside him now. "The Fiat must have come off there." Barry pointed up an embankment only fifteen or twenty feet steep. This part of Highway 1 was bracketed with low cliffs.

Just south of Davenport, about ten miles north of Santa Cruz, the road was cut like a channel through a hillside of farmland sloping toward the Pacific. Tonight the waves crashed loudly and the fog smelled of sea salt and cold kelp.

A siren could be heard—sheriff, most likely, maybe Highway Patrol returning. John pulled out his flashlight. A firefighter was shining a light under the back bumper of the top car, probably assessing its stability.

John crouched, aiming his light through the slit formed by the crushed frame of the driver's window. A few beads of safety glass still clung to it. The driver's torso, bleeding profusely, was visible. The seat had collapsed on impact and the driver was pinned almost supine. That was good. He'd never have survived being crushed upright.

John shifted the light, trying to get a look at the driver's head. He told Barry, "Head's cracked open; I think I see brain matter. But he's foaming, definitely breathing; he's still alive. We'll have to get him to a trauma center. We're going to need a helicopter."

John walked around the cars while Barry got on the radio and ordered helicopter transport. He quickly realized Fire was right. To get to the driver, John would have to wait for the back door to be cut away.

A highway patrolman approached, saying, "There's almost no traffic. We can make a landing zone for the helicopter right up the road. If you think this guy's going to make it."

"Yeah, good, the closer the better. Tell the 'copter to watch out for those power lines. You've got the highway blocked off?"

"Yes," a fireman told him.

"Any chance this thing's going to catch fire?"

"We've got flame retardant under the lower car."

For the first time, John noticed a thick sprinkling of something that looked like Kitty Litter.

"There's not much we can do about the upper car," the fireman admitted, "except keep the hoses handy."

"I'm going to need you to get this back door off pronto," John said. Barry had oxygen and IV bags ready.

"Jaws-of-Life is on its way from Santa Cruz," the fireman explained. "Our hydraulic cutter can't handle this one. They should be here any minute."

And in fact, the siren was audible.

Within minutes, firemen were leaping from a red engine and attacking the car door as single-mindedly as leaf-cutter ants. John was right behind them. The minute the opening was big enough, he contorted and squirmed his way inside to check on the driver.

He was fighting claustrophobia, shouting at Barry to aim the flashlight a little lower, when he heard the helicopter overhead. John could see its red side lights and bright searchlight reflect off twisted chrome. Its whirling blades were deafening.

By the time the helicopter landed, he'd made sure the driver's airway was clear, and he'd started a trauma line. But he knew the guy wouldn't survive, not with such severe head injuries. He'd be lucky to make it to the helicopter alive. Too bad—he was fairly young, maybe sixty. Not a bad-looking old man either, plenty of hair and reasonably slim.

John squirmed out of the car. Despite the seacoast chill, he was drenched in sweat. He'd been worried the Fiat would shift and collapse the passenger compartment completely, crushing him along with his patient.

He stepped away to let Fire cut out the seat back. There were two fire trucks on scene now, one in front and one behind the ambulance. A Highway Patrol car and a sheriff's car were parked on the shoulder. The helicopter was just up the road, smack in the center of the highway on the white line. Six vehicles, their lights swirling and flashing, and twelve men—quite a congregation for a single-injury car accident.

The MediVac helicopter began spilling out trauma nurses, bent at the waist to avoid the rotor.

When the firemen motioned to him, John squirmed back into the car to keep the patient's head and spine stable while they yanked the seat back out from under him. The trauma nurses were at their elbows, peering in at the driver while John shouted over the noise, describing the patient's condition.

"What about the driver of the other car?" one of the nurses asked.

"GOA," a fireman explained—gone on arrival.

"Hit-and-run, huh? Stupid son of a bitch, I hope they catch him."

When they helped load the patient through the helicopter's back doors, John thought his eardrums would burst, the blades beat the air so loudly.

John and Barry stood with Fire, watching the helicopter lift off and turn inland toward the trauma center. When they could no longer see its red lights in the sky, Barry called County Comm and cleared. They could return to quarters and go back to sleep.

The sheriff and Highway Patrol were still walking around the cars, shining their lights inside. A tow truck had pulled up alongside the ambulance.

Barry remarked, "Hit-and-run. Boy, that guy's in a world of trouble."

"Not as much trouble as the guy he landed on." John looked up the slope. "Jeez, that Fiat came down hard. I wouldn't mind taking a look up there."

Barry was about to say something when his pager went off. He clicked the button to hear the radio squawk, "SC-2, respond to a medical emergency at the end of San Vittorio Road in Davenport."

While Barry got details, John jumped into the back of the unit and stripped off his bloody jumpsuit, replacing it with the clean one. He'd be driving this time: Barry's turn to be patient person. But he still might have patient contact. And besides, he didn't like being bloody any longer than he had to.

It was less than two minutes before he was behind the wheel, threading carefully past the stacked cars and the fire engines. San Vittorio was just up the highway, not even a half mile away, right before Davenport itself.

They barreled down the rutted country road, their lights glinting off the dark windows of run-down houses. There was no traffic, so they kept the siren off. No use waking everybody at three-thirty in the morning.

Barry commented, "There's sure been a lot of calls around Davenport lately."

Davenport was a minuscule village—a deli, a P.O., a B&B on the highway, and a few hillocks of houses rising up around a cement plant. For a town with just a couple of hundred residents, they'd had an inordinate number of dispatches this past week.

"Yeah, well, this last call takes the cake." Then John predicted, completely erroneously, "We're not likely to see anything any weirder for a while!"

1

Ironically, I was watching the movie *Inherit the Wind* when I got the phone call.

Inherit the Wind is a fictionalized account of the Scopes "monkey trial," where Clarence Darrow—perhaps the last lawyer in America to be admired and respected—defended a teacher charged with the crime of explaining evolution to his 1920s high school class. Darrow lost the case despite some heavy oratory. That's because there's no defense against orthodoxy; by definition, too many people believe in it.

Today, evolution is part of our orthodoxy. But I managed to find out the hard way what its modern equivalent is. I managed to find the one idea that, despite volumes of supporting evidence and testimony, even a modern-day Darrow couldn't comfortably advocate. And unfortunately, I'm no orator; natural selection bred that quality out of lawyers to make room for creative billing.

I'd been perfecting my double-billing skills for the last year, working for a firm specializing in high tech, especially multimedia law. The job sounded hip; that's why I took it (and also because I'd been unemployed for the previous half year). But to the low woman on the totem pole it meant a lot of copyright-infringement, unfair-competition, and breach-of-contract suits. It meant way too much time in conference rooms with techie lawyers.

7

These shouldn't be confused with stereotypical nerds of either the geek or cyberpunk variety. Lawyers have huge, spun-glass egos, so having the best equipment (computer equipment, that is) isn't just a way of mainlining more data, it's a way of putting their claw marks higher up the tree. And with plenty of money to waste, lawyers can afford a little bark under their nails.

After almost a year of hearing three lawyers, two paralegals, and four secretaries lust after technology that was "almost there"—that is, almost equal to their transcendental or business purposes—I was sick to death of computers. Even my stereo seemed offensively digital. All I wanted to do was get away, go someplace where suits weren't required and hardware wasn't deified. I was longing for the tech-free simplicity of my hippie youth; I was looking for one of those cabin-with-no-phone kinds of vacations. Instead, I got the call from Fred Hershey.

I was comfortably cocooned in bed watching *Inherit the Wind* when the phone rang. In the ordinary course of things, I'd have let my answering machine pick up. But in my hooray-I'm-free-for-three-weeks bliss, I'd unplugged it.

So along about the sixth or seventh ring, I became groggily concerned. What if my father was sick? What if my mother, the world's oldest Yippie, had broken her vow to stop getting herself arrested?

I staggered out of bed, cursing my inconvenient Ludditism, and picked up.

Fred Hershey said, "Willa Jansson, time for you to return the favor you owe me."

I would later learn that Fred can be pathologically blunt, an odd trait in a psychiatrist, and one that natural selection will, perhaps, eventually eliminate from the breed. This night, it surprised me. I'd spent only a few hours with Fred last year, just long enough for his brother, my old boyfriend, to put me deeply into Fred's debt.

I said, "Who is this?" But I suppose I knew. Being generally cranky and antisocial, there are few people to whom I owe phone calls, much less favors.

"Fred Hershey. I need you to come down to Santa Cruz first thing tomorrow morning."

"I'm leaving to go on vacation."

"Perfect. You'll enjoy the weather here."

Fred's brother, Edward, had driven me crazy years ago when we lived together. And he'd made himself a pain in the butt several times since. Now it seemed to be Fred's turn. I could only wish their mother hadn't spared the rod.

On the other hand, Fred and Edward had helped me hide out a friend. But for them, he'd be in prison now. I might be there, too.

"Willa, listen. A patient of mine is about to be arrested for vehicular manslaughter and felony hit-and-run. I need you to represent him."

"I'm a business lawyer," I protested. In the five years since graduating from law school, I'd also been a labor lawyer, a corporate lawyer, and a federal judge's clerk. Lest Fred think me versatile, I added, "And I'm on vacation."

"You're the only lawyer I know who's crazy enough to take this case."

"Thanks a—"

"And you're the only one who owes me a favor."

The evening chill penetrated my sweat clothes. I hugged myself. I remembered Fred in therapist mode, his voice as modulated and mellow as an FM deejay's. I'd also seen him under stress, swearing and barking out cross orders. But I hadn't spent enough time with him to recall the details of his face; I kept visualizing Edward's, which engendered a Pavlovian impulse to bicker.

"Why don't you get him a local lawyer, a criminal lawyer? That's what he needs, not a—"

"I'll explain when you get here. Can you make it by lunchtime?"

"Who did your patient hit?" I could just see myself representing some jerk who'd sped off after mowing down a nun.

"They say his car went over a cliff and landed on the highway."

"What do you mean, 'They say'? Did it or didn't it?"

"It landed on top of another car, yes. The driver was crushed."

"And your patient drove away?"

"No. He wasn't in the car."

"So who was driving?"

"No one."

"It went over by itself? He didn't set the hand brake?"

Fred didn't answer immediately. "It's a lot more complicated than that, I'm afraid. But I think you should hear it from Miller."

"Miller being the guy who wasn't in the car when it killed someone?" Shades of Stephen King's *Christine*.

"Yes."

"Where does he say he was? Does he have an alibi?"

"That's the part that gets a little sticky. That's why I need you."

Why oh why didn't I ignore the ringing phone? Why didn't I leave for vacation just a half day sooner?

There was no getting around it; I did owe Fred Hershey a favor, a great big one.

"Yeah, okay, I can be there by lunchtime."

I went back to watching *Inherit the Wind*, little realizing I was about to be transformed from a thirty-seven-year-old, slightly graying, too-short blonde with an uninspiring résumé. I was about to hobble a strange, modern mile in Clarence Darrow's shoes: Willa Jansson, heretic lawyer, counsel for the infidel.

2

Alan Miller seemed like an okay guy; I didn't really care much one way or the other. My agenda was to convince him and Fred Hershey that they didn't need me, they needed the local public defender. I'd even packed my suitcase, hoping to keep driving south, maybe to Big Sur, preferably to Mexico.

Miller was in a Catholic hospital. He looked pale, sitting in a cramped bed in a tiny room with a window slit and a big crucifix on the wall. Miller's face, pained, scared, strangely resigned, was a match for any plastic Jesus. Beside his bed, an IV dripped clear fluid into his vein. I noticed they'd shaved a patch of dark hair off his hand before taping in the needle. His other hand, presumably unshaven, was hidden beneath the sheets.

Miller was a big man, maybe thirty, with a square stubbled jaw, unkempt dark hair, and slightly dazed eyes. He winced occasionally, either uncomfortable in the too-narrow bed or battered beneath his flimsy gown and blankets.

"There's no way I'd have left the highway, no reason I'd have driven through a Brussels sprouts field." His Fiat sports car had landed atop a northbound Buick on a lonely part of Highway 1 ten miles from Santa Cruz. Miller's voice was deep, even in exasperation. "Why should I pull off the highway just so I could cut back toward it a quarter mile

11

later? That's assuming I could even get my old Spider across a sprouts field, which I'd probably break the damn axle, the car's such a piece of shit." Tears glinted in his eyes, a clear green ringed by black lashes. "God, I'll miss that car!"

"So let me understand this. The cars were . . . stacked?"

"Yeah. I've seen pictures. The sheriff took some, mostly out of the weirdness of it, I think. The Fiat was right on top of the Buick, not perpendicular like you'd expect. You'd have to drive along the cliff edge of the field for a while to come off at that angle. Even so, I don't see how you could land pointing straight up the road."

I'd just experienced the glorious drive down from San Francisco, two hours of sun on crashing surf, winding cliff highway, and, close to Santa Cruz, cultivated land on a thin verge between the road and the drop-off to the sea. Apparently the hills on the inland side of the highway were Brussels sprouts farms. But they were hardly "cliffs," they were only ten or twenty feet above the road.

"The cars were within sight of Davenport, facing north toward it," he continued.

Davenport, from what I recalled, looked like a group of giant scrub-covered gumdrops with a few houses laced between them. A cement plant, a couple of restaurants—that seemed to be the extent of the tiny town fifteen minutes north of Santa Cruz.

"They're saying I turned off the highway, went up the hill, cut through the field—which probably would have blown my tires and wrecked my muffler—and went over." Miller gestured with his IV'd hand, wincing when the line tugged the needle. "Only they can't say why—because it didn't happen. I would never have done that. The road I live on is south of Davenport. Why would I be heading north at two-thirty in the morning?" He glanced at Fred Hershey. "And no way I'd run from an accident. Not with someone hurt; no way."

Fred was sitting in a corner looking like a psychiatrist, sympathetic and noncommittal and very prosperous. He was tan and fit, his tight curls lightly gelled. He wore a flaxen sport jacket with pushed-up sleeves, a vanilla cotton shirt, twiny slacks, and glove-leather boots. Despite the same heavy brows and strong nose, he didn't look enough like Edward to be recognizable as his brother. But then, I'd never seen Edward so well groomed.

Miller said to him, "I don't know what I told you in hypnosis, but I can't think of any reason I'd do what they say I did." Miller sounded plaintive, maybe a little scared.

"You hypnotized him?"

"Yes." Fred didn't offer any details.

"And he told you where he was that night? Whether he did it or not?"

"He certainly doesn't believe he did it." Fred spoke slowly, tranquilly, turning on the verbal Prozac.

If a distinction was being made, I wasn't getting it. "Does he have an alibi?"

"I think it's best if you finish interviewing Alan before we discuss the hypnotherapy session." His tone was as bland as the voice programmed into my computer at work. *You have mail, Ms. Jansson,* I expected him to say. "He's already been interviewed by the police and the district attorney and myself about this, so I assume there's no confidentiality problem?"

"I have no idea—I'm a business lawyer."

"I want him to stay," Miller put in. "I want him here."

"I guess it's up to you." "I guess" is not a good thing to hear your lawyer say. But Fred was right; Miller was already on record. And presumably, at some point Fred would overcome his reluctance to tell me what Miller said under hypnosis. I assumed the delay was a psychiatrist thing: no quick (or cheap) insights. "But, Mr. Miller, let me get the accident scene straight. They found your car still on top of the other car? It didn't bounce off, drive off, roll off?"

"Right smack on top. With nobody inside when the police and paramedics got there. And the guy"—he gulped—"underneath, in the Buick, I guess his car had a lot of rust damage, it was an oldie. The roof wasn't strong. The Fiat just squashed the shit out of it. They told me the driver's head cracked open like an eggshell." His color changed from ashen to ghostly. "The nurses here are—I guess they knew him from a few years ago, when he had cancer. One of them yelled at me about it; said she heard pieces of his skull were sticking out through his forehead." He glanced at his IV as if the nurse had taken vengeance with the needle.

"And this was how close to your house?"

"About a half mile from where I turn off. I live on San Vittorio, a funky little country road. I've got but two neighbors."

"So what were you doing that night?"

"I was up in San Francisco, up at a symposium all day. Then, you know, a buffet at the hotel with some of the people there. Gabbed with them awhile. I left maybe at eleven or so." He looked like he was hiding something.

"What kind of a symposium?"

"Mycology. Mushrooms. That's my specialty. I do regional field guides, teach classes through the natural history museum, take people out mushroom hunting, that kind of thing."

"He's something of a local celebrity," Fred Hershey added.

"No." Miller smiled slightly. "But I've helped out a couple of times here at the hospital when the docs needed spores identified. You know, in cases of mushroom poisoning when they didn't know what they were dealing with."

"Okay, so you were at a mushroom symposium in San Francisco until eleven o'clock or so?"

"Uh-huh. I stopped in Half Moon Bay for a cup of coffee. There was a girl standing out by the café door, asked me for a ride down the coast. I told her I was only going to Davenport, but that was okay with her."

"So she rode with you? All the way to Davenport?"

"I let her out at the beach, the one across from the Cash Store—I guess that's what you'd call downtown, for Davenport. But that was at like one o'clock, one-fifteen."

"Oh." I tried not to sound disappointed. An alibi witness would be a godsend, even if it took a while to locate her. "Then what?"

He glanced at Fred Hershey. "I'm not . . . I don't know,

14

I'm not totally clear. I remember I pulled over to drop this girl off, and I was worrying about it. She looked awful young to be hitchhiking, and I thought maybe I should offer to let her crash at my place. It can be cold down on the beach. But she didn't seem to want to talk about it, she was acting pretty tough. And after that, I just can't . . ."

I waited a moment, then prompted him. "After that?"

"I can't quite get clear on it, can't seem to get a handle on the time. I don't really remember anything else until I woke up in bed the next morning."

"The accident was at two-thirty?"

"That's when it got reported. A Highway Patrol car spotted it."

"And you believe you were home asleep by then?"

Fred stirred in his chair. "Actually, the Highway Patrol went to his house at around three o'clock. They got his address by checking his license plates."

I could guess where this was going. "But he wasn't there?"

"No."

Miller's brow furrowed. "I can't explain it. I don't remember. I just woke up at home."

"What time?"

"About ten-thirty."

"But they'd checked your house at three."

"It's worse than that. The Highway Patrol went back at around five, and then the sheriffs checked at eight."

"So, as far as anybody knows, you were gone all night. Did they find you in bed at ten-thirty?"

"No. In the shower."

"The deputies slammed him to the floor, handcuffed him, and were reading him his rights before they noticed the kind of shape he's in." Fred's lips pinched tight. "He ended up being transported here by ambulance."

I tried to telegraph a silent *Help* to Fred. What did he expect me to do for Miller? The man couldn't offer an alibi. Moreover, he was injured, just like he should be if he'd been in a car wreck. In fact, the more I heard, the more likely it seemed that he was guilty.

"Do you think he might have hit his head in the crash? Wandered off? Wouldn't a concussion account for the memory lapse?" I checked my watch. Mexico or bust.

"His injuries aren't consistent with a car accident." Fred was keeping something to himself.

"They aren't?"

"After an accident, you'd expect compression fractures of the neck and vertebrae, maybe broken knees and a crushed chest from hitting the steering wheel, head trauma, facial trauma, cuts from broken glass, that type of thing."

"And that's not the case here?" It seemed to me Miller moved like a man with plenty of aches.

"No."

"So what kind of injuries does he have?"

"We'll go into more detail about that later." Fred Hershey was either a control freak or he didn't want to discuss it in front of Miller.

Well, the hell with that. To Miller, I said, "What have the doctors here told you?"

"They haven't really wanted to say much. They're the ones who called Dr. Hershey." Miller looked scared. "I can tell you how I feel."

"Yes?"

"It's like my head's stuffed with cotton, sinuses killing me. My leg hurts. But mostly it's my kidney. Man. I've been passing blood."

"So the sheriffs found you at home at around ten-thirty yesterday morning, and either they were too rough or something was already wrong with you and you needed an ambulance. They brought you here, checked you in. The doctors examined you, and then called Dr. Hershey." It's a lawyer's habit to make clients agree to some version of the facts before retrospection begins to airbrush them.

Miller's eyes filled with tears. He nodded.

"And you assume the sheriff will be back to arrest you?"

Using the hand with the IV needle taped to it, he tugged down the sheet covering his other hand.

It was handcuffed to the bed rail.

"Oh." I glanced at Fred.

"They came last night and charged him with gross vehicular manslaughter and felony hit-and-run. They'll take him straight to jail, formally book him, as soon as the hospital's ready to release him."

"I wish they'd take this thing off!" Miller clattered the handcuff. "It means bedpans—I hate it. It drives me nuts."

"As far as you know, they haven't proved yet you were driving?" It sure didn't look good: it was Miller's car, and he admitted being in it an hour or two before the crash.

When Fred shook his head, I asked him, "Why exactly did they call you in?"

"He was in a great deal of emotional distress, especially about his memory loss. And I was the on-call psychiatrist. Alan and I talked for a while, and I suggested he might be a good candidate for hypnosis. I explained the procedure and the part it might play in a legal proceeding."

"Did the DA have anything to do with the decision?" If I remembered correctly, prosecutors could request that witnesses, but not suspects, be hypnotized.

"The district attorney signed off on it. His approval was required."

"And you went ahead with this?" I asked Miller. "Without consulting a lawyer? Without having one present?"

"I had to know," Miller protested. "I couldn't believe I'd done what they thought I did. I'm the one that pushed for hypnosis."

"The DA had Alan sign a document stating that he knew the session would be tape-recorded, and that if charges were filed, the recording could be used as evidence against him."

"But I was sure I didn't go driving through a field off a cliff, no way," Miller put in. "I was all for it. I never thought I'd end up like this." He raised the cuffed hand as high as it would go.

I was trying to understand Fred's part in this. "So your tape recording ended up getting him arrested?" He'd helped Miller incriminate himself, then hired him a business lawyer instead of a criminal lawyer. Did Fred have it in for the poor man?

But Fred didn't seem abashed. "It obviously didn't prevent his arrest. When I realized it would be a matter for the public defender, I called you."

I sighed. "Mr. Miller, Dr. Hershey and I have . . . worked together before. But I wasn't acting as an attorney then." I was acting as an accessory to an assortment of crimes. "And I've got to tell you, I'm not a criminal lawyer. I'm a multi-media lawyer—basically business and intellectual-property law. I really don't think I could be of much use to you. Especially compared to a public defender, who tries criminal matters day in and day out."

Fred raised an imperious hand. "I don't think a public defender is a good idea."

"They're usually highly accomplished—"

"A PD would plea-bargain," he insisted. "They are very good lawyers, I agree; but they just wouldn't know what to make of this. It'll take someone creative. And preferably not from around here."

"What does that mean?"

"Let's just say it will have to be a rather . . . eccentric defense."

" 'Eccentric' as in, get an out-of-town lawyer to come here and make a fool of herself, then vanish?"

With barely a smile, Fred nodded. "You'll understand after you hear the tape recording."

Miller sat forward. "You'll let me listen?"

"You haven't heard it?" I was surprised.

"Dealing with this kind of memory loss, without knowing the reason for it . . ." Fred seemed to be struggling not to overexplain. "I thought it would be best to wait and see whether Alan began recovering the memories on his own."

"I haven't." Miller looked as frustrated as he sounded.

Fred removed a small tape recorder from his briefcase. "Under the circumstances, and especially since the district attorney has a copy of this tape, I think you're entitled to hear it, Alan." Fred didn't look happy about it. "I would certainly have preferred to work with you first. I would have liked to have seen the memories begin to reemerge on their own." He set the recorder on his knee. "Rather than blind-side you with them, as it were."

Miller sat forward, his eyes round, his lips slightly parted, staring at the tiny tape recorder as if it were Pandora's box. "Just play it," he begged. "I want to know what I said. I want to know where that time went." He flicked me a glance. "It's not like I haven't *tried* to remember. I've tried every way I can think of. I really have."

Handcuffed to a hospital bed, he probably had done his best, all right.

"Let's hear it," I agreed. Fred's hints had piqued my curiosity. What kind of case would send someone scrambling for an "eccentric" hired gun from out of town?

Probably the same question Clarence Darrow asked when he got the call from John T. Scopes.

3

"What *is* that? What is that thing? Oh, my *God!*" Miller's voice screamed out of the tape recorder.

The sound of it, hysterical and tinny, emanating unnaturally from a plastic box, made this seem like an old radio drama. *Carjackers from Mars.*

"Oh, my God, the light; it's paralyzed me. It's like being dipped in glass, invisible restraints all over me. I hate the light, I hate it, I could just burst out of my body, just blow up like an overcooked wiener or something. Oh, my God, it's *awful!*" Miller's voice quivered on the verge of a freak-out.

Watching Miller listen to himself, I'd have bet his shock was genuine. He sat very straight, his neck craned forward, his face so attentive the muscles were slack.

"I can see I'm moving, I can look out the car window and see I'm moving. Not my body; it's paralyzed. But the car's moving with me inside it!"

Miller's muscles jerked as he listened. His head started shaking slightly. He looked like a man about to say, *No way!*

"Something's wrong, something's wrong. Moving so fast, like getting sucked up, but I don't feel it; there's no wind to it, no rushing noise, no engine noise. It's all wrong. I must be going crazy. God, I've gone crazy. Just like Grandma. Oh, my God!" The voice on the tape was tight, wary. "What the hell is that? What is that thing?"

Fred Hershey's best FM voice intruded. "Remember, Alan, you're here now, not there. You're remembering this from a place of safety, recalling something that happened in the past and is behind you. Try to stay with the memory. What do you see?"

"Man, I don't know. Some kind of a *thing*. It's gray. It's skinny, it's got little legs and arms as flimsy as a spider's. There's four of these spidery guys. Big black eyes, tiny noses, little slits for mouths. Skinny chested. They're like gray insects standing up, like little grasshopper men."

"What are they doing, Alan?"

"They put their arms into the car like it's not solid. And then I'm going right through the car, right up through the roof, through it like it's just a cloud. They pull me right up through the roof. Oh, my God. I must be crazy!"

"You're okay, Alan; you're safe now. Try to stay with it."

"It's like they're floating me. We're in some kind of room. They're floating me into a chair. Except when I sit down the chair molds itself to me, straightens me out. It's more like a gurney now, but it's shaped to me and I'm . . ." The voice on the tape whimpered. "They took my clothes! Oh God, I'm claustrophobic, can't stand it, can't stand it, I'll go nuts if I can't move."

"You're safe now, Alan. You're only revisiting the past. Try to stay with it if you can."

"One of them is taller and bigger. It's like a big old praying mantis or something. I must be insane. I must be dreaming." He screeched. "It's touching me! It's touching my face. I'm so cold, its touch is so cold. It puts words into my head."

"Words?"

"It says I'm not scared. But I am. It says it won't hurt, but it does hurt."

"What hurts, Alan?"

"It's like a syringe with two needles. It's filled with something hot and gold colored. It burns like hell going in. The tall one says it doesn't hurt, but goddam it, it does, it really does hurt."

Miller's shoulders were hunched. He was shaking, staring down at the thumb of his cuffed hand.

I strained for a look. I could barely make out two small puncture wounds.

"He keeps saying it won't hurt, but it all hurts, it all does. Not as much as before he put the words in my head, but I know that underneath his words, it still hurts. It's like I don't feel it, but I know it hurts."

"You say, 'It all hurts.' What else hurts, Alan?"

Miller hung his head, listening to a long description of tissue taken from the back of his leg, an apparatus placed over his genitals to extract something, a huge instrument lowered over the table and used to bore beneath his rib cage into the general area of his kidney, something pushed up his nostril deep into his sinus cavity.

The tale was as harrowing as it was preposterous. And Miller's voice was as terrified as any I ever expected to hear.

Miller, in person, looked like he might leap up and run screaming down the hall, dragging the bed by his handcuff.

When the tape ended, we were all silent for a moment.

"Well . . . ," I said, "I guess I agree the public defender would want to plea-bargain this one."

"What does it mean?" Miller's voice was intense. "Am I crazy? I don't remember anything like that. I mean, how could I? It's crazy, right?" He looked at Fred as if begging him to concur.

Fred crossed his legs, scowling. "Perhaps I should explain the dynamics of hypnosis, Alan."

"I mean, I must have hit my head or something. It must have been some kind of nightmare." Miller rubbed the punctures on his thumb as if trying to erase them.

"Hypnosis is a way of getting into your perceptions, your own highly individualized and filtered view of reality. It doesn't give us the quote-unquote facts, or the truth, or any of those abstract concepts. It only gives us what *you* make of what *you* see. It gives us your memories, in short. And memories are more personal than most people realize. They're shaped by your worldview, your history, the unique way you process impressions. Does that make sense?"

Miller lay back as if deflated. "So if I'm crazy, my memories are going to be crazy."

"But you see, your other memories, the ones you've shared with me—what you did that day, where you come from, what you do for a living—those memories appear to be competent. It would be unusual for you to have only a few hours' worth of 'crazy' memories, as you call them."

"But Fred," I interjected, "say he did hit his head. Couldn't that put weird ideas into his brain?"

"There's no sign of trauma to the head." Fred sounded cranky. "On the contrary, if we're going to look at the physical indications, we have puncture wounds on his thumb, an apparent generalized allergic reaction to an unknown agent, kidney problems, genital swelling, pain in his calf, a sinus ache, and a tendency to nosebleed."

I was beginning to think Fred was the crazy one. "You're not saying this really could have happened?"

Fred sighed. Miller closed his eyes, breathing shallowly, quickly.

"Fred, are you saying you want me to go into court and argue that this man got abducted by gray aliens with spider legs who put words into his head?"

Fred scowled. "Would you be surprised to know people all over the world are telling similar stories?"

Miller's eyes were shut so tight his lids looked like prunes. Tears leaked down his face.

"I've been doing some research," Fred continued. "The founder of the Cambridge Psychiatric Hospital compiled seventy-some case studies. There are hundreds of others in other collections. Reputable scholars believe there are literally hundreds of thousands of Americans with recovered memories of similar experiences. Some of them put the number at close to four million."

"Yeah, well, millions of people believed Richard Nixon had a 'secret plan' to end the war in Vietnam, but that didn't make it true! People believe all kinds of crap." I glanced at Miller, hoping I hadn't given offense.

But his eyes popped open. He watched Fred hopefully, as if wanting him to agree.

Encouraged to see it, I continued. "I thought the whole repressed-memory thing got discredited." I recalled some lawsuits about it—a woman who kept "remembering" her father slaughtering her childhood friends; women who, at the instigation of their therapists, began attributing their problems to sudden "memories" of sexual abuse.

"Discredited, no. Controversial, yes. Ordinarily, when a traumatic event occurs, the memories around it might become distorted, sometimes highly distorted—compressed, expanded, forgotten—but memories of the trauma itself tend to be unnaturally sharp and focused. That's why Vietnam veterans have such a hard time, for example; they can't forget the horror, not even one detail of it, though they may have blotted out the day-to-day occurrences."

"So Mr. Miller should have remembered very clearly . . . whatever happened. Which probably means it didn't really—"

"This has been used to discount so-called repressed memories of childhood sexual abuse. But there *have* been documented cases of recovered memories being independently verified. In fact, attacks on repressed memories seem to be more an assault on certain kinds of therapists than a bona fide scientific position."

Great. I could just see myself jumping into the whole repressed-memory quagmire.

"But Alan isn't experiencing the usual pattern of some memories being repressed and others remaining intact within the same period. He's lost an entire well-defined, recent block of time. Amnesia, basically. And that's one of the recognized areas where hypnosis can be very helpful. It can be a problem when it's used to enhance existing memories—people are prone to embellish and confabulate. But when you're trying to get to the memory itself instead of getting at the details . . . I'm sure that's why the district attorney went along with its use in this case."

"I'll bet he wasn't expecting this."

"Memories of alien abduction . . ." Fred glanced away. He seemed embarrassed even saying the words. "If the case studies can be believed, they're unique in that they almost always follow a period of amnesia, what they call 'missing time.' They may slowly leak back into conscious recollection. Or a person may experience difficulties that take him into therapy, where close work or hypnosis jars them free."

We continued watching Fred.

He added, "One theory is that they are forced into suppression."

"Forced? You mean, the bug-eyed creatures *tell* everyone to forget?"

Fred looked like it was hard for him to nod.

"No," I said. "No way. I'm sorry. But I am not going to go into court and say that." I'd spent years trying to prove I wasn't a flaky hippie like my parents; I wasn't going to undo it in a single close encounter of the legal kind.

Miller surprised me. "I agree with her. I won't go into court and say I got sucked into a—" He stopped, hyperventilating again. "I can't do it. I mean, I'll be honest. I'll say I don't remember what the hell . . . But not this. Nuh-uh."

Fred sat up straighter. "I'm not advocating anything, I hope you understand that. But I do want you to consider two points. One is that stories like yours are being told all over the world—and personally vetted by reputable therapists. And secondly,"—he spoke quickly, before we could scoff—"none of the doctors here is likely to testify that your injuries are consistent with a car accident. If you accept a plea bargain simply out of embarrassment at what you'd have to claim in your defense, you could be doing yourself a disservice."

That was cause for nonspacey optimism. "What about the injuries? Why didn't they keep the DA from filing charges?" Perhaps I could just stay the night, have a talk with the DA tomorrow, persuade him he couldn't prove Miller was in the car when it crashed.

"The sheriff didn't find anyone else's fingerprints on the steering wheel; that's number one." Fred leaned forward, ticking the numbers off on his fingers. "They have his statement that he was driving the car earlier. And the car didn't run itself off the cliff—so they believe. As far as the DA is concerned, the accident speaks for itself. The simplest explanation is that Alan walked away unhurt. That his condition now is the result of something that happened later."

I tilted my head, watching Fred. There was something else, something more. I couldn't believe he'd accept alien abduction so easily, otherwise. "How long have you believed in this stuff, Fred?"

"I don't 'believe in' it. I'm just telling you this isn't an isolated, unique recollection."

"You heard about this at some point, right?"

"I heard that John Mack, the Harvard psychiatrist, had written a book about it; that he believed the seventy-plus cases he described were legitimate recovered memories of alien abduction."

"Did you read the book? Were you persuaded?"

"No, I didn't read the book." He ran an exasperated hand over his curls. "I was rather appalled when Harvard spent a year deciding whether or not to censure him for his public stance, but I had no particular interest in the subject."

"And you'd never heard this kind of story before, yourself?"

Fred didn't answer.

"Did you?"

"Not until this week," he replied.

I was about to ask whether he meant Miller, but he raised a hand to shush me.

"The crucial thing is for Alan to make an informed decision. What if he doesn't offer an explanation of what happened that night? What are the possible penalties?" He turned to Miller. "Would it make a difference to you to know you could go to prison for five or ten years?"

Miller blanched.

Fred continued. "I don't know what the penalty is for manslaughter, Alan. But it's likely to be stiff. Stiff enough to be worth some public embarrassment."

"That's true," I agreed. Might as well jump in with something vaguely lawyerly. "But you don't want a business lawyer. If there's a good criminal lawyer here in—"

Fred leaped to his feet. I assumed he was going to get

ballistic about the favor I owed him. But he was staring behind me at the hospital door.

I turned, alarmed by the shock on his face.

An older woman, perhaps sixty, perhaps a hard-drinking fifty, stood there glowering at Alan Miller. Her hair was dyed blond, arranged in a country-bar bouffant that needed tending. Her eyes were ringed with black liner streaked by tears. Her face was wrinkled and lean. She wore tight black jeans, boots, a black top that looked home sewn, and black plastic earrings. Her hand fumbled at the zipper of a big vinyl handbag.

She looked for all the world like a Texas divorcée with some serious hell to raise.

I glanced back at Fred. He'd reacted so strongly to the intrusion. Did he know her?

Fred was sidling close to the bed, putting himself between Miller and the visitor. He'd puffed himself up somehow, looking bigger and more authoritative.

Behind him, Miller seemed to cower. I could hear the handcuff rattle on the bed frame.

By virtue of their reaction, the woman earned my full attention. I turned back to her.

She was clearly agitated, her head twitching slightly, her eyes wet, her stare fixed. The corners of her mouth turned down, lipstick bleeding into her wrinkles.

She said, "You can't hide forever!" I was almost surprised she didn't have a Lone Star accent.

Miller was stuttering something about how sorry for her he was, but that it wasn't, he didn't . . .

Fred interrupted him. "This is highly inappropriate. Do the nurses know you're here?"

She barely glanced at him. To Miller, she shrieked an outraged "Sorry? *Sorry*'s all I get? 'I'm sorry?' " She stepped into the room, the door swinging shut behind her, bumping her forward another inch. The stink of cheap liquor entered with her. "You ever been married, you jerk-off son of a whore?"

Fred strode toward her, almost stumbling over my feet as

he passed my chair. He wore the determined scowl of a nightclub bouncer.

He was already grabbing her as she added, "Well, 'sorry' don't cut it, asshole. Don't cut it. You never been married, much less a second time. What are the damn odds I die alone? How many men you think the good Lord made like Francis? Hunh, Mr. I'm-so-sorry, bastard?"

I finally realized she was the dead driver's widow.

Fred, grappling with her as he tried to reach around and open the door, looked like he was doing the Texas two-step with her. He was using the Voice again, telling her her grief was understandable, but that her actions were inappropriate and must cease immediately.

That sent her over the top. She spewed profanity, struggling to shove Fred aside. Fred, in the fray, didn't notice what she was doing with her hands.

She was reaching into her big purse.

I stood, almost toppling my cheap plastic chair. I've grown to accept the fact that I'm more paranoid than most people. But then, my parents have been arrested seventeen times, two of my former bosses have been killed, and Fred's own damn brother gave me herpes. I think people are crazy to expect anything but the worst.

I closed the short distance between me and the widow's ugly vinyl bag.

I knocked Fred's elbow aside. The widow made eye contact then, and I knew I was right.

Her eyes, a little jaundiced, a little red, were as mean and angry as a gargoyle's.

I threw myself against the handbag, trapping her hand inside it. We were in a tight huddle now: Fred in front of the widow, me to one side, the bag hard between us, and the door behind us.

The next moment, a blast sent me stumbling across the room. My ears felt like they'd been boxed.

The widow's gun had gone off in her purse. Through smoke that smelled like saltpeter and melted plastic, I could see a ragged hole in the bag.

Fred staggered back, mouth agape.

Miller was saying, "Holy shit," about an octave higher than his usual speaking voice.

Only the widow kept her head. She opened the door and slipped out.

Seconds later, two nurses ran in. They stopped short, looking at Fred with his hand over his forehead, and me, sinking back into my chair. "What was that noise? What's that smell?" They turned to Miller and demanded, "Do you have firecrackers?"

I pointed to a corner of the room. The bullet had to be there somewhere, lodged in the wall or the floor. "A gun." I was out of breath.

Another nurse came up behind them. "Was that a shot? I'm going to get security up here."

Fred regained his composure. "Hurry!"

Miller slumped back against his pillows. One of the nurses bent over him.

"Come on out into the hall, both of you," the latest nurse commanded. "We'll talk out there."

Fred turned and murmured something to Miller as I walked out.

God damn, the widow had come here to shoot Miller, just cold-bloodedly shoot him for (she thought) driving his car off a cliff onto her husband's. With so many other elements —fate, coincidence, rust damage (never mind alien abduction)—she'd chosen to blame Miller.

She could as easily have railed against kismet for putting her husband on that bit of highway at that moment, or for sending Miller's car over at that spot. She could have wished they'd owned a sturdier car or installed a luggage rack. She could have picked the incident apart, regret by regret. Instead, she'd kept it simple. Miller killed her husband; Miller must die. It was as direct, and as dumb, as the plot to a Hollywood movie.

I looked down the quiet corridor, beige and peach with subdued prints. The nurses' station had a few peeps of color —pictures of children, potted violets—but nothing incongruous. Nothing operatic, nothing crazy.

Nothing like a tape recording of a man recalling medical

experiments aboard an alien spacecraft. Nothing like an in-furiated Kmart shopper with a loaded gun.

I glanced at Miller's room number, 2120: you have just been admitted to the Twilight Zone. I memorized the number as if to localize the insanity, label it and keep it on the other side of a closed door.

I sniffed my sleeve, suddenly convinced my clothes must stink of gunpowder. My semidressy sweater did indeed reek.

Fred was standing beside me now, nagging me about something.

"Willa! Willa, talk to me."

"What?" My tone was cross. I pulled up my collar to see if it stank, too.

Fred gripped my shoulder, forcing me to make eye contact. "How are you doing?"

I wanted to bat his arm away. This was his damn fault. I'd be doing some leisurely packing right now, planning a restful trip, but for Fred.

"How are you?" he repeated. His brows were knit so tightly a couple of the hairs touched his lashes.

"How should I be? I'm freaked out."

He nodded, looking relieved. He let go of my shoulder. "Of course you are," he said complacently.

As a tubby security guard trotted toward us, Fred added, "You will represent him, won't you?"

I'd very likely saved Miller's life in there. Didn't that repay the favor I owed Fred? Or did it add Miller to my karmic load?

I hesitated.

"Good girl," Fred said, as if the matter were settled.

4

Fred Hershey sat me down in his office, which was decorated to look like someone's sunroom. Glass-topped tables matched white rattan love seats and chairs with green cushions. A wall of windows overlooked a gulch of young redwoods and hardy ferns. I'd been to Fred's office once before, in the process of sinking myself into his debt.

Now he sat opposite the love seat I occupied, staring out the window at his picturesque gully. He sat low on his spine, legs splayed, arms crossed. His suntan was the only cheerful thing about him.

"I want you to hear something," he said slowly. "I'm trying to think of some rationale—any rationale—to play it for you."

"What is it?"

"A session with a patient early last week."

I was surprised. Surely that would violate the doctor-patient privilege.

"It would have to be strictly on the QT, off the record. I'd have to have your assurance that you wouldn't mention it to anyone. That you wouldn't allude to the tape's contents or to the fact that you'd heard it."

If I couldn't use it in any way, why even bother? "You're making me feel like a lawyer, Fred." A rare and not completely pleasant thing. "How can I promise? What if it could help acquit Alan Miller? I have a duty to my client." My client; Christ—I'd caved. I'd made the business equivalent of a shotgun wedding.

"If you can get this information from a different source, fine; use it. But what you hear in this office you've got to swear you won't use or refer to in any way."

"There's no loophole in the patient-doctor privilege, Fred." I might as well go the lawyerly distance. "If you tell me, you've violated it and it ceases to exist."

"That's why you can't let anyone know I did this."

Did Fred assume, because of the way we'd met, because I'd been on the run from the police, that my ethics were shaky? Did he assume I was, in general, a sleazy rule-bender?

On the other hand, it must be important for him to rationalize doing it.

Sleaze on: "Tell me."

Fred reached behind him, finessing open a drawer. From it, he extracted an audiotape. He held it up. "It's another one," he said.

"Another tape of Miller?"

"No." He fumbled his tape recorder out of his briefcase and popped the new tape in.

His voice, crackling out of the small speaker, was almost sickly sweet. "Now we're going to talk about what happened to you yesterday morning, okay? But if we get upset, we'll go right back to that nice safe place you described; do you understand? The dog pillow in the kitchen is right there for you if things get hard. But remember, where we're going is all in the past. It's all done with, and you're safe now, okay?" He sounded like Mr. Rogers.

When the other voice piped up, I understood why. It was a young boy's, a grade-schooler's high-pitched "Okay."

"Now let's go back to where you and Joey were that morning. Let's go right back to when you left your mom's house. Can you do that?"

"Uh-huh. We go to the store and get cinnamon buns and Snapple."

"What store is that?"

"Davenport Cash Store." The squeaky voice seemed to relish the memory. "The buns are sticky there. And big."

"Then where did you go?"

"Beach," he replied. "I want to find agates. Joey says beaches don't make agates, but do so. And shells. I got mussels with the hinges still on." A silence. "I looked up and Joey's not there anymore. Where's Joey? It's so sunny I can't see." The boy's breathing quickened. "It's too sunny. I can't see Joey."

"What can you see?"

"It's too sunny. And the beach is getting little."

"Getting little?" Fred sounded confused, if still avuncular.

"I'm on top of the beach. It's little, like if I'm on a mountain, but I'm not."

"Is there . . . anybody with you?"

"A gray man with big sunglasses."

"What's he doing."

"He gots my arm. He gots a silver suit and he's little like me but he's a grown-up."

"How do you know he's a grown-up."

"I just know. When he talks to me, he talks like a grown-up."

"What does he say?"

"He doesn't say. He talks straight into my head. That it won't hurt."

"What won't hurt?"

"They gots a table like at the doctor's but invisible. And stuff to put on me." His voice sounded frightened now. "I want my clothes. I'm cold."

"Don't be scared. That time is all over with. You're just remembering something that's all done. And you're safe now. Do you understand that?"

"I go, 'I'm cold.' But the doctor with the sunglasses says no, I'm not. He says it won't hurt and I shouldn't be scared. Like you."

"Does it hurt?"

"Nope."

"Were you scared?"

"Nope. Not after he says I'm not."

"What is he doing, the doctor with the sunglasses?"

"He's taking sperms."

There was a brief silence on the tape. "What kind of sperms?" Fred asked.

"Sperms, you know, like eggs and sperms."

"How is the doctor taking the sperm?"

"With a box."

"Does he ask you to put your sperm in the box?"

"No. He puts a box like a glove on me and says I don't feel it on me, and then he takes it off and says I was good and gave good sperms. But the next thing hurted."

"What was the next thing?"

"The invisible table turns over and they have to put a cold snake inside me." The boy sounded matter-of-fact, not frightened. "It even hurted after the doctor said it didn't. He had to touch my eyebrows with funny gloves to make it stop hurting."

"He touched your eyebrows with funny gloves?"

"Like at the Halloween store."

"What did the gloves look like?"

"Gloves."

"What shape were they?"

"Hand shaped!" The boy seemed to find this a silly question.

"Like the gloves that took your sperm?"

"No. That was like a box with a glove. This was like a Halloween glove."

"And he touched your eyebrows with it?" Fred apparently decided to move beyond the gloves.

"He says it doesn't hurt, and then it really doesn't. He's a good doctor. Better than you!"

Fred clicked off the tape recorder. He scowled at it for a moment. "This boy, Mickey, and his brother Joey were missing from Davenport Beach for almost three hours. His mother had everyone she could round up out there looking for them. And then all of a sudden, there they were walking in the surf, arguing."

"Arguing?"

"Mickey claimed he bent over to pick up a shell, and that Joey wasn't there when he straightened up. Joey says the same thing about Mickey. They were fighting over who lost whom."

"Where does Joey say he was?"

"Joey's a year younger than Mickey, which is why I played Mickey's tape; it's a little clearer. They both say they were at the beach the whole time. Only, to them, it seemed like about twenty minutes. Whereas in reality, they were gone over four hours." His frown tightened like a spring. "Their mother—there's a restraining order against the father; he abused the boys."

"You mean that day? At the beach?"

"When they were younger." Fred seemed sincerely pained. "It was a terrible thing. Their memories of it are fragmentary, confused, as the memories of young children tend to be. But, of course, when the boys didn't come home on time, the mother panicked. Her immediate fear, her first assumption, was that their father had kidnapped them. And frankly"—he rubbed his eyes—"that was my assumption, too. I was sure these were screen memories."

"Screen memories?"

"A psychological mechanism to deal with memories that are just too painful or frightening. A father who's raped you, for instance: you erect a screen in front of your mental images. Something that accounts for the actual event while diminishing its horror. You quote-unquote 'remember' a gray alien instead of your father. And the physical sensation is no longer a rape, it's a medical procedure. Instead of your father insisting he's not hurting you, you take the fact that doctors often say that. You try to transform the memory into a visit to the doctor's office. But you know deep down you didn't see your doctor; and you know your mother knows it. So you have to work a little harder, construct a screen that can't be seen through so easily."

"So, in essence, the boy made this up."

"Not consciously. But on a level so deep, it isn't retrievable as a regular memory. Getting to it requires hypnosis." He straightened, stretching slightly. "On the surface, both boys were convinced they'd been at the beach only a short time."

"Are screen memories common?"

Despite better posture, he looked tired. "Common? No. But they happen. I've encountered them before, usually in children. Children have a greater tendency to blend memory and fantasy, just in general."

"So you thought this was a screen memory. And then you hypnotized Alan Miller."

Fred winced. "Yes."

"What do you think now?"

"I think there are an astonishing number of similarities in their stories. Not to mention a locational connection." He scowled. "What can I say beyond that?"

"That wouldn't sound ridiculous?"

He raised his hands as if to say, *Well?*

"I can't do it, Fred. I can't let Alan Miller testify that he was abducted by aliens. He'll get laughed out of court."

"Unless there are other people in Davenport who might also come forward . . . ?"

"They'd all be laughed out of court. And they should be! This is stupid! This is crap!" I felt my cheeks grow hot. I felt tears sting my eyes.

Fred handed me a box of Kleenex, saying, "You were almost shot. You're entitled."

I waved the tissues away. "Psychiatrists are supposed to think everyone's entitled."

Fred's snort made it clear their private assessment didn't always match the party line. "The real question is, *can* you defend Alan Miller without bringing his hypnosis session into it? Can you defend him based on his word that he wasn't driving the car at the time?"

"The jury would wonder what he *was* doing," I conceded. "And to tell you the truth, I do, too. I don't buy this space aliens stuff. What about a screen memory?"

"In a man Miller's age?" He shrugged. "The possibility is remote, at best. I say this because, number one, he shows no overt symptoms of a serious psychological disorder. And absent that, screen memories are rare in adults. Adults have learned so many other coping techniques."

I mulled this over.

"And it would defy the laws of probability," Fred added, "to find matching screen memories among unrelated individuals from entirely different age groups and backgrounds."

"You're saying it stretches your credulity?" I couldn't keep the sarcasm out of my voice. "But alien abduction doesn't?"

"Well, let me put it this way. Mickey and Joey's father certainly didn't abduct Alan Miller." He sighed. "And after hearing Miller's story, I wonder whether Mickey and Joey's father abducted *them.*"

"You're not about to talk me into representing the father, too?"

Fred smiled. "Take on Miller and we'll call it square."

"Only if I can do it without bringing up spacemen. That's where I draw the line, swear to God."

Fred couldn't guess how out there my parents were. He didn't realize I'd spent my childhood elbowing past loonies in their Haight Street flat. He didn't know my landlord traced his lineage back to the Martian quarter of Atlantis.

I had worked long and hard to be the least weird person of my acquaintance. To end up as counsel for an alien abductee carjacking victim?

"I'll talk to Miller's neighbors—maybe we can find some alibi evidence. I'll go have a look at the field he supposedly drove through. Maybe we can get a mechanic to say his car couldn't have made it. There might be something we can argue—something terrestrial. But we can't go into court with *I was on a spaceship at the time.* That just doesn't cut it as an alibi."

"I'll drive you up there," Fred offered.

I took a hard look at him. Miller wasn't a longtime patient or even a personal acquaintance. Why was Fred putting himself out for the man? "It's the boys, isn't it? You want to know for sure what happened to them."

"If you can find an explanation for what happened to Miller—"

"You can go back to your screen memory theory."

"And not worry that their father is being unjustly reaccused." He rubbed the back of his neck as if it ached. "But it's also about Alan Miller. I believe him when he says he had no reason to drive across that field. I believe him when he says he wouldn't have left the scene of an accident."

"How can you believe that without believing the rest of it?"

"I don't know yet," he admitted. "I'm working on it."

5

Fred bought me lunch at the Davenport Cash Store, a restaurant and ethnic arts emporium whose brick walls and high ceilings lent it a bistro air despite the musty smell of African carvings and Persian rugs. Fred's patient, Mickey, had told the truth about one thing: the cinnamon buns there were sticky. And big.

Davenport was right on the coast highway, but two lanes of traffic didn't spoil the lonely, Hitchcockian charm of the town. Hillocks flowed with spring weeds overrunning tough perennial scrub. In seams between them, streets converged like veins in a leaf. Untended houses with wet yards rose toward an adobe church with an arch and bell, and a tiny building with a Western facade dangled a shingle reading Jail. Up the highway, a cement plant with tall digesters backlit the camel-hump hills.

After lunch, we got back on Highway 1 and headed south, pulling onto a gravel shoulder about a quarter mile down the road. Beside us, a rise blocked what I presumed was a view of the beach. I could hear waves crashing on nearby rocks. I could smell seaweed and wet sand, even from the highway.

Fred climbed out of his immaculate Lexus and came around to open the passenger door. "This is where the accident happened," he told me. "That's the hill, across the highway."

I wasn't sure what he expected me to notice. But I climbed out of the car for a better look. The hill was even shorter than I'd supposed. It rose, clifflike, to a height of perhaps twenty feet. The rise on our side was less than ten. The route had obviously been cut through a slope running down to the sea.

I stared at the highway, zipping with Sunday traffic now that the fog was burning off. Up the road, a dozen parked cars were jammed onto a dirt verge. A few surfers were stripping off wet suits.

Fred was saying, "You can still see beads of safety glass over there. Near the poppies."

The sun was catching side-of-the-road bits of windshield like sprinkled glitter.

"You haven't seen the pictures," Fred continued. "What a sight. Miller's car was about the same length as the Buick from the driver's window to the taillights. And it wasn't just sitting on top, it was wedged into the Buick's interior with its tail end sticking up." He shook his head. "I understand it was a complicated extrication."

"I see what Miller means about the angle," I mused. "You'd think any car coming off that hill would be pointing more toward the ocean."

Fred nodded, opening his door. "Let's go take a look up there."

A few minutes later, we turned left onto a rural road. We passed more shrubs overrun with tangled greenery as if everything was trying to grow everywhere at once. We turned onto a bumpy road that was paved in spots and graveled in others. It went sharply up a short hill to a Brussels sprouts field.

The sprouts had been harvested some time ago. Chopped stalks, about six inches high, were ringed with broad, wilted leaves. There were perhaps a hundred neat rows of them, too close together to drive between. But the dry stalks looked as tough and stiff as bamboo; it would be a hell of a bumpy ride over them.

Fred didn't try to get the Lexus across the field. He parked at the end of the road and hopped out of the car.

I joined him at the edge of the field.

"A lot of farmers let their land sit for a while between crops," Fred explained. "They're just starting to plow it under and replant with artichokes."

"I assume the sheriff and the DA have been here?"

"If they found Miller's tire tracks, they didn't mention it to me or to him. The ones we're looking at are obviously from a bigger vehicle, probably the farmer's truck."

"If they didn't find Fiat tracks, I'll put the sheriff—or whoever checked this area—on the stand. I wonder if they brought a forensic photographer up here."

Staring out across the field, I felt utterly inadequate. In the last year, I'd never once worried about tire imprints. I'd worried instead about securing patents for an Internet broadcast company's hardware and negotiating its "rent" on preexisting cable and telephone wires. My newfound expertise wasn't likely to be of much use to Alan Miller.

We started toward the "cliff," walking slowly, looking for tracks. We stepped over quite a few that were too wide to belong to a sports car. Fred was probably right about them belonging to a farm truck or a small tractor.

It didn't take long to get across; the cultivated area wasn't much bigger than a football field. Where the chopped stalks ended, the ground was bare and hard for perhaps four feet. It was too dry to show tracks, instead showing scuffs that could as easily have come from boots. Beyond that, tough, dusty-leafed plants competed with yellow-flowered sorrel and wild radish, holding the cliff edge together.

"This should be just about the spot." Fred prodded the shrubs with his chichi ankle boot. "You'd think the greenery would be crushed if he drove over it."

The plants appeared hearty and unbroken as far as I could see.

I looked beyond the brambles onto the road. Even with cars speeding by, I could tell where the accident happened. Traces of the Highway Patrol's orange spray paint still marked the scene. In addition, the pavement was noticeably smeared with oil and gasoline. A few twists of metal and piles of safety glass littered the shoulder. But there was a similar spot down the way; apparently the area had had its share of crashes.

Across the highway, beyond where the shorter hill bracketed it, the land tapered quickly down to the ocean. I could make out a long line of pelicans skimming the horizon. I inhaled ocean mist, car exhaust, and fertilizer. Eau de Highway 1.

I turned, hearing an engine. A big pickup truck was cutting a bumpy diagonal across the field. Dirt rose around it, making a corridor of murk behind it.

It stopped a few feet away. A cranky-looking man in jeans and a checkered shirt jumped out. He was short and swarthy, with a drooping black mustache and a sunburnt bald spot.

"This is private property, posted 'No Trespassing,' " he barked.

Fred pulled out his wallet, extending a business card. "We're here about that car crash Friday night—or rather, Saturday morning—the one down below on the highway."

The man came closer, snatching away and scowling at Fred's card. But if he wondered why a psychiatrist was investigating an auto accident, he didn't say so. "A doctor, huh?"

"That's right." Fred gestured toward me. "And this is my associate from San Francisco."

The man looked much friendlier now. "Jesus"—his tone was confidential—"I heard the Fiat landed right on top of the Buick. Now what are the odds of that?" He looked up and down the field. "I drive through here, but it's no place for a sports car. You'd have to be crazy or stoned to try something like that in the middle of the night."

"The sheriff was up here after the accident looking for tire prints?"

"Not till dinnertime. My house overlooks the access road, so I know when I've got company."

"He didn't come first thing Saturday morning? With photographers, evidence collectors?"

"No, I seen him drive up for a quick look about three-thirty in the morning—just shined his light around. Checking nobody was up here, I suppose. But they didn't really walk the field till dinnertime, like I said." The farmer grinned. "But hell, it's clear enough the fella drove across here. There's no other way to land on a car down below."

"How tough are these plants?" Fred wondered. "Over here on the edge? Because I don't see where they were run over."

The farmer glanced down at Fred's boot. "They're tough enough; they hold the hill together when it rains. But you should be able to notice—not that I've ever seen them run over. I took a look yesterday morning."

"Before the deputies came out?"

"My field, so of course I'm curious."

"Did you notice anything?"

"No." The farmer looked concerned. "It's posted 'No Trespassing,' " he repeated. "You couldn't mistake this for a road. He must have been stoned on something."

"You didn't know either of the drivers, did you?"

"I don't know anybody drives a Fiat. I believe in buying American."

We stood in silence for a minute.

"Can I show you something?" the farmer asked unexpectedly. "I'm wondering what to think about it."

"Please do," Fred said.

The farmer gestured toward his truck.

There was plenty of room for three in the cab, but that didn't make it comfortable. The leather seat was cracked and collapsing, and it stank of manure and dust. There were dirty skeins of spiderwebs where the windshield met the dash, making me imagine spiders on my ankles and neck. I was a car slob myself, but I drew the line at driving an ecosystem.

It was a bumpy ride across the field and onto the road. The farmer turned inland, barreling over ruts and potholes. A few minutes later, we reached a meadow of tall grasses, mottled beige and green, with flecks of pink and yellow from wild radish.

"It's the damnedest thing," the farmer said. "Come and

take a look. I don't know if I'm supposed to report this kind of thing or what."

We walked into the field. As beautiful as the knee- and thigh-high grasses were, I couldn't help but wonder about snakes, ticks, jumping spiders. In the city, greenery is corralled into parks, where it can't hurt anybody.

About five minutes later, we stepped into an area of flattened grass. It didn't look crushed or dead, just lying flat. The downed area extended at least twenty feet ahead.

"Some kind of camp?" Fred guessed. "For tents and the like?"

"That's what the other fellows thought," the farmer agreed. "But I sure didn't notice the traffic, if folks have been camping here."

"The other fellows?" I repeated. I watched Fred walk farther out, following a swirl pattern in the mashed-down grass.

"The paramedics." The farmer wiped his forehead fretfully. "The ones that took the call, that tried to save the fellow in the Buick. When they got off work in the morning, they came up to look at the sprouts field, same as you."

It seemed to interest everyone but the sheriff.

"And you brought them over here to see this?"

"Uh-huh. You know, one summer, they drove their ambulance right across my artichokes to get me when I was hurt out in the field. If they were more worried about their ambulance than about me, they sure as hell didn't show it."

"The same medics who came to see you on Saturday?"

"No, no. On Saturday, they were young fellas. Nice as can be. You could see they were still shook up about it. One of them had to crawl into the car and start an intravenous line. You know, while the firemen cut the driver out. But to hear him tell it, he knew the poor fellow wasn't going to make it. His head was cracked open with chunks of his brain hanging out—he died on his way to the hospital." The farmer's eyes glinted with empathy. "You could tell it had got to him. And just think how much those boys see every day."

"Is there any way to reach this field besides the road we took?"

"On foot, sure. You could come from over that way." He pointed past Fred to a rising hill. "Off-road maybe a half mile from San Vittorio, where the barn is."

"San Vittorio Road?" I tried to sound nonchalant. But I remembered Alan Miller saying he lived there.

6

When we finally climbed back into his Lexus, the first words out of Fred's mouth were, "Crop circle."

I was a little tired and more than a little distracted by itches. "Crop circle?" To me, this signified some kind of farmers' union or grange.

"It's a crop circle," he repeated. "That thing in the farmer's field. It's like the ones in England."

"What in England?"

He didn't engage the engine. He shifted on the plush leather seat to look at me. I could see his furrowed brows through the gray lenses of his sunglasses. "I met someone a while back, someone who was researching them. There have been thousands of these things in England. Hundreds of them appear every summer. And they've appeared in more than a dozen other countries."

"So what causes them?"

"They think . . ." He glanced away.

"They think . . ." I prompted. I suppose I expected him to say sinkholes or fungus or whirlwinds. Even after our strange morning, his reply caught me by surprise.

"Spaceships. They think crop circles are their landing patterns."

"Oh, Fred—please." I rolled my head back against the buttery leather.

"I'm just telling you the popular view there," he protested. "I'd like to get a better look at it from uphill, see if it forms a pattern."

"Make it so," I agreed. "Warp three."

San Vittorio Road was longer than I'd imagined, a rutted, winding few miles bordered by tangled hills occasionally leveling to lush fields. There weren't many houses on the road, and they tended to come in clusters. Most were rural to the point of looking third-world, with scrubby, terraced gardens, cars on cinder blocks, and untethered goats. At Alan Miller's end of the road, only two houses were visible. One was freshly painted with bright trim and hollyhocks climbing the porch supports. Lace curtains dressed the windows.

The other had green paint showing through weathered patches of yellow, and a driveway piled with auto body parts overgrown with ivy. The porch was so swollen it looked mossy, and an old sofa beneath the eaves sprouted mushrooms from its arms and back.

I suspected this one was Miller's.

When we stopped to gawk, a white van, parked between the two houses, started up and pulled a U-turn. As it sped past, I caught a glimpse of the passenger, a thirty-something man with a graying buzz cut.

"Where's the barn the farmer talked about?" I could see the end of the road, but it looked like these two houses were the only structures here.

"I don't know." Fred drove the Lexus a few hundred yards forward into a turnaround. At that point, we spotted a dilapidated structure behind some trees.

A broad path curved up a steep grade. We climbed out of the car and continued on foot. When we rounded the first bend, a big, new house confronted us. What we'd taken for a footpath was apparently wide enough for a car; a Toyota sedan was parked near the front door.

"Wonder what happened here," Fred muttered.

The otherwise well tended house had a boarded-up front window, a dangling porch light, and a slashlike gouge in the door.

As I stared at it, the door opened.

A heavy, balding man with a long nose, wide mouth, and pale eyes seemed surprised to see us. He reached unconsciously toward his shirttail as if to tuck it in. "Hello?"

"We wondered if you'd mind . . ." Fred tilted his head, scrutinizing the man. "Dr. Joseph Huizen? The author of *Simple As Pi* and *Sweet As Pi?*"

"Yes." The man squinted as if a clearer view might help him identify Fred.

"We met at the last University Night." Fred stepped forward, extending his hand. "Dr. Fred Hershey. I guest-lecture the psychology graduate students now and then."

"Oh, yes?" But it was clear he didn't remember Fred.

"This is Willa Jansson," Fred continued, as if any friend of his must be a friend of Dr. Huizen's. "She's an attorney from San Francisco. She's representing your neighbor, Alan Miller."

"My neighbor?" He looked bewildered. "Is he buying land or something?"

Lest I seem like Mrs. Fred, I spoke for myself. "He was involved in a car accident; charges have been filed against him. The accident was close by here and there's a possibility that we might have a view of . . . something relevant from a hill behind your house."

Dr. Huizen shook his head as if I'd spoken Greek to him. "He had an accident on my property?"

Before I could reply, Fred blurted out, "Did you know you have a crop circle back there?"

I was surprised by his chattiness. The tendency is trained right out of lawyers. Surely psychiatrists were also in the habit of being closemouthed?

"Really?" Dr. Huizen looked interested.

"It's an odd coincidence, isn't it?" Fred added. "Don't you remember? At University Night, the Oxford scholar who was researching crop circles?"

"Ah!" His face lit up. "The fellow who kept on about 'sacred geometry.' Not that I don't appreciate geometry"— he turned to me—"I teach mathematics at the university. But good heavens above, what's sacred about it?"

48

"That's right—the sacred geometry of crop circles; he was writing a book." Fred looked excited. "The geometry of the patterns within the circles or something. I only remember because he wouldn't let anyone change the subject."

"How long ago was this?" I wondered.

"Not even a month," Fred guessed.

"The fifteenth of last month," Dr. Huizen confirmed. His face was friendlier now, a sparkle in his pale blue eyes. "Would you like to come in? You can get oriented from my patio."

When we followed him into the high-ceilinged foyer, we saw other signs of damage: a pile of shattered porcelain, scarred parquet, a broken chair leg.

The professor must have noticed our eyes on the disarray. He sounded apologetic "Apparently I did this."

"You?" Fred's tone was neutral, a nice, nonjudgmental, psychiatrist's reaction.

"Mr. Hyde . . ." He motioned us all the way in. "Would you like a cold drink?" His gaze strayed to a photograph of a young woman, circa 1950. A now-dead wife? One who'd trained him to offer refreshments to guests?

Fred glanced a question at me. "Cold water would be nice, thank you," I answered.

"The same for me," Fred said.

We followed our host into a square, white-walled kitchen with plenty of windows. He poured us water from a cooler.

Just when I began to doubt we'd get the skinny, he explained, "It was night before last. My first diabetic emergency. I didn't know I had diabetes." He handed us the water, looking rather ashamed of his condition. "It was a miserable shock, I'll tell you."

He opened a sliding door to a small patio with the usual white tube furniture. We had a view of a slight decline, and then a steep incline, all tangled with vines and flowers.

"I suppose I've been trying to take refuge in the chemistry of it, to use my training to make it more real to myself. It seems my body depleted my blood sugar and then began leeching it from my brain. I've never tolerated alcohol well and I'm not one for mind expansion, as they call it. So I've never been seriously altered before." He smiled wanly. "It put me nose-to-nose with something unimaginable to me. And I didn't care for the experience, not a bit."

"It must have been very disorienting." Fred sounded sympathetic—and maybe a little surprised. It wasn't easy to visualize Joseph Huizen, with his white hair and soft build, busting up a foyer.

"At the time," he continued, "I felt unfettered—I remember the sensation so distinctly: I felt lightened, as if my body were a weighted vest I'd managed to shrug off. I remember feeling joy at being free of this inconvenient mass —a sign I should go on a diet, I suppose. And then I started trying to dance. I had a notion of dancing across a tetrahedron buried in my floor like a fly in an ice cube."

"A tetrahedron?" Fred seemed to take a professional interest, as if he were documenting yet another case of pesky tetrahedral delusional disorder.

"It makes a funny kind of metaphorical sense. I've been flirting with tetrahedral mathematics, specifically tetrahedra within spinning masses like planets. For my next book, *Pi in the Sky.*"

"Wonderful title."

"It may sum up my likelihood of ever truly grasping the subject." The professor sighed. "But I suppose, when my brain suddenly flew into chemical chaos, that I *would* see myself dancing on a tetrahedron." He looked down at his hand. The back showed a big bruise around a puffy vein. A bad IV stick? "It must have been at that point that I called nine-one-one. I really don't recall doing it, but they assure me I did. Apparently I babbled at some length about tetrahedra. If an ambulance hadn't already been in Davenport finishing other business . . . they say I'd be dead now. My brain, damaged from the lack of sugar, would have forced me into a coma; and they tell me I wouldn't have awakened."

"That's a difficult realization for anyone." Fred remained in psychiatrist mode.

"By the time the ambulance reached me, I was outside,

communing telepathically—I thought—with a pattern of stars that had descended to eye level to discuss tetrahedra with me." He grinned sheepishly. "They made a few good points, too. I've been working on them."

"The unconscious can put together a lot of data for us," Fred agreed.

"Then I saw this dazzling, impossibly bright white light. And a strobing blue and red. I was utterly blinded by it."

Fred cast me a glance. I sat forward. Was this elderly math professor about to describe the descent of a spaceship?

"I became terrified. I recall backing toward the house, then stopping, immobilized. Two strange beings approached . . ." His voice became dreamy, subdued. "They were speaking gibberish, clad in some type of uniform."

"What else do you recall about them?" Fred asked.

"At the time, I seemed to know instinctively that they meant to harm me. But I wasn't able to back up any farther. I must have thrashed about on the porch a bit before making my way back into the foyer. I have cuts to show I broke lamps and a chair. But it seemed only seconds before these evil beings pinned me down and strapped me tight. I felt I would die of fright, truly—it was such a horrific shock. But I couldn't overcome their restraints. They carried me along a river of light into an enclosure. And then one of the beings sliced away the sleeve of my shirt and began torturing me with a needle."

Beside me, Fred had grown pale under his tan. He ran a finger under the wire frames of his aviator sunglasses, wiping away sweat.

Joseph Huizen glanced at him, a smile spreading across his face. "And then, the ordeal ended quite abruptly. The being with the needle injected me with glucose and . . . he suddenly became a paramedic. The blindingly bright vehicle turned out to be their ambulance."

I had to laugh. Poor Fred looked so relieved.

"Yes, quite an experience for someone who skipped all that sixties LSD business!" The professor grinned. "The medic said hello to me and started asking questions—who was I, where was I, that type of thing—obviously designed to see if I was back in reality. Then he explained the mechanics of diabetes, the warning signs, the seriousness—"

He looked so troubled, Fred patted his arm. "Quite an experience."

"It's odd, you know. We hadn't gone fifty yards down the road before the ambulance stopped. The paramedic who was tending me seemed mystified. The driver called to him to come up front for a minute. I remember he looked rather angry—you know, checking the IV, then me, looking like he meant to protest. But when he did go up front, it was a few minutes before I heard the driver say, 'We'd better go.' "

"That certainly is odd," Fred agreed. He glanced at me. "And I would think potentially actionable."

Dr. Huizen dismissed the suggestion with a good-natured wave.

"What night was this?" I wondered.

"Friday night."

"What time Friday night?"

"Perhaps three-thirty, four o'clock. Saturday morning, actually."

"And your ambulance stopped just up the road?" I wondered what to make of it.

"Yes. Whatever happened, the medic looked upset when he came back to me. Not that he didn't seem competent and concerned. But he was also flustered."

"My client's accident happened that morning. I wonder if the ambulance stopped near his house. Maybe the medics saw something going on there. Do you remember their names?"

"The one who tended me, his name badge said 'Barry.' I imagine the hospital's paperwork would tell you more." His gray brows were raised. "Well, I hope I've inadvertently helped you. I was beginning to feel guilty about being so long-winded."

"Not at all," Fred assured him. "I hope your condition is easily kept under control?"

"I suppose I'll get used to it," he said glumly. "They sent me home with the latest blood-testing kits and stacks of pamphlets apparently written for sixth-graders—you know the kind, illustrated with competent-looking women in shirt-dresses smiling at their children."

"If you need to talk this out, let me know. I'd be happy to recommend someone, Dr. Huizen."

"Please call me Joseph." The professor appeared embarrassed. "I'm fine, really. Just old age—we all have to make some accommodations . . . Why don't you tell me what you're trying to get a look at, and I'll walk you to the best vantage point. They say I need more exercise."

Five minutes later, we started up a tangled hill with no path.

Close to the top, the greenery dried to a less dense incline of tough-leaved shrubs. They smelled spicy.

"The fog line," Joseph pointed out. "It sits in a trough between the hills, keeping the lower part wetter than the upper."

When we reached the top of the rise, I looked down a steep hill and over smaller mounds to a series of meadows. One of them showed the big circle. I was surprised to see how many smaller circles ringed it.

Apparently, Fred was, too. He let out an appreciative whistle. "That's quite a footprint."

"My Lord," Joseph agreed. "It reminds me of something —I wish I could put my finger on it."

"It looks like a six-planet solar system with one too-small planet and one multiple-mooned planet," I ventured.

"How was it made?"

"Your guess is as good as mine," Fred told him. "It's smashed into the grass in a kind of spiral pattern. The circles inside circles are grasses swirled in different directions."

"It looks like something," Joseph repeated tentatively. "A schematic I've seen recently."

"Do you have any idea who could have done it? Or why? Have you heard any commotion out behind your house?"

"No. But I haven't been home since Friday night."

I continued staring down at the pattern. The way it reflected sunlight, it gave the impression of hovering above the meadow. Maybe that's what suggested spacecraft to the British.

Fred started down the hill, presumably for a closer look.

By the time we joined him, he was pacing off the size of the inner circle.

Maybe it had to do with pitching tents. Maybe it was performance art. Maybe it was some kind of cult thing. Or maybe Alan Miller had made them. Maybe he'd done it in the wee hours of Saturday morning, crashing the car on his way home.

Beneath my feet, at least three kinds of wild grasses bent to the left in a broad swirl, coming together in the circle's center. I squatted, examining a few stalks. They weren't bruised or broken. The only signs of damage were in the joints, some of which seemed browner than they should be. Most of the stalks were bent at the lowest joint, as if sudden heat—or something—had wilted them from within. Some grass leaves showed a rumpling like stretched crepe paper on one side.

Fred returned, saying, "The big circle's about twenty-five yards across. Five of the smaller circles are about five yards. That one over there is only about three yards. And one of the five-yarders has a three-yarder up above it, with three even smaller circles around it."

"Does it mean anything to you?"

The look he gave me said, *Oh right.*

Joseph Huizen was squatting in the center of the big circle. The droop of his head told me there was more to his posture than simple interest in the wild grasses.

I hurried to him. "Are you okay?"

Without looking up, he asked, "Don't you feel it?"

I motioned for Fred to join us. To Joseph, I said, "Why don't you sit down. You must be tired."

As Fred trotted over, Joseph murmured, "There's some kind of a charge here. Don't you feel it?"

Fred looked worried. He dropped to his knees, easing Joseph out of his squat so that he sat in the spiraled grass. "What's your insulin dose and when did you last take it?"

"No, I'm not unwell." But sweat beaded his cheeks. "It's like a static charge. Can't you feel it?"

"No." Fred was checking Joseph's pulse.

Joseph insisted, "Look at the back of my neck."

The hairs there were standing up.

Fred seemed a little nonplussed. "Your pulse is strong."

"And that crackle," Joseph added. "Did you hear it?"

"No. Willa?"

"No."

"It zipped by, a minute ago."

I reminded myself that Joseph had just been in the hospital because of a blood sugar imbalance. And, as Fred had pointed out, he'd begun taking a new medicine.

But I was afraid the truth was simpler than that. Fred, by bringing up crop circles, had slipped Joseph the most potent drug of all: suggestion.

7

It was a relief to leave before Fred reiterated the theory that spaceships create crop circles. I tried to sit quietly in the car, suspecting Fred wouldn't enjoy my sarcasm any more than his brother, Edward, had in years past.

Fred backed out of the dead end turnaround, starting to say something. But he stopped midword, abruptly braking.

Up ahead, smoke tumbled across the road.

Fred cut the engine, fumbling for his dash-mounted cell phone. I got out of the car and started down the road. The smoke was coming from Alan Miller's house.

As I passed his tidy neighbor's, I noticed no sign of life there—no one peeping through the window or the door, no interior lights, no chatter from a television.

Even before I reached Miller's gate, smoke stung my eyes. It hung over his porch like a billowing gray curtain. I paused where the road met his yard. His windows were opaque with smoke. I doubted it was safe to get closer.

Even from here, I could see that the front door hung strangely, as if a hinge had snapped free of the wood frame. I wished Fred and I had checked it earlier. I wished I knew whether sheriff's deputies had damaged it bursting in to search for Miller. If it happened today, it meant arson.

I heard Fred shouting, "Back up! Get away from there." I turned, coughing, to find him running toward me, still holding his cell phone. "Into the field."

I joined him in a tiny pasture across from Miller's house.

"There's a fire station a stone's throw from the Cash Store," Fred panted. "They should be here any second."

"That white van. Remember the white van parked here when we first drove up?"

Fred nodded, eyes glued to Miller's house. He stuffed his cell phone into his slacks pocket.

"Did you notice the license number?"

He shook his head.

A moment later, an explosion of flames knocked the front door down, licking over the porch and curling over the eaves before retracting into the house.

Fred grabbed my shoulder, pulling me several yards farther into the field.

We could hear sirens now. Fred was saying, "It's smoke inhalation that kills people. All the toxic matter in houses now, the fumes are poisonous."

"Do you remember the men in the van well enough to describe their faces?" I only had a clear enough memory of one of them.

"Holy sh—look at this!" Fred crouched to pick something up. Still squatting, he held up a black bauble of an earring. I took it from him while he searched the ground more thoroughly.

I let the earring dangle from my fingers. I wasn't completely sure, but it looked like those clipped to the ears of the widow who'd tried to shoot Alan Miller this morning. I imagined her, sometime since, standing in this spot. Before we got here, waiting for Miller to return home? Or more recently, waiting for his house to catch fire?

I glanced at Fred, examining the ground between fluffy grasses and low weeds. Funny that he'd happened upon this earring. If it were anyone but Fred, I might suspect the widow had dropped it in the hospital room and that Fred had palmed it to "discover" later.

It was easy enough to suspect a man who'd dragged in an out-of-town business lawyer and then championed an alien-abduction defense.

But I tried to quiet my worries. Fred had saved my neck

last year. He was Edward's brother, and I trusted Edward.
And he had no reason—none I knew of—to do Alan Miller
a disservice.

Fire engines were barreling down the road now. Fred
rose, standing beside me.

Miller's house was wrapped in smoke so thick that interior
flames glowed dimly, like a lightbulb through a scarf.

The fire trucks stopped in the middle of the road. Men
leaped off, some working valves and yanking huge hoses,
while others ventured closer to the house. One firefighter, in
thick protective garb, ran next door and began pounding at
the doors and windows. A moment later, he kicked open the
door and disappeared inside.

Fred walked briskly toward the trucks.

I watched the firefighter emerge from the neighbor's
house a moment later, speaking into a radio and gesturing
for another man to join him.

Fred was giving a fireman his card, presumably explaining
that he'd phoned in the call. The man nodded,
gesturing him away from the scene.

Fred returned to where I stood, telling me they'd asked
us to remain on hand until someone could question us. Considering
their fire trucks blocked the road, we had no choice.

Fred hustled me toward his Lexus, several yards past
Miller's neighbor's house. "Let's get well clear of the
smoke. The air in my car should be good. You're all right?"

Assuring him I was okay, I let him hand me into the
passenger side. He slid in behind the wheel, and for a while
we just sat and watched.

One of the firefighters climbed onto Miller's roof and
poked a hole into it. Another positioned a huge fan at the
door. Within minutes, smoke from the porch and front of
the house was being funneled up through the roof. Firefighters
went inside.

I was still gripping the black plastic earring. I put it on
Fred's dashboard. Against the backdrop of hardwood and
glove leather, it stood out like a cheap hooker.

I considered all the phone calls I had to make. I had to
talk to Miller's doctor, see how quickly we could get him

released—I didn't want him to remain a sitting duck. I wanted to get him booked and out on bail as soon as possible. I wanted to examine the forensics reports, see how much evidence the DA had; look over what was left of Miller's Fiat; hire a detective to search for the hitchhiker he'd picked up; interview his neighbor.

It made me tired just thinking about it. In the leather womb of Fred's fine car, I wanted to curl up and sleep. This was supposed to be my vacation. I was supposed to be resting and relaxing.

But another siren made me sit up straight. An ambulance was bumping across the shoulder of the road, edging past the fire trucks.

It pulled close to Miller's neighbor's house. Two medics, both women, leaped out, one of them joining a firefighter on the porch and the other opening the ambulance's side doors. She grabbed three large black bags and followed the other medic into the house. A few moments later, a firefighter returned to the ambulance, pulling a gurney from the back.

Fred said, "I'd better see if they need a doctor in there." When he opened the car door, acrid smoke stung my nose.

I remained in the car a few more minutes, debating whether to follow him. I reluctantly decided that something at the neighbor's might bear on my case.

I got out of the car, gagging at the stench. But hardly any smoke rose through Miller's roof now. And several firefighters were gathered at the truck, retracting the hose. The fire, I assumed, was out. I just hoped Miller could salvage something from it.

When I started up the walk to the neighbor's, a firefighter trotted toward me, shouting at me to get back.

I pointed to the house, calling, "I'm with the doctor." I hurried before he could block my way.

I stepped into a tidy house with buffed wood floors. A firefighter and a medic were crouched on either side of a supine woman. The medic was pumping a bag attached to a tube taped to her lips. The firefighter had both hands positioned on her chest, exposed where her T-shirt had been cut away. He was doing chest compressions. Fred knelt at the woman's head, shining a tiny flashlight into her open eyes. The second medic adjusted some kind of monitor.

I staggered back a step. The woman was waxy white and her eyes didn't blink.

The firefighter noticed me, but he didn't say anything.

I could hear a slight pneumatic wheeze from the air bag. And I could hear a cracking sound with each compression of her chest.

Damn, the woman looked so young, younger than me. What could have happened to her?

I looked around her house. Every surface gleamed. Bowls of wildflowers sat on colored straw mats. Bookcases were loaded with novels. The back window curtains were nailed into an artistic drape against the wall. Through it, a wild-flower-dappled hillside showed no sign of anything to invade her privacy.

On a corner desk, a small computer was still on, its screen saver glowing with a stained-glass pattern. Amid the flowers and waxed wood, it created the impression of being in a small rural church.

But I didn't see any open windows. And the stink of smoke was lighter in here than outside. Could the woman possibly have succumbed to smoke inhalation?

Fred was murmuring to the paramedics. He took over pumping the bag while they went tête-à-tête over the monitor. Whatever it should have measured, it showed only a flat line.

I edged toward the door. Maybe if I didn't hear them pronounce her dead, the image of her lying there exposed to the view of strangers, her ribs cracking, her mouth stuffed, her eyes glassy, would fade from my memory more quickly.

As I turned to go outside, I glanced at a small table next to a coatrack. It was stacked with library books. Poor woman, I wondered if she'd had a chance to read them.

I touched the topmost cover, opening the book. The liner showed a due date thirteen days away. She'd checked out the books only yesterday.

I glanced at the title: *Abduction,* by John E. Mack. I

tilted my head to see the spines of the other books: *Close Encounters of the Fourth Kind*, *The UFO Encyclopedia*, *Communion*, *Roswell Revisited*.

I stood there, hardly breathing. Why? Why had this woman gone just yesterday to check out a stack of UFO books?

I looked at Fred, wishing I could ask him, wishing he could give me some answer that would make my flesh stop crawling.

But Fred was shaking his head, watching the paramedics remove leads from small round pads on the woman's chest.

He approached me, saying, "She's been gone some time —probably a massive heart attack. They had to go through the motions. But it's time to get the coroner over here."

8

Miller was released from the hospital Sunday night and booked into the County Jail. He was arraigned Monday morning and out on bail by afternoon. Tuesday and Wednesday we selected his jury. And through it all, I waffled.

I never thought I could be so discouraged in a case where the District Attorney's Office had so little tangible evidence. In fact, the assistant district attorney had almost nothing: no Fiat tire prints in the field above Highway 1, no eyewitness to the accident, and absolutely no proof Alan Miller was inside his car when it landed atop poor Francis Everett Addenaur.

What the assistant DA did have was Miller's admission he was driving the Fiat earlier that night, his inability to provide a credible alibi, and—most persuasive of all—the notion that cars don't just fall out of the sky.

So even though the ADA's case was purely circumstantial, one of the circumstances was our basic understanding of how the universe works. I could cast doubt on every other aspect of the charge. But it was no use relying on reasonable doubt to suggest the car hadn't sailed off the cliff, tracks or no tracks. I either had to prove someone else was driving, prove Miller was elsewhere, or—God help me—prove that cars did indeed just drop out of the sky sometimes.

I'd get nowhere trying to prove someone else was driving.

Where were his or her fingerprints on the door handle, on the steering wheel, on the hand brake? And where the hell was the person? Barring a stroke of magnificent good fortune—finding the hitchhiker and having her confess to carjacking, for example—I wouldn't get far with this argument.

Nor had Miller budged on his alibi. His memory was returning, but so far—to his distress—it continued to match the wild tale he'd told under hypnosis. And that was no more of an alibi than *My car fell from the heavens* was a defense.

With the trial just around the corner, I was forced to make the choice I'd dreaded since first hearing Fred's tape. I could ask the jurors to agree the state hadn't met its burden of proof, hadn't proved beyond doubt that Alan Miller was driving his own car at two-thirty, even though he admitted having driven it a little earlier and refused to say where he was at the time. And I could wave good-bye to Miller as they led him away to jail.

Or I could put on an affirmative defense, the only one available to me: that Alan Miller's car and person had been outside his control that morning.

The absence of tire tracks worked in our favor. So did the nature of Miller's injuries. So did Fred's audiotaped hypnosis session and his expert opinion. So, according to Fred, did many other experts' opinions. But how much good did expert opinions do John T. Scopes?

And though it might be the best defense, I just couldn't make myself believe it. I reminded myself lawyers don't have to believe, only defend. But most lawyers only risk losing their client's case. They don't end up tarred with the same brush.

I was in San Francisco when I finally made the decision. I'd returned to grab some clothes and do a little late-night computer research at my law firm.

I was still hedging when I stopped by my parents' flat for dinner. Maybe a dose of there-but-for-practicality would put me right.

As usual, my mother got up a dozen times during dinner

to take phone calls, most of them about a caravan to deliver used computers to Cuba. Never mind that the Cubans had only two hours of electricity a day and precious few phone lines—my mother was sure socialism would flourish in cyberspace.

I poked at my stir-fry until my father, a slender, dimpled man, observed, "It's only been thirty years since the household went vegetarian—maybe you haven't given tofu a fair chance."

"What do you think of this alien-abduction stuff, Daddy?"

"Alien abduction? Coyotes at the border trucking in Mexicans?"

"No, space aliens, little gray men with bug eyes."

My mother reentered the room. Frowning as she was now, her skin looked as puckered as a deflated balloon. She wore her hair in the classic Women's International League for Peace and Freedom do—medium short, uncolored, and conscientiously unstyled. She was only a little overweight but she'd burned her bra thirty-five years ago, and it showed. The scary thing was, she'd looked a lot like me when she was my age.

She was seething as she crossed the dining room—if one could call it a dining room. Every sideboard and shelf was stacked with fliers, pamphlets, petitions, and diskettes. A sheet was tacked over the far wall for quick slide shows on the immorality of NAFTA.

Mother pushed away her half-eaten meal. "They're punishing him"—Castro, I presumed—"for being the last unrepentant socialist in the world."

"At least there's one left."

The doorbell rang, sending Mother through the door again. My father's chopsticks were poised partway to his lips as he waited to see which invading army would encamp here tonight. Would he spend the evening discussing Chinese labor camps, congressional e-mail box stuffing, or the politics of AIDS?

This time, Mother ushered in a group of aging cyberpunks, a recent coterie. My father, a true infoaddict, looked pleased. He'd recently fallen in love with the Internet. And my mother, grasping an opportunity for cheap mass mailing, was determined to work cyberspace like a street corner whore. The cutting edge had always managed to slash into our home life. It was a rare evening that every living room cushion wasn't a soapbox for someone with a monochromatic world vision. I'd grown up assuming we lived in a nation of ranters.

Tonight's cyberians were high on virtual avatars and erotic Web pages. They thought I was cool because my firm represented a group developing an Internet broadcast system. They didn't realize the damage done by recent movies glorifying techies, hackers, and nerds. Geeks in tight leather now talked kiss-kiss, do-lunch Hollywoodese. It was not a pretty sight.

Eventually, my father recalled the question I'd asked him over dinner, posing it to the group.

Moag, a thirtyish white guy with a bad Klingon haircut, immediately said, "I've been abducted."

I guessed they'd thrown him back.

"Not by the Grays, by the Pleiadeans." He crossed his plump legs into a half lotus. "They're not into the experiments. They're into communication and soul advancement."

My mother snorted. "Advancement doesn't come from other galaxies. It comes from a strong, united workforce—right here on earth!"

"There's more to life than the minimum wage," Moag pointed out. "Why should a guy dying of Ebola in Africa care how much some white asshole at the Ford plant makes? So imagine the rest of the universe giving a shit."

"And someone from the Pleiades is going to tell you what to care about?" Mother's cheeks were flushed.

Another netnerd spoke up, a ponytailed man with a bald spot and a squinty leer. "Have you seen the UFO Web sites? The video clips are great."

I turned to him. "What video clips?"

"Spacecraft mostly. A lot of sightings in Mexico, as usual. Another wave recently in Gulf Breeze, Florida."

"And the sightings were videotaped?"

"Tons of footage. In Mexico during the eclipse, home videos from people all over the city all showed the same ships."

"They weren't airplanes?"

"No way. Get on-line. Take a look."

"If there's video footage available, how come it's not broadcast?" But I already knew CNN and other stations had an aversion to news.

"In Mexico, it's on all the major channels. My wife watches their news all the time. Her English isn't very good."

A woman sitting beside Moag said, "There's a UFO conference here now."

"In town?"

"In the East Bay somewhere. I know the alien-propulsion-systems guy."

"The what?"

"He explains the antimatter reactor and space-bending mechanism used in the space ships."

My mother waved her arm impatiently. "This is just another way of turning our faces from the problems we have at home. Spaceships in Mexico! Let's talk about car manufacturers slinking down there. Let's talk about penniless, exploited Mexican truck drivers being manipulated into coming up here to undercut the Teamsters!"

My father chimed in, "I understand quantum physicists believe parallel universes might be intersecting this one. That might account for some of what people have been seeing." He glanced guiltily at my mother. She had forbidden him to mention his new hero, physics guru Brother Mike. To Mother, physics was just one more distraction from politics.

I still hoped to talk myself out of an alien abduction defense. So I egged Moag on: "You were saying the Pleiadeans differ from the Grays?"

"The Pleiadeans are called Nordics. They basically pass for good-looking Scandinavian types. And they don't get into the weird experiments, they don't do anything nonconsensual. They're not like the Grays. There's no way they'd sign that kind of treaty with us."

"You're saying we have a treaty with the Grays?"

He nodded emphatically. "Area Fifty-one in Nevada, the military's got a huge underground bunker there. Everybody's known about it for years, way before *Independence Day*. The government doesn't even bother denying it anymore. Instead, they land-grabbed the ridges overlooking it from the Indian reservations. But there's all kinds of videos of spaceships flying out of there, getting test-driven. Even Las Vegas news filmed one and showed it." He scratched a spot beneath his Worf goatee. "In return for the Grays giving us the technology, they get to abduct whoever they want —nobody high-ranking, just plebes—and the government doesn't try to stop them. And it keeps it out of the news as much as it can. Or makes it look ridiculous if it does get reported."

My mother jumped to her feet. "People actually put their energy into these beliefs?" Versus hers.

I wanted to reassure her: people believing in this government conspiracy might also be inclined to credit her conspiracies of choice.

"Area Fifty-one's for real," Moag insisted. "Just take a look at the videos."

"Well"—my father's tone was meant to soothe my mother—"but you're a computer videographer—you know how easy it is to fake video."

"There's been footage around for years—way before undetectable fakeability. One guy's Gulf Breeze pictures are in stereo film—that stuff's impossible to fake—plus people all over town took pictures of the same object. And look at the Mexico City eclipse films. How do over a dozen people in different parts of the city all fake the exact same thing from different perspectives? Same with the videos from Nevada and Florida. You've got footage from different people at different times in different cities of identical objects. They're here. They've decloaked."

I turned to the woman. "How can I find out where the UFO conference is?"

She looked at me pityingly. "Use a search engine."
Search engines guided one through the Internet.

Presumably some UFO Web site would have posted a full schedule. It was getting so much more convenient to be flaky.

9

The trial would begin on Tuesday. I didn't have the luxury of waiving the speedy-trial date and cobbling together a brilliant defense—or even taking a crash course in oratory. I'd barely had time for my quick trip back to San Francisco. But I made time to stop by the UFO conference.

I was explaining to Alan Miller, "It changed my mind."

"About alien abduction?" Miller looked alarmed. In spite of his precarious legal position, he still seemed to hope someone would disprove his story.

"No—not about that. About your defense." A major distinction.

Though Miller looked better than he had at his bail hearing, he still looked fragile and pale despite a strapping frame and manly jaw. He still looked shell-shocked.

Today we sat in Edward Hershey's living room. Edward had locked the place up for three months while undertaking a macho-man sail through the Panama Canal. Fred decided his brother wouldn't mind a house-sitter for the few weeks remaining until his return.

I'd been to Edward's several times. The place hadn't improved over the years. The wood floors were little better than rough planks after being repeatedly soaked with salt water from fishing gear, rubber boots, and wet suits. The kitchen was stacked with accumulating mail and fly-fishing lures. The living room was a musty accumulation of old sofas and easy chairs with broken springs. The bedroom— well, I'd vowed never to set eyes on it, and I saw no reason to change my mind now.

Alan Miller, with his mushroom-sprouting porch sofa, was probably not offended by Edward's decor, however. Miller's major regret about the fire seemed to be that he'd lost most of his slides and photographs of mushrooms. His obsession was to teach enough classes to replace his camera.

And his worry was that he'd go to jail instead of getting the chance. So I definitely had the man's full attention.

"You changed your mind about my defense?" he repeated. "But not about the plea, right?"

I'd come this morning with news that Assistant District Attorney Patrick Toben, your typical suit with a smug smile, had offered a deal. He'd drop the felony hit-and-run charge if Miller changed his plea to guilty of vehicular manslaughter. It would shave some years off the sentence.

"No, not about the plea. I still think we should go for broke. That's what I'm here to talk about. Going for broke means more than trying to disprove their case. It means putting on one of our own."

He finger-combed a curtain of dark hair off his forehead. "I don't get the difference."

"We probably can't win unless we put you on the witness stand and have you tell your story."

His eyes widened as he pressed himself against the back of Edward's couch. Either he hated the idea, or a broken spring had lanced him. "But you said I'd get laughed out of court."

"I talked to some people yesterday who are willing to offer expert testimony." I could feel myself flush. "They're all credentialed to the hilt."

Miller was looking distinctly mistrustful. "Psychiatrists?"

"One of them's a psychiatrist. One of them's a science librarian. One's a detective. One's a retired air force colonel."

"What would they testify about? None of them's looked at the Brussels sprouts field or anything?"

I never thought I'd give such crazy advice: "We need them to testify that UFOs are real. That's their area of expertise. I found them at a UFO conference. I handpicked the most credible, least eccentric of the lot."

And what a lot it had been: a best-selling science fiction novelist weeping over the beauty he'd found in his (he claimed nonfiction) abductions; a "forensic" artist who specialized in drawing the sixteen races of aliens housed in secret government compounds; Roswell experts faulting a recent alien autopsy video because the alien had too many fingers; the founder of an abduction support group specializing in child abuse survivors; a muttering sharp-eyed man tracing the government's "conspiracy of silence" back to the Freemasons and (inescapably) the Trilateral Commission; a "freelance exohistorian" documenting gene manipulations by aliens throughout our evolution; members of an alien-human hybrid organization; crop circle investigators so moved by "agriglyphs" that they became enraged by mundane questions about how they were formed.

But the conference was also packed with intelligent-looking post-docs and computer wizards, as well as hippies and "experiencers" of every stripe. It was totally devoid of *Star Trek* uniforms and *Dr. Who* T-shirts, which surprised me. And many of the presentations were impossible to dismiss. The information was impressive, if only for its volume and consistency.

"The psychiatrist is prepared to present the statistics: thousands of reported abductions. At least, I'll coach him to say thousands—he puts the figure at five to seven million, but I don't want to blow our credibility. He'll say that nothing we know of—mass delusions or the power of suggestion or the Jungian unconscious—can account for it. He'll say it has to be a real phenomenon."

Miller kept gulping as if he might cry. I knew he was in a bind. If he didn't believe this, he was crazy. If he did believe it, he was the victim of something too horrible to accept.

"The detective has video footage and still shots of UFOs. He'll talk about interviewing four hundred people who've reported sightings. And he's got scientific analysis of crop circles—showing that some are hoaxes but most of them couldn't be man-made. We'll use him as more proof that something physical is definitely happening, something that can't be explained away."

As way-out as some of the people at the conference had been, the fact remained: there was a mountain of pictorial evidence that something weird was going on. I just wished I'd remained in hidebound ignorance of it; seeing, in this case, was bewildering.

"I don't know, Willa. I don't know. Just because you've got experts saying it doesn't mean people won't laugh at it."

"A lot of people believe in this stuff already. Who knows how many of your jurors are in that boat?"

I'd tried to choose young, open-minded folk without overly conventional accessories. I'd favored Birkenstocks over Naturalizers or even Nikes. I'd stayed away from vinyl handbags with matching pumps. I'd rejected double-knit slacks and Nancy Reagan hair. It was a far cry from hiring a jury consultant, but I hoped it would help.

"You said you had a scientist?" Miller tried to sound hopeful.

"He used to work for NASA's library. He ended up using old NASA photos to prove they're hiding a lot of their current space images from us—apparently they're censored by the National Security Agency. And the last guy, the colonel, he's got charts and diagrams of secret military installations he says are hangars for alien spacecraft. It sounds nuts, but it's pretty convincing when he runs through it." I gave Alan a moment to digest this. "That's the game: to make the jury think it might be possible, and to show them smart-looking men with credentials and documentation who believe it. Then we'll hammer on the fact that the assistant DA, with all his forensics people, can't prove you drove through the sprouts field."

Miller looked glum. He slumped, elbows on his knees, staring at Edward's filthy rag rug.

"I wish I knew what really happened," he told me for the hundredth time. "I wish I had something certified real, a piece of paper like my doctorate, something I could hang on to to tell myself I wasn't crazy."

I didn't know what to say. I wished a law degree were that potent.

I'd barely managed, in the last few days, to acknowledge the evidence behind claims I'd previously dismissed as bogus. After what I'd seen and heard, after meeting Alan Miller, I could no longer be blithely derisive. But making a case for something is a far cry from believing it.

And if I was having trouble in this tiny corner of the Twilight Zone, I could imagine Alan's struggle.

"I won't do it if you insist that I don't. But I think it's your best chance." I never thought I'd hear myself say so, but, "I'm willing if you are."

He threw his head back, letting it loll on Edward's none-too-clean afghan. I noticed the tapered end of a deep scratch disappearing into the neckline of his "Fungus Amongus" T-shirt.

"That scrape—it's not from the night of the accident?" One argument for Miller's not having been in an accident was that he should have been cut: his windshield had popped out and shattered. But as I understood the doctors' reports, Miller's injuries had been internal, including impaired kidney function and inflammation associated with "sharp instrument trauma"—through unmarked skin—into a calf muscle and a kidney. I didn't recall a notation about scratches.

Miller shot me a shamefaced look. "You won't— It's not a big deal, okay? I don't want you to mention it to anyone, all right?"

"What happened?"

"I ran into her again."

"The hitchhiker?" She was very much on my mind. I'd just spoken to the detective I'd hired to track her down; he'd picked up a lead at a homeless camp. There was a possibility she could help establish Miller's alibi. But even if her story incriminated him, I wanted to find her before Assistant DA Toben did. It had been a long time since I'd tried a criminal case, and I didn't want to be blindsided. I'd do an amateurish enough job, I was sure.

"Not the hitchhiker. Addenaur's widow."

"Why didn't you tell me? You ran into her—or she stalked you?" Didn't he understand she might have burnt his house down? We'd shown him the earring. We'd handed it over to the police. They'd remained tight lipped about the arson investigation, except to say kerosene had been used. But clearly they suspected her.

"I saw her in the courthouse the day of the jury stuff."

"You saw her during voir dire and you didn't say anything?" I felt like slapping him.

Bad enough he'd told the sheriff that she hadn't threatened him with a gun, that the whole thing looked to him like an accident. The only reason she wasn't currently under arrest was that no one could find her.

"Sorry." He glanced at me. "I was going to tell you, but . . ."

"But what? She tried to shoot you and she probably burned your house down. For all we know, she scared your next door neighbor to death."

"Poor lady."

I hoped he meant thirty-two-year-old Donna Nelson, who'd moved next door to him earlier that month. Tough luck to have a massive heart attack at that age.

"I don't believe she was going to shoot me," Alan persisted.

"I know it's hard to think about how the accident affected her, but—"

"No, no—I get it that she's devastated, I'm not in denial. I just think she was raving. I didn't feel from her that she'd go to that length. You'd feel it if someone was really going to kill you."

"No, you wouldn't." Unfortunately, I spoke from experience.

"Another thing . . . don't you think Dr. Hershey could

have gotten her earring stuck on his jacket when he wrestled her? It doesn't seem very likely that he'd come across it by accident in a big old field. I mean, isn't that a little hard to believe?"

I was with him on that one. But as to the rest of it: "She was going to shoot you, all right. Even if you couldn't 'feel' it, I could. That's why I grabbed her handbag."

But he continued looking unconvinced. Why the hell did he feel so guilty about her husband's death if, as he believed, he wasn't even in the car?

"Tell me about the courthouse. What did she do to you?"

He pulled down the neck of the T-shirt. Even through his dark weave of chest hair, I could make out healing claw marks. "She kind of got my back a little bit, too. It's not bad, though."

"What did she say? What else did she do?"

"The same stuff—that she'd never find anyone like him again, that she'd die alone." He looked pained. "I don't suppose you've got an alcoholic in your family?"

"No." Just a couple of old radicals drunk on politics.

"I've had to deal with a few—basically, my mom and my aunts on her side. That's what's going on here, if you want my opinion. People get worked up when they drink, and she's been hitting it."

"How did you stop her?"

"A couple of deputies came out of the men's room."

I humphed. "What are the odds of that happening next time? We need to tell the sheriff about this."

I wondered if Toben could possibly use Miller's failure to report this against him. Could he infer Miller's guilt from it? Could he argue that Miller's consciousness of wrong-doing was behind his silence?

Questions like this just don't come up in patent searches.

10

I worried about the fact that Fred was picking up the tab for the expert witnesses. It might become an issue in the trial, where his audiotape and psychiatric testimony would figure prominently. I vowed not to mention Fred's name to any of the witnesses; I didn't want them blurting it out in response to a fee question from the assistant DA. I didn't want it to look like Svengali Fred had hypnotized the story into Miller's head, then hired experts to lend it credence.

I sent plane tickets to each of the four UFOlogists and arranged to put them up at a local hotel the day before I expected them to testify. I would meet with each the evening he arrived. It's customary to spend some time going over a witness's testimony. But I'd blocked out extra hours to get up to speed on a subject I'd never deigned think about. The UFOlogists had been amiable about staying on an extra day, perhaps two, if there was a delay in the proceeding. (It certainly helped that Santa Cruz had miles of beaches and lots of cute bars to spend Fred's money in.)

So I was expecting to turn my attention to UFO experts. I just wasn't expecting to turn it so soon, and to turn it toward the one UFOlogist I'd resolutely crossed off my list. The ironic thing was, I wouldn't have had to deal with Reginald Fulmer at all if I hadn't stupidly asked him a few questions at the UFO conference.

At the time, he'd seemed so scattered and unfocused I'd doubted he was listening to me. Unfortunately, he was.

He'd just presented an hour-and-a-half slide show of crop circles in England. His comments on each slide had been effusive, extravagant, full of upper-class British stutters and pedantic drawls. As fascinating as the crop circle patterns had been—triangles within circles, orbit rings, spiderwebs, flower shapes, concentric swirls—this man, who'd spent every summer for the last eight years sleeping in grainfields to try to see a crop circle being formed, bombarded us with hyperbole until I was numb.

With his long flared nose, thin cheeks, down-turned lips, and flyaway bush of hair, he resembled a commedia dell'arte version of Mr. Ed. He alternated pacing manically or dropping into a chair to sit on his spine with his knuckles dragging on the floor. I'd seen fewer dramatic flourishes at Finocchio's.

Though I learned that over two thousand increasingly complex crop circles had been appearing as if by magic in British fields for decades, I didn't learn much else from the presentation—it was, ironically, mostly chaff. But because there were circles so close to Alan Miller's house, I toyed with the idea of inviting Reginald Fulmer down to testify.

I cornered him after his slide presentation, waiting while a gaggle of organic-food hippies rhapsodized with him. From one of them, I learned that hundreds more circles had appeared in a dozen other countries.

When I finally got Fulmer to myself, I still felt as if I were in a crowd. I couldn't cut through his posturing and gesticulating, had to weather a long word-spree about how he hoped he'd done well, but really, if people were going to want to cover the same ground every year—facts available in all the books, for goodness' sake—rather than looking, really *looking* at the pictograms themselves ... after all, these glyphs must be allowed to speak for themselves, to speak directly through the visual cortex into that part of us that isn't tediously fussing over the same old dry statistics about when the circles are formed and in what direction the grain is swirled and whether it's suitable for harvest—really, why can't people separate out what's important, why can't they look at the damn circles and see them and experience them at the level at which they choose to communicate with us?

Since I'd stayed behind especially to ask him the questions he scorned as philistine, I kept it short.

"The crop circles that looked like a solar system—rings with circles around bigger central circles—do you know of any like them in this country?"

A plain, sensible-looking woman appeared behind him and began putting away his slides. He glanced at her as if she were an intrusive servant.

"Solar systems?" He rolled his eyes. "What a stupid assumption. They aren't solar systems, for pity's sake."

"I just meant that's what they looked like to me. Do you know the ones I mean?"

"Of course I know the ones you mean." His tone was sarcastic. "Americans always want to call them solar systems, God help us. It's all your *Star Trek* and *Star Wars*—you've no imagination left. What about the so-called solar systems?"

We were off to a brilliant start. "Have you seen anything similar to them in this country?"

"You don't get crop circles in this country." His tone made it clear we didn't deserve them. "Perhaps the odd one here and about, I don't know. It may be you people mow them down as a nuisance, just as you do your redwood forests." He began stuffing papers into a briefcase full of protractors and straightedges.

"Can I draw a crop circle for you, one I've seen? I'd like to know if you've encountered anything like it."

He raised his supercilious brows as if to say that wasn't bloody likely.

Nevertheless, when I drew the thing in the field behind Joseph Huizen's house, he spent several minutes scowling at it.

"Where is this?"

"In Santa Cruz county. A town called Davenport."

He squinted at me suspiciously. "You're quite sure it's a crop circle and not something else entirely?"

"You tell me—what are the hallmarks of a real crop circle?"

"The grain's not broken. It rather wilts at the growth nodes. And it's precisely swirled and woven, not pathetically, raggedly stomped down like the hoax circles by Doug and Dave, who fooled no one but the media with their amateurish grab at the limelight. Occasionally, there might be a sort of charge in the air—an indescribable physical effect— if the circle's quite fresh." This was more information than he'd provided in his entire slide presentation.

I wondered whether, with precise questioning, he might be useful on the witness stand, after all.

He answered my silent question by wadding up the paper I'd drawn on and throwing it at me. "Solar systems! Idiots raised on telly pabulum. Why, why, why must we always be looking for spacemen muttering *'Klatu barada'* and dum-dum-dum-dum?" He hummed the notes from the movie *Close Encounters.* "You find yourself in the presence of a communication from an ancient other, brilliantly editing itself, elaborating upon its previous utterances to produce the magnificent geometries I showed you today, and what do you Americans always think? *Oh, Mildred, turn off* Wheel of Fortune; *the spacemen have landed."* He gestured with both arms. "Have you any concept of how ancient a thing we're dealing with here? Think Merlin, not Mork! Do you suppose it's a coincidence that two thousand agriglyphs have appeared in the exact area where we have nine hundred stone circles, including Stonehenge?"

I backed away, saying, "Guess not."

The woman behind him dropped a slide tray. He turned to her with a vexed "For godsake! What now?"

I left quickly.

Luckily, I encountered a detective later in the conference who'd accumulated botanical data about crop circles, including microscope analysis of the affected grain. He could prove the grain had dramatically enlarged "cell pits," suggesting an unknown physical process involving intense microwave energy (like a spaceship landing?). By that time, my brain was awash in statistics—I'd been to several presentations by UFOlogists backing their claims with math (and math goes over my head at the point beyond which I can use it to balance my checkbook).

I had hoped never to set eyes on Reginald Fulmer again. I never dreamed my drawing—the one he'd crumpled and thrown at me—would bring him to Davenport.

I'd spoken to him on Saturday. That night, he contacted a colleague, the Oxford scholar who'd met Joseph Huizen and Fred Hershey during University Night. He, in turn, spoke to Joseph, who verified the circle's existence and provided the exact location.

As elaborately detailed as recent crop circles in England had been, the one in Davenport was at least as complex. This was especially remarkable because the wild grasses were a less dense, uniform palette than grain. So the following morning, Reginald Fulmer came to take a look.

And he didn't go away soon enough to keep his weirdness from tainting Alan Miller's trial.

On Monday morning, I picked up the local paper and saw a color photograph of the Davenport crop circle on the front page. Half a column inch later, Reginald Fulmer was effusing: "The earth is speaking to us directly, if we will only turn off the boob tube and take the trouble to look."

That seemingly innocuous statement must have touched a nerve: it was picked up by the wire services and reprinted in the *L.A. Times* on Tuesday. By Wednesday, it started pilgrimages: "Wicca" (witch) covens, New Agers, UFO "experiencers," the curious, the flaky, minor gurus and their coffee shop followers, and, of course, Reginald Fulmer himself, charging $40 a head for on-the-spot seminars that probably amounted to no more than "Look at the circle, and don't bother me with questions!"

The pilgrimages, in turn, brought puff-piece newscasters from ten counties—*look at the hippies, Ma.* If I'd been worried before about my defense being noticed and laughed at, now I felt doomed.

The local newspaper went on a full-out assault to prove

that Santa Cruz was a levelheaded, business-friendly haven of rational consumers. One local columnist slammed the crop circle pilgrims as "superstitious, gullible throwbacks to an era of inquisitions and charlatans, willingly preyed upon by mental midgets pushing New Age snake oil."

And onto the stage I'd inadvertently set myself, Alan Miller and I had to make our courtroom entrance.

11

On the first day of trial, I awakened early. There was still a deep-night chill in the air and the light was sallow. I was disoriented for a moment, missing the familiar smells of old apartment and heaped laundry, the pencil line of sunlight through gapped curtains.

Instead I smelled a fabric-softened duvet. I opened my eyes, surprised to find myself beneath a white eyelet comforter in a white room dotted with peaceful watercolors. My first thought was the Betty Ford Clinic—this level of tranquillity suggested upscale recovery. Then I sat up: Fred's guest room was a dream of expensive blandness, matching the rest of his waxed-hardwood-and-matte-white townhouse.

I climbed out of bed, perversely missing my messy, downscale flat. But I'd managed, even on so short a stay, to put my stamp on this place. My suitcase, on an upholstered bench beneath a window, appeared to have erupted with clothes and clutter.

I crossed to it, rummaging for underwear. I looked out the window into Fred's backyard, where severely pruned shrubs flowered meekly. Except for a few big pines, it was the most castrated garden I'd ever seen. Like Fred's condo, it showed little regard for profusion.

I heard a sliding glass door open below, and watched Fred

step outside. In shorts and a T-shirt, he began trotting down his walkway. I figured I'd be out of the shower before he finished his morning run, so I didn't bother taking my business suit into the bathroom with me.

Later, drinking coffee in Fred's Swedish wood kitchen, I went over my notes obsessively, never calming down enough to really read them. I'd lost the last case I'd tried. I hadn't considered hara-kiri, but the experience had left me feeling unimpressive.

I was surprised, leaving for court, to find Fred standing beside my car. He stiffened when he saw me, taking a backward step.

"I'm off to the wars," I told him.

He didn't say anything. When I got closer, I noticed he wasn't sweating, didn't even have a runner's blush.

Frowning slightly, he cleared his throat. "That time already?"

"Yes." I was surprised to find my Honda door unlocked. I slid into the driver's seat, tossing my briefcase onto the seat beside me.

I glanced up at Fred, expecting some comment of encouragement. And some reason to believe he hadn't just been snooping in my car.

But Fred seemed wrapped in his own thoughts. He was still standing there when I turned the corner.

12

I sat at the defense table with Alan and watched the jurors. The judge, a beagle-faced man with half glasses, took his time shuffling through papers.

The jurors appeared expectant and alert. I hoped they weren't mulling this morning's news about multiple arrests of beach campers in Davenport, the first wave arriving to gawk at the crop circle. I hoped they weren't irritated about morning traffic through downtown streets inconveniently clogged with Grateful Deadheads, barefoot Rastafarians, and crystal-wearing blessing givers. As they fought for parking places around the courthouse, I hoped they hadn't been muttering about yet another influx of grooving, oh-wow transients.

I glanced over at Assistant DA Toben, a thin, buffed-out boomer with comb lines in his hair. He was leaning back in his chair, a corner of his mouth curled as if he was trying hard not to smile. With my expert witness list in front of him, he had every reason to look like the cat who'd swallowed the canary. We were going ahead with the *Outer Limits* defense; he didn't look too worried.

The courtroom itself was standard issue, with wood paneling and a big state seal between an American flag and a California flag. Below the judge, flanking him, a clerk and a court reporter sat looking patient and practical. Their lives were made up of delays.

The pews seemed a little on the full side for a vehicular manslaughter case. But Addenaur's widow hadn't shown up; that had been my main concern.

That is, until Alan Miller glanced at the audience and bent close to whisper, "Leonard Deally's here."

I turned to look. Leonard Deally was a columnist who in this morning's paper equated believing in crop circles to devolution into pre-*sapiens* ignorance. He wasn't likely to have much respect for our defense. But who'd tipped him off? Why had he come here?

"Which one?" I whispered. There were a few men in the audience with unstyled hair and sport coats, underdressed for lawyers and overdressed for passersby.

"With the three-piece."

I was surprised. I'd taken the portly young man for a stolid financial planner with a Rotary meeting later in the day. I'd met a lot of reporters, but never one who looked like a banker manqué.

The judge was looking over the rim of his half glasses as if our whispering demeaned him. Put a man behind a maple bench and he thinks he's Zeus.

There was a stirring in the courtroom, pure anticipation. The judge had already welcomed the ladies and gentlemen of the jury and thanked them for performing this valuable civic duty. So I knew what he was about to say: batter up.

I watched my opponent walk suavely toward the jury and smile like a genial MC. He greeted them, then launched straight into a rap about circumstantial evidence: "You've probably heard the term on television dramas and in the news. You might know already that it means evidence drawn from looking at the circumstances of the crime. It's not an eyewitness account or a confession, but that doesn't make it any less reliable. Circumstantial evidence asks you to reach logical conclusions from the facts of a case; that's all. We'll do our best to explain those facts to you. And the judge will give you careful instructions on how to reach your conclusions from them. All of us representing the People of the state of California will do our best to ensure that the ends of justice are served. And we know you'll do your best . . ." Blah blah blah.

If I was no Clarence Darrow, at least he wasn't William Jennings Bryan.

But the opening statement wasn't about engaging jurors' intellects, it was about winning their trust. Patrick Toben, detailing the accident scene, previewing the testimony of highway patrolmen, sheriff's deputies, and paramedics, wasn't merely presenting his data—he'd do that later. He was, instead, showing his compassion and his grit: on behalf of the People of California, he cared about a life cut short; and any caring juror would trust his perspective and take him at his word.

I watched him critically. The jurors looked interested, even when their thoughts might have begun straying toward lunch. But they weren't in his pocket, not yet. I'd have to be careful not to put them there.

So the lunch hour would have been a perfect time for some sort of Zen centering or method lawyer's affirmation to improve performance. Maybe I'd have even thought of one. But I didn't get the chance.

As I sat with Alan Miller in the basement cafeteria, he glanced at the front page of the local paper's "Living" section. It showed two color photographs. One was an aerial view of the crop circle, shaggier than the day Fred and I stood atop the hill. The other was an on-the-ground shot of happy pilgrims circling it, holding hands.

Alan grabbed my arm, pointing to one of them. "That's her! That's my hitchhiker!"

13

A breathless phone call to our detective resulted in a busy lunch hour with no time to rethink my opening statement. Before I knew what hit me, I was introducing myself to the jury, half my mind still on the hitchhiker.

To make matters worse, Alan caught my eye and rubbed the lapel of his borrowed sport coat. When I glanced at my own lapel, I saw fuzzy little blooms from a tree near the outdoor pay phone I'd used to avoid eavesdroppers. There was no inconspicuous way to brush it off, so, with a sigh, I did it conspicuously.

I was off to a Willa Jansson start, that's for sure.

"The assistant district attorney has explained circumstantial evidence to you and promised you detailed instructions on how to weigh it. What he hasn't promised you, and can't promise you, is enough circumstantial evidence for you to find Alan Miller guilty of vehicular manslaughter or hit-and-run."

God, I already had the flop sweats. I'd be looking for a demure way to wipe my cheeks in a few minutes.

"You'll learn that no one saw the accident that killed poor Mr. Addenaur. You'll learn there isn't a single tangible piece of evidence to prove that the accident happened the way the prosecution says it did. And you'll hear physicians testify that Alan Miller's injuries weren't consistent with his being in a car crash."

I went through these points more fully, hammering on evidence the prosecution should have found but didn't.

Then I took a deep breath. "The prosecution says its case depends on circumstantial evidence. But don't confuse circumstantial evidence with nonexistent evidence. A lack of evidence is not a circumstance, it's only a lack of evidence." Well duh, Willa.

I was getting nervous, conscious of Leonard Deally behind me in the pews. Toben must have tipped him off, told him to come here and listen to me talk about space aliens. No one but the assistant DA knew the guts of my defense, no one but Fred. No one else had a stake in seeing it ridiculed in the newspaper.

I looked at the jurors. They seemed like nice, white-collar people with polite faces. Before Leonard Deally made me doubt my strategy, I'd decided to prepare them for what they would later hear from me. I'd decided they needed all the time I could give them to get used to the idea.

But they weren't sequestered. And there was no way to insulate them from Deally's derisive ink.

When in doubt, hedge. "An implication here, an *It stands to reason* there, an *it must have happened that way*—these don't add up to circumstantial evidence. These are guesses made in a void, made precisely because there is no evidence. And multiple surmises don't equal a fact. Three times zero is still zero."

I could hear a stirring behind me and wondered if Toben was standing up to object, to make it look like I was mischaracterizing the evidence. The strategy had worked for O. J. Simpson's prosecutors; they'd won that round, though they'd lost the case.

I forged ahead. "Alan Miller isn't obligated to do anything but sit back in the courtroom and watch the prosecution try to add up the zeros: zero witnesses, zero tire tracks, zero accident injuries to Mr. Miller. Alan Miller isn't obligated by any rule or law or even stratagem to testify before you or to bring others here to testify on his behalf. But he will."

I launched into a syrupy biography of Miller: how he'd

put himself through college after his parents died, how he'd helped shape a mycology graduate program out of the university's botany curriculum, how he'd come to be a respected mushroom expert, teaching classes through the museum and writing local field guides.

"The fact is," I concluded, "Alan Miller cares about this community and is an important part of it. He cares too much about his reputation to sit back and let the prosecution fail to prove him guilty. Alan Miller is going to do something he's under no obligation to do: he's going to prove his innocence."

During closing arguments, I'd remind the jurors a dozen times that the prosecution had the burden of proof and that they must find Miller not guilty whether he'd "proved his innocence" or not. But for now, it sounded good.

And for now, it would have to be enough. I didn't want to preload Leonard Deally's gun for him. Let him wait a few days until the first of our experts spoke the A-words: "alien abduction."

I managed a concluding smile. I hoped I looked more confident than I felt. They say jurors, like dogs, can smell fear.

Whatever impression I'd made on the jury, Alan Miller was ecstatic. His color was almost as high as his denial. He whispered to me, "That was great! Great! You were so good, maybe—" His eyes were bright and hopeful. "Maybe we could just stick with that. You know, not even bring up the other stuff."

The judge scowled at us for whispering. I shushed Alan until court was dismissed for the day. I was glad he'd liked my opening statement, but if he trusted jurors to acquit him based on little more than an absence of eyewitnesses, he was being naive.

We discussed it in my car on the way to the detective's office. By the time we arrived, Miller looked deflated.

The detective I'd hired, Carl Shaduff, had been recommended by Fred. It seemed that Edward, also a private eye, hired him whenever he needed backup.

Shaduff worked out of a studio in front of his house. The

neighborhood, just a block over from Edward's, was a mix of shabby rental Victorians and yuppified bungalows. It was close enough to downtown that I could see the sprawling deck of a café crowded with students.

I'd expected to find Shaduff alone, I hoped with news of the girl pictured in the newspaper. I didn't expect to walk in and find her there with him, sitting at a rickety conference table finishing a take-out Mexican dinner.

Beside me, Alan choked back what he'd been saying. The girl glanced up, dropping her fork when she saw him.

She looked barely postpubescent, with freckled round cheeks, shoulder-length brown hair razored short above the ears, and full lips ravaged with cold sores. Her sweater, though stretched tight, appeared warm and new beneath a layer of dirt. At her feet, a big backpack was almost empty.

I glanced at Shaduff, a strapping buzz-cut blond obviously of Scandinavian descent. Despite his tidy gray suit, his red face suggested he'd just come in from ice fishing.

He said, "This is 'Mackenzie.' " He spoke the name as if he didn't believe it for a minute. "Just Mackenzie."

The girl flashed him an annoyed look.

Alan was stuttering, "I'm—look, I'm glad—glad you're —Are you okay?"

"Uh-huh." But her posture changed. She seemed to curl around an invisible weight on her chest.

"I found her at the crop circle," Shaduff explained. "There's a regular encampment out there."

I sat at the table opposite the girl. The room was spartan: the table, a desk, some computer equipment, filing cabinets. Right now, it smelled of burritos.

"My name is Willa Jansson. You've met my client, Alan Miller?"

She hugged herself, nodding.

"Would you tell me the circumstances of your meeting?" I didn't want to lead her. I wanted to know the worst, if that's what she had to offer the prosecution.

"Why?" Her tone wasn't the sullen default of many teenagers. She sounded worried.

I caught Shaduff's eye, wondering what he'd said to get

her here. He rubbed his thumb over his fingertips, letting me know he'd had to pay her.

"There was a car accident involving Alan's car. It was at two-thirty the morning of the night you met. We're talking to everyone Alan saw that night. The time line is very important in our case."

"He told me," she glanced at Shaduff, "that I wouldn't have to testify in court."

"That's not what I said," Shaduff objected. "If your story doesn't have any bearing, the lawyers won't call you to testify; that's what I said."

"That's right," I assured her. "If your statement isn't relevant, you won't be asked to testify." But the prosecution would almost certainly find her testimony relevant, if only to prove Miller was driving his car earlier that night. "In the meantime, you're considered a material witness, and the district attorney is searching for you."

She looked alarmed, tears springing to her eyes. "Why?"

"We're trying to find out what happened between the time Alan left San Francisco that night and the time the accident happened. That's all. There's nothing for you to worry about. Let's just start with when and how you met Alan, okay?"

"I don't want to talk to the district attorney." She pushed away from the table.

She displayed more than the usual amount of anxiety about becoming a witness in a court case. She was probably a runaway.

"Why don't you tell us what happened that night? And I'll be honest about whether I think the DA will want you to testify, all right?"

"Will he arrest me?"

Alan stared at her with openmouthed intensity. Wondering if her question meant she was involved in the accident?

"You won't be arrested unless you participated in the crime. The DA just wants to know what time you accepted a ride from Alan and what happened after that. Look, I can answer your questions much more fully after you've answered mine."

"What's your name again?"

"Willa Jansson."

"And you're a lawyer?" She sounded as if that were a marvel, an attainment not remotely within her grasp.

"That's right. Can you tell me where and what time you first met Alan?"

She hesitated.

"You *have to* tell me." I gambled she was young enough to be in the habit of doing what adults commanded.

"Friday night." She leaned forward as if monitoring my face for early signs of hostility or danger. "Hitchhiking. In some little town."

Alan began, "It was—"

But I held up a hand for him to be quiet. The last thing I wanted was for him to feed her answers—answers she might change for Patrick Toben.

But she just sat there. I finally offered, "Half Moon Bay?"

"I guess so," she confirmed.

"You'd never been through there before? Where were you coming from?"

"Just . . . I was just traveling. I have some friends here." She flushed. She might have friends here now, but I doubted she'd had any when she arrived.

"So you saw Alan in Half Moon Bay. Then what happened?"

She looked at Alan again. For another answer?

"I asked him for a ride, and he said okay."

"Where did he take you?"

"I don't know. Here. I'm here, aren't I? I don't know the exact spot." She was sounding a little panicked.

"Well, why don't you tell me the circumstances when Alan stopped the car. Did you get out in a town, a beach, a residential area, a business district? You don't have to know the place-names, just describe the general area where you stopped."

Her breathing grew audibly ragged. "I don't know. It was weeks ago."

"Not even two weeks," I pointed out. "You remember

meeting Alan and accepting a ride from him. I'm only asking you when and where you got out of the car."

"I don't know!" she repeated. "I can't testify if I don't know."

"That's not true." I had to make her understand that feigned ignorance wouldn't help her. "Even if you don't remember anything else, your testimony would prove Alan was driving earlier that night." I let it sink in. "It's only if you answer our questions fully, and both sides decide we don't need your information, that you won't have to testify. That's why you're better off searching your memory and cooperating with us."

Her mouth tightened to an I-won't-cry line.

"You're a runaway, aren't you? You're afraid the district attorney's office will send you back home."

She remained statue still.

"If you're having problems at home, you're much better off talking to someone in the DA's office about it. There are probably a lot of alternatives you haven't thought of. They can help you."

She shook her head.

Shaduff piped up. "This is not a good town to be on the streets at night, believe me. I can take you to a friend of mine at Child Protective—"

"No! I'm staying with friends. I'm not a runaway. I'm nineteen." She looked barely sixteen.

"Mr. Shaduff's just saying we'd like to help. I wish you'd trust me; I want to help." I waited until she looked a little calmer. "But for right now, you've got to make an effort to remember when and where you left Alan. He's been charged with two very serious crimes, and his freedom's on the line. It's really important that you be honest with us."

I glanced at Alan, leaning against a wall. He pressed a thumb and finger into his closed eyes as if trying not to cry. The stress of finding this girl but getting no information from her seemed too much for him.

The girl watched him, too. Her shoulders drooped. She looked nearly spent by her effort to appear decisively nineteen. But after a pause, she repeated, "I don't remember. It was weeks ago."

"How about the next morning? Did you wake up in Santa Cruz? In Davenport? On a sidewalk? In a bed? On the beach? This would be your first morning in the area. You'd remember your first morning, right?"

"On the beach, I guess; I don't really remember." She sat as still as a mouse facing a snake.

"Here in Santa Cruz?"

"Maybe. I don't know."

"What did you do that first morning? Did you walk on the beach? Talk to kids downtown?"

"It was too long ago! How'm I supposed to remember?" But she certainly remembered something: her lips curled downward and her brows furrowed. Whatever had happened, it had been a hard morning.

"Okay, then"—maybe if I started over, nice and friendly —"let's go back to Half Moon Bay. Were you having a bite to eat there?"

For the next hour, I did my best to act supportive, to win her trust. But I battled an accelerating desire to shake her.

Carl Shaduff sat behind his desk, rubbing his chin and looking tired. Alan slumped in a chair against the wall, apparently lost in thought. The girl kept her eyes on the remains of her burrito. Spellbinding I'm not.

In a last-ditch effort, I laid it on the line. "I'm going to tell you exactly what this case is about. I want you to know what Alan's up against here. Maybe then you'll understand why it's crucial that you make an effort."

I described the accident. I described the police search for Alan. I described his condition when they found him, his hospitalization, his amnesia, the difficult alibi he'd offered under hypnosis.

Only my description of Alan's hypnosis won me her full, startled eye contact.

"Do you understand what I'm telling you? Long after you really are nineteen and things are going fine for you, Alan Miller could still be in prison. Think how you'd feel then, knowing you held back information. Your memories of that night could make all the difference—if you'll just put your mind to it." My voice was rising in pitch. I was going to lose it soon, stand up, reach across the table, and try to slap an answer out of her.

She continued staring at her dinner as if it were a television screen. Her eyes flickered with thoughts and unspoken comments, as if some story unfolded in her paper plate.

Finally she repeated, rather huskily, "I don't remember."

"Would you be willing . . ." Toben might object. And it could turn out badly for Miller, I didn't know. "There's a psychiatrist named Fred Hershey. He's a very caring person, and you can trust him. What he could do, if you'll consent, is try to hypnotize you, try to nudge your memory."

She rose suddenly, knocking over her chair. "No! No way!"

Alan Miller freaked out, too, though less dramatically. "You don't think—Are you saying she was with me when they abducted—"

"No." I gestured for him to shut up. I didn't want to plant memories she didn't have. "No. I'm just suggesting we try to jog her memory."

The girl was backing toward the door. With a smooth inconspicuous motion, Shaduff slid out of his seat and stood between her and the exit.

She was so young—maybe she had comic book ideas about hypnosis. "Hypnotism is a very well respected, non-harmful procedure. Dr. Hershey would relax you and invite you to recall what happened that night, that's all. I've been hypnotized. It doesn't hurt, and the doctor doesn't intrude on other—"

"No! I won't do it! I don't have to!" She'd grown so red faced she looked like a toddler having a tantrum. "I don't remember anything. And you can't make me stay here saying so over and over."

"At least tell me this: What have you been doing since that night? Where are you living? How did you end up in that newspaper photo?"

"I haven't been doing anything. Just staying with friends. I have a right to do that, don't I?"

Only if you really are nineteen. "Have you spent much time in the crop circle?"

The change of subject seemed to calm her a little. She shrugged. "It's raggedy now. Some of the grass is standing back up. And all the people walking to it, a lot of the field's mashed." She sounded apologetic. "It still looks sacred, I guess."

"Do you know much about sacred geometry?" I wanted to ask if she'd been taken under the tiresome wing of Reginald Fulmer. But she didn't do well with direct questions.

"Yeah." She didn't sound sure.

"Maybe you could explain it to me sometime? We could go out there together."

She didn't exactly look like an ad for Little Sisters of America. "I might not go back."

"What does the pattern look like to you? A solar system?"

"No!" Her scorn made me positive she seen Fulmer. "The pattern is understood on a deeper level. That's where the geometry comes in." She backed up, looking defensive. "Why are you asking about the circle?"

"It's close to Alan's house." The remains of Alan's house, that is.

"Well, I've already told you everything I—" She turned to find Shaduff blocking her. "Hey! You can't keep me here."

"Better make the call now," Shaduff suggested.

"I'm sorry," I explained. "You're wanted for questioning because you might be a witness to a crime. That means I have to contact the assistant district attorney in charge of the case."

She turned back to me, looking flabbergasted. "You're going to call him? I thought you were on opposite sides."

"We are. But I have to let him know you're—"

"You were going to call him all along, weren't you? You knew you were going to call him, but first you tried to sneak answers out of me."

Well put. "I'm entitled, as Alan's lawyer, to question you before the DA does. What I can't do is question you, then sit back while you disappear. I can't cheat the DA out of his opportunity. I can stay close by when he questions you, if you like. Anytime you need me there, you can reach me through Mr. Shaduff or Dr. Hershey."

Her eyes were wide and wet with betrayal. "So what you said about me trusting you, you were only trying to get the answers you wanted. And just because you didn't, you're going to call the police on me!"

"No, you heard me say from the beginning that you'd have to talk to Assistant DA Toben." I tried to see it from her point of view: I was calling in the State to stomp around her fragile new life. "A man's freedom is at stake—of course the lawyers on both sides need to talk to you. We can't have a fair trial without all the witnesses."

Shaduff seemed to think I was being verbose. He motioned toward the phone.

I gave the girl a minute to respond. Instead she whirled around, trying to knock Shaduff aside.

I quickly made the phone call. We couldn't put ourselves in the position of restraining her. But there would be hell to pay if she got far.

Luckily, Toben was at his desk. "We have the hitchhiker at Carl Shaduff's office," I told him. "You'd better get someone over here. She's determined to leave."

He was no slouch; he dispatched deputies to cruise the area. They found Mackenzie less than twenty minutes later, not half a mile away.

After my hour with her, I suspected she'd be just as reticent with Patrick Toben as she'd been with me.

If only.

14

I've had many horrible days in court. My first year practicing law, I represented a kid who refused to register with the Selective Service even though we hadn't had a draft in over a decade. He insisted on scorning my advice and making a political statement; he practically clawed his way over me to get into jail. When I watched the bailiff take him away, possibly to four years in federal prison, I thought being a lawyer couldn't get much worse.

I've also been arrested twice and convicted once for protesting the war in Vietnam. I spent two horrible months in the San Bruno jail. I still get night sweats, dreaming I hear women's sobs echoing up and down the cell block. The judge who sentenced me became a personal enemy; it had been hell facing him again in court as a lawyer.

Plus, I'd been to most of my parents' civil-disobedience trials. And believe me, it's not easy watching the people you love most led away to prison. It's wrenching for an adult, but it's terrifying for a child—huddled alone in a sleeping bag at some acquaintance's house, fretting over what might be happening to them in prison, seething over being subordinated to their political ideals.

So I'm no stranger to things going wrong for me in court. But the first week of Alan Miller's trial, while the prosecution presented its case, things spun so far out of control that it was all I could do not to slink out the back door and jump a tramp steamer.

It wasn't just that the assistant DA did an excellent job. I expected he would. Patrick Toben presented the accident as a case of *Res ipsa loquitur,* "The thing speaks for itself": a car doesn't land atop another absent malfeasance by the driver. He made the most of the fact that Alan, when questioned by police and doctors, steadfastly failed to provide an alibi. He put up poster-board diagrams of the accident and the Fiat's trajectory off the cliff. He displayed a four-color map: green for Addenaur's route, purple for Alan's drive down from San Francisco, blue for the road to Alan's house, and red for the next turnoff, leading up to and across the field. Questioning a highway patrolman about the map, he suggested a scenario: Alan missed the turn onto San Vittorio Road, took his next left in order to backtrack, and ended up cutting through the field, crashing his car, and running away.

A serologist testified that it takes four to eight hours for blood alcohol levels to dip from legally drunk to zero. The DA was able to suggest that Alan left San Francisco later than he admitted and stopped to do some drinking; that he fled the accident to avoid drunk driving charges, staying gone long enough to sober up.

But I'd expected all that.

The hitchhiker was the problem. Mackenzie, as she continued to call herself, spent two nights in custody after leaving Carl Shaduff's office. A material witness is required to give information, and Toben refused to believe she couldn't remember anything. He also refused to believe she was nineteen. She was required, as a juvenile, to explain why she wasn't in school and wasn't living with a parent or guardian. She didn't. Hence, the nights in lockup.

What she told Toben Thursday morning, after a night of suicide threats, sent us reeling. She claimed she'd been abducted, along with Alan, by a UFO. She would give no descriptive details, nor discuss the time of night this happened, nor consent to hypnosis.

She would say only that gray aliens performed an experiment to make her pregnant.

And it turned out she was, indeed, pregnant. This was confirmed by a minute level of a hormone in her system. She had been impregnated anywhere from nine days to six weeks prior.

Needless to say, Toben didn't believe she'd been abducted and impregnated by aliens. It only gave him more fodder for scoffing at Alan's tale.

It also gave him a hell of a big stick.

I met with him Friday night to discuss Mackenzie's bombshell. He ushered me into a little conference room in the county building, a cement box attached by a glass-walled walkway to the courts.

As usual, he looked in fine fettle. He was a handsome man, I suppose, too conventionally tailored and muscled to be my type. But he didn't flirt, which set him above most jock lawyers.

"You'll be interested in the latest, Ms. Jansson." He motioned me into a chair, then dropped a stack of files onto the conference table. Behind him, windows glowed with the golden light of late afternoon. Only two hours south of San Francisco, the weather here seemed latitudes better.

"The latest being?"

"We've consulted experts, child psychologists, psychiatrists." He paused, as if waiting for me to debate Mackenzie's age. "Not Dr. Hershey, of course."

"Of course." Fred was on my witness list; I had dibs.

"I'm giving you their names and vitae. And I don't mind discussing what their testimony will be, if we decide to call them to the stand."

"Please do." I braced for bad news. If he was cocky enough to lay it out in advance of adding them to his witness list, he knew it would make me squirm. He wanted a ringside seat.

"Your client told the deputies he dropped Mackenzie off at around one o'clock in the morning. He claims a memory lapse after that." The corner of his mouth twitched; he was making an effort not to gloat. "Here's what our psychologists think: your client pulled the car off the road, but not to let Mackenzie out. To rape her."

"What the—!"

"Hear me out; we're not just whistling in the wind. We think this accounts for a number of things—including your client's memory lapse, if it's genuine."

"If Alan Miller was capable of raping a teenager to begin with, he wouldn't be traumatized enough to get amnesia about it." My God, were they serious? Or just maneuvering, trying to bargain?

"It would explain your client's swerving off onto the wrong road. He could have attacked her up there in the field. Or he could have been flustered afterward and missed his turn. And also . . . are you acquainted with the term 'screen memory'?"

"Yes. But it's not applicable here."

"Oh, come on. Miller says aliens touched his genitals. Mackenzie makes the same claim. We know there aren't little green men running around this planet touching peepees." He shook his head as if to say, *We're all rational lawyers here.* "Either they're both lying or they're both dealing with a traumatic experience."

"Or one of them's lying—she's lying. It's obvious she ran away from home because she missed her period, she was afraid she was pregnant. You should be looking for her family, maybe for a rapist father or brother. She's only talking about alien impregnation because I discussed my defense with her."

Toben tilted his well-groomed head. "Why would you do that?"

"To persuade her to answer my questions."

"By telling her your client was kidnapped by space lechers?"

"The point is, I brought it up. And she saw a way to get herself off the hook for becoming pregnant."

He simultaneously chuckled and sneered. A neat trick, and one he'd mastered. He continued to sit in easy hubris, not bothering to reply.

"Is there any more information you'd like to share with

me?" I asked him. "Because I didn't come here to discuss my defense. Or your opinion of it."

"Just wanted to let you know about the two new experts." He grinned. It's customary to amend witness lists by mail or fax.

I stood. "You've got some papers for me?"

He handed me a file folder, and I left.

If I couldn't persuade the judge to disallow this testimony, Toben would finesse the time discrepancy. In the process, he'd offer a reason for Alan's careening onto the wrong road and off a cliff. And he'd explain why Alan might erase his own memories, masking them behind false images of sperm-extracting aliens.

Where Toben had previously scoffed at Alan's recovered memory, he would now welcome my introducing testimony about it. He would use that testimony to piggyback in his own psychiatrists. He was lying in wait, rubbing his hands in anticipation.

But my biggest problem wasn't the assistant district attorney. It wasn't even his new experts. It was that almost *any* story is easier to believe than alien abduction.

15

My meeting with the assistant DA was a wake-up call. I realized the trial wouldn't wrap up quickly. I began to doubt I'd make it back to work a week from Monday.

Because I'd taken the case pro bono and on my own time, I hadn't bothered letting my firm know. Now, barring unforeseen luck, I'd have no choice. As hard as it would be to tell a courtroom full of strangers that my client had been fondled by space aliens, it would be even harder to explain in proper legalese to a group of business lawyers.

But I didn't make the mistake of thinking things couldn't get worse—I try not to tempt fate.

That evening, Mackenzie showed up at Carl Shaduff's office. She threatened to kill herself if I didn't come immediately and talk to her.

Shaduff, thinking I was with Alan, called him at Edward's. Alan reached me at Fred's.

"I'm just around the corner from Shaduff's," Alan pointed out. "You want me to go over? I could wait with her till you come."

"No. Stay by the phone." He was still crashing at Edward's. "I'll call if I need you."

Fred, too, was champing at the bit. "I should come along. She's obviously having a lot of problems. You could use me."

103

"No—it's weird enough I'm camping at a witness's house." If it came out during Fred's cross-examination, the jurors might discount his testimony, thinking I'd pillow-talked him into it. "I don't want you to know any more details. Anything you blurt out on direct becomes fair game on cross."

He'd just come in from running, and he looked hot and damp and cross. He kept pacing his white-walled, white-carpeted living room. I couldn't tell if he was agitated or just cooling down. "Do you have any experience with troubled adolescents?"

"Only if you count my parents." I grabbed my jacket. "I'll be fine."

"It's her I'm worried about. You say she—"

"I'll call you if I need you."

I left Fred's townhouse and rushed to Shaduff's.

I found Mackenzie prowling his office like a caged cat. Her first words to me were, "You said you wanted to help me. You said I could trust you. You've got to hide me!"

Shaduff sat behind his desk. The look on his face said he'd raised no daughters and congratulated himself on the choice.

I ushered Mackenzie into a chair.

"Hide you? From who?"

She was definitely the worse for wear. Her eyelids were swollen from crying, her cold sores had turned into furious scabs, she looked puffy, pale, exhausted.

"That jerk Toben."

"Are you feeling all right?"

She bowed her head, her lower lip trembling. "He put me in jail. He had a doctor come and . . ." She'd had an obstetrics exam, courtesy of the county of Santa Cruz. "I hate him. He just wants to use his power against me. Lock me up, and what he had the doctor do. Now he's going to try to send me back home. Isn't he?"

Ten minutes with him exceeded my tolerance threshold, so I could empathize with her. "Well, he doesn't believe your alien abduction story."

"It's not a story!" She regarded me defiantly. "You believe Alan."

I didn't reply.

"They were this tall." She held her hand about three feet off the ground. "They had gray skin and black eyes with no white part. They put me on a steel table and put a needle-tube kind of thing in through my belly button. And a taller one told me telepathically that I was pregnant now and they'd be back later to take the baby." Her cheeks glowed with hot red patches.

Her story was no crazier than Alan's—not surprising, since it was modeled after his. The difference was that Alan refused to accept it, would have preferred to be thought delusional. And her story sounded like a convenient excuse, the synopsis of an *X-Files* episode or a cheesy television movie.

"It just . . . it sounds like the only lie you could think of." I tried to keep my tone nonthreatening. "Did you run away from home when you missed your period? Did you take a home pregnancy test? Because you do have choices, you know, even as a teenager."

She swallowed hard several times. "I told you how I got pregnant. It was the aliens. But now . . . they'll find out."

Did she mean the aliens? "Find out what?"

"My grandparents." She slumped in her chair. "They're from—well, they're foreign. My grandmother and grandfather came here after my mom was born. Their country's like some old-fashioned planet, at least they think so. It probably changed, but they don't know that. They visualize it being like it was when they left." Her lower lip trembled. "My mother wasn't married. So after she had me, they . . . they say they told her to leave the house because she disgraced them. But really?" She looked at me with big wet eyes. "They killed her."

"How do you know that?" I was relieved to hear a likelier story, however sordid.

"She never tried to call or come back."

"But you say she was banished, sent away in disgrace.

You don't know how that might have affected her. I gather she was young?"

Mackenzie nodded. "But she'd have tried to phone her friends in town. They all think so. I talked to them. I looked them up in my mother's old yearbook. My grandparents forgot to burn it."

"They burned your mother's stuff?" Jeez, no wonder this girl was a mess.

"Uh-huh. If they ever find anything of hers in an old box or whatever, they tear it to shreds like crazy people. They swear and scream and rip it up like wolves killing something." She looked terrified just thinking about it. "I know they killed her. My mother would have called her friends"—her eyes said, *and me*—"if she was alive."

"So you thought your grandparents would kill you when they found out you were pregnant?" I was singing a silent hallelujah. As sorry as I felt for this girl, this was something I could put on the witness stand. And Patrick Toben could eat his damn expert witnesses.

A canny look crossed her face. "I told you: I got pregnant after I left. On the spaceship."

I supposed she was hedging her bets, keeping this story as insurance in case her grandparents found her. But I could hardly imagine them believing it. "Then why did you run away?"

"Because they killed my mother. And they . . ." She looked ashamed. "If they thought I was sneaking out with boys, if a guy phoned me or one of my friends made a comment about someone—you know, an innocent comment . . ."

"They'd beat you?"

She didn't say anything.

"Tell the assistant DA about this. I know he's—" I stopped myself from calling him a jerk. "Regardless of what you think of Mr. Toben, he can help you. His office can arrange a new home for you. They won't send you back to an abusive family." I hoped.

"No! It would kill them." Tears spilled down her cheeks.

"But if they beat you—"

"Sometimes. Most of the time they're crazy about me. They cook for me and make me things. They love me. It's just that, about boys . . ." She stopped to catch her breath. "They're different, you know? Like they were raised on another planet with upside-down ideas about things. They love me, but they're not like Americans, they're not calm, they're not from this century."

"But if they love you, wouldn't they rather know you were safe? Even if it meant you were with a foster family?"

"No, no, no. You don't get it." She leaned forward, as if proximity would help her explain. "The DA's going to find them and call them and they'll come here. And all he'll see is how nice they are and how much they love me. And then they'll take me home and we'll be alone and they'll kill me. Just like they killed my mother. They'll stop being relieved that I'm back, that I'm okay; and they'll just snap. They can't help themselves, they're not like Americans." She wiped her tears away. "You don't know what it's like to have a crazy family."

I wish. "Let me to talk to Mr. Toben about this. If he knows what to expect from them—"

"No! You've got to hide me from him. It's the only way! Otherwise, they'll kill me."

I watched her. Why come to me? Why not just take off? Hide on her own?

"Do you need money? Is that it? Help getting an abortion?"

She pulled herself straight, nodding.

"Look, I'm sorry, but I'm Alan's lawyer. That means I've got to put his welfare above everything else. If I hid you and the assistant district attorney found out—God, especially if I paid for an abortion—he'd assume it was an admission on Alan's part."

"Huh?"

As much as I hated to add to her burdens: "Mr. Toben is suggesting Alan raped you two weeks ago. Your pregnancy could be as recent as nine days."

"Alan?" She swayed with the shock of it.

"It's a way for the prosecution to offer a theory that guilt made Alan drive recklessly and have an accident. Mr. Toben will say you both concocted false memories to cover up what really happened, that it was too traumatic for you."

She shook her head, murmuring inaudibly.

"So if I help you, everyone will take it as proof. They'll say I hustled you away so you couldn't testify that Alan raped you. If I pay for an abortion, it'll look like an attempt to avoid a paternity test. Or like I was bribing—"

I didn't get a chance to finish my sentence. Carl Shaduff's front window exploded into shards of glass, spraying the floor and tabletop.

Shaduff dove across the room, pushing me off my chair.

I could tell by the smell it was a shot. A gunshot—Jesus. I scrabbled toward Mackenzie while Shaduff crawled back to his desk. He took something from a drawer.

Mackenzie had leaped to her feet, keening with panic. She kicked me in the face, as clumsy as a spooked colt.

Shaduff edged along a wall, loading a gun. Mackenzie lurched past him, pushing the front door wide.

Shaduff shouted, "Chee-rist!" and ran out after her. I could see him pause, aiming left, then right, like a cop in a shoot-'em-up movie.

I hid behind Shaduff's desk, my heart pounding, waiting for a gunman—Addenaur's widow?—to burst in and finish the job. I pulled the desk phone to the floor and dialed 911.

A few minutes later, Shaduff returned. He slammed the door, his face so red he looked skinned alive.

"Whoever it was, he's gone."

I remained on the floor. I touched the cheek Mackenzie had kicked, feeling for broken skin. I could hear night breezes stirring shards of glass near the window.

"What happened to Mackenzie?"

"Who knows?" He looked at me as if it were normal for a lawyer to cower behind his desk. "Are all your cases this interesting?"

"Only the ones here on Earth."

16

While I was leaking angst all over a hypercalm policeman, Patrick Toben showed up.

Shaduff, by then, had said his piece and was sweeping up broken glass. As the cop finished his report and handed me his business card, Shaduff produced, from somewhere in his house or yard, two rectangles of plywood. He began nailing them over the window, leaving me to Mr. Smug.

"So what was Mackenzie doing here?" Toben was as nonchalant as someone asking for a football score.

I wished I could be equally cool: *Nothing much, she just wanted me to hide her from you and pay for her abortion.* "She came to talk to me."

"About?"

I was obliged to give him notes and recordings of meetings with witnesses. Period. "We were interrupted." I gestured toward the window.

Shaduff was hoisting the second sheet of plywood, holding it in place with his shoulder while he positioned nails and swung the hammer.

Toben said, "We found her folks."

"Where?"

"We matched her with a missing-person report from up in Grants Pass, Oregon."

I sat, feeling suddenly exhausted. "Who are they? Who is she?"

"Her name's Maria Nanos. She's fifteen. She lives with her grandparents." He sat, too. He glanced at his wrist-watch, looking tired. "I wish we'd run this down last night, while we still had her in custody. But we know where she's been staying. And she doesn't know about this. So hopefully we'll find her there."

"What's the story on the grandparents? Why'd she run away from them?"

"Everything I know, you know." He cocked his head as if to ask if I could say the same.

"They're not here in town, are they? The grandparents?"

"I couldn't tell you. I suppose if they hopped a direct flight the minute they heard. But I doubt it."

"They haven't checked in with your office?"

"No."

My attention strayed to Shaduff, hammering in the last of the nails.

Patrick Toben followed my gaze. "You're not suggesting the shooter was after Maria Nanos?"

"No, I'm not." Especially since Toben would be likely to suspect Alan Miller of the crime.

"Okay, then, I'm taking off. We're doing our best to find Betty Addenaur—soon, I hope. Keep safe tonight. Where are you staying?"

"I gave the officer the local address." Let him learn from the police report that it matched that of a witness. "But I'm heading back to San Francisco for the weekend."

"I wrap up Monday morning. Who's first up for you?" His expression was ingenuous.

"It's in my papers," I reminded him.

I'd bought into the lawyers' trick of withholding direct answers, of making my opponent jump through hoops for no reason except that I'd jumped through his. Reciprocal dickhood, the first thing lawyers learn in the field.

Toben was too seasoned to react to minor chain jerking. He gave a huge yawn, not bothering to cover his mouth.

110

17

I thought about the unself-conscious guyness of that yawn the next morning, as I stood atop Joseph Huizen's hillside, doing the same.

It was quarter to eight. I wanted to get to my apartment early, try to get in a full day of slovenly hermitry.

But first, I took a detour into Davenport to look for Mackenzie/Maria.

Longing for home, I'd tried to talk myself out of it: Maybe Maria Nanos was self-dramatizing, like most teenagers. Maybe she was lying about her grandparents beating her. And probably she was wrong about them killing her mother.

But I wanted to talk to her again before the police found her and reunited her with them. I couldn't hide her, and I wouldn't warn her—that would only result in her flight. But I could offer to go with her to the DA, to intercede with Child Protective Services.

I'd even toyed with the idea of asking Fred to follow me here, to stand by to do his therapist thing. But I'd gotten no reply when I knocked at his bedroom door; either he was out jogging or he was a very sound sleeper.

Stifling another yawn, I looked down at what had once been a distinct pattern of circles in circles. The field, though lush, wasn't as dense as a wheat field. Some grasses had withered and been replaced by wildflowers. Footpaths criss-crossed the now-ragged circles. The swirls within swirls had been mashed till they lost definition.

But even at seven-forty-five in the morning, there was a group inside the large central circle. They sat on blankets, watching a gesticulating figure.

I thought I recognized his extravagant arm-flinging and manic loping back and forth. It was almost certainly Reginald Fulmer.

I was even more startled to see checkpoint sawhorses and a table under a café umbrella where the field met the farmer's road. Between it and the circles was an encampment of at least a dozen tents.

As often as the farmer had emphasized to us that his fields were posted No Trespassing, he'd allowed all this. I wondered why.

I backtracked past Joseph Huizen's house to my car. If Maria Nanos was camping beside the farmer's road, I wanted to be parked nearby. If I persuaded her to come with me, I didn't want to risk leaving her to second-think the decision while I retrieved my Honda.

I went back along San Vittorio, stopping for a moment at Alan's house. Yellow plastic tape was liberally laced in front, warning passersby that it wasn't safe to go inside. But except for a boarded-up door, a plywood-covered hole in the roof, and some blistered paint, it didn't look a great deal worse from the outside.

I sped farther down the road toward the highway, past ratty yards crowded with old trucks and lounging dogs. I turned onto and almost immediately off the highway, going up a hill and beyond the Brussels sprouts field. I parked behind the sawhorses, in a row of dusty cars. But if someone was supposed to be manning the table beneath the umbrella, he didn't show himself. I cut straight over to the encampment.

About a third of the tents were zipped shut. I didn't see Maria in any of the others. Instead I found friendly neo-hippies spreading blankets and breaking bread. More than one advised me to have a nice day. None knew or would admit to knowing a girl calling herself Mackenzie or Maria.

"Are you here with permission?" I asked a plain-faced woman with long graying hair and a flowered jumper.

She'd run a clothesline from her tent to a ground stake. She was hanging purple thistles upside down from it, presumably to dry them.

"We pass the hat every morning," she told me, in a cheerful contralto.

"For what?"

"To pay the use fee." She looked with satisfaction at the row of large, thorny flowers.

"You're being charged money to stay here?"

She nodded. "A farmer comes and collects every morning. There's a separate fee for the seminar."

"Reginald Fulmer's seminar?"

"Uh-huh. He started about twenty minutes ago, if you want to do it today."

"How much is it?"

"Forty." She looked wistful. "We don't have that kind of money. But the ones who go try to keep the rest of us filled in."

"What does he say about the circles?"

"It's exciting: this is the first one he's encountered with a recognizable pattern." She glowed with satisfaction. "Right here in California! The ones in England, as fabulous as they are, only speak to the unconscious. 'Only'!" She laughed. "Communication on that level is probably the most powerful kind there is. But if our conscious mind can't grasp it, well . . . it's a little frustrating. Like a Zen koan."

In a neighboring tent, someone began hacking and coughing. Nearby, a man shouted to a frolicking dog.

"We traveled in Peru for a while," the woman continued. "We got so deep into Andean jungle we met a tribe that had never set eyes on the modern world. They wove their clothes out of wild cotton; true hunter-gatherers. We had our guides show them pictures, photos we'd taken, magazine pages, but they absolutely couldn't see anything in them. Not anything at all, just colors. They'd never seen printed images

113

before. And our perceptions depend so much on what we're used to looking at." She grinned. "Maybe that's us with the crop circles. We don't know how to perceive them yet."

"Except for this one? This pattern's recognizable?"

"Mm-hm." She sniffed the air, apparently distracted by the scent of nearby coffee. "I wonder where that's coming from? We're not allowed to cook here—no campfires or stoves; the fire hazard is too high."

"So what is it?" I asked her. "What's the pattern?"

"One of the sugar molecules."

"Sugar." I took a backward step. "Not glucose?"

"That's right." She continued sniffing, head turned, like a dog.

"Glucose? You're sure?" The substance Joseph Huizen nearly died for lack of.

"You could ask Reggie," she pointed out. "I think that's what he said: the simplest form of sugar. I'm going to go track down that coffee!"

As much as I longed to follow her and get myself a cup, I traipsed through the field toward Reginald Fulmer and his small audience.

As I approached, Fulmer stopped talking. He took a few steps toward me, shouting crossly, "Two rules: no interruptions, and no trooping in late. If you can't be bothered to greet the dawn with us, then go piss away the rest of the day, I don't care. But don't distract the group with—"

He stopped, arms arrested midgesture. "The solar systems lady! From that ghastly conference."

"Yes. I'm sorry to interrupt, but I need to speak to you."

His half dozen students watched us. Tired looking and older, they might have been left over from a Pete Seeger concert.

"I'll be done in an hour."

"This won't wait." And then, to forestall protest, "It's a legal matter."

"Oh, not that bloody girl again!"

I gathered the police had already been here looking for her.

"Among other things," I admitted.

"Bother!" He scowled at his seminar. "Sit here for five minutes. Remember your techniques."

The techniques seemed to involve sitting cross legged with head bowed and eyes closed. He strode past them and over to me.

"Now, what do you want?" he demanded. "A legal matter, indeed."

I looked up at the man, who was at least a foot taller than I was. With his flaring nostrils and extraordinarily narrow face, he looked like a caricature from an illustrated Dickens or Swift.

"I'm a lawyer. I'm trying a case in which Maria Nanos, probably known to you as Mackenzie, is a material witness."

"Well, bully for you. As I've already told your policemen, I'm a scientist, I am not a baby-sitter."

"When was the last time you saw her?"

He waved his hand impatiently. "Oh, who bloody remembers?"

"Did you see her last night?"

"Certainly not. I'm not sleeping out here, you know. The first two nights, when it was fresh, yes. But there's no point anymore, is there? It's been fairly well squashed, hasn't it? Tomorrow's the limit, I'd say." He looked over his shoulder, shaking his head at the crop circle's disintegration.

"Where have you been staying?"

He snorted. "As if I have a choice of accommodations! The Davenport Bed and Breakfast, if one can call it that. They don't serve breakfast until after dawn—and a lot of damn use to me that is."

The bed-and-breakfast was directly over the Cash Store. In a town of a few hundred people, I could well believe they didn't get much call for predawn meals.

"Can you tell me anything about Mackenzie? Any observations at all?"

He bent closer, as if gawking at a madwoman. "Do you suppose she could be of the least interest to me? When I've got all this to worry about?" He nodded toward the circle.

"I hear you've identified it as a glucose molecule." I was

afraid if I phrased it as a question he'd find a way to be nonresponsive.

"So much for your solar system." He flicked a finger as if I were a gnat. "Solar system! The minute I set eyes on it, I knew it couldn't be anything but a molecule. I should have guessed immediately which one. Sugar is the bloody basis for plant life, the basis for food preservation. It's also the greatest reward we can give our taste buds—our most primary sensual delight, the first thing children crave. Only think of what this tells us in terms of a communication uniquely tailored to us! Glucose is the basic unit of that which is most pleasing and precious and crucial to us." He nodded, flushing with excitement. "And here it is—right here. Within a stone's throw of me! And the timing of it: the one scholar likely to decipher the pictogram is in the neighborhood—not in his own backyard in southern England, where the circles usually form. To think I've worried about leaving on lecture tours. Well, this shows how silly I've been." He nodded solemnly. "They follow me, when they have to."

And I'd thought the assistant DA guilty of hubris.

"Yes, they follow me!" he repeated. "Can you fathom the urgency they must feel? Can you begin to understand how hard they worked to lay down a pattern of such complexity? To use this shabby mess of weeds as a medium?"

"To use me as a middlewoman?" It was all I could do not to smile.

He raised his brows, apparently not wanting to dignify me with the title.

Back to business: "You say you're leaving the area soon?"

"Oh, yes. I've had people out to photograph it. I've got what I need. I expect it'll cause the sort of stir we saw with the Mandelbrot Set."

I shook my head to indicate I didn't know it.

"Mandelbrot? As in the inventor of fractal geometry? As in chaos theory, the degree of irregularity remaining constant across different scales?" When I didn't say, *Oh, that Mandelbrot,* he rolled his eyes. "And I suppose you've a college degree? Well, take my word for it. If you feed Mandelbrot's extremely famous"—another roll of the eyes —"iteration into a computer, it gives one a pattern, a very distinctive shape. A perfect reproduction of which turned up in a field not so very far from where he happened to be at the time."

"Really? Like a message to him?"

He looked at me as if I were hopeless. "To a few more people than that!"

"Have you analyzed the plants here?" I mentioned a test one of my expert witnesses had recommended.

"Cell pits and growth nodes—what rubbish! These are *pictograms,* darling! One need only *look* at a picture."

"Would you be interested in lab results from the local university?" What I really wanted was his address. I might, in dire circumstances, need him to testify.

"Don't trouble yourself." His tone was snide. "We've all had our fill of Colin Andrews by now."

I'd watched one of Colin Andrews's videos at the UFO conference. An early crop circle researcher, Andrews focused on their physical features, including botanical changes. Unlike Fulmer, I'd appreciated his lack of pretense and bullshit.

"It's no trouble; I'll be happy to send them. Let me jot down your address."

With a twist of the lips and a sour sigh, he rattled off something that sounded more like directions than an address. "It's near Avebury. That's in England, so do put the extra stamp on."

He turned away, returning to his fidgeting groupies.

I wondered what he'd do if I shouted a few parting comments: That the crop circle had nothing to do with Reginald Fulmer. That just over the hill, a mathematician was writing a book about the spin of planets. That, on the night this pictogram appeared, Joseph Huizen would have died without an injection of glucose.

Glucose. Sugar might be the basis for plant life, a fine food preservative, and a child's first delight. But in addition, just two weeks ago, it kept alive the author of the forthcoming *Pi in the Sky*.

I walked back to my car in a daze. I didn't know what to think.

I made a call from a phone booth in Davenport. I asked Carl Shaduff to contact the paramedics who'd picked up Joseph Huizen the night of his diabetic emergency. They should be easy to find. They were on the prosecution's witness list because they'd tended Francis Addenaur earlier that morning. The ADA hadn't called them, relying instead on the testimony of cops and doctors. But he'd have their home phone numbers handy.

"I'm going to subpoena them, maybe put them on the stand toward the end of next week; I'm not sure. And one other thing . . ."

"Yes?"

"Find me some drawings of a glucose molecule?"

"Okay." His voice told me he envisioned a highly eccentric direct examination.

I drove home wondering why none of the news features about the crop circle had mentioned the resemblance to glucose. Was it because journalists had done their research and found none? More likely, Fulmer hadn't reached his conclusion until after they went home.

Maybe it didn't matter, one way or the other. Until I powwowed with my experts, I couldn't be sure it would pay to mention the circles.

I spent the weekend mainlining coffee and going over my notes, preparing questions for direct examination of my first witnesses. I jittered around the apartment telling myself I could budget in a break, take a short walk. But I knew how I'd feel if Alan Miller went to prison. My stomach would clench every time I thought about it; I'd second-guess every question I'd asked, every motion I made. I thanked God I wasn't (usually) a criminal lawyer—and I made myself keep working.

18

I was both relieved and disappointed on Monday: Patrick Toben didn't manage to wrap up his case before lunch.

I was still in the courtroom, stuffing my notes into my briefcase and looking forward to a bad lunch, when he approached me.

"I just got word," he said. "Maria Nanos's grandparents are in my office wanting to talk. You're welcome to join us."

Alan, leaning against the counsel table waiting for me, suddenly straightened. "They don't think I—? You didn't tell them I—?"

Toben clobbered him with a how-dare-you-speak glance. To me, he said, "If you want to come, come now."

"I'm right behind you," I assured him. To Alan, I said, "I'll join you in the cafeteria when I'm done."

I left him standing with his mouth open, poised as if to persuade us to take him along.

I followed Patrick Toben through the courthouse hall and into the adjoining county building. He walked past coworkers and clericals as if they were invisible. He led me into the usual conference room.

A short man in a well-fitting blue suit and cashmere vest stood behind a woman in dignified green wool. Her old-fashioned patent handbag, on the table, was as black as her dyed, sprayed hair. Her age showed in her choice of accessories, not in her skin.

Her husband strode toward us. His round face and sleekly combed hair made him look drawn onto a balloon.

His accent was so slight I couldn't identify it. "You have Maria?"

The DA extended his hand. "Mr. Nanos, hello. I'm the assistant district attorney trying *The People versus Alan Miller.*" He withdrew his hand when Nanos didn't shake it. "Mr. Miller is the man who picked up your granddaughter hitchhiking in Half Moon Bay and brought her to this county."

Nanos bared a hint of teeth. His nostrils flared slightly. "You have Maria?" he repeated. "Friday you are telling us you know where is Maria. And so we pass a day on the bus and another one in the hotel. Today they say we will wait and talk to you. We are waiting since you phone us three days ago!" His voice was growing high pitched with exasperation. "You have Maria ready? She is ready to go home?"

But Toben was not to be rushed. "This is Mr. Miller's attorney."

"Hello," I said.

Mrs. Nanos flinched, rising partway out of her chair. The motion was slight, but her rush of feeling went further. I took a backward step.

"Where is Maria?" The grandmother braced her palms against the table edge. It seemed to be the only thing keeping her from flying at me. "What your Miller did with my granddaughter?"

"Please have a seat." Toben seemed to be performing some kind of hosting ritual. "Let's discuss why Maria left home and where she might be now."

"You can have no reason to keep my granddaughter!" The woman's voice was rising.

Her husband said, "We will take care. Where is Maria?"

"Please sit down." Toben's tone made it clear this conversation wasn't happening until they did.

Finally, Mr. Nanos sat beside his wife. He yanked her back into her seat.

Toben and I took the other side of the table.

"We don't know Maria's exact whereabouts, I'm sorry to say." His tone was brisk; for him, this was business as usual. "Ms. Jansson last saw her Friday night. Since then, we've been trying to locate her, for many reasons. One of them is that we'd like to call her as a witness. Do you know if she has any friends here in town?"

I watched the elderly couple. Toben's cool tone seemed to increase the heat of their seething.

He waited a moment before adding, "Maybe we should start with why she ran away. What can you tell us about that?"

"I tell you I will break her legs!" Nanos's words were barely audible, whispered like a prayer. His lips hardly moved. "Before she will hitchhike with men, I will break her two legs."

Beside him, Mrs. Nanos nodded, tears streaming down her face.

"Mr. Nanos," Toben said patiently, "that's no kind of solution. It's also illegal. I know you're upset, but I hope you realize that we need to address the underlying problem here. All of us do. That's the reason I'm asking you, why did Maria run away?"

Nanos looked appalled that anyone would be in doubt of the reason. "This criminal, he has convinced Maria."

Toben's brows rose. "Our information is that she met Alan Miller just sixty miles north of here. So most of Maria's trip would have been in other company. She may have left with someone she knew or she may have hitched rides with strangers. Either way, the question remains, why did she leave in the first place?"

"Television!" Nanos spat the word out. "What a young girl she sees on the television . . . men and women going together like pigs." That drew a moan from Mrs. Nanos. "Even good children they are ruined."

"You think television influenced Maria to seek out more freedom?"

"Not just the television, even the teachers at Maria's school. Even the teachers in America they are like pigs, they are like animals."

"Was there a particular teacher? A male teacher? Someone she had a crush on?"

Mr. Nanos looked angry enough to pummel Toben just for hinting it.

"I'm asking for a reason, Mr. Nanos. Maria is pregnant."

It was obviously news to them.

Mr. Nanos dived across the tabletop, grabbing Toben's lapels and cursing him in a voice so high pitched it was difficult to resolve into speech.

Mrs. Nanos fell over backwards in her chair. I watched it happen, but I still don't understand how a person could arch her back and go over like that.

Christ, and I thought my family was strange.

I went around to Mrs. Nanos, assuming the DA didn't need my help handling a man twenty years his senior.

Mrs. Nanos made no move to rise. She lay partly splayed over the chair, the opaque tops of her panty hose showing and the weight of her torso forcing her neck into a painful-looking angle.

I thought for a second she'd had a heart attack and died. But then I saw her face contort with sobs so strong they sounded like a slow hiss. She seemed to have no energy left for rearranging her body.

When I tried to help her up, she was dead weight. I looked over at Patrick Toben, hoping he could help. But he had his hands full. He was no longer protecting himself from Mr. Nanos. He was trying to prevent the man from bashing himself repeatedly in the face.

Nanos was smashing his fists against his head. Toben was trying to get a forearm between Nanos and his fists. He was shouting for help.

Two men in suits ran in. They stopped for a minute, apparently shocked to find two well-dressed seniors causing such commotion.

The grandmother still seemed catatonically unable to do anything but cry. I suggested the men call for a medic, and one of them left. The other helped Toben force Mr. Nanos into a chair.

Nanos was screaming, "Kill me yesterday, God, kill me yesterday!"

A woman in a red suit entered the room, her elbows lifted as if bracing herself for an imminent tackle. Toben shouted, "Over there."

She went around to Mrs. Nanos. I backed out of the way, trying to imagine how this scene would have played had Maria been here. Would her grandfather have dived for her, trying to punch her, trying to break her legs?

One thing was sure: Maria had worried too much about her grandparents fooling the DA. She'd worried too much about being handed back over to them, at least right away.

I considered the places a kid without money might be. I'd slept under a few bridges in my hippie youth, flowing with a river of protesters to Washington, D.C. My main memories, besides endless political debate, were of being cold and hassled. But that was before Reagan emptied the mental hospitals, before the war on drugs incited dealers to buy guns.

The streets were an armed madhouse now. But I supposed anything beat getting your legs broken.

I stayed until paramedics arrived for Mrs. Nanos. Then I left the conference room.

But I'd lost my appetite for lunch. In the twenty minutes before court reconvened, I strolled to a park near the courthouse.

It was about seventy degrees out. The sky was streaked with clouds. Ducks squabbled in a jade green pond. I sat on a bench and watched them.

When the bailiff called court back in session, Toben seemed a little distracted, a little off. It took him the rest of the day to wind up his case in chief.

It was probably just as well I had the extra night to prepare. I played phone tag with the paramedics who'd picked up Joseph Huizen. Carl Shaduff said they'd been chatty about picking up and treating Joseph, but evasive about stopping the ambulance near Miller's house during transport. I prepared subpoenas in case I decided to put them on the stand.

I touched base with my four UFO experts, confirming their arrival on Wednesday.

I went through my questions for the next day's witnesses.

And I pretended to be surprised that it had grown too late to phone my boss at Curtis & Huston.

19

I put on a parade of witnesses Tuesday: investigators and forensic photographers to discuss the inconclusive evidence of the Brussels sprouts field; sheriff's deputies, paramedics, and doctors to establish that Alan Miller had been injured but that his injuries weren't typical of a car accident. I asked the deputies and doctors whether Alan remembered how he'd gotten hurt. Toben objected that this was hearsay, and I countered that it was offered to explain the witnesses' subsequent conduct. What it really did was set the stage for Fred Hershey's testimony and audiotape.

But something happened Tuesday night to make me worry about my most important witness.

I was preparing Fred's testimony, going over questions the assistant DA was likely ask on cross and suggesting ways he might couch his answers. My notes were strewn across a blond wood table in a kitchen that looked like the Swedish Modern nook of a home improvement store. Fred, ever the good host, had set out bagels and toppings and juices, any of which would have lain like lead in my nervous stomach.

"I'll start by running through your résumé at some length —your credentials are impressive, so I'll beat them to death. I especially want the jury to know you've testified in over a hundred trials, eighty of them for the DA. It'll give your testimony weight, make you seem unbiased." With luck, Fred would be a dream witness. He was old enough to have authority but young enough to exude vitality. His clothes looked expensive without being too New Yorkish. And he came across as confident, concerned, relaxed. "I'll ask how you came to interview Alan Miller; why you suggested hypnosis; whether the DA consented to it; the conditions and circumstances under which hypnosis is considered most reliable. I'll zip through these questions with you tonight, but I'm just laying a foundation for introducing the taped hypnosis session. After the jury hears the tape, that's when the thing gets tricky. I want you well prepared for anything Toben's likely to ask on cross."

Fred leaned back in his chair, sighing. His testimony could only invite ridicule. He'd be associated with the tale on the audiotape even though it wasn't his.

We were about half an hour into it when I excused myself to take a bathroom break. I returned to find that Fred had clicked off the kitchen light. The sliding door to Fred's backyard was partway open.

"Fred?" I crossed the dark room, glancing out into the yard. One of his walkway lights was flickering. Maybe he'd gone out to check it?

I pushed the door open farther so I could get through. But a quick glance told me he wasn't out there.

I stepped back inside, walking through the downstairs rooms. Then I went upstairs, calling for him. His bedroom door was open, but the spare, well-ordered room was empty.

He'd certainly made a speedy getaway. But where the hell had he gone?

I spent the next hour and a half going over my notes and fuming. How could Fred flake out on me? Why would he take off like this?

I'd left the sliding door open. The air was sweet with the smell of jasmine and cool enough to keep me alert. At about ten o'clock, I heard a sound outside. Footsteps?

I jumped to my feet. By the time I reached the door, I could see Fred standing in front of the walkway light, tapping it as if to get it to come back on.

"Fred! Where did you go?"

He looked up, startled. "I just came out to check on . . ."

I hated to sound like a shrewish wife, but he didn't seem to have any more to say. "To check on what? What have you been doing all this time?"

I couldn't see Fred's face. The bit of light from the flickering lamp didn't reach that high.

"What time is it?" Fred asked.

"Ten! And we've still got a lot of ground to cover."

"Ten?" He just stood there. "I'm sorry, I must have dozed off on the bench."

"What bench?" I stepped out into the garden. How could I have missed him?

Fred pointed to some rhododendrons pruned to look like boxes. I hadn't thought to check behind them.

"I called your name. You didn't hear me?"

"No, I'm sorry. I just sat down for a second. I don't usually nod off like that."

I turned to go back inside. I couldn't afford the doubts I was having. Fred Hershey was a key witness; my whole case depended on him. But he'd hired a lawyer who didn't usually try criminal cases. Then he'd sneaked out and stayed gone for much of the time allotted to coaching his testimony.

I didn't know what to think. Fred was the brother of someone I'd known since I was eighteen. And he'd helped me out last year, big time. Surely I could trust him?

When we resumed our seats at the table, I looked him over carefully. He seemed a little distracted, but ready to get back to business.

I just prayed he didn't have something up his sleeve, didn't have some agenda that would end up backfiring on Alan Miller.

20

Audio- and videotapes are always fun for the jury, like watching movies in class instead of listening to lectures. I could see the jurors perking up, especially after an hour of hearing about Fred's résumé and background.

But I hadn't prepared the jurors in my opening statement for what they were about to hear. As I produced the tape and handed it to the bailiff to feed through the court's audio system, I tried to keep the worry off my face.

I looked out into the pews. As usual, columnist Leonard Deally looked hot and cranky in his undertaker's three-piece. He was shaking his head, lips pursed, already writing in his notebook. He knew what was coming, I was sure of it.

A moment later, Alan Miller's voice screamed out of the speakers, "What *is* that? What is that thing?"

As the tape rolled on and the jurors realized what they were hearing, they sat very still, sneaking peeks at one another. One appeared to be stifling nervous laughter.

In the pews, someone did giggle.

The sound made Alan jerk as if he'd been struck. He stared at his hands, braced against the table, and struggled to keep his face blank. But his blush was painful to see.

Leonard Deally would later print that Alan "smirked like a man enjoying his big joke on the court."

After signaling for the tape to be turned off, I asked Fred,

"Is this an accurate recording of your session with Alan Miller?"

"Yes, it is."

"What is your professional opinion, as an experienced psychiatrist, about Alan Miller's condition at the time you made this recording?"

"He appeared fully hypnotized."

"At the time you hypnotized Mr. Miller, what kind of story, if any, did you expect him to tell you?"

"Nothing like this." He looked surprised. "I had no set expectation, but I certainly didn't anticipate hearing about aliens or spacecraft."

"Did you have any interest in his mentioning spaceships or aliens?"

"None whatever."

"During this session, did you make any kind of hand gestures or signals, or do anything else that wouldn't be apparent to someone listening to the tape?"

"No, I didn't."

"What was your reaction when Mr. Miller brought the subject up?"

"I was very surprised." Fred nodded firmly. "Yes, I certainly was."

A few titters.

"Can you tell us, what is the role of a therapist during a hypnosis session?"

"It's a hypnotherapist's role to listen carefully and help the patient explore his recollections, not to point him in some particular direction by approving or disapproving of what he says."

"On the day you hypnotized Alan Miller, had you heard of other hypnosis sessions in which patients claimed to have been abducted into spaceships?"

I expected an objection on the grounds that this was irrelevant. Other therapists and patients might be flakes or red-hot UFOlogists, their sessions might further some obscure goal, their memories might be fantasies or screens.

I'd prepared a response to this. But Toben didn't object.

Presumably he preferred to wait and hammer these points on cross-examination.

"I was slightly acquainted with the work of Dr. John E. Mack of Harvard University," Fred admitted.

Again, Toben might have objected. Mack wasn't on my witness list; he wouldn't be available for the assistant DA to cross-examine.

But my rebuttal—that these questions were intended only to shed light on what Fred knew at the time and could therefore "implant"—was again wasted. Patrick Toben sat there looking bemused and unruffled.

"Dr. Hershey, can you tell us what you knew about Dr. Mack's work before you hypnotized Alan Miller?"

The judge, hand straying to his gavel, watched Toben.

Fred answered, "I knew he'd collected some seventy-five accounts of people claiming, usually under hypnosis, to have been abducted by aliens. But I hadn't actually read his book at that time. I'd only followed the controversy around it."

"So when you hypnotized Alan Miller, you didn't know details of other alien abduction stories?" Recalling the boys Fred had hypnotized, I quickly amended this: "That is, you knew these accounts existed in Dr. Mack's book, but did you know any details of the accounts?"

"No, I didn't. I only knew that Dr. Mack had worked with these people and believed they were sincere. I knew their stories involved alien abduction, but I didn't know any particulars. I didn't know how they claimed to have been abducted or what happened to them after that."

"You said a moment ago that you'd followed the controversy around Dr. Mack's book. What did you mean?"

"I'd read in a number of professional journals that Harvard University put together a panel to decide whether to censure Dr. Mack for his involvement with UFO abductees."

"To your knowledge, does it violate some medical or psychiatric code of ethics to work with people who claim they've been abducted by UFOs?"

"No, it doesn't." Fred frowned. "But judging by Harvard's reaction, it's risky to believe their claims."

"So, speaking hypothetically, a psychiatrist who knew that Dr. Mack had risked censure by his university for believing claims of alien abduction . . . do you think that psychiatrist would purposely steer a client toward claiming he'd been abducted?"

"No. I doubt it very much." Fred's tone made it clear it was the last can of worms he'd want to open.

I was beginning to think Patrick Toben was on quaaludes. It's a rare hypothetical that isn't assailed for being confusing, improperly presented, or too different to be relevant.

"Immediately after your taped session with Mr. Miller, did you discuss with him what he'd said on the tape?"

Fred said, "No, I didn't."

"Why didn't you?"

"He seemed to have no recollection of the events he'd described. I didn't want to suggest them to his conscious mind. I wanted him to have the opportunity to recall them at his own pace, if possible."

"Would you say you were being particularly careful not to endorse or reinforce his memories of alien abduction?"

"Yes. Very careful."

Not even an objection that I was leading the witness. Man, if all DAs were this easy (or this confident?), business lawyers would try criminal cases as a lark.

"Dr. Hershey, can you tell us what a repressed memory is?"

"In certain instances, particularly involving psychological trauma, a person can choose, as it were, not to remember something that would cause him what he would consider unbearable stress or hardship."

"Have you encountered repressed memories in patients before?"

"Yes, I have."

I knew Toben would be prepared to dismiss repressed memories as controversial, at best. I was also afraid the jurors had heard of hotly contested cases of repressed memories of child abuse. I was afraid they'd watched women on

Oprah or *Geraldo* recanting false memories that had ruined their families' lives.

"How, if at all, do repressed memories differ from what laypeople call 'amnesia'?"

We spent a long time distinguishing between forgetting everything within a certain block of time, as Miller had, and selectively repressing some memories within a larger time frame. I wanted the jurors to know this case was different from those they'd heard blasted on tabloid television. Miller might claim spacemen had abducted him for his sperm, but at least he wasn't slandering his daddy.

"As a psychiatrist and licensed hypnotherapist, are you trained to decide, based on your patients' demeanor, whether they themselves believe what they're saying?"

The judge himself almost objected to that one. Expert witnesses can offer conclusions, but they've got to be supported by facts. Arguably, a patient's demeanor wasn't a fact.

"We look at a number of factors to assess whether patients are sincere, yes."

I let Fred know with a quick "Thank you" that he'd answered my question. I didn't want him making any distinction between "sincere" and "truthful"; let Toben do that.

"Dr. Hershey," I continued, "were you present when the audiotape we played here in court was first played back to Mr. Miller?"

"Yes, I was."

"What, if anything, did you notice about Alan Miller's demeanor then?"

Fred glanced at the assistant DA, expecting to be silenced. When he wasn't, he said, "It was my strong impression that Mr. Miller would have preferred to be thought quote-unquote 'crazy' than to actually believe what he'd heard himself say on tape."

There were murmurs behind me in the pews. I almost turned around to check on Toben, to make sure he was still in the room.

Fred's "strong impression" could be considered a conclusion outside his area of expertise, a mere guess about a stranger's veracity. I'd never ever gotten away with this much in civil court.

What the hell did Toben have up his sleeve? Moses himself swearing there were no alien beings in the universe? A videotape of Fred and Alan in bed together?

I stood there stewing for a minute, trying to figure out prosecution's strategy.

Finally I said, "Thank you, Dr. Hershey. No further questions."

No doubt Patrick Toben would have plenty more. And unless there was Thorazine in the courthouse water supply, I was bound to object to some of them.

But so far so good, especially since I hadn't prepared Fred as well as I'd hoped to.

Over lunch, I fretted to him, "I can't figure out why the ADA didn't object to any of my questions. He's planning a sucker punch. Just try to stay cool, okay? Look professional, bring up your education and credentials whenever you can. Try to keep it on your turf: if he uses derogatory phrases, correct him with the proper psychological terms."

Fred nodded, looking a hell of a lot calmer than Alan or me.

A half hour into his cross-examination, he flicked a glance across the courtroom, meeting my eye. He was about to take my advice.

In response to a prosecution question about "false memories," he said, "The term I would use in this case is 'recovered memory.' The fact that a memory is not immediately retrievable doesn't say anything one way or another about whether it's true or false."

"I understand that, Dr. Hershey." Toben sounded ever so patient. "But I'm asking if you're aware of a phenomenon called 'false memory syndrome'?"

"I'm aware of the term. I wouldn't agree that it's a phenomenon. It's a hypothesis."

To give Fred his due, he looked cool, all right—maybe a little too cool. It's not good to have your experts appear overly detached and cerebral. Juries are, above all, just folks.

"Would you say it's a hypothesis for which there's considerable support in the psychiatric community?"

When Fred hedged further, Toben began asking if he'd read various tomes, papers, and journal articles on the subject. Fred said he had.

"Don't these authors conclude that a large percentage, more than a majority, of 'recovered' memories, as you call them, are false?"

"More than a majority of *non*recovered memories might be false," Fred pointed out. "Our memories are highly colored by our emotional, intellectual, and economic context. They are notorious for being out of line with verifiable history."

"What is usually meant in the literature by a 'false memory'?"

"Often it refers to something that never happened, but which a patient believes happened."

"By way of an example, are you familiar with . . ." He mentioned an experiment Fred knew nothing about. Then he asked about one Fred said he'd heard of.

"Isn't it true that in the course of this experiment, psychologists, during their therapy sessions with—"

"Objection, Your Honor. Counsel is testifying."

"Overruled."

"During therapy sessions," Toben continued, "psychologists repeatedly referred to a bogus childhood incident involving a patient being lost at a shopping mall, isn't that correct?"

"Yes, I believe so."

"Did the patients eventually begin to 'remember' the incident and elaborate upon it under hypnosis?"

"Those therapists drew on biographical data about the patient. I didn't know Mr. Miller at all when I hypnotized him."

"Are you aware of an experiment in which volunteers were asked to imagine, to simply make up, an alien abduction while under hypnosis?"

"Yes, I am."

Toben glanced at the jury, looking gratified. "Isn't it true that, while hypnotized, they were able to offer detailed and convincing abduction stories?"

"Well," Fred hedged, "but they were given permission to do so."

"Permission to lie under hypnosis?"

"Yes."

"Are you saying that without permission," Toben spoke the word sarcastically, "a person can't lie under hypnosis?"

I tried not to squirm. Toben wouldn't be asking unless the answer was no.

"I'm saying that experiments of the type you describe are fundamentally flawed because the subjects have the therapists' permission to lie. No conclusion can be drawn one way or the other."

"Let me understand this, Dr. Hershey. Are you testifying that people do not lie under hypnosis?"

"No. I'm testifying that the experiment you described doesn't answer that question."

"Do people lie under hypnosis?"

"Properly hypnotized, people faithfully describe their unconsciously edited and often inaccurate perceptions. That's all memories are."

Though I hoped the jury was persuaded, I found myself fearing that Fred protested too much. Was he worried that somehow, however subtly, he'd influenced Alan Miller? Was that why he'd skipped out on part of witness prep last night?

"So," Toben continued, "it is your testimony here today that no one willfully and knowingly lies under hypnosis?" This was lawyer code for *I have a truckload of experts ready to say they do*.

Fred seemed to know it. He sat straighter. "No therapist could make such a broad claim. I can only repeat that experiments designed to prove that point are inherently flawed because the subjects were *asked* to lie."

"Dr. Hershey, have you ever heard the term 'confabulation'?"

With a slight sigh, Fred said, "Yes, I have."

"What do you understand the term to mean?"

"It is the filling in of details not actually recalled. The replacement of fact with fantasy on an unconscious level."

"Does this occur under hypnosis?"

"It occurs in all states of consciousness."

"Is it considered a particular problem with hypnosis?"

"By some therapists, yes."

Without skipping a beat, Toben moved on to screen memories, asking Fred if he'd read certain articles about them.

I debated whether to object. All this harping on false memories and confabulation and screen memories would no doubt give the jurors additional reasons to dismiss Miller's story. But Fred was handling the questions well enough, and his familiarity with the literature might make him seem more, not less, credible.

And I worried that objecting too often would backfire, would make me look scared—especially after Toben's sanguine silence during direct.

Toben knew local juries. He knew the judge. I hoped I wouldn't regret it, but I decided to adopt his strategy: I wouldn't dignify my opponent's implied arguments with objections. I wouldn't let Toben make me look histrionic. When in Santa Cruz, lay back as the locals do.

I boiled redirect down to one question: "Dr. Hershey, given your extensive study and experience, do you feel that Alan Miller, under hypnosis, recovered genuine memories?"

Though I'd asked him this very question in last night's practice session, Fred seemed taken aback. He paused for a moment as if holding his breath. Then he blinked and straightened. He leaned a little closer to the witness microphone.

"Yes." He cleared a slight rasp from his throat. "I believe Mr. Miller recovered genuine memories."

21

I'd chosen my UFO experts based on how rational they seemed, how much scientific data they'd marshaled, and how good their résumés looked. It never occurred to me that there might be warring UFO camps. I didn't realize UFOlogists were no more monolithic than leftists. I'd spent decades watching communists denounce socialists, Yippies denounce liberals, the New and Old Left denounce each other, and just about everybody denounce the ACLU. So I was in no mood to hear UFOlogists accuse one another of spreading "disinformation."

My first mistake was putting them up at the same hotel, a local landmark advertising that every room had an ocean view. I thought having them at the same place would be convenient for meetings with them. I also thought it would give them a chance to walk on the beach. Instead, they apparently spent the afternoon in the hotel bar, bickering.

I'd asked them to meet me for dinner in the adjoining restaurant, a beige-and-mauve family-friendly place with piped-in elevator music. I was late because I'd stopped to see Carl Shaduff, and he'd put me on the phone with the medics who'd picked up Joseph Huizen.

Now, I spotted the four men at a bar table far from the ocean-view windows. The tabletop was cluttered with beers and chasers, soggy napkins and pretzel crumbs.

Three of them were speaking simultaneously. I lingered in the doorway, getting a hit of my witnesses.

The psychiatrist, Dr. Gene Karollas, a natural baritone, was the loudest: "Bart, Dan, this is a lose-lose. You're getting way off track. You're not discussing the same aspects—"

He was being squeaked down by Bart Bustamonte, a human Jabba the Hut, sweating in his tent of a shirt. "We've got so much verification it's ridiculous." He stabbed his finger at ex–NASA librarian Dan Fichman. "How can you possibly whine about sloppy science when we spent seventy-two hours running the data through a supercomputer?"

Dan Fichman, not a perfectly sprayed hair out of place, scoffed, "You could spend seventy-two *hundred* hours on computer analysis of your data and still reach a completely erroneous conclusion." Even with his collar open, he was as natty as a TV newsman.

"How? How can you argue with a perfectly clear ultrasound of an atomic reactor four hundred and fifty feet under a mesa?" Bustamonte's fleshy face was blotching red. "It's just like we've been saying, just like the Hickory Apaches out there have been saying, just like the nearest rancher neighbor has been saying. There's a multilevel military complex under that mesa, and it's hiding alien spacecraft. Hell, you can go sit on Apache land and watch ships fly out of there for your own damn self. The rest of us have done it. You've seen the videos we took."

"I'm talking about methodology, Bart." Fichman's words were precisely pronounced to full patronizing effect. "It's no use bothering to interpret data—however thoroughly—if you have a flaw in a major design parameter. It's going to be garbage in, garbage out. Look at what you piped through your buried transceivers to get that ultrasound: the woo-woo-woo Billy Meier *claims* he recorded from beamships visiting him over thirty years."

"Because of its sonic range. Other sounds would have worked. They chose Meier's because it has thirty-two bands, six of them subsonic, meaning—"

"Meaning zilch. Because we know now that Billy Meier

is a fraud—leaking out pictures and videos from reclusion in Scandinavia, feeding us the latest quote-unquote wisdom from his Pleiadean buddies. Making himself the hermit guru of feel-good abductees." Fichman shook his head. "Korff's book proves Meier's lying, which means you used an invalid parameter—"

"Are you even listening to me?" Bustamonte shook like Mount St. Helens. "It's the range of sound that matters, not—"

Fichman made a sarcastic noise. "Then what was all that hooey about expecting Gray aliens to come screaming out of their underground labs and hangars because they'd think their Pleiadean enemies were after them?"

"Now that's disinformation! Who the hell told you that? And why the hell would you believe it?" Bustamonte looked close to pushing the table over.

A few other bar patrons, over near the windows, looked up in alarm. I fought the urge to turn around and leave. I'm rarely in the mood for bombast.

"Bart, Bart," Fichman continued, as if perfecting his pitying tone. "If we don't adhere to the standards of good science, if we aren't rigorous in our testing procedures, then our results are not scientific!" He took a calm sip of his drink.

Fichman's presentation at the UFO conference had certainly reflected his determination to appear scientific. He'd shown NASA slides of planets and moons, collected during his years as a science librarian. He'd overwritten them with geometric notations purporting to prove that certain features were too precisely and identically arranged on too many planets to be natural. His presentation had been methodical and intense, and he'd shown no sign of slowing even after three hours. Every discipline had its Trotskyites.

Dr. Karollas, a lean psychiatrist in regulation Izod, jumped back into the discussion. "I don't see any purpose to attaching negative tags to our disagreements. Words like 'disinformation' shoot us all in the foot. We've got enough to worry about on other fronts without sniping at one another, gentlemen, and you know it." He glanced at the fourth member of the group for support.

But Melvin Kraduck, a retired air force colonel with a white crew cut and mean gray eyes, remained deadpan. He sat back as if it would take an army of Grays and Gordon Liddy himself to get a word out of him.

So I was surprised when he boomed, "Science be damned, Fichman! Science is a different animal altogether every decade. Science is just a bad guess with money behind it."

Fichman shook his head. "Applications and theories change. But the scientific method got us to the stars. And it can get the stars to give up their secrets to us. Unless we abandon it in favor of—"

"Of what?" Bustamonte slapped his hand onto the table, making pretzel salt bounce. "You want the evidence to jump through hoops for you? Twist itself into math formulas? Well, I'll tell you something I've learned from twenty years as a private investigator, Dan. Evidence comes like it comes, not like you want it."

I'd eavesdropped too long already, observing this pack of UFOlogists in the wild. I forced myself to walk to their table. I'd grown up among ranters; it wouldn't do to become squeamish about vehemence now.

"Hello," I greeted them. "Thank you all for agreeing to meet me tonight."

Dan Fichman stood suavely, smiling like a product representative, a Scientific Method salesman. He was wearing quite possibly the only double-breasted jacket in all of scruffy Santa Cruz.

"Our pleasure," Fichman said. "We've just been having a collegial discussion."

Bart Bustamonte snorted.

Dr. Karollas and Colonel Kraduck murmured greetings.

"I'm sorry I'm late. I had to make a stop."

Dr. Karollas checked his wristwatch. The colonel had already risen. Bustamonte still scowled at Fichman.

Fichman took on the role of host, leaving money on the

bar table, clapping Colonel Kraduck on the back, taking my elbow and leading the group into the dining area.

Once seated, the men looked at me. The colonel said, "So? What do you expect from us?" He pushed away the menu as if military men were always ready to order.

"I've told you generally what the case is about. Let me tell you where we are in the trial so far." I brought them up to date. "Now I want to offer expert testimony to convince the jury that Miller's alibi isn't crazy, that this stuff . . ." I couldn't quite make myself conclude, *really happens.*

Dr. Karollas said, "I've seen about a hundred and eighty patients personally. And I can tell you about hundreds of others."

"Your testimony will be the most directly relevant," I agreed. "It will let the jury know my client's not alone in this. The danger is . . . the DA could turn it around on us. If there are books full of these accounts, if they're featured in movies of the week, then they're available as alibis of last resort for the desperate and the delusional."

Karollas nodded. "Yes, I've heard that many times. My usual response is that even if you discount some percentage of the stories, you can't discount them all. No one who's met abductees can fail to be struck by how ordinary they are. Just regular, bewildered workaday folks, most of them. So even getting draconian and ignoring three quarters of the claims, what about the ones that remain? The most modest estimate puts that reduced number in the hundreds of thousands. Worldwide, it may be several million."

"Are the claims believable?"

"There are hundreds of multiple-abduction cases where groups of people are abducted together and all recover the same memories under hypnosis—the same craft and same type of examination, down to minute details. Plus, I've had two dozen people from different parts of the country, with no knowledge of one another, write down for me a series of symbols they've seen inside a craft. It's always the same unusual glyphs in the same odd pattern. And I have purposely never published this information! Add to that the fact that abductees repeatedly pass polygraph tests. And this is simply abduction cases. There have been millions more UFO sightings."

I couldn't hide my skepticism.

"There was a mass sighting by a million people in China in nineteen eighty-three," Bustamonte put in. "At least that many sightings in Mexico in the corridor between Mexico City and Oaxaca since the solar eclipse in ninety-one. Reports in this country are almost never picked up by the wire services, so it's hard to get numbers. But it's at least in the hundreds of thousands. Plus over four thousand trace cases."

"Trace cases?"

"Scars, scorched earth, radioactive ground, radiation burns on witnesses. You've heard of Cash and Landrum?"

"No."

Bustamonte raised his brows. "Famous court case. Betty Cash and Vicki Landrum got horrible radiation poisoning—nausea, hair loss, oozing sores, eventually cancer—from a huge spaceship that flew over their car on a highway in Texas. The craft was being escorted, or at least followed, by army Chinook helicopters, so the women ended up suing the government to recoup the cost of six weeks in the hospital. The court said their physical conditions alone didn't prove anything. So they had someone photograph that part of the highway—it was black from the heat where the ship flew over it. Within days, unmarked machinery dug up and replaced that whole piece of road."

"Did they win their case?"

"Against the government?" He snorted. "Of course not."

The waiter was at my elbow now, asking if we needed more time to decide.

The colonel said, "Steak medium and fries, black tea, and more water."

The rest of us needed quick consultations with the menu. The colonel sat back looking like a man disappointed in his troops.

To cover my inefficiency, I told him, "After Dr. Karollas testifies, I'll put you on the stand, colonel. I guess what I'm looking for is a list of credible people—astronauts, military men, scientists—who say they've seen UFOs."

The colonel nodded. "Plenty of astronauts: Ed White and James McDivitt saw them over Hawaii, James Lovell and Frank Borman spotted one from a *Gemini* capsule, Neil Armstrong admitted at a NASA symposium that he saw one while he was on the moon. Gordon Cooper and Donald Slayton reported them when they were fighter pilots. Cooper was on television a while back talking about it: an armada of saucers higher than the fighters could fly. Other pilots saw the same ones, hundreds of them over the next day and a half. Air force finally had to say something, so they wrote them off as airborne seed pods." Kraduck shook his head. "Imagine telling your best pilots they're so stupid they can't tell seed pods from manufactured craft."

"We've got forty-two hundred confirmed sightings by military and commercial pilots," Bustamonte added.

"What do you mean, confirmed?"

"The pilots reported the sightings. There's paperwork on it." Bustamonte had cooled down. He looked more like Sydney Greenstreet now. "We couldn't begin to estimate the sightings pilots don't report. Military pilots and astronauts who report UFOs run the risk of getting grounded for two weeks while they have psychological tests and most of their orifices probed. They definitely get the message that it's best to shut up about it if you see something up there."

Colonel Kraduck took back the floor. "Presidents Reagan and Carter saw them. Scientists: Hermann Oberth and Robert Oechsler, fathers of modern rocketry; Wehrner von Braun, Robert Sarbacher. Military men: General George Marshall, Admiral Roscoe Hillencoetter, first director of the CIA—he even joined a UFO group after he retired."

"You should have the colonel talk about the CIA's role in all this." Bustamonte's glance suggested he'd have plenty to say. "When one of our groups hit the CIA with a Freedom of Information Act request, they said they didn't have a thing on UFOs. Not a thing—can you believe the chutzpah? Then after years of appeals, they cough up nine hundred pages—nine hundred!—of information on UFOs . . . with most of the text blacked out. And that's only a fraction! They admitted they were holding back dozens upon dozens of documents from other agencies—OSI, FBI, Department of State, DEA, NSA." Bustamonte dabbed his forehead with his paper napkin. "We tracked down hundreds of National Security Agency documents, but they convinced the judge not to let us see most of them—too sensitive. So don't let anyone tell you the government's not hiding what it knows about UFOs!"

"Government's right to worry about spies." The colonel buffed his scant crew cut. "The aliens have propulsion systems that blow away anything we've got. Whichever country figures it out first has a tremendous advantage; we can't be sharing what we learn from downed spacecraft. And you don't talk to your friends without your neighbors finding out —that's where the FBI and NSA come in. If you want to keep a secret, you've got to deny everything straight across the board, to your own citizens same as to the Russians or Iraqis."

"There's more to it than that." Bustamonte waggled his hand. "The government made a deal with the aliens, probably back in July of fifty-two, after they showed up en masse in D.C." He looked at me. "You didn't know about that little sky show? People always say to me, 'If there really are aliens, why don't they just fly over the White House?' Well, they did. I could show you photos from several sources— seven glowing objects in formation over the Capitol dome. They showed up on three different sets of radar. We had fighter planes ready to go after them, but they kept disappearing from the radar screens, playing peekaboo with us. Thousands of people saw the formations two Saturdays in a row. It made the front page of the *New York Times,* the *L.A. Times,* the *London Times,* all the D.C. papers. And Eisenhower got the message, all right: *We can fly rings around you and we can mess with your radar. Nyah nyah nyah.*"

I looked around the table, expecting Fichman, at least, to deny it ever happened. But the men all seemed to agree on the mass sightings.

"After that, from all appearances"—Bustamonte shrugged—"the government let the aliens abduct anyone they wanted. It protected them with disinformation, and it made sure whoever reported UFOs got ridiculed and ghetto-ized in tabloids—isolated behind the 'laughter curtain.' And for what? What did we get in return? The technological equivalent of their Model T's."

Fichman shook his head. "You're behind the times, Bart. The news leaks, the tabloid stories, the TV shows—ever ask yourself *why?* Why would the government be feeding information to *X-Files, Sightings,* and *Unsolved Mysteries?* Why the public celebration of Martian bacteria inside that meteor? They're getting ready to make an announcement."

"Announcement, my butt. The information's out there because *we* dug it up. Hell, you're the one who keeps com-plaining about the NSA taking jurisdiction over NASA." He turned to me. "*Apollo, Gemini,* the space shuttle, *Or-biter,* they used to video-feed live to universities, news-rooms, amateur astronomers. Now everything goes through the NSA and they decide what to release. Remember the moon landing? If it happened today, you wouldn't see it. You might see some photos weeks or months later—*if* the NSA was feeling generous."

Fichman smiled. "Ah, but NASA is an organization of scientists, and scientists just won't put up with restricted information, not for long. NASA's already drafted protocols for a formal announcement of alien visitation."

"You're waiting for the good scientists to save us? To storm the Pentagon in their white lab coats?" Bustamonte waved dismissively. "In your dreams, Fichman. They all work for the damn military, one way or another. If they aren't actually in uniform, they're on the payroll of some company with a big defense contract. Besides, that NASA protocol's been on the books for years. Along with Federal Regulation one-two-one-one, saying it's illegal to come in contact with an alien. Five thousand dollar fine and one year imprisonment."

I must have looked surprised.

"That's right." Bustamonte read my mind: "Convince

the jury your client got abducted by aliens, and the FBI could march right into court and arrest him. Pretty serious stuff considering the Feds supposedly don't believe UFOs are anything more exotic than weather balloons and swamp gas!"

22

For four hours after dinner, I talked to the UFOlogists individually, ensconced in their respective rooms. The first thing each of them said to me was that one of the others was not what he seemed.

Bustamonte was adamant: "Colonel Kraduck's one of the biggest disinformation specialists the government has. Try to get hold of his military records—you won't be able to. Rumor has it he was an aide for one of the bigwigs in Project Blue Book, an air force commission put together back in the sixties to discredit and hush up UFO reports. Its members admitted later their orders were to release flaky reports to the press and bury valid ones. So this is not a man who decided to join UFO groups for fun after he retired. He's career military! Just because he wears civvies now doesn't mean he's out of uniform."

"You're afraid he'll give me false information?" I moved my feet farther from Bustamonte's strewn changes of clothes lying between the hotel chairs.

"Not if you limit your questions to which astronauts saw UFOs and that kind of thing—that stuff's too well documented for him to lie about." Bustamonte sat on the hotel bed because none of the chairs were wide enough. "But he'll put you on the map. Everything you say to him, everything he finds out you know, it'll get reported back to his superiors. And watch what kind of harassment you're in for when the shadow government learns about you! You'll get your house searched for sure. A few times out in the desert, they practically bounced their unmarked helicopters off our cars—all we could do not to crash. They've got deep pockets—some Pulitzer Prize–winning articles back in eighty-seven put the black budget at thirty-five billion, and you know it's higher by now. That's a hell of a slush fund. And they are mean sons of bitches! And Kraduck's their man."

Colonel Kraduck, on the other hand, pointed the finger at Dan Fichman.

"I hope you don't trust that phony bastard!" he barked to me from his hotel wing chair. "Anybody can scribble lines all over NASA photos and call it geometry. The man's a smooth talker, running a mathematics shell game, that's all. He gets the liberal arts majors out there all het up with his razzle-dazzle numbers and angles, and he's got half the UFO community convinced our ancestors came from Mars." He shook his head in gruff disgust.

"You think he's distracting UFOlogists from something more important?"

"Hell yes! What's his point?—just ask yourself. That a bunch of aliens traveled through the cosmos building pyramids and interbreeding with local humanoids? That we're part alien ourselves? Don't you see where that takes you? Don't you see the danger in a knuckleheaded story like that?"

"Well . . ."

"The rest of us are worrying about real aliens who kidnap and torture American citizens. Whereas Fichman's going around flim-flamming people into believing they're our long-lost cousins. The man's a menace. He'll have people walking up to the aliens with bouquets in their hands—*Uncle Henry, welcome back*—when they're here to steal our goddam genetic material!"

When I got to Dan Fichman's room, he warned me about Gene Karollas.

"Just a word in your ear," Fichman said suavely. He still wore his sport jacket and his hair remained wig perfect. "I know your defense is based on the alien abduction phenomenon. But I wouldn't question Gene Karollas too extensively. He doesn't have the stature of a John Mack or a Budd Hopkins, and there's a reason for that."

"There is?"

Fichman nodded portentously. "I'm not saying this is true of your client, but far too many so-called abduction cases are bogus. And Gene Karollas seems to specialize in them. Actually, I'm sorry to admit this to you, but I think this abduction stuff . . ." He shook his head.

"You don't think it's real?"

Fichman leaned toward me, his tone intimate. "Here's the mistake well-meaning investigators like Bustamonte make. They see the government engaged in an obvious cover-up, hiding hard evidence of flying saucers. Then they hear reports of aliens taking abductees, and they conclude the two things are related. But what we've really got is separate phenomena. One of them is flying disks, which the government certainly is studying for strategic military purposes. That's why they're hiding as much evidence as they can of alien artifacts here and on other planets. But the presence of extraterrestrial beings now and in the past does *not* mean they're kidnapping humans and playing with our genitals!"

Oh, great. I hoped he didn't say this under cross-examination. "So how do you explain the alien abduction reports?"

"Oh, *something* is happening. Up here." Fichman tapped his forehead. "Succubi, incubi, elves, demons . . . we humans have been visited and kidnapped by other kinds of beings without pause throughout our history. I think that whatever it's about, it involves a quantum-mechanical dimension of mind, shall we say? A psychophysical part of the human machinery—but nothing *extra*terrestrial."

"So you're saying these unwelcome visitors aren't aliens, they're . . . some kind of mental manifestation?"

"That's right—somehow part of us, emanating from us or coexisting with us. The infusion of aliens into our popular culture, starting with science fiction movies and pulp novels of the forties and fifties, causes us to interpret our timeless abductors as gray aliens with laser scalpels. But the experience, in its essence, is exactly the same as that of a thirteenth-century girl being raped by succubi. It's the Gene Karollases among us"—Fichman cocked a brow—"who encourage people to fill in memory lapses to match recent fictional portrayals of the future."

Needless to say, Gene Karollas's take on this was completely different.

"I could have had the kind of lucrative, satisfying practice my medical school classmates have now." Karollas stared out the hotel window as if lost in a happy fantasy of curing rich bipolar women. Two floors below, spotlit surf raced over packed sand. "But once I'd heard a few dozen of these abduction stories, I no longer had the luxury of disbelief. The trauma to the abductees is simply indescribable to anyone who hasn't met them. For people to imply they're after some kind of notoriety, well, comments like that could only come from the pettiest ignorance. That's our real enemy: the closed mind. And the easy put-down."

Just when I thought I was going to have a normal witness prep session, he added: "That's why fellows like Bart Bustamonte are so dangerous."

"But Bustamonte believes in—"

"He's simply over the top! How can we ever convince people of the truth when we've got overgrown kids sneaking around the desert piping spaceship music through underground speakers? He makes us all look foolish! Telling wild tales to a news media already laughing at our expense . . . Do you believe him? Do you believe there are subterranean hangars full of flying saucers? I hate to use the word, because it hurts us all to have it bandied about, but Bustamonte *is* passing along disinformation. He may not be aware of it, but he's the best friend the government could have in its cover-up of alien abduction!"

By the time I walked out to my car, I was sick to death of all of them. And despite being barraged with evidence —Bustamonte's photos of flying saucers, Karollas's case studies, Fichman's NASA photos of artifacts on other planets, Kraduck's government cover-up documents—I was too overloaded to believe any of it. Even the Business and Professions Code made more sense.

I'd also spent about as much time in company—especially paranoid, big-ego male company—as I could stand.

Unfortunately, I didn't even make it out of the parking lot before my solitude ceased. Our detective, Carl Shaduff, suddenly appeared in my headlights, waving for me to stop.

I slammed on my brakes, unlocking the door for him. He climbed into the passenger seat, looking rattled. "You okay?" he said.

"Yes. What are you doing here?" I could see his car parked on the street a half block down from the hotel.

"The question is, what the hell are *they* doing here?" He slumped so that he could squint out the windshield at something in the sky.

I felt my chest tighten with panic. Was Shaduff about to point out UFOs? Were we about to get abducted?

I followed Shaduff's gaze, but I didn't see anything. Only stars, nice and stationary. "What's who doing here?"

"Let your eyes get used to the dark a minute."

We were hardly in the dark. The hotel parking lot was bathed in the glow of searchlights trained on the tide line. I kept looking at the sky.

"I knew you were here talking to your witnesses," Shaduff said, still watching whatever he saw in the sky. "I came about the paramedics. One of them decided to 'fess up. I've been over to his house interviewing him." Shaduff's eyes moved slowly to the left as if following something.

" 'Fess up?" I finally made out shapes in the sky. "Are those helicopters? Why don't they have any lights on?"

"Not your usual helicopters. I'm not sure about this because it's so dark up there . . . but it looks like they're unmarked."

"Unmarked helicopters? Is that legal? Aren't they required to have identifying numbers like planes? And shouldn't they have their lights on?"

"I've heard about black helicopters." He followed them with his eyes, looking as excited as a teenager. "They're supposed to be almost silent, almost invisible in the night sky."

"If they're designed to be invisible, why are they flying so low?"

"The rumor is they show up when one of the alphabet agencies is working with the military. CIA, NSA, DEA—when these babies pop out of the clouds, somebody's running special ops."

I could barely see them, a few hundred feet out over the tide line, hovering like black dragonflies.

"Of course, our view's not the greatest. And the surf's going to cover some of their noise. They could just be police choppers looking for something on the beach. Or coast guard, I suppose."

"Or they could want the UFOlogists to spot them," I realized. "From the hotel windows."

Shaduff nodded. "They could be making a statement. To one or all of them. Maybe to you."

"Do you have a camera?" But I knew it was too dark to get a picture.

"No, but it wouldn't—"

The helicopters turned then, flying seaward until they were out of sight.

"Where did they come from?" I wondered.

"There's an airport up in Bonny Doon above Davenport, another one down in Watsonville. There's military bases all over central California; Travis Air Force is probably the closest. You could ask your experts."

I hesitated. The last thing I wanted to do was go back into the hotel and talk to them some more. I shifted in the Honda seat to face Shaduff. Fred Hershey would be paying plenty of overtime, it seemed.

"What did the paramedic say?" I asked him.

"He admits now that he and his partner stopped on San Vittorio after they picked up Joseph Huizen." Shaduff's eyes remained on the horizon, ready if the helicopters came back into sight. "The one I talked to, John Bivens, he was the driver. He says as soon as he turned out of Huizen's drive onto the road, he was almost blinded by a bright light.

He slammed on the brakes about fifty yards short of Donna Nelson's house."

"Miller's neighbor." I was disappointed; I'd hoped to hear something involving Miller.

"Get this: the bright light was pointing straight into her window. Bivens couldn't see what the light was coming out of, but it was up in the sky at the height of a four- or five-story building. It was as bright as daylight and as big as a water-slide tube at an amusement park—his words."

"What would create a light beam like that?" I was getting scared. It was night and I was far from home.

"It might not have been as bright as he remembers." He nodded toward the shoreline. "Or maybe it was a helicopter. But Bivens says he's used to MediVac helicopters, that he'd have recognized a searchlight."

"Did the light do anything?"

"They couldn't stay long. Bivens says he slammed on the brakes and called his partner up front. But they couldn't hang around to watch."

"Donna Nelson went to the library the next day and checked out an armload of UFO books," I told Shaduff. "It's obvious what she thought it was."

"I could probably get her library records," Shaduff offered. "If you're thinking of trying to do something with this."

"The paramedic seems credible?"

"You never know. But it's hard to figure his reason for making it up. Imagine the shit he'll get at work. He stops an ambulance in the middle of transporting a patient. And you could certainly construe his statement as a UFO sighting. Even if his bosses don't care, he's bound to get a ration from his coworkers."

Shaduff was right. Paramedic John Bivens was likely to join my client behind what Bart Bustamonte had called the "laughter curtain."

I would soon learn what an uncomfortable place that could be.

23

I was jittery driving back to Fred Hershey's. I found myself watching the sky as much as the road. Try as I might, I could no longer dismiss space as an empty expanse with the occasional floating rock or distant gas ball. Now it seemed like some teeming ocean with strange life-forms breaching the surface.

I reminded myself that I didn't have to believe or debunk or even decide. I didn't have to get caught up in it; I only had to plead Miller's case.

And I didn't have to do that until tomorrow. Right now, I needed a respite. I needed some solitude and maybe some ice cream. I hoped I'd find Fred Hershey already in bed.

But when I rounded the corner onto Fred's street, I knew I wasn't going to get a break. There was a police car parked in front of his townhouse. Fred's front door was wide open. Every light in the place was on.

I pulled up behind the cop. Last night someone shot out Carl Shaduff's window. The bullet, lodged near the ceiling of the back wall, hadn't come close to hitting anyone. But it had scared the hell out of me. I tried to make myself stop for a second and get a grip.

Instead I ran up the walkway, trying to assure myself I wouldn't find Fred dead inside. There would be more police cars if anyone was hurt. There would be an ambulance, a fire truck, paramedics. There would be a commotion, a police line.

Nevertheless, I was so relieved to see Fred, looking frazzled in black sweat clothes, that I lowed like an ox.

"Willa." Standing beside a policeman, Fred waved his arm and snapped, "Can you believe this?"

The living room had been trashed: sofa cushions strewn, magazines scattered, paintings and pictures yanked off the walls. Through the kitchen door, I saw utensils on the floor.

"Every room in the house is like this," Fred complained. "This is Officer Groom."

"Hi." I didn't look at the cop; there was too much else to notice. "What's missing?"

"Nothing, I don't think. You'd better check the things in the guest room."

I ran upstairs. My clothes were tossed around the floor. So were a few of my papers. Most of them, luckily, were in my briefcase in my car.

I picked up my blue suit jacket, brushing white carpet fibers off it. I did a quick count: suits, blouses, shoes, everything was still here.

I rejoined Fred and Officer Groom. "My stuff's okay. Were they searching for something? Or just being malicious?"

Officer Groom stopped writing on his clipboard.

"I mean, nothing's taken apart. The couch cushions aren't unzipped. My bed's barely mussed. Did they mess with your computer, Fred?"

"Not that I know of."

"So . . ." The officer circled a number from a list on his paperwork. "You think this might be an act of mischief? Spite? Do you know who might have done it?"

"If it's spite . . ." Fred sighed.

"Fred testified in a trial today. The widow of"—I didn't want to go into the merits. "An aggrieved party, Betty Addenaur; she might have done it."

Fred added, "If you contact Sheriff's Deputy Brazel and Police Officer Rose, you'll find out she tried to take a shot at us, and that she's also under suspicion for another shooting incident."

I was surprised Fred knew the name of the officer who'd come to Carl Shaduff's Friday night.

Groom, a round-faced, freckled man who would probably always look too young, scribbled down the information. Fred spelled Addenaur's widow's name for him.

"Obviously you weren't here," I said. I was surprised by the note of suspicion in my voice. I recalled tapping on his door early Saturday and getting no answer, returning to the kitchen last night to find him gone. Last week, he'd claimed to be running, but I'd found him beside my car without a bead of sweat on him. What wasn't he telling me? Where was he really going?

"I went straight from the gym to dinner," Fred explained. "I'm thinking I must have left the kitchen window up—it's open now. Anyway, I came home about an hour ago and found this." He waved his arm. "I hope my insurance will pay for a cleaning service."

Straight from the gym to dinner, then home an hour ago. It was close to midnight now. Had he really eaten so late?

I glanced at the cop uncertainly. "Another witness in the case I'm trying . . . she expressed concern that her grandparents might be unstable, might be out to harm her. I have no reason to think this is related, but her name is Maria Nanos. She was with me when a shot was fired through a private investigator's window Friday night—Officer Rose can give you the police report." I gave him Patrick Toben's number, too. "He can give you details about the grandparents, if you want to check on them."

Fred was nodding. "I guess it's possible."

"Anybody else?"

Fred flushed. I knew he had three ex-wives and a brood of kids. I didn't know anything about his relationship with them.

I wondered whether to bring up the black helicopters. I kept hearing Bart Bustamonte's warning: now that "they" knew about me, I could expect a visit to my house.

"Let me call my client before you go. Let me just make sure he's okay."

I crossed to the phone and dialed Alan at Edward's house. I got Edward's answering machine.

"Alan, if you're listening, pick up," I urged. "Alan?" I waited. "Call me at Fred's if you check Edward's messages."

Very likely, Alan was asleep. But I hung up feeling troubled.

Fred wrapped things up with the policeman. I added my name and address to the information already on his clipboard. He scribbled the case number across two of his business cards, handing us each one. I was getting quite a collection of cops' cards. Maybe they'd be valuable someday.

When we were alone, Fred put his arm around me and gave me a brisk squeeze. "Tell me you're not anal retentive."

"Hardly." My apartment didn't look much better than this at the best of times.

"Then we'll leave it. Let's get some sleep and worry about the mess in the morning."

I'd be putting the UFOlogists on the stand in the morning; I had a worse mess to worry about.

24

I found Fred in a slightly tidied kitchen reading the newspaper and shaking his head. When I greeted him, the look on his face—startled, hesitant—told me there was bad news.

"Leonard Deally?" I guessed.

"Afraid so."

I took the editorial section from him. Deally's column was headlined *Twinkie Defense Meets Lost in Space*. "Dan White got away with murder because he ate too many Twinkies," it began. "Now Alan Miller, whose car crushed local contractor Francis Addenaur, is trying to get away with murder . . . by claiming he *is* a Twinkie. Or I should say that he was abducted by *alien* Twinkies."

"The laughter curtain," I murmured, skimming further.

"What?"

"That's what one of the UFOlogists calls it." I set the paper down on the table. "It's what I expected. There's no reason for Deally to be in court every day unless he plans to milk it."

Fred handed me the front page.

Another article, also under Deally's byline, discussed the trial. It quoted Fred's testimony and talked about the upsurge in reports of alien abduction since the topic had been popularized by novelists and screenwriters. It quoted Carl Sagan sneering at abduction reports and accusing therapists of implanting false memories. A sidebar listed bizarre defenses in other trials. Another interviewed Addenaur's friends and grandchildren, all of whom were outraged by the sleazy depths to which Miller's lawyer and therapist would sink to get him off.

"We're lucky they didn't find some preachers willing to call us satanic."

Fred smiled wanly.

"Look, Fred, I don't live here. I'm not even a criminal lawyer; I'll go back to multimedia law like none of this ever happened." Even if I did go back in dire need of a vacation. "What about you? Is this going to affect your practice?"

"I can't let that matter to me, can I?"

But I couldn't shake the feeling he was keeping something from me, some purpose beyond or even at odds with helping Miller.

He continued, "A good part of my work is for county agencies. If this tarnishes my credibility with them . . ." He sat back in his chair. "But I expected this. I'm okay with it. I just hope you are, too."

An hour later, in court, I was sincerely doubting it.

"The defense calls Dr. Gene Karollas." I tried to sound confident. But I worried that my UFOlogy experts would find ways to slander one another on the stand as they had in their hotel rooms.

Dr. Karollas was sworn in, looking at least as well tailored as Fred, in his silk turtleneck, a blue blazer, and gray slacks. No bargain basement experts for me.

I questioned him about his résumé, got the scoop on how and why he'd started working with abductees, how he checked patients' claims of "missing time," his reasons for and methods of conducting hypnosis, his experience with multiple abductees whose stories matched, and his documentation of abductees' physical effects, such as scars, bruises, and nosebleeds.

Just when I was beginning to congratulate myself on how sane and dignified the doctor seemed, he went and got strange on me.

"Dr. Karollas, is there any reliable estimate of how many of these cases have been reported?"

"The estimates range from several hundred thousand to several million worldwide." Unfortunately, he added, "I'm talking about alien abduction cases, mind you, not the cases attributed—wrongly, in my opinion—to abduction by so-called black budget elements of our own government."

I quickly asked a question about something else entirely. But I supposed Toben had noticed the perverse little toad hopping out of my witness's mouth.

During cross-examination, he could barely keep the smirk out of his voice. "A few moments ago, you mentioned cases of abduction not by aliens but by United States military personnel. Can you tell us how many *non*alien abduction cases have been reported, Dr. Karollas?"

"That's irrelevant," I objected. "These claims are not the same type made by the defendant."

"Your Honor," the assistant DA said patiently, "there's already been a great deal of testimony about unverifiable abduction claims. The People have the right to impeach based on how broad these claims are."

"Your Honor, the witness stated that his testimony does *not* take this type of claim into account. So any follow-up about them is irrelevant—on par with asking about abductions by the Symbionese Liberation Army."

The judge disagreed, overruling my objection.

Dr. Karollas looked upset. Maybe he realized he'd shot himself, as well as the rest of us, in the foot.

And boy, what an "us" I'd let myself get drafted into.

"I don't know of any estimate," Karollas answered the DA.

"Can you tell us how these stories differ from the ones you claim number in the hundreds of thousands?"

Dr. Karollas's lean face looked pinched. "Air force personnel are either alongside the aliens in the examination area or are working alone, using memory-wiping techniques such as those employed by the aliens."

I could hear a stirring in the pews, a pre-snicker, if there's such a thing. With a sharp look, the judge silenced it.

Toben paused as if to control his own smile. "So there are individuals who believe that air force personnel fly around in spaceships?"

"They don't necessarily believe or disbelieve anything."

"Well, in your experience, how do therapists interpret these stories?"

"Too often, as evidence of an alliance between our military and an alien race referred to as the Grays."

"Do you believe that, Dr. Karollas?"

"Objection. This is not the doctor's area of expertise."

"Overruled."

"No." Karollas was emphatic. "I do not believe, as some people do, that our government would ally itself with creatures capable of inflicting so many indignities and causing so much pain and trauma!"

Obviously he hadn't heard of Joseph Stalin or the Shah of Iran, of Pinochet or Duvalier or Somoza.

"You stated under direct examination that you began hearing accounts of alien abduction from your patients in nineteen eighty-two?"

"Yes."

"Are you aware of a book published in nineteen eighty-one by Budd Hopkins, titled *Missing Time*?"

"Yes."

"Doesn't this best-selling book describe case histories of individuals supposedly abducted by gray alien beings?"

"Yes."

"Are you aware of a nineteen eighty-seven best-selling book by Whitley Strieber titled *Communion*?"

"Yes."

"Isn't it a detailed account by a popular horror novelist of abductions by gray aliens?"

"Yes."

"Does it describe, among other things, intrusive physical exams and the taking without consent of a sperm sample?"

"Yes." Dr. Karollas was squirming with the desire to say more, to explain why he didn't think his patients' stories were mere paraphrasings.

But Assistant DA Toben kept his questions narrow:

"Since nineteen eighty-seven, have any of your patients told you stories similar to the one in *Communion*?"

An irritated "Yes."

"Would you say, in fact, that the majority of your patients' stories track this one, give or take some details?"

Alan scribbled a note to me. It read, "I've never heard of *Communion*! Or that other book!"

Karollas replied, "A substantial number of my patients have experienced ordeals similar to Mr. Strieber's at the hands of the Grays."

"Are you aware that a movie was made of *Communion*?"

And on the ADA went, implying that Dr. Karollas's patients had been so enamored of Strieber's tale of alien torture that they'd claimed it for their own.

But then, who knew? This was a country that had re-elected Nixon and Reagan; we obviously weren't above embracing painful debasement.

Toben continued his list of "Did you know's": that after the 1951 movie *The Day the World Stood Still*, UFO sightings "skyrocketed" to a then record fifteen hundred; that reports of gray aliens did the same after the publication of *Missing Time* and *Communion;* that reports of mysterious government agents in black did so after an *X-Files* episode? Did he know that after forty years of popular fiction, there were five times more believers in UFOs than there were fundamentalist Christians, twice as many as there were Catholics?

I repeatedly objected that the ADA was testifying, and I was repeatedly overruled.

I began to suspect that Toben's silence during my questioning of Fred Hershey owed less to strategy than to long acquaintance with this judge.

Toben then began raising problems with the use of hypnosis to recover "alleged memories of alien abduction." He'd covered much the same ground with Fred Hershey, but seemed delighted to do so again. He concluded with a series of questions about "sleep paralysis," about which Fred had claimed ignorance.

Unfortunately, Dr. Karollas was able to describe sleep

paralysis as a condition where, for a few moments upon awakening, the sleeper was conscious but unable to move.

"Dr. Karollas, isn't another characteristic of sleep paralysis being prone to hallucinations?"

"I've never encountered a case of sleep paralysis with hallucinations. But I've seen mention of it in the literature."

"Isn't it true that most so-called alien abductions occur when a patient is wakened from sleep?"

"Most of them occur late at night, so, yes." Karollas glanced at the jury as if hoping they appreciated his point.

When I stood, a few minutes later, to do a little witness rehabilitation on redirect, I noticed Leonard Deally slipping out the courtroom doors. I guessed he wasn't interested in my rebuttal. He had all the negative stuff in his notes; he was ready to go write his column.

Ah, if only.

It turned out Deally left the courtroom to go phone his pal Timothy Elgin, the head of the news bureau for a local network affiliate. By the time I was halfway through questioning Bart Bustamonte, news cameras were being hoisted onto the shoulders of cameramen in the corridor outside.

I saw the broadcast later.

It began with a long shot of the chipmunk-cheeked newsman on the courthouse steps. His voice was both mellow and emphatic. "Just another day in court? Well, yes . . . if you live in Santa Cruz, California." He smiled, showing many white teeth. "Yes, Santa Cruz, where Jerry Garcia's Deadheads gathered in the thousands to mourn him . . . and never quite left. Where every year lesbian activists parade topless to show their, uh, *liberation*. Where just last week, hundreds of New Age pilgrims congregated to feel the vibes from so-called crop circles . . ."

They cut to film footage of kids in tie-dye dancing inside the main circle.

"Well . . ." Now the newscaster was shown in a wood-paneled portion of the courthouse corridor. "You wouldn't expect Santa Cruz to have the usual kinds of legal cases, would you? But just how far out *was* Courtroom Number

Two today? Would you believe . . . in a far-distant solar system called Zeta Reticuli?"

They showed Bart Bustamonte outside the men's room, looking cranky after an afternoon of bad treatment by the assistant DA.

Bustamonte, sweating profusely, was trying to hold up UFO video stills and photographs he'd brought to court. But the cameraman was making no effort to zoom in on them. No doubt they'd rolled plenty of film of Bustamonte rattling off his data—thousands of sightings per year, types of craft sighted repeatedly in diverse locations, mass sightings, video-recorded sightings, radar-verified sightings, authentication of the film and photographs, trace-evidence cases showing irradiated ground and burnt grass—Bustamonte had plenty of statistical and pictorial backup.

But the only snippet the news chose to run was Bustamonte's comment that the aliens were widely reported to be small gray humanoids from Reticulum 4, the fourth planet of the Zeta Reticuli system, which had a binary sun that might account for the dark film over their eyes.

Having made Bustamonte look like a flake, Timothy Elgin then goaded Colonel Kraduck into a temper tantrum.

Kraduck, my final witness of the day, had been unshakable on the stand. There were over four thousand UFO sightings reported by American pilots, and by God, the colonel wasn't going to let the assistant DA get away with calling thousands of American boys liars.

But the colonel, confronted by a crew of derisive newspeople, became as testy as Ross Perot. The television segment cut straight from Bustamonte's pronouncement that aliens came from Reticulum 4 to Kraduck snapping, "Of course the air force knows about it! Don't be stupid! Contrary to popular belief, the U.S. military knows how to keep a secret!"

The camera returned to Elgin, alone in the corridor. "Well, it's nice to know that someone, in this era of news leaks, has faith in our government to keep a secret! Let's see if Dr. Eugene Karollas, a therapist specializing in alien abductions, agrees."

They segued to Dr. Karollas, who fielded their curveball with the pronouncement, "Hundreds of thousands of people have had contact experiences. So no, no, no, this is not a secret in any sense of the word."

A last shot showed Elgin again alone in the courthouse corridor, a glass wall behind him. Through it, a skinny Rastafarian with long dreadlocks could be seen approaching. "But what does any of this have to do with Courtroom Number Two? Let's ask attorney Willa Jansson. Her client, Alan Miller, is accused of killing Francis Addenaur when his car drove off a cliff and landed on top of Addenaur's."

I was suddenly ambushed by cameras as I left the courtroom. My face looked like a companion piece to Munch's *The Scream*, something titled *Oh, Shit.*

"Miss Jansson, your client says his car didn't go off a cliff, as the police have charged. He says it fell out of a spaceship?" Elgin sounded like he might burst out laughing.

I noticed Leonard Deally standing behind one of the camerapeople, looking satisfied.

Without a word, I went back inside the courtroom to warn Alan, a few seconds behind me, not to come out.

The news segment concluded with the assistant district attorney saying, "Well, I really can't comment." Then, piously, "But I will say that it's tragic Francis Addenaur lost his life."

"Do you believe the car that killed him fell out of a spaceship?"

Toben grinned sourly. "No, of course not."

"Well," Elgin wrapped up, "San Francisco had the Twinkie defense, and now Santa Cruz has the space cadet defense." He sighed telegenically. "As we love to say here in Surf City: 'Only in Santa Cruz' . . . and Zeta Reticulum Four. This is Timothy Elgin reporting."

25

I found Alan Miller in Edward's backyard, an overgrown weed patch and parking lot for a kayak, a surfboard, an inflated boat on a small trailer, and a filthy Jeep that had once served as my getaway car.

Some getaway: I'd escaped last year's police problems only to become obliged to Edward's brother this year. I'd traded last year's escape for this year's vacation.

I put my hand on Alan's shoulder. He was sitting on an upside-down kayak supported by cinder blocks. He was staring at Edward's eight-foot plank fence, his back to me.

"Alan?" He'd certainly heard me rustle through accumulated leaves and dry grass. But he hadn't even glanced over his shoulder.

"It's just so stupid," he said.

"The reporters today?"

"All of it. Everything we're saying. Everything the witnesses said."

Uh-oh, we were back to basics. "You can't help what you remember," I pointed out. "You're just trying to be honest."

"What about those studies the DA talked about? Maybe Dr. Hershey was, you know, suggesting alien abduction to me. Without being too obvious."

I was a little worried about that myself. But we were

committed now. "You heard the tape. It didn't sound like it to me."

"Or maybe it was that sleep paralysis thing. Maybe I'm one of the people that gets hallucinations along with it."

"Have you ever experienced sleep paralysis before?"

"No." He looked up. His eyes were rimmed red. "But it makes more sense than getting snatched by aliens, doesn't it?"

"It's no use worrying about what makes sense. We have to go with the evidence we've got."

"Yeah, well you don't have to live in this town."

"If you're acquitted, you won't have to, either." It came out sounding harsh. "Look, I'm sorry all this got heaped on you. But I've got a few more things to add to the pile."

He sighed, staring back across the yard at the fence.

I walked to the other side of the kayak. I was still in my suit, so I didn't sit on the filthy plastic. But at least I could look Alan in the face, even if he was determined not to look at me.

"I just talked to Patrick Toben." I'd stopped by his office to discuss what happened to Fred's apartment. "Maria's grandparents are still refusing to go home. They seem to hold the DA's office—and us—responsible for losing her. Toben suggested we be cautious, keep an eye out for them and report any harassment." I hastened to add, "In a way, this is good. It's shut Toben up about screen memories for rape, at least for now. It seems obvious Maria's just trying to keep her grandfather from breaking her legs." But the charge, I was afraid, would surface again when Maria did.

Alan covered his face with both hands. His shoulders rounded.

"I didn't get a chance to talk to you about this today, but I think you should know. Someone broke into Fred's condo last night and tossed his stuff all around. They didn't take anything, but it was a mess." Still no response. "Please be careful, Alan. You're the flash point for all this."

Finally, Alan looked up.

"The other thing is, remember I mentioned going back to

the crop circle Saturday morning? I told you about Reginald Fulmer. I've decided to put him on the stand."

I reached into my briefcase and pulled out one of the science-book Xeroxes Carl Shaduff had provided. I handed it to Alan, saying, "Glucose."

He stared at it a minute or two, tilting his head from side to side.

Rendered as connected spheres, like most molecule diagrams, it didn't look much like a crop circle. But I'd done my share of head tilting, too.

"Imagine it as a two-dimensional line drawing. It can be sketched to look like the crop circle." I waited for him to agree. Finally, I continued, "I'll put Dr. Huizen on the stand and have him mention he's writing a book about the mathematics of spinning planets. He'll describe his diabetic emergency the night of your car crash. He'll testify that the medics gave him glucose, and that it saved his life. That if the ambulance hadn't been right in the neighborhood—they'd just put Addenaur into a helicopter—he'd have died."

Alan stared up at me, his face flushing. He swallowed a few times before saying, "Why? What will it prove? That there was a goddam silver lining?"

"There's more. On the way to the hospital, the ambulance slammed on its brakes in front of Donna Nelson's house. The medic who was driving admits now that he saw a bright light from the sky shining straight into her window."

Alan murmured, "No." He scowled. "The medic could be lying. Or he could be mixed up in this."

"Mixed up in what?"

"Maybe it's a drug thing. Maybe Fred's part of it—paramedics, a psychiatrist. Maybe they're drugging people to give them false memories. Maybe the medics made the crop circle."

He closed his eyes, looking exhausted.

I told myself Alan was weaving stories from the tatters of his denial. But Fred's level of involvement—including paying all expenses—troubled me, too. "As long as you know everything I know, I've done my bit. Right now, I've got to make a phone call. I'll come back out in a while and we'll talk some more."

If I couldn't persuade my own client his defense made sense, how would my boss, Cary Curtis, react?

As I walked inside to use Edward's phone, I decided the best tactic was to avoid details.

So, after some desultory "How have you been's" and what's-happening-at-work chat, I kept it general.

"Cary, an old friend of mine needed a favor. He asked me to defend one of his patients on a vehicular manslaughter charge. He contacted me the day my vacation started, and, well, I just assumed the case would be wrapped up by now."

Silence.

I continued. "It isn't. The trial was scheduled to last a week—it should have concluded Tuesday, yesterday at the latest. But now it looks like it could go maybe three or four more court days."

Cary cleared his throat. "It hasn't been easy without you around here. We've been going crazy with the extra work, to tell the truth. We've got the digital signatures . . ."

Several states were making it possible to "sign" Internet and e-mail documents using a private encryption key, with the receiver using a public unencryption program. This was supposed to make each "signature" as unique, theoretically, as handwriting. But disputes were already arising over types and ownership of encryption software.

"Plus we've got more domain name troubles."

Two of our corporate clients had been blindsided by clever young men registering Internet domain name addresses that matched corporate business names. When the corporations saw the wisdom of Internet advertising with online ordering, they found they couldn't use their own names in cyberspace—not unless they paid someone off or fought him in court.

"And we've got a shitload of copyright work, as usual."

The Internet was a copyright lawyer's dream come true. Art, literature, and music were swiped, reproduced, and sent all around the world every day.

"We need you back," he concluded.

"I want to be back, Cary, believe me. I never dreamed this case would drag on like this. But what can I do? I can't leave this guy twisting in the wind."

"If I may be blunt, shouldn't you have thought of that before? Before you went and took on a case? And as to that —you know, you *do* work for us. We do have a contract provision about other employment."

"I know. But this is completely outside our area of practice. And I'm doing it on my own time, pro bono. It's just a favor for a friend, Cary. I didn't think it would take so long, that's all."

"Jesus, the position you put me in here! What am I supposed to do? You don't leave me a hell of a lot of choice. If I say come back—as you are obligated to do—you leave your client in the middle of a case and he sues you for malpractice, and ends up going after this firm because we've got the friggin' pockets!"

Cary was taking this less well than I'd hoped. Though an excitable man, he almost never swore.

"I'm sorry, I really am. If I could make it go away today, I would. But like you said, I can't leave my client in the middle of trial. You can charge this time off against my next year's vacation. But what can I do?"

"What's this case about, anyway?"

"Vehicular manslaughter and felony hit-and-run. They can't prove my client was driving the car at the time, so I didn't want him to plea bargain."

"Where does he say he was when the accident happened?"

"It was two-thirty in the morning. He doesn't remember being awake then." True—as far as it went.

"So what is it, his word against what?"

"They didn't find anyone else's prints on the driver's side. And he wasn't home right after the accident."

"So what's the basis of your case—anything besides his denying it?"

"The way the prosecution claims the accident happened . . . well, they can't produce any evidence."

"Of what?"

"Look, it's no use arguing the merits. The problem is that both sides ended up bringing in expert witnesses. It's dragging out longer than I'd hoped." I prayed Cary wouldn't get stubborn about hearing the details.

"I guess I'm troubled that you would take a case without so much as running it past anybody here. I mean, really, your reputation is our reputation. We can be harmed by your representing certain kinds of clients. You must realize that?"

"Yes, I do. I really do." I'd been pacing Edward's ratty living room, cordless phone in hand. Now, I dropped into his dusty sofa, tired with the effort of remaining contrite. "Like I said, it's a small pro bono thing on my own time. The client is a nice Ph.D. who honestly doesn't believe he did anything illegal. I owed his therapist a favor. I thought I'd be done by now. I'm really sorry, Cary."

During the ensuing pause, I prayed: If Cary let me leave it at that, all might be well. If he asked for details, if he dug deeper into my defense, who knew what would happen?

"I'll discuss it with the others. Call me tomorrow and I'll be speaking for more than just myself. In the meantime, what's your number there? What's the case name?"

I gave him Fred's number. "It's a Santa Cruz County case, *People versus Alan Miller.*"

Little did I know Cary would go to his Palo Alto home that night and see Timothy Elgin's news story. Elgin's network affiliate, it seemed, reached as far north as Palo Alto and as far south as Big Sur. And who knows, maybe as far up as Zeta Reticuli.

26

I don't know why I found the article in the newspaper more disturbing than the television news story. Maybe because Elgin's story was as shallow as it was clichéd, whereas Leonard Deally's acid burned deep.

A PREMEDITATED EXCUSE, Deally's headline read. "Maybe it's just the system," he began,

> that encourages lying: All's fair in court and war, and everyone's entitled to the best defense —just ask Nicole Simpson's family. But what happens when a defendant is so flagrant in his lying—whoops, I mean defense—that the hypocrisy itself seems criminal? Case in point: Local mushroom expert Alan Miller says his car fell out of the sky when he was abducted by spacemen. Laughable, you say? The jury couldn't possibly buy it—you hope! Well, but this is California, where Dan White served three years per corpse and O. J. Simpson's out on the golf links right now.

Deally inserted a brief biography of Francis Addenaur, who was driving along minding his own business when he got squashed like an unimportant little bug, first by Miller's car and now by a legal system that lets slick city lawyers substitute trendy hokum for the truth.

As if that wasn't bad enough:

> There are larger issues at stake here. When a lawyer can pass off UFO buffs as expert— yes, *expert!*—witnesses, what does that do to science? Aren't we reintroducing medieval demons to run amok in a world that supposedly outgrew them with Galileo?

Deally missed the irony of Galileo's having been laughed at and imprisoned for taking an unorthodox stand.

> Isn't the court leading us right back into the middle ages, when the truth cowered in fear while superstition wore judicial robes and turned the thumbscrews?

Then Deally got personal.

> But here's the kicker: Alan Miller's dishonesty is premeditated, reaching all the way back to his college years, when he wrote his doctoral thesis on—can you guess?—outer space aliens. That's right. Our own UC Santa Cruz awarded Miller a Ph.D. for the preposterous theory that mushrooms are an alien life-form. And here you thought they were something you smothered over T-bone steaks!

"What does this tell us," Deally concluded, "about what passes for science nowadays? And what does this case tell us about what passes for law?"

I reread the part about Alan Miller's Ph.D. thesis, then put down the paper.

I sat back in the kitchen chair. I was alone this morning. I assumed Fred had gone early to his office, but for all I knew he was sleeping on his backyard bench again. I'd nearly been driven out myself by the stink of industrial cleaner from the janitorial service he'd hired to tidy his place.

I pulled the phone closer and dialed Alan at Edward's house.

I was leaving a message on the machine when he picked up.

"Hi. I'm here. I just don't like to answer if it's not for me."

"Alan, what was your Ph.D. thesis about?"

"My doctoral thesis?" He sounded surprised, obviously hadn't seen the morning paper. "The ability of spores to survive for long periods without any of the apparent prerequisites for life."

"Such as?"

"Oxygen, carbon dioxide, water, light, pretty much any kind of atmosphere or nutrient; you name it, spores can survive without it. They won't fruit, but they don't lose the potential."

"So basically they can survive in outer space?"

"Uh-huh. They've been collected in samples of what should be empty space above our atmosphere. So we know they drift up through the ozone layer. And they're able to germinate even after bombardment with solar and other kinds of radiation. Spores are probably the hardiest life-form on Earth."

"Do you think they could drift all the way to other planets?"

"Given enough time, I don't see why not."

"Do you think they could have come from other planets?"

"It's possible. There's a growing body of thought that solar systems and planets are like archipelagos. So particles and spores and what-have-you may be slowly washing up on each other's shores. They could also be hitching rides on asteroids or meteors. Why do you ask?'' His tone was cheerful, what you'd expect from someone discussing pet theories. He didn't seem to connect them with aliens and abduction.

"So you did write a doctoral thesis saying spores may have reached Earth from some other planet?"

"Millions of years ago, but sure. Fungi are such a boon to plants—they sheath and protect rootlets and help them absorb nutrients, they were pivotal to evolution. Things didn't really start to rock-and-roll botanically until the fungi kicked in. But they're different from plants, that's for sure. On a cellular level, they're closer to beetles, did you know that? Their cell walls are made of chitin, like insect shells. They're heavy on protein, like bugs. They're like rooted animals—different from anything else in the world." His voice glowed with proprietary happiness.

"Leonard Deally's column makes it sound like your thesis says mushrooms are spacemen."

There was a long silence. "I love fungus," he said, as if Deally had attacked it, not him. "My thesis is about what spores can endure. What they can survive. It just looks at possibilities."

"We're going to have to put you on the witness stand to say that."

"I thought you didn't know yet if I should testify."

"Deally's forcing our hand. I don't think we can count on the jurors not to hear about this. And we don't want them thinking you've been obsessed with space aliens your whole life."

"Oh." His tone told me how depressed he was.

I hung up to take a call-through.

It was Cary Curtis. "Willa, what the hell are you doing down there?" he demanded.

"What do you mean, Cary?"

"I mean I saw you on the news last night. Luckily I know someone who got it on tape so I was able to show it to the others this morning. What the hell are you doing?"

"Trying a case."

"Shoveling shit! What kind of a case is that? Abducted by aliens—come *on!*"

"There's a lot more to it than you saw in that tabloid puff piece, Cary. The prosecution says Miller's car went over a cliff, but they didn't find his tire tracks in the dirt up there. They say Miller was driving, but he doesn't have any injuries you'd expect from a car accident. And when he was hypnotized to find out where he was, this is what he came up with."

"The hypnotist probably suggested the whole story. You hear about these quacks all the time."

"He's a respected psychiatrist—and a friend of mine."

"Well someone's sure as hell lying! Or crazy."

"I'm just arguing the facts, Cary. Just like any good lawyer would. I'm not doing anything weird."

"The hell you aren't! Alien abduction? Are you trying to make us all look ridiculous here? Look who our clients are—high-tech companies, for godsake. Do you think they want their law firm associated with this kind of antiscience?"

"Antiscience? There's plenty of evidence—photographs, videos, traces of—"

"Of what? Maybe some Martian bacteria from billions of years ago. But spacemen roaming the earth? Are you *nuts?*" Cary's voice was reacquiring its New York accent, something that happened only under stress.

"Science means looking at the evidence, right? Not dismissing it just because it's strange. *That*'s antiscience. Four hundred years ago, astronomers called heliocentrism heresy; two hundred years ago, doctors attacked the idea of germs; a century ago, scientists swore machines could never fly. Science always thinks it knows everything—until it's proved wrong! Besides, the issue is simpler than that. The evidence supports Miller. If I don't argue the evidence, he loses. That's not the way it's supposed to work. That's not fair to him."

"You work for us, you know. How about what's fair to us?"

"All I'm taking away from you is a few days of my time."

"Let's talk about credibility, let's talk about accountability, let's talk about the prestige and goodwill this firm has accumulated over the last eight years!"

I groped for my coffee as if it were Valium. I waited for the pronouncement I hoped wasn't coming.

"The others agree: we want you to withdraw from the case. Today. For the sake of this firm's reputation. I'm afraid this isn't a request."

There it was.

I took a swallow of room-temperature coffee, trying to remain lukewarm myself. "Cary, if you let me give you a nontabloid account of this case, you'll feel differently about it. I'm only doing what any lawyer would do. I'm arguing the facts."

"You'll have to withdraw," Cary repeated. "Right now. Before your verdict gets national press and you're linked to us."

"I can't do that. You said yourself I'd be sued for malpractice."

"Yes, and you will indemnify us for any judgment against the firm. We're drawing up the papers now."

"What if I were to win the case?"

"Either way, the unwelcome attention—Good Lord, how could we reassure clients this firm didn't mean to rely on astrology or palmistry when we went to try their cases? No, either way, we refuse to be burdened by the publicity."

We were both silent.

He added, "You know, we're being generous even offering you this option. You didn't discuss this with us, clear it with us, even warn us we'd be linked to news reports like the one last night. You've put us in the terribly unfair position of scrambling to do damage control. We expected better treatment from you, Willa!" With that, he hung up.

I replaced the receiver slowly. I stood up and finished getting ready for another day in *Space People's Court*.

I walked into the courts building just in time to see my

mother get up on her toes and lean close to Colonel Kraduck's face.

She was shouting, "I recognize you, all right!"

"Oh, no!" I couldn't have been more horrified to see my mother sucked into a beam of white light. At that moment, it might have been a relief.

She wheeled to face me. "Do you know who this man is?" She looked unusually tidy in unfaded jeans, a relatively new blue sweater, and clean white sneakers. Her dress protest clothes—worn, no doubt, to avoid embarrassing me.

"Colonel Kraduck," I said contritely, "I'm so sorry. She doesn't—"

"So you do know! You know this man is an officer in the air force?" This seemed to settle something, as far as my mother was concerned.

I walked up to her, flung an arm around her, and began marching her down the hall toward the ladies' room. Pushing the door open, I demanded, "What the hell are you trying to do to me? Why are you hassling Colonel Kraduck?"

"Don't you recognize him?" From the look on her face, I expected her to tell me he was Josef Mengele. "He used to work at Travis Air Force Base. He was there twice when we got arrested. You were with us one of the times."

"No, I don't recognize him. And even if he was there, so what?" I could see myself in the mirror above the bathroom sink. I looked like I was going to jump out of my skin. "The military police arrested you for trespassing, not because a particular colonel didn't like the look of you." I took a breath. "What are you doing here?"

"Moag called me. He saw you on the news." She looked disgusted. "Of course, he thought it was marvelous. But I just had to come and talk to you—I didn't get a chance the other night."

"Talk about what? Make it fast!" I had to go assuage Colonel Kraduck. And I had a case to try in less than half an hour.

"The Republican plan to resurrect the Strategic Defense Initiative, Star Wars! They're going after more funding."

She shook her head as if the topic were obvious. "Three different times, Ronald Reagan made remarks about what would happen if we learned about a threat from outer space. Three times! Because he knew Russia wouldn't be our excuse forever. And when George Bush—former head of the CIA!—couldn't shake enough money out of Congress, he started funneling Iran-Contra money into the Star Wars project. The government's been working on this weapons system for over ten years now, Willa, making up for shortfalls with secret operations and black budget money. And the whole time, they've been planting and exploiting paranoia about an alien invasion, about alien abduction. They've been doing it to justify SDI, so they can pressure Congress to—"

"I've heard this all before, Mother. You could have saved yourself a trip."

"But don't you see? When Democrats object, the Republicans will just point up to the sky. They'll have the people believing all this aliens nonsense by then. That was the whole point of *Independence Day*—Hollywood's playing right into their hands. And Congress will do anything it thinks their constituents want." She scowled, hot red spots appearing on her cheeks. "People will applaud an immoral waste of resources—resources diverted from desperately needed social programs—because they're afraid of little gray men invented just to scare us. And you're helping them do it!"

I knew from long experience that it was useless to argue with her. I cut to the chase: "What are you planning to do about it?"

"Some local members of WILPF"—Women's International League for Peace and Freedom—"are going to meet with me to discuss a teach-in."

"Fine. Have a teach-in." The Republicans would quake in their boots, no doubt. "Just leave my witnesses alone. And stay away from the courthouse!" I took a step toward her. "You hear me, Mother? My client's got a lot at stake. I'm not kidding."

I left her in the bathroom. I try to walk away early when

I fight with her. If I stay too long, I say too much, and I just feel guilty later. I've learned the hard way: You can't change your mother, and you can't stop loving her. All you can do is watch your mouth.

When I got back out into the hall, Colonel Kraduck was nowhere to be found. I stepped into the courtroom for a quick discussion with the bailiff. I described my mother and told him to keep her out of court because she'd harassed a witness. I didn't trust her to put my wishes above her dogma.

Leonard Deally was already in the pews, fifteen minutes early. I turned and glared at him.

He met my gaze and cocked his pudgy face forward like a turtle's. His eyes told me he hated me and everything I represented. Or maybe just every*one* I represented.

At that moment I realized it might be personal, having nothing to do with antiscience and the flaws in our judicial system. It might be a lot more simple.

Maybe Leonard Deally had it in for Alan Miller. Maybe Deally knew Alan better than either of them let on—well enough to know the topic of Alan's Ph.D. thesis and well enough to hate him.

I checked the corridor again. Colonel Kraduck hadn't returned. I peeked into the ladies' room. My mother was gone, too. Before reentering the courtroom, I made a decision. Everyone was so damn sure stories like Miller's were ruses, lies, or antiscientific scams. They were sure enough to denounce me, harangue me, and even order me to withdraw from the case.

I went out to the pay phone and made a call.

When I got back, I ran into Dan Fichman on a padded bench in the corridor, awaiting his turn on the stand. I thanked him for coming and warned him that there might be a delay.

I entered the courtroom to find Alan sitting at the defense table, looking tired and listless. I murmured a greeting, then approached the assistant DA. I told Patrick Toben I wanted to add four more witnesses to my list. He knew their identities because I'd already subpoenaed them, just in case.

I then spent almost an hour in the judge's chambers persuading him the eleventh hour additions were relevant and necessary and not a waste of the court's time. In the meantime, Carl Shaduff alerted the witnesses that they would be expected at the courthouse this afternoon.

It was time to get serious, time to give Alan Miller everything I had.

I tried not to think about Cary Curtis's demand.

It looked like I'd get my vacation, after all.

27

Dan Fichman should have made a better first impression. I could see the jurors looking away, as if in embarrassment, when he began showing NASA photographs with circled anomalies. I didn't ask him to offer theories about the unexpected, unexplained objects and blips of light. Instead, I asked him to authenticate the photographs based on his experience cataloging them for NASA's library.

I asked him if similar features had shown up in recent NASA photographs, and he explained that only *some* new photographs were released to the public by the National Security Agency.

I asked him if he considered himself a scientist, and if he felt that science was well served by this change.

I watched the jury, hoping that Fichman's cheerleading for science would show them that not all scientists had rejected the possibility of UFOs and alien contact.

By the end of Fichman's direct examination, I could see the jury beginning to make a little timid eye contact with him. I'd saved him for last because his testimony was the least directly relevant. But I also thought he'd play best, looking as well groomed and practical as a TV anchorman.

And with luck, the jury would carry away the idea that there was some context, including NASA pictures, for the thousands of alien abduction stories.

Because we'd spent an hour in the judge's chambers, questioning Fichman took us up to lunch.

I was too wound up to eat. I spent the time preparing my afternoon witnesses—if harried conversations can be called preparation.

I noticed, when I started back into the courtroom, that news trucks were parking out front. Apparently, Elgin's feature had chummed the waters. There would be infotainment sharks aplenty by the close of the court day.

My first witness that afternoon was Joseph Huizen. I was disturbed to see him looking tired, with his suit hanging badly. Though he'd needed to lose weight, sudden illness had stripped the pounds off too quickly.

I asked him about his credentials and publications, especially his forthcoming mathematics-of-spinning-planets book, *Pi in the Sky*.

I asked if he was Alan Miller's neighbor. I asked where he was on the night Miller's car landed atop Francis Addenaur.

I asked about his medical problem that night, inviting him to describe his ambulance ride—especially the part where it stopped partway down the road.

Since he'd offered undisputed facts and no opinions, there wasn't much for Toben to cross-examine him about. He asked whether Joseph had seen or heard anything going on at Alan Miller's that night.

My next witness was John Bivens, the paramedic who'd driven the ambulance. His partner hadn't been reachable this morning. And for all I knew, he wouldn't have supported Bivens's testimony.

Bivens was a tall young man with short black hair, a friendly face, and a sport coat he didn't seem used to. He glanced nervously at the jurors. I felt a pang: he hadn't wanted to get dragged into this, and I could hardly blame him.

"Mr. Bivens, can you tell us what you and your partner did when you arrived at Joseph Huizen's home?"

"Well, first off, we had to restrain him."

"Why is that?"

"It happens in diabetic emergencies. The body uses up

the blood sugar and then starts leeching it out of the brain. It makes the patient altered and combative." Bivens looked confident, discussing a medical matter he'd handled many times.

"What did you do after you restrained Dr. Huizen?"

"My partner started an IV—an intravenous line—on him."

"You didn't wait until you reached the hospital?"

"No ma'am," he said, making me feel old. "You don't want to let the body steal too much of the brain's sugar or the patient will go into a coma."

"What substance did you give Dr. Huizen intravenously?"

"Glucose."

I introduced into evidence my science-book Xerox. I asked the medic to verify that it represented a glucose molecule.

I could hear the jury stirring, probably wondering what possible relevance the drawing could have.

"What happened after you left Dr. Huizen's house?"

Bivens scowled. I could feel his unhappiness. "Down the road a few hundred feet . . . I know this is going to sound crazy, but . . ."

"Please go on."

"There was this incredibly bright light."

"Where was it?"

"Coming out of the sky." He stopped, looking like a deer caught in headlights as he recalled the moment. "I couldn't tell where it came from. It was like a tunnel of bright light leading to a fixed point maybe seventy-five, a hundred feet up."

"Where was the light aimed?"

"Into the window of a house."

"How many houses down the road from Dr. Huizen's?"

"The first house."

I'd made a point of asking Dr. Huizen where his house was in relation to Alan Miller's. With luck, the jury realized we were talking about Miller's next-door neighbor.

Apparently the audience got the point. The judge had to ask for silence in the courtroom.

"Did you stop to observe this light?"

He hung his head. "Yes."

"What did you observe about it?"

"It was bright, majorly bright. Aimed, like I said, into the window of this house."

"Did you observe anything else about it?"

"That's about it."

"Did anyone else observe the light?"

"I . . ." He flushed. "It was so bizarre. I called my partner, Barry, to the front to look."

"How long were the two of you parked there?"

"Maybe a minute."

"Was the light still there when you left?"

"Yes. But we had to go, obviously. We had a patient to transport."

On cross, Patrick Toben asked him if it was customary for medics to stop an ambulance during transport of a sick patient. He asked if it was a company policy for the driver of an ambulance to hold up transport to stare at "bizarre" sights. He asked if Bivens had ever done so before. Never? Or had he stopped at times, but not bothered to report it? Had he reported this stop to his employer? Did he think his employer would approve of him stopping an ambulance, even for a short time, with a sick patient in back? Bivens, tongue-tied, rattled, and shamefaced, answered no to every question.

My next witness was the farmer whose field hosted the crop circle and the stragglers who'd come to camp around it. He'd already testified for me once, stating he hadn't noticed Fiat-sized tire tracks in his Brussels sprouts field the morning after the accident.

Now I asked him to describe the location of his land in relation to Joseph Huizen's and Alan Miller's houses. I asked him if he'd seen anything unusual on his property the day after the accident.

I asked him to describe the crop circles. I offered into

evidence a newspaper photograph of the circles, asking him to verify that this was the pattern in his meadow.

My next witness worked in the university's botany lab. He didn't have anything relevant to say—the tests had shown "inconclusive amounts" of cell-pit and growth-node damage. But I thought the jury would think the crop circles were phony if I didn't offer some kind of botanical analysis.

"You were asked to collect wild grasses from the circles and analyze them, is that correct?"

"Yes." He was a longhaired man with a balding crown and a cranky squint. I'd hated to put him on the stand because he was needlessly combative. I hoped to keep him to simple yesses and noes.

That worked until it was time to ask what he'd noticed about the grasses.

"Some cellular damage, and lateral splitting in some growth nodes. Easily caused by any number of stresses to the plants."

"Would ordinary farming techniques such as fertilization cause this type of stress?"

"Not the fertilizers I've seen."

"Frost?"

"No."

"Whirlwinds?"

"No."

"Microwave radiation?"

"What?"

"Microwave radiation."

He all but rolled his eyes. "Conceivably."

I had to leave it at that.

The assistant DA went over the lab results more thoroughly, having him point out several times that no test results struck him as unusual.

Then Toben asked him, "Did you see anything in your test results to rule out the so-called crop circles being made by ordinary human beings?"

"No, I didn't."

"Can you suggest a method by which they could have been made?"

"Objection. Calls for speculation."

"He's an expert on grasses, Your Honor," Toben pointed out.

"But not on how to make crop circles."

"It's within his expertise," the judge agreed. "Overruled."

"Lawn rollers should work," the witness guessed. "Even a board should flatten that stuff out."

"Is there anything in your laboratory results that's inconsistent with the circles having been made by, say, people with lawn rollers?"

"No."

"To your knowledge, are others in the botany department familiar, in general, with crop circles?"

"Oh, yes," the witness said dryly. "About a month and a half ago, we had a professor from Oxford over here who wouldn't talk about anything else."

By the time Toben was done, he'd created the impression that the English crop circles scholar, the same one Fred met during University Night, had inspired botany students to conduct a local circle-making experiment.

I cursed my decision to give the jury an expert it "expected."

All I could do on redirect was ask, with feigned assurance, "Do your tests rule out exposure to microwave energy?"

"Common sense does that."

"Please answer the question."

"No, they don't rule out microwave energy."

"Could microwave radiation cause the cell-pit damage and the crepey effect you observed on one side of the grass leaves?"

"It would have to be a pretty short exposure. Very long, and the grass would start to look cooked."

"No further questions."

I tried to look cheerful. Testimony about cell-pit damage was bound to be confusing to the jury. Maybe they'd interpret my confidence as a sign they'd missed something exculpatory.

The good news was that I had an ace up my sleeve: Toben didn't know why I'd shown the paramedic a glucose molecule drawing. He'd simply indulged me by not objecting.

The bad news was that there was only one witness I could call to make the connection between the molecule and the crop circle. My final witness that day was Reginald Fulmer.

Fulmer flounced into the courtroom like Scarlett O'Hara in high dudgeon. The phone call from Carl Shaduff had caught him at the checkout desk of the Davenport Bed and Breakfast. Only Shaduff's promise of getting him on a later flight—and paying him $500—had persuaded him to delay.

"Mr. Fulmer, can you tell us your educational and employment background?"

Fulmer crossed his legs and arms so that it appeared he had a couple of extra limbs. With his hawk nose, flyaway hair, and sour expression, he looked like a caricature in *Anglophobe* magazine.

"I took a first at Oxford in philosophy," he began pompously, "and I have, at times, been a public school teacher. What you would call private schools here," he added hastily, lest we suspect him of mingling with commoners.

"Do you consider yourself an expert on crop circles?"

"I am a well-known cereologist, yes."

"What have you done to gain expertise in this area?"

He shot me a look. "Merely camped out in the corn for eight consecutive summers, personally mapped and photographed roughly a hundred agriglyphs per season, and traveled all around the world lecturing and showing slides on the subject."

"Have there been very many crop circles appearing over the last eight years?"

"About twenty-four hundred in ten countries. I suppose you would call that 'many.' "

I could feel the jury begin to dislike him. I kept it short. "Have you seen the crop circle located in Davenport?"

"Seen it? Good Lord, I've been there all day every day for the last nine days!"

"That would be this one in the newspaper photograph?" I named the exhibit for the record.

"Yes, yes."

"Does the pattern of the circles suggest anything to you?"

"It's a sugar molecule."

I thought I heard the assistant DA's chair scrape; for once, he might be planning to object.

I quickly asked, "Glucose? Do you mean the form of sugar called—"

"I object, Your Honor. This is outside the witness's area of expertise. He's no more qualified to interpret a pattern than anyone else."

"Sustained."

Talk about an inconvenient time for the word to appear in the judge's vocabulary.

"But Your Honor," I pointed out, "Mr. Fulmer's opinion that it's glucose is based on eight years of experience mapping and photographing crop circles."

"His photography expertise is irrelevant to pattern interpretation," Toben repeated. "He's no more qualified to do that than—"

"I have already ruled!" The judge looked ready to throw his gavel at us. "Objection sustained."

But it didn't matter: I'd repeated the word I wanted burned into the jurors' brains: glucose.

Reluctantly, I said, "No further questions."

There was no way Fulmer would help me make crop circles seem "real" to the jury. He'd refuse to discuss botanical traits and ramble instead about pictograms, snapping out rude responses until the jury discounted everything he said.

Nor would he point out, as Bart Bustamonte would have, the relationship between increased sightings of lights in the sky and the appearance of circles.

It was my own damn fault. I should have asked Bustamonte about it during his testimony yesterday. But I'd still been waffling about introducing the crop circles. I hadn't wanted to overwhelm the jury.

Or maybe I just hadn't been ready to pull out all the stops. Nothing like getting fired to make a person get serious.

I looked at the jury, and wished I could repeat the word "glucose" one more time. I wished I could say *Joseph Huizen* and *Pi in the Sky*. But they must have gotten the point—they looked a little stunned.

I could hardly blame them. Eventually this case would end and we would all leave behind the crutch of duty—to a client, to the court, to the community. Then we'd have to make up our minds for real.

Maybe the jurors were ready to do that. I sure as hell wasn't.

28

Outside the courthouse, Reginald Fulmer encountered a trio of television cameras. He postured, preened, and declaimed in front of them so long that he missed his second flight. I waited beside my car like a patient chauffeur, ready to deliver the promised ride to the airport. But he was too damn busy strutting to heed my semaphoric signals.

When he finally tore himself away, I broke the news, with some satisfaction, that he'd never make the evening plane.

He demanded to be put up for the night. I reminded him he'd known the plane's departure time and had missed it through his own blabbing fault. I told him he was on his own. We proceeded to have a shouting match in the parking lot of the county building.

The last straw was him calling me a wren-tit. I have no idea what kind of bird that is; maybe it's adorable, maybe it looks like a short blond lawyer. I didn't care. I lost it. I called Fulmer a pretentious dick, a New Age drama queen, and an insult to rational discourse. And that was before we raised our voices.

About the time he was commenting on my lawyering skills ("I've heard better oratory from Harpo Marx—honk, honk!"), I noticed a white van cruising slowly, one row of parked cars away.

I struggled for a glimpse of the driver, convinced it was

the same van I'd spotted on San Vittorio Road before Alan Miller's house burned. Fulmer, annoyingly, was in my way. Thinking only of catching sight of the van's driver, I put my hand on Fulmer's arm and gave him a bit of a push, the slightest jostle so I could see past him.

Fulmer responded with an oath, then punched me just below the collarbone. In addition to having the wind knocked out of me, I was as mad as a hornet (certainly madder than a wren-tit). And I remained determined to see more of the van, if it wasn't too late. I shoved Fulmer again, harder this time.

He started shrieking and slapping at me as if he were shooing away a mosquito. I slapped back. And then, abruptly, a wall of deputy sheriff stood between us.

The deputy, his car parked just a few feet away in the sheriff's section of the lot, began barking out instructions: "Hands up, don't move. I said, let me see your hands. I mean it, don't move! Move again, and you'll find yourself under arrest."

And so I might have been if Patrick Toben himself hadn't come out and vouched for me. As it was, Fulmer and I were warned at humiliating length that the matter would be dropped only if neither of us wished to press charges.

Fulmer assured the deputy I didn't deserve the title of criminal, not for shoving one about like a bloody fishwife and hurling paltry insults!

It was all I could do not to lunge at him again. (A fishwife was clearly a demotion from a wren-tit.) I was especially peeved to realize I hadn't gotten the van's license number.

When Fulmer stomped off to go God knew where, the assistant DA invited me into his conference room to discuss Maria Nanos. I went along, despite his annoying little smile.

As we climbed the charmless cement stairs, Toben commented, "I don't think I've ever duked it out with a witness, especially not my own."

"I didn't want to call him as a witness, believe me."

"Well, I probably shouldn't admit this, but I wasn't expecting that glucose thing."

I nodded. "It surprised me, too, when I found out."

"Coincidences are like that," he said blandly.

I trailed after him. As he held the door of the conference room open for me, he added, "We'll be calling the guys who made those circles as witnesses."

I turned. "What are you talking about?"

"We just picked them up making some more. Botany graduate students. You know how they are at that age."

"You're saying you found students making crop circles?"

"That's right."

"Making them today?"

"Uh-huh."

"And they claim they made the glucose molecule?"

"I haven't talked to them yet, so I'm not sure what they claim. But it stands to reason, doesn't it?"

"It stands to reason they heard about the crop circle—saw the picture in the paper, saw it on the news—and decided to try to copy it." I hoped. Oh God, did I ever hope. "Where's this circle you caught them making?"

"I'm not sure yet. We'll let you know."

He wouldn't "let me know," he'd tell me the exact location before I left the damn building. If there was one thing I'd learned from my mother, it was how to make a nuisance of myself.

A young man in a dark suit intercepted us at the conference room door. He asked Toben for a minute. Toben waved me inside before stepping away for a quick in-the-hall conference.

When he joined me at the table, he said, "Good news! They found Maria Nanos. They've got her in a car on her way here."

"Who's they?"

"Big Sur park rangers turned her over to some deputies. She should be here in a couple of hours."

"Are the grandparents still in town?"

"They were yesterday." He didn't look very happy about it. "And they sure didn't express plans to leave."

I remembered Monday's scene. "You're not turning Maria over to them, are you?"

"That's up to Child Protective Services."

"Her grandfather threatened to break her legs."

Toben ran a casual hand over his hair. "And if he meant it, that's one thing. If it was just shock, that's another." He smiled. "They'd just heard for the first time that their fifteen-year-old grandaughter was pregnant. I think you'd get a pretty strong reaction to that from a lot of people." When I started to protest, he added, "You're not going to tell me you don't lose your temper sometimes?"

I felt myself blush. Goddam Fulmer.

"Where have the grandparents been staying?"

"Holiday Inn." The hotel was a stone's throw from the courthouse. "Waiting. To some purpose, luckily."

"What are you going to do with Maria tonight?"

"We'll have to keep her in custody until she testifies."

Unfortunately, I'd been right. The rape/screen memory theory had returned with Maria.

As if to confirm my fear, Toben said, "So this puts her back on the witness list. She'll be our first rebuttal witness. Followed by our psychiatrists—you've got their names already."

I sighed. The case would last another week for sure. But what the hell, thanks to Cary Curtis, I had the time.

29

I'd planned to go home for the weekend. In fact, I'd planned to leave that evening. But thank goodness I'd stowed a pair of jeans in my trunk. It would be hours before I knew when and whether I could get away.

I went straight from Toben's office to Edward Hershey's. I wanted to talk to Alan Miller about Maria Nanos's return. And because the DA was going to put her in custody, I wanted to see her as soon as possible, let her know she could call me anytime.

"She might admit the truth—who the father really is— once she's confronted with her grandparents. Who knows?" I felt guilty offering Alan this slight hope. But he needed it; he'd just heard himself ridiculed on the evening news. "In the meantime, Carl Shaduff's coming by for us. Some botany students made a crop circle up near the university. I want to take pictures of it, see if there are enough similarities for Toben to link it to the one behind Joseph's."

Alan looked alarmed, so I was glad to hear a knock.

But when I opened the door, I could tell by Shaduff's face he hadn't come about the crop circle.

He said, "Kraduck's been shot."

I took a backward step. "The colonel?" As if he'd tell me about some other Kraduck.

"In the hotel parking lot. I heard the news on a police

scanner—private frequency, which I'm not supposed to have access to. I've been over there the last half hour."

"Is he—? He's not—?"

"He's fine. Bruised as hell and possibly a broken rib from the impact."

"Who shot him? Did they catch the guy?"

"He was shot from a car driving by the parking lot, he says. Didn't get the license number, all they have is a description." Shaduff stepped past me into the room. His red face made his hair look like polar bear fur. "He'd have two bullets in his chest except for the vest."

"Why was he wearing it?"

"Beats the hell out of me. I didn't get anywhere near him. I did get one of the city cops to talk to me a little bit. Was Kraduck wearing a vest in court?"

I recalled the colonel in a blazer and open-collared shirt. "I don't think so. He might have been wearing one today when I saw him; he had on a bulkier jacket."

"The better vests aren't too obvious. He was wearing a windbreaker over it tonight. Climbing into a rental car." Shaduff jerked his head toward the door. "We should go."

"To the hospital?"

"No, they won't let us near Kraduck, not for a while. I was thinking we should talk to Bustamonte and Fichman. Neither of them's checked out yet. They might know something."

I turned to grab my jacket, and found Alan flattened against a bookcase. His eyes were wide and he seemed to be holding his breath. "Do you want me to come?"

"We should minimize your contact with witnesses; it just complicates things." I didn't want to be answering subpoenas for nonexistent notes and tapes of Miller's meetings with them.

Alan exhaled, looking relieved.

I followed Shaduff out to his Road Ranger.

"I tried Fred Hershey's pager when it happened," Shaduff said. "Tried to get a message to you."

"But Fred didn't get back to you," I guessed. Fred had a way of being gone when one was looking for him.

Shaduff, scowling as he got his truck into gear, didn't reply.

Ten minutes later, we were in Bart Bustamonte's room, a hovel of heaped clothes and scattered notebook pages. Dan Fichman hadn't checked out, but he wasn't in the hotel.

Behind Bustamonte, a picture window framed gulls spinning over a silver gray sea.

He was saying, "I don't get it, I just don't get it. Kraduck's one of the government's biggest disinformation specialists. Why would they try to whack him?" He ran a beefy hand over his cheeks, wiping away sweat.

"You think the government had something to do with it?" The man was as paranoid as my mother.

"Who else gets off a couple of nice, clean shots, then gets away? It's got to be the military or one of the alphabet agencies."

"The shots," Shaduff pointed out, "weren't so nice and clean—torso shots from a moving car right there in the parking lot. Seems to me the military would have put a marksman somewhere farther away. And they'd have aimed for the head. If they even do shit like this, which, who knows?"

Bustamonte waved the suggestion aside. "They'd only do it that way if they wanted to leave a calling card! Kraduck's military—he'd know the current weapon of choice and the standard approach. It's no coincidence he had on a bullet-proof vest."

"Whoever did it might have it in for UFOlogists in general." Shaduff seemed to be baiting him. "Not Kraduck in particular."

"Come on. A man's shot twice and it turns out he's wearing a vest? Kraduck saw it coming. Maybe a few nuts have it in for UFOlogists, I don't know. But I'll tell you this—the only times I wished I had a bulletproof vest, I was in the desert near Area Fifty-one being chased by black helicopters!"

"Maybe someone who watched the news about the trial," Shaduff continued. "Some religious nut, someone who thinks you guys are full of shit."

"Yeah, yeah, plenty of people think we're full of shit. But so what?" Bustamonte demanded. "Who isn't?"

"When did you last see Kraduck?" We could get existential some other time.

"About six o'clock he knocked on my door to say so long. He said he was on his way to Travis."

"Travis Air Force Base?" My mother had hassled him in the courthouse corridor just this morning, accusing him of having her arrested at Travis. "Why was he going there?"

"He didn't say; I didn't ask." Bustamonte shook his head cynically. "I assumed he was going to report in. I'm telling you, Kraduck's not retired."

"Did he mention needing to talk to me?" Why had he come to the courthouse this morning? What would he have done there if he hadn't been set upon by my mother? Watch the rest of the trial? Or relay a message, confide some problem?

"No, he didn't mention you. Except to say you put us up in a better hotel than Fulmer."

"Reginald Fulmer? What did he mean?"

"He said you put Fulmer at the Holiday Inn."

"Why did Kraduck think that?" Had he witnessed the scene in the parking lot? Spotted Fulmer flouncing toward the nearest hotel?

Bustamonte shrugged. "I didn't care, so I didn't quiz him. He's probably got operatives watching everything we do."

Shaduff looked puzzled. "Why did he say good-bye to you? You in particular?"

"Good question," Bustamonte agreed. "We're not pals, no. But Karollas is already gone. And I suppose Fichman wasn't in his room."

I knew from my interview with Kraduck that he didn't approve of Dan Fichman.

"He puts on a bulletproof vest," Bustamonte continued, "then he knocks at my door and tells me where he's going. Like he wants me to know, in case he doesn't make it back."

"I heard someone . . ." I didn't want to drag my mother into this. "Someone mentioned he'd been stationed at Travis."

"Well, I doubt he was on his way to a reunion party, not in that vest."

Shaduff stood at the picture window. Outside two gulls hovered, caught in an updraft. They were as motionless as the other night's unmarked helicopters.

"We're going to lose our daylight," Shaduff pointed out.

I stood. I needed to photograph the new crop circle before it got trampled. "There's something else you could do for us," I told Bustamonte. "If you don't have other plans?"

Bustamonte glanced at his papers. "You pay me, and my plans can wait."

We left immediately, Shaduff driving his Road Ranger as if it were a monster truck. He sped past the university entrance up a steep, winding mountain grade. He pulled up to a fire access gate hung with university No Parking signs.

As we climbed out, Bustamonte nodded up the road. "You know they're building parts for stealth bombers just ten or so miles from here?"

"No, I didn't know that."

We skirted the gate, starting down a path through an oak-studded meadow. I was surprised my mother hadn't mentioned a manufacturer of stealth bombers, one so close to home.

"Wait a minute . . ." Years ago, we'd reached a moutain-top Lockheed plant by taking a turn somewhere off High-way 1. A group of us protested their building first-strike nuclear weapons. We sat for hours in front of a chain-link fence while security guards milled around a distant, inaccessible guardhouse. I'd returned home covered with mosquito bites. "Is it a Lockheed plant? Building nuclear missiles?"

"Used to build missile triggers; now it's stealth bomber guts." Bustamonte nodded. "Scary looking place way up where this road dead-ends; all fenced off, warning signs everywhere, not even an intercom for visitors to try to talk their way in."

The path wound through mixed forest with madrones blossoming as if hung with white piñatas. Tiny irises dotted the duff.

Bustamonte added, "That's probably why you get UFOs

up here. Most sightings are near air force bases, nuclear test sites, weapons research and development plants. Lockheed's probably your magnet."

I wondered if I should bring it up in court. Or would jurors resist the suggestion they were living near a UFO "magnet"? Especially one that presumably employed hundreds of locals.

"They seem to monitor us," Bustamonte continued cheerfully. "Regular sightings started over Nevada the year we began testing A-bombs there. The more bombs we dropped, the more of them we spotted. We've still got them in droves over the Nevada and New Mexico desert, where we fly fighters and test weapons." He stopped abruptly when the path reached another meadow. "There it is."

The new crop circle was only some twenty yards to our right. The trail, I'd been told, ended above a science building housing the botany labs.

As if reading my mind, Bustamonte commented, "They weren't out to fool anyone, putting it so near their own department."

I noticed he was wheezing with the exertion of the short hike, sweating profusely despite a cool evening breeze. But then, he carried more weight than Shaduff and I combined.

We waded through thigh-high grasses with fluffy beige and green heads. Out of the shade, the air buzzed with insects and the warm meadow smelled like hay.

Shaduff unslung his camera and snapped the cover off the lens.

Bustamonte stopped us a few feet from the circle, looking at it. "Classic pattern," he commented.

It was a smallish circle, perhaps fifteen feet across, with four smaller ones bracketing it like a cross.

"A quincunx," he continued. "A Celtic cross. They show up a lot, sometimes several times per season. The kids who made this obviously did their homework."

I scrutinized the main circle for the swirl pattern I'd seen behind Joseph Huizen's house.

Bustamonte followed my gaze. "Nice clockwise spiral. They definitely know their stuff."

"A crop circle expert visited the university last month. I'm told he talked about them nonstop."

Shaduff was starting to snap pictures. I'd hoped they would show a shabby, asymmetric mess, not a fine forgery like this.

"So it could pass for a real crop circle?"

"Oh, no," Bustamonte scoffed. "It doesn't look like a real circle. I'm just saying the hoaxers tried hard. They went to a lot of trouble and they did a good job. I'm impressed."

He walked to one of the smaller circles.

I followed. It, too, looked like Joseph Huizen's circles. The mix of grasses might be slightly different, but they were flattened in the same spiral pattern.

"What's wrong with this one?" I asked. "How can you tell it's a fake?" I motioned Carl Shaduff over to take a picture of whatever the problem might be.

I almost cursed when Bustamonte said, "You can feel it, for one thing." He noticed the look on my face. "No, really. A crop circle's got a whole different energy signature— measurable, if you have a dowsing rod. And if you've been inside enough of them, you get to recognize a certain je ne sais quoi."

"Yeah, well, je ne sais quoi doesn't exactly hold up in court."

Shaduff was squatting, looking at the swirled grass. "The grass looks a little different."

"Of course," Bustamonte agreed. "It's smashed, mashed, and torn." He plucked a stalk, holding it out to me.

The base was held together only by stringy plant fibers.

"If this were a real circle, you might have some splitting at the lowest growth nodes. You might have swelling or darkening of the nodes. But usually you find healthy-looking grain with very little rupture or splitting where it bends. You don't find trampled-looking, broken grass like this." Bustamonte nodded. "They probably attached a plank or a lawn roller to a central spool of string to get the spiral; you know, basically walked around the maypole. But they put too much pressure on the grass as they went around."

"The DA will use this circle to discredit the other one.

Even if the students admit they didn't make that one, the DA will show all kinds of photos of this. He'll go on about how perfect and well swirled it is. And the jury will think, If someone faked this one, someone else faked the other one."

"Probably," Bustamonte agreed. "I've seen it happen: Multiple UFO sightings somewhere, and next thing you know, the air force is all over the sky flying everything you can think of. The next time there's a report, they say, *See, it's just us.* Same with the crop circles. This isn't the first time I've seen phony circles get made to divert attention from real ones."

It was hard not to have a knee-jerk reaction to his conspiracy talk; I'd been supersaturated by my mother. On the other hand, I was standing inside a hoaxed crop circle that could ruin my case. And one of my expert witnesses was in the hospital.

Shaduff began photographing individual mashed stalks. "So who's making the crop circles? Really?"

"Not who, what. Some of them are phony, no doubt about it—you can tell when you get down and look closely; it looks like this. But the genuine circles, the grain's not broken—the cell-pit and growth-node changes are similar to what you'd get if you microwaved the grain for thirty or forty seconds. The ground underneath isn't marked at all, no crumbling of fragile dirt clods. And the grain isn't just swirled, the stalks are interwoven. A lot of those circles are preceded by sightings of small balls of light, sometimes high in the sky, sometimes down low, just a few feet off the ground. And I don't mean a few sightings—we have dozens and dozens of witness statements."

Shaduff looked skeptical. "Little light balls? How little?"

"Six inches, a foot."

"And how do they make the circles?"

"Our best guess? Remember, no one's actually seen them getting made—at least, not that we can verify; you always get claims, some of them pretty ridiculous. But judging from the microwave-zapped look of the grain and zero disturbance to dirt underneath . . ." He stared at the quincunx.

"We assume the patterns are painted into the crop from above. Quick swirling strokes of light or energy or radiation, like an expert's brush on a canvas."

Shaduff sighed, shaking his head slightly. He went back to photographing stalks.

"So you think Fulmer's right?" I perished the thought. "About them being pictograms?"

"Pictograms? How could I begin to guess? We could be dealing with something that doesn't visualize or process images the way we do. Would you hold up a bit of greenery chomped by a snail and call it a pictogram? What about the pattern of dots when an octopus moves its legs? Or the trail a beetle leaves in the dust? The whole concept of pictograms is meaningless if you don't know what you're dealing with. That's what makes Fulmer an idiot. He's so sure we're being given an *answer*. Well, I'm sorry, but we don't even know what the question is. *If* there's a question. We've only got what we've got. We've got what's in front of our eyes."

Shaduff rose from his squat, appraising him. "So you don't have a pet theory? Based on what you've seen?"

"What I've seen? Look, when white men first weighed anchor in the New World, the Indians saw the rowboats the sailors were using to get to shore, but they couldn't see the big European ships farther back in the water. They thought they saw some clouds, but they couldn't recognize ships. Because they'd never seen any craft bigger than a canoe before." Bustamonte waved an arm over the phony crop circle. "We're just as culture bound in our perceptions. You know, I was just having this conversation with that damn chihuahua Fichman. He's up in arms over funding cuts to SETI."

Knowing Fichman's unbridled faith in scientific projects, I wasn't surprised he supported NASA's Search for Extraterrestrial Intelligence.

"Here's SETI," Bustamonte continued, "with its big old antennae pointing out into space listening for radio signals from beyond. What are the odds that anything out there communicates like we do, and on wavelengths we can monitor? I mean, good heavens, isn't that like assuming they drink black tea with two lumps of sugar? It's so culture bound it's embarrassing."

"And so is trying to interpret the crop circles?" I followed up.

"Did you know you can buy crop circle Tarot cards now? The pictograms have been interpreted by channelers—Change, Renewal, Dissatisfaction." To Shaduff, he said, "You're a private investigator, just like me. You go where the evidence is, and you look at it and you record it, and you believe it because it's right in front of your nose. You don't scientific-method yourself out of seeing what you see, like that prissy Fichman. And you don't force it into a Tarot deck, either. If crop circles are symbols, they're not *our* symbols. If they were, we'd have agreed years ago what they meant."

"The Celtic cross is one of our symbols," I pointed out. "You say it shows up in the wheat fields pretty often."

"Yeah, yeah. But you know, the Celtic cross comes from the area where these circles appear. It could be the Celts took something they kept seeing in their fields and hung it on their buildings, who knows?"

"What about the glucose molecule?" I pressed. "Showing up behind Joseph Huizen's house the same night glucose saved his life?"

"I think it's a bunch of baloney. You say the formation looks a little like a glucose molecule—*if* you twist up and flatten a drawing of what we *think* the molecule looks like. You want to bet me fifty bucks I could find something it looks even more like, something meaningful to me?"

I must have looked a little miffed.

He added. "I know you're trying a case and you're going with what works. You're doing your best to convince people there's a real phenomenon going on here. But see"—he mopped his cheeks with his shirtsleeve—"I already know it's real. I don't have to buy every circle or every theory; I can keep an open mind."

"So just out of curiosity," Shaduff chimed in, "what do you think of Alan Miller?"

"Hiding something," Bustamonte said. "He's lying about

something." An apologetic glance at me. "Judging by how he acts. I've met almost four hundred abductees. They're in denial, they're emotional, they're a lot of things. But they're not furtive, they don't have that weird extra thing Miller's got."

"They're not on trial for manslaughter," I pointed out.

"That's true. That could be it." Bustamonte shrugged. "But also, his story's so . . . generic. Usually, they have some weird little signature, some observation that's part of who the person is, not part of what happened. Miller's tape, it didn't have anything like that; it sounded like an abstract, it sounded phony to me." He lowered himself to the ground as if unable to support his bulk any longer. Beads of sweat glistened through his thinning hair. "But again, I've got the luxury of knowing these stories are true. I've interviewed a lot of folks, and I believe them, so I know it's not bullshit. I can point to an individual story and say, *That's a piece of crap.*"

"Whereas I have to believe Miller or I got fired for no reason." I spoke before thinking.

Shaduff whistled. "Your law firm fired you? Man, that's cold."

Bustamonte looked up at me. "Fuck 'em if they can't take the truth." He smiled. "Now there's a slogan for your new business card."

30

We barely made it back to Shaduff's Road Ranger before night fell. I was exhausted from a long day and itchy from standing in a bug-filled field.

But after picking up my car, I stopped at Edward's house. I told Alan the new crop circle was different from the one behind Joseph Huizen's. I hoped he'd be relieved to hear Bustamonte would testify to that effect.

Alan, it turned out, was less than effusive. Presumably he wanted to be acquitted, but he definitely didn't want any of this to be true.

I didn't like to add to his burdens, but I couldn't forget Bustamonte's suspicions. "Alan, is there something I should know?"

He squirmed on Edward's couch. "What do you mean?"

I voiced my most concrete suspicion: "There's history between you and Leonard Deally, isn't there?"

His face went blank. It looked like an expression he'd practiced. "No."

"You didn't know him in college?"

"No."

"But you met him somewhere—you pointed him out to me in court."

"I've seen his picture in the paper. Sometimes they run it next to his column."

"But you seemed afraid of him."

Alan jumped when the phone rang. We sat in silence while the machine screened the call.

It was Patrick Toben. I picked up.

"We've got a problem," Toben said. "We were doing okay with Maria Nanos till she saw her grandparents. Then she got hysterical—you ever watch a cat when a big dog comes in the room? She practically ran straight up a wall. Anyway, don't ask me how the kid managed it, but she got away from us."

"She got away? From you and the deputies?" I couldn't keep reproach out of my voice. Maria might never get her life straightened out now, might never have a second chance. "You let her run away?"

"We didn't want her handcuffed, not for the family meeting. And deputies in the room just add to the tension." He didn't even sound defensive. "She absolutely flipped. We weren't prepared for it. She was so hyper she made it past everybody—right out the building. We've got cars cruising the neighborhood now, looking for her."

"What are the grandparents doing?"

"I have to tell you, they're not calm. They're talking a lot of crazy talk. We had to get some Family Support people up here to deal with it."

"When you find Maria, you're not going to send her home with them, are you?"

"That's not up to this department."

"What about murder investigation? That's up to you. Maria thinks they killed her mother."

I was distracted by the doorbell.

"Why don't you go ask them—?" Watching Alan answer the door, I lost my train of thought.

When I saw who stood on the porch, I said, "Oh, never mind," and hung up.

Maria Nanos stepped inside, looking over her shoulder. She almost collided with Alan, who was stuttering out sentence fragments.

"Oh, good; it's you!" She slammed the door shut. "I

wasn't sure what address . . . the phone book under 'Hershey.' I guessed Fred was short for Edward."

I was confused. Had I mentioned bunking with Fred?

She leaned against the closed door, looking none the better for her days of camping. Her hair was stringy, her sweater streaked with dirt, her jeans stiff. Her backpack was gone, probably still in a County Jail locker.

She spoke in a rush. "I have to leave here, they'll look here. You've got to help me—please!"

"Maria, I know this is hard, but you have to go back and face—"

"No!" She flattened against the door as if I'd struck her. "You've got to help me get away! I'll kill myself if they put me in jail again!" Her face twisted like a sobbing toddler's.

Within seconds, she snapped out of it, looking manically around the room. "Is there a back door? Could I have some money?"

Alan was reaching into his pockets. I stepped up behind him and grabbed his arm. I shuddered to think what the assistant DA would do with his giving her cash.

"You have to go back, Maria. I'm sorry, but you really do. I guarantee you won't end up with your grandparents again." Somehow I'd make good on the promise. "You can't keep running. You'll never be free of this, you'll never have a chance to get past it. And your baby—"

But she was already dashing into other rooms, looking for a door. She was muttering, "Oh my God, oh my God, they'll *be* here."

Alan looked at me as if I were a monster.

As Maria backtracked from the bedroom, she pushed me aside, knocking me into the bookcase. She ran into the kitchen. Alan followed.

It took me a second to regain my balance. I got to the kitchen as Maria flung open the back door. But I wasn't in time to stop her from erupting out into the yard. Alan, hand digging into his pocket, was right behind her.

I watched him follow her through the back gate.

By the time I got there, they were halfway down the

208

alley. I could see that Alan wasn't chasing her, wasn't even passing her cash. He was running with her.

I started after them, my mind boggling at what this could do to my case, to Alan's life.

But worry didn't make me any fleeter of foot. When I emerged from the alley onto the street, I saw that they were already at the next corner.

Gasping for air after an unaccustomed sprint, I stood in the chilly night. Down the street, a coffee shop with a porch full of outdoor tables lit the pavement.

As Alan and Maria ran past it, he reached out his hand and she took it. They rounded the corner moving fast, holding hands.

Holding hands.

I stood there awhile trying to believe I was mistaken. Then I walked back to Edward's, hoping Alan had joined her out of sympathy and compassion, not self-interest or complicity.

But I was shaken by Bart Bustamonte's take on Alan. I was rattled by the sight of him running off with Maria. And I had trouble believing Maria had found us by misinterpreting the phone book.

I wondered what the police would make of it if they caught them together. I knew how Patrick Toben would argue it.

I went back through Edward's gate and yard, stopping for a glass of water in the kitchen. When I entered the living room, I saw someone there. I screamed.

"Willa! Don't do that! You scared me!" My mother, still in this morning's dress jeans, was sitting on Edward's couch.

"I scared *you?*" Even from here, I could smell cigarette smoke on her clothes. Since she didn't smoke, it meant she'd been to a meeting. "How did you find me, Mother?"

"I assumed you'd stay with Edward." Her tone was carefully neutral. We'd had a few battles over her lingering fondness for my former boyfriend. "You didn't answer, so I came inside to wait."

"Edward's sailing through the Panama Canal. I'm staying with his brother, Fred."

"But this is Edward's house," she pointed out.

I dropped onto the couch beside her. The afghan stank of fish lures and mildew and visiting dogs. "It's Edward's house, but I'm not staying here. My client is. It's lucky you caught me."

"I wish you'd have let me come listen to your case today," she pouted. "I haven't heard you in court in ages."

"Next time." I shuddered involuntarily at the idea of Leonard Deally interviewing her.

"I didn't mean to embarrass you there at the courthouse, Baby. But when I saw *that* man . . ." Her expression again reflected an encounter with Dr. Mengele.

"Tell me about Colonel Kraduck. You say you remember him from Travis. What year was this?"

"Oh, about the time you got back from Boston. Right before you went to—" She stopped herself, knowing I hated any reference to the two long, painful months I'd spent in jail.

"What was Kraduck doing then? Do you remember his uniform? His rank?"

"A uniform's a uniform." Strands of flyaway yellow-white hair drooped over her forehead. With her bright blue eyes and old-handbag skin, without makeup or jewelry, she looked like the Minnesota-Lutheran-turned-union-activist-turned-radical-dinosaur that she was. "It was quite a few years ago."

"But you remember Kraduck's face? Are you sure?"

She nodded. "You know me and faces."

"He was shot tonight," I told her.

She jerked as if I'd slapped her. "He's dead?"

"He might have been. But he was wearing a bulletproof vest."

"Oh, good—then it has nothing to do with your case." She looked mostly relieved, maybe a little disappointed.

"Why do you say that?"

"Well, if he knew somebody was after him, then it has to do with his life, not yours. Right?"

"Maybe you have a point." I didn't tell her I'd been shot at twice since coming to town. "They didn't catch whoever did it. It was a drive-by."

She didn't comment.

"So you came down here to hassle me about SDI and alien abduction stories?"

"I came especially on a Friday so I could ride back with you." My mother wasn't one for polite denials. "I'm so glad I caught you."

"I was going to stay here this weekend. There've been a lot of developments." I had a sudden horrifying vision of my mother in Santa Cruz for the duration of my trial. "But . . ."

It was only two hours each way. For a mere four hours in transit, I could assure myself of a Mother-free courtroom. I could also pick up my mail and sleep in my own bed.

A pounding on the door interrupted my musing.

I opened it, expecting the police. I got a two-fer. Patrick Toben stood beside a cop.

"We had a lead Maria Nanos was in this neighborhood," he said. More likely, he'd attributed my suddenly hanging up on him to Maria appearing on the porch. "Is she here?"

"No." Without actually saying I'd put down the phone to greet my mother, I made a point of telling him she'd just arrived.

I'd have liked to be honest, to admit Maria had shown up here, then bolted. I wanted to help him; I wanted Maria to get counseling, find a foster family, go to college—things she'd never manage without intervention.

But I couldn't say more without getting my client into trouble we might never talk his way out of.

"Do you mind if we look around?" Toben asked.

"Go ahead. But you know this isn't my place. Don't touch any of the owner's stuff, okay?"

My mother jumped to her feet, clearly indignant over his request. I told her with a gesture to shut up.

Toben noticed. "We just want to look in the other rooms," he assured me. "We won't disturb anything."

The cop started in the kitchen. I could hear him open the back door and go out into the yard.

My mother was scowling, lips pursed as if to break into speech.

I didn't want a confrontation; I didn't want Toben asking point-blank if I'd seen Maria.

I babbled, "What did you do with the grandparents?"

"They're at the Holiday Inn again. Waiting."

The cop came back inside, leaving the kitchen and crossing to Edward's bedroom.

"That's Edward's private area!" my mother protested.

I flashed her a Medusa look. "I'm sure his underwear's all put away, Mother."

I moved close enough to elbow her, if need be.

"So where's Miller?" Toben wondered.

I was honest: "I don't know."

"He was here when I called."

"Why do you say that?" I'd answered the phone. Miller hadn't made any background noise, not that I recalled.

Were the police watching the house?

I felt myself scowl. If they were watching the front, they'd seen Maria enter. They'd seen her arrive, but not leave.

Was that why they'd come here? To catch her—and to catch us harboring her?

Toben and I had a staring contest. Finally he said, "I just had the impression Miller was here when I called."

The cop came out of Edward's bedroom. "Nobody," he confirmed.

"Well, what did you expect?" my mother fumed.

I squeezed her arm. I didn't want her prolonging the encounter. But I shot Toben a look telling him the accusation wasn't lost on me, either.

He chewed the inside of his cheek. "Okay, well . . . We'll call you when we get her back."

"If it's tonight, try me at my San Francisco number. I'm going back right now." Ten minutes with my mother had convinced me I couldn't risk her showing up in court next week.

Star Witness

Toben glanced at the cop, then asked, "You're returning to Santa Cruz when?"

"In the morning." I sighed for another lost weekend.

"I'll be in the office all weekend if you need me." Toben sighed, too.

31

My apartment was stuffy and stank of neglected perishables. My mail was mostly junk. And my bed wasn't as comfortable as I remembered.

I had a funny thought as I packed a fresh suitcase. Maybe I should move to Santa Cruz. Put a little distance between myself and my parents.

I'd spent a week in the Santa Cruz mountains last year. This year, in town, I was still liking what I saw. I could find a place near the beach. Maybe I needed a change.

Maybe not. First, I'd have to see if I got laughed out of town.

I stopped in Davenport on my way down the coast. I drove along San Vittorio Road. Yellow Caution Do Not Enter tape was still strung between fire department sawhorses in front of Alan Miller's house.

Alan had been escorted in by fire marshals and allowed to take some of his things from certain rooms. He'd been kept out of the living room, where the floor and walls were unstable.

As far as I knew, the arson investigation continued, but no one was saying anything beyond the fact that a space heater had sparked some kerosene. I'd have to try to get more details by Monday, before I wound up my case in chief.

I continued down the road. Donna Nelson's house looked vacant. The shades were pulled and the hollyhocks were wilted. The gate was wide open. A yellow dog moseyed through the yard.

The hill behind the houses was dotted with purple wild-flowers that hadn't been in bloom last week. Overhead, big white clouds drifted through a pale blue sky. The field across the street rustled in the breeze. Even this far inland, I could smell the ocean.

It was a perfect Saturday. If I didn't get back on Highway 1 soon, I'd certainly get caught in beach traffic.

But first, I continued down the road, turning up Joseph Huizen's bumpy driveway. Yesterday, he'd left the court-room before I'd had a chance to talk to him.

We'd had only minutes to prepare his testimony, so I'd decided not to tell him the crop circle resembled a glucose molecule. I hadn't wanted him to become self-conscious; I hadn't wanted him stumbling over a description of the IV, overemphasizing it or giving it short shrift.

But I wondered how he'd reacted to later testimony, what he'd thought of Fulmer's theory.

I knocked at his door, assuming he was too much a scien-tist to buy it. I imagined he'd agree with Bustamonte that it took an inordinate amount of twisting to make the molecule model two-dimensional. And that the model was just a con-ceptual guess, anyway.

Maybe I'd come here for a comforting dose of conven-tional science.

When Joseph opened the door, I stepped back in alarm. He wore pajamas and a robe, he needed a shave, there were circles under his eyes, and his thin white hair hung in limp, uncombed strands.

"Are you okay?" My manners didn't equal my concern.

"Oh, the pajamas; I'm sorry. I didn't make it to bed last night. Last night was *marvelous!*" He grinned like a boy on a bumper car. "Please, come in."

I stepped inside, hoping his mania hadn't led to more smashed lamps and broken furniture. I followed him into his airy kitchen, relieved to see things unharmed, if untidy.

He practically skipped to the table—not something I expected from a man his age or his size. Behind him, picture windows framed a flower-dotted hill. A hummingbird with invisibly quick wings stared in at us, then flew off as if jerked by a string. I felt as if I'd suddenly wandered into an outtake from *Mary Poppins*.

"I got it, I really got it. I can hardly believe it, but I've been checking it and checking it, and it still works." His pale blue eyes glittered. "I solved it. The tetrahedron inside the spinning mass, it—Oh, never mind the details. If there's one thing I've learned over the years, it's that it doesn't make sense to people one invites in for coffee." He pulled out a chair. "Is coffee all right? Is there anything you'd rather have?"

"Coffee's perfect."

I sat at a table an inch deep in scratch paper anchored with calculators, rulers, and protractors. The calculators had about forty extra buttons. The papers were penciled with equations and diagrams and measured angles. Some were marked in red pen. A few numbers were circled in blue. The floor around my chair was also littered with paper, most of it traversed with impatient cross-outs.

Joseph bent close to the tabletop, setting his cheek on the papers. He turned his face and kissed them several times. Then he went to the counter and began making coffee.

"I'm sorry to be so selfish. You probably have things you want to talk about." He cast me a look that said, *If so, get it in now.* "It's just that I've never had such a breakthrough, such a 'Eureka!' moment."

"I take it you discovered something last night?"

"Not just discovered something. Not the way academics 'discover' things today. This is *real*, not a mere embellishment on so-and-so's footnote in someone else's journal article. This is . . . well, I don't want to explode with hubris, but it may be the kind of thing that comes along only once in a generation. Unless I've gone completely foolish." He looked stricken by the notion. "But I've checked it over and over again. It seems to work, it really does."

"The mathematics of spinning bodies?"

"To drastically oversimplify it, yes."

"Is this . . . ?" I hated to bring up anything so flaky. "Is this what you were talking about—you know, outside with the imaginary lights—when the medics picked you up?"

"That's right! I was consulting a pattern of stars—I mean, as part of my hallucination. And they gave me a suggestion. What a suggestion!" He grinned. "It took glucose starvation for me to get this clue. And perhaps I should be embarrassed that it came to me in an altered state. But it works! I finally figured out what I was trying to say to myself that night. I finally got the numbers to click."

He finished pouring water through the coffee cone. I noticed his hand was trembling.

While the coffee brewed, he fumbled through his notes, trying to explain to me, in layman's terms, what he'd concluded. It was so far over my head it would have taken a spaceship to get me anywhere close to understanding it.

But I was grateful for the coffee. And he gave up blessedly soon on the explanation.

"Did you stay for the rest of the court session yesterday?" I asked him.

"Oh, yes! The glucose molecule crop circle! Only this" —he nodded at the notes he'd just gathered and stacked— "could have driven it from my mind."

"So you heard Reginald Fulmer's testimony?"

"My first thought was that it couldn't be possible. It gave me such a case of heebie-jeebies I could hardly drive home." He looked alarmed recalling it. "It seemed the most oppressive burden. Imagine the universe leaving graffiti in your yard."

"That's why I came to see you today. It gave me the heebie-jeebies, too," I confessed. "And I wanted to make sure you weren't angry."

"Angry?"

"That you didn't think I'd exploited you or played up a weird coincidence at your expense; something like that."

"Heavens, no. You have to do your job as a lawyer." He patted my hand. "When I got over the, well . . . *physical* reaction to the strangeness of it, I started to think, What if it's true, old man? What does it mean?"

He looked at me as if expecting an answer.

"I flipped it this way and that way and every which way," he continued. "But it continued to suggest an interest in me. An interest large enough, cosmic enough . . . Well, I'm afraid I'll get stricken down dead if I go on in this Olympian way. But thinking about it put me in the oddest mental state, almost a meditation. It was so shocking, it drove everything else from my head." He looked puzzled. "I've never gone in for Eastern religions, but this must be close to what they're talking about. Emptying your mind of all its noisy little thoughts to make room for something larger. That's what it was like. It was like a mantra. A marvel that I turned over and over like a jewel."

"But you were okay?" I needed to know, even in the face of his obvious bliss, that I hadn't harmed him.

"More than okay. That's when the insight struck, just like that, in an instant, a nanosecond. My life's toil didn't amount to a hill of beans by comparison. I just . . . *got* it. It suddenly made perfect sense. I saw how it worked and why it worked."

His smile was so young, so dashing. I felt I saw him, for the space of that quick grin, as the boy he'd been fifty years ago.

"You can work with mathematics for an entire career, write books, teach others, and have it be mere industry. You might as well work in a numbers mine, chipping and piling and equating. It's so easy to forget that mathematics is magic, that it's the poetry of the universe."

He sighed, taking a long swallow of coffee. "Actually," he confided, "I hate poetry. It always seems like too many words, spoken with more meaning than they really have. I've been dating a poet since my wife died. So I never get to say how I feel about it." He snickered. " 'Open mike,' in my opinion, is a synonym for 'purgatory.' "

I laughed. The universe had chosen a worthy recipient for its glucose-shaped love note. Even if it had, possibly, spoken through botany students armed with twine and a lawn roller.

32

On my way down the coast, I slowed at the scene of Miller's accident. Naturally, there was no trace left. And naturally, the cars behind me honked.

They were even less glad to see traffic stalling up ahead of me.

In no mood for a traffic jam, I pulled onto the access road to the farmer's sprouts field. I might as well have another look up there. Maybe I'd see something I'd missed before, some clue we'd all ignored. Or maybe the universe had decided to leave me a cosmic Post-it, like Joseph's.

The field, I found, had been rototilled and replanted with rows of spiky-leafed plants. I had a vague idea they were artichokes. Apparently the time had come to segue from Brussels sprouts to something edible.

I parked near the No Trespassing sign and started picking my way through plants so jaggedly pointed they looked like they were being grown as weapons. About a third of the way across I stepped over ruts left between rows by the farmer's truck. The tire tracks, deep in irrigated dirt, were easily a foot across. Two of my Honda tires would have fit inside.

The prosecution was right about one thing: If this truck had driven over Fiat tracks, it would have obliterated them.

I continued toward the "cliff" and began walking between the cultivated area and the weedy verge dropping off to the highway. Now that the field was irrigated, the dirt was softer near the unwatered edge, still dry but less like hardpan. Three weeks ago, Toben and the deputies argued, this margin had been too hard to show tracks. When I reached the spot where the accident happened, I looked down.

Twenty feet below, northbound traffic clipped along. But the other lane wasn't moving at all. Perhaps a quarter mile up, two shirtless men pushed a Jeep toward a turnout.

I wondered, with a commuter's impatience, why it was taking them so long. As I turned, I almost fell over the wooden handle of a gardening tool sticking out of the weeds.

Annoyed, and a little concerned that a clumsier person (if one existed) might stumble off the cliff, I yanked it out of the greenery. It was a rusty metal rake, twice as long as I'd supposed.

I prodded the vegetation. Uneven growth made the edge appear level, made it look like three feet of flat, weed-covered ground ending abruptly. But beneath the plants, the ground dropped off at a forty-five degree angle before plunging straight down to the highway. Never having poked through the flora, I hadn't realized it.

I looked out across the field. If Miller's car really had sailed off the cliff here, sailed off at sufficient speed, his tires might not have made contact with the hidden slope. There was a chance, at just the right spot, that a car wouldn't crush plants between the ground and the wheels, after all.

No wonder the sheriff's deputy testified that a "disembanking" car wouldn't necessarily damage any greenery. But he hadn't made his reasoning clear; not to me, anyway. Not even under cross-examination, when he'd merely cited the "slope angle."

I could only hope the jury had missed the point, too. And that Patrick Toben didn't prepare a diagram to use in closing arguments.

I walked back to my car worrying: That the farmer really had overridden Miller's tracks sometime before the sheriff arrived to check the field. That Alan Miller did indeed sail off this field onto the highway. That he was lying about the alien abduction. Or that he was crazy, as he seemed to fear.

That he was guilty of manslaughter, after all.

I climbed into my car recalling how Miller had taken hold of Maria Nanos's hand last night, how he'd run away with her. I hoped it was impulsive gallantry. I feared there was some preexisting attachment between them.

I was relieved to find Highway 1 traffic moving again. I slowed down out of curiosity when I passed the stalled Jeep. It was up on jacks with two tires off. Two flat tires: easy to see why it had taken so long to push it. I was impressed the men had rolled it so far on its rims.

But suddenly, it made me wonder. Having opened myself to one paranoia, I found another piggybacking in.

No one had witnessed Miller and Addenaur's accident. No one knew how long the cars had been stacked there before discovery.

What if Addenaur's car hadn't been crushed beneath the sprouts field at all? What if the accident happened a little farther south, where another field rose above the highway? What if the cars had been rolled to the spot where they were found?

I remembered noticing, when Fred and I looked down from the Brussels sprouts field, the stains of another accident on the highway.

I tried to calm down. Think of the cleanup it would have involved: sweeping and moving glass beads and twists of metal. All at night. And easily foiled by a single passing car.

No, it didn't make sense. Not unless someone didn't want the police looking in the right field for tire tracks.

I slowed my Honda. I guess I was afraid not to check. I was afraid an unjustified lack of confidence in my client would show, that the jurors would smell it on me, hear it in my voice.

I turned onto the next inland road. There, I found an easily accessed field that dropped straight off onto the highway. It was freshly tilled, stinking of fertilizer. Any tracks that might have been on it were gone now.

I told myself it didn't prove anything. What would Miller be doing here in the wee hours of a Saturday morning? As with the sprouts field farther north, there was no reason for him to take the side trip.

On the other hand, this would be an easier field mistakenly to veer into and across—if one were already heading west on this road.

Instead of returning to the highway, I followed the road inland to see where it went. I climbed through redwoods and oaks and pine-lined curves up into the coastal range. I'd spent a week in these mountains last year. Funny how much more beautiful the scenery was when the police weren't after you.

I turned onto another road, thinking I recognized it as the road to Lockheed. I'd been in the back of someone's VW when I'd gone there to protest with my parents, so my memories of the route were hazy. But it seemed worth a ten-minute detour to try to find Santa Cruz's UFO magnet.

I soon found myself at an end-of-the-road military-looking facility. But if it was Lockheed, it was totally unidentified.

A sign on a twelve-foot Cyclone fence read, "Absolutely No Trespassing or Loitering; Forbidden by Law." Slightly smaller signs read, "No Entry Without Permission; Closed to Public," and, "Trespassers Will Be Prosecuted Under Penal Code Sections 602," followed by a long list of subsections. Another sign read, "Photography Strictly Prohibited." Through the fence, I could see a guard station with one-way mirrored glass. Squinting, I could barely make out some of the writing on the sign beside it: "No Smoking, No Firearms, No Tape Recorders, No Cameras. All items to be deposited with guard until leaving facility." Beyond the guard station, a road wound through a compound of barrackslike structures. Behind them, a stand of trees blocked further view.

It had all the welcome signs I vaguely recalled decorating Lockheed's fence. But it should have been labeled "Lockheed Missile and Space Company." I remembered staring at the words, years ago, while mosquitoes rose out of roadside duff to bite every inch of me.

I wasn't sure if I'd found Lockheed or stumbled upon some other mountain stronghold. I made a mental note to ask Bustamonte.

I was turning my car around, backing onto the shoulder of the road, when I saw helicopters. There were two of them, big, dark ones, flying inland toward this facility. I couldn't guess whether these were the same type I'd seen at the hotel; it had been too dark that night, and these were too far away. I couldn't tell if either pair was "black." But they couldn't have scared me more if they'd been Black Riders from *The Lord of the Rings*.

The UFOlogists had spooked me with their shadow-government stories.

I was tucked beside the road, under cover of redwoods. For once, I was glad my Honda was a drab green. I cut the engine, hoping I wasn't visible from the air.

I watched the helicopters fly overhead, over the fence. I decided to wait a few minutes rather than risk being seen—and perhaps pursued—by them.

The next thing I knew, I was startled out of an uncomfortable doze by two large deer rustling along the shoulder of the road not two feet from my windshield. I looked at my car clock. It was past noon.

How could that be? How could I have lost almost two hours? I sat up, feeling achy and a little nauseated. My unintended nap had left me anything but refreshed.

I glanced at the guard station down the road, on the other side of the warning-laden Cyclone fence. It occurred to me —a little late in the game—that anyone inside could see me. If there was a guard in there and he had a radio, he might send someone out after me.

I took off down the mountain.

I careened around curves, remembering Bart Bustamonte's tale of black helicopters chasing him through the desert, bouncing off the roof of his car. I tried to take reassurance from it: Bustamonte was still around to tell the (maybe not so) paranoid tale. And he was a bona fide investigator, presumably a thorn in their side.

Except that I didn't know who "they" were. For all I knew, this compound belonged to a conservative committee of the State Bar, gunning for flaky lawyers.

I raced the rest of the way to Highway 1. Once there, I rolled down my window, drinking in the salty perfume of a sunny seacoast day.

I made myself stop wondering what kind of facility hides on a mountaintop without a single identifying plaque. I stopped thinking about the helicopters I'd watched fly into it. Because I couldn't afford to reflect on my sudden nap, not now. After the stories I'd heard lately, I was afraid I'd put a label like "missing time" on the experience.

No wonder Alan Miller couldn't believe he'd been abducted by a spaceship. I couldn't even come to grips with a couple of helicopters and a two-hour siesta.

33

I prayed, as I knocked at Edward's door, that I'd find Alan Miller there. When I didn't, I used one of the duplicate keys Fred made for us. I looked around. There was nothing in the living room to indicate whether Alan had returned.

Nor could I tell by the number of cups and dishes in the kitchen sink. I have an untidy woman's way of not noticing clutter, so it was hard to measure what I saw against last night's mess.

I was forced to break my long-standing vow and set eyes on Edward's bedroom. The room was surprisingly spartan, with old-fashioned wood furniture and a bed with no backboard.

The curtains were closed, but enough light filtered through the cheap weave for me to appreciate Edward's Navajo blankets and his dresser display of Northwest Indian carvings.

Right now, the cedar objects were pushed aside. The dresser top was covered with waxed paper, and several clusters of mushrooms were spread over it. I picked through them, amazed at how different they were from the ones in the supermarket. One group had frilly-looking caps with edges melting into black goo. A few were fluorescently bright red or yellow and seemed made of wax. Some weren't even shaped like mushrooms; they looked like little brains and corals and glops.

226

A tattered field guide lay beside them. I picked it up and began flipping through it. I saw pictures of fungi resembling fingers, clubs, nets, octopi; others you could dye with, write on, bake into cookies; some that attracted spore-transporting flies by stinking of carrion; carnivorous ones that invaded beetle bodies and consumed their flesh until only fungus filled the shiny insect shell (the photo showed a mushroom protruding from a beetle's back). I could understand Alan's thesis that fungi might be an alien life form. But then, I felt that way about Republicans, too.

I was about to replace the book on the dresser when my attention was caught by a section headed "Poisonous Mushrooms":

> The most lethal of commonly occurring mushrooms in North America is the *Amanita phalloides,* or Death Cap, and it's springtime relative, the *Amanita ocreata,* or Destroying Angel. Its toxins typically do not cause illness for several hours or even two or three days, when they have caused enough liver and kidney damage that those organs no longer screen out everyday toxins. The body will, as it accumulates toxins, become susceptible to bruising, and there may be blood in the urine and delirium from poor liver function. Depending on the amount eaten, liver and/or kidney transplants may be the only hope for sustaining life.

I sat down on Edward's bed, book in hand, straining in the darkened room to read the rest of the section entitled "The Deadly Amanitas." Not only were they common, according to this author, but their survivors often remarked that the flavor was good. The picture showed big, standard-shaped mushrooms with nothing about them to disgust or deter.

Delirium and blood in the urine: it sounded like Miller's experiences before the sheriff's deputies came for him.

I slumped on Edward's bed, thinking. Alan had been at a

mycology conference in San Francisco before the accident. Could a fellow fungus expert have poisoned him?

Or, given how long it took for the effects to be felt, maybe he'd been poisoned before he left Davenport. Maybe he was supposed to collapse at the conference, where other mycologists would be suspected of some kind of mistaken mushroom identification.

Maybe mushroom poisoning had made Alan Miller disoriented enough to take the wrong road, drive through a field, and land on top of Francis Addenaur.

I snickered, wondering if the jurors were having even half the doubts plaguing defense counsel.

I stood, about to return the book to the dresser. I checked the title page for author and publisher, thinking I'd buy a copy. It was published by an arty press in San Francisco, and I'd never heard of the author, K. L. Korlovatz. But the inscription made me catch my breath.

It was autographed, "To Leonard, Thanks for the great publicity."

Leonard Deally?

The possibility sent me on a brief detour through downtown, a bustling row of Italianate buildings, corner flower stands, and outdoor cafés. I picked up a triple espresso and a less soiled copy of the mushroom book. Maybe K. L. Korlovatz, if I tracked him through his publisher, could tell me how Leonard Deally and Alan Miller were connected.

Then I drove on to Fred's house.

Fred wasn't there. But for once he'd made himself easy to find. He'd left me a note asking me to phone his office. I stared at his tidy handwriting. Good news was easily jotted down. Only bad news needed telling.

Fred answered the phone with a clipped "Yes?"

"Hi." I couldn't quite bring myself to ask.

"Come to my office."

"Is it—? Have you talked to Alan?"

"Just come. We'll talk here."

"Is it about Alan?"

"Not directly. I'd rather talk here," he insisted.

"But—"

He hung up before I could finish objecting.

I found I was reluctant to meet him. It seemed to me that, once too often, Fred hadn't been where I'd expected him to be. I was beginning to worry that he had a secret agenda. Or worse, that he was following someone else's, perhaps reporting in to that person.

So before I rushed to oblige him, I made a few other phone calls. My first was to the hospital. Colonel Kraduck had been discharged. I tried the hotel, but he hadn't reregistered—perhaps being shot in its parking lot had soured him on the place.

Then I phoned the assistant DA. True to his word, Toben was in his office on this sunny Saturday.

"It's Willa Jansson. I'm back from San Francisco. Did you find Maria Nanos?"

All morning, I'd been in a fever to know. But I'd wanted to appear calm, no more concerned than I should be, not like someone whose client had run off with a witness. My unscheduled nap had made it easy to wait until afternoon.

"No. We've got deputies and city police looking. But it's hard on the weekend. We get anywhere from fifteen to fifty thousand tourists on a nice day like this. Unless she shows up at a beer brawl or a boardwalk knifing, everybody's pretty busy."

"What about her grandparents? Did you ask about their daughter, Maria's mother?"

"Yes." A pause. "I asked them."

"What did they say?"

"They were very . . . excitable on the subject. But their basic point was that she was a prostitute. That she left Maria with them and took off to live that life."

"They called her a prostitute? That's probably just their old-fashioned ideas. They're so—"

"Maybe." He sounded a little peeved. "We have the mother's name; we're checking for arrests. But you know, it could be Maria's romanticizing things—girls come up with the most amazing *Perils of Pauline* stuff at her age. And if her mother really was a prostitute, you can see how the grandparents would want to keep the brakes on Maria."

I had a sudden suspicion: "Do you have teenage daughters?"

"Two of them."

No wonder our conversation was going nowhere. In part, he was talking about his overdramatic daughters and I was talking about my crazy parents.

"Call me if you find her." I gave him Fred's number.

On the way to Fred's office, I drove past beaches with high waves chasing flocks of shore birds. I dangled my arm out the window to feel the sun on my skin: the ten-minute vacation.

As I walked across Fred's tiny parking area, my worries begin to synergize. I tapped at his outer office door, feeling like just another patient with a panic disorder.

Fred, in a polo shirt, linen pants, and boating shoes without socks, looked like a man who should be lounging with a pink drink in his hand. But his face was anything but relaxed. His brows were pinched and he looked pale. His shoulders were hunched.

He said, "Those boys I told you about, Joey and Mickey?" He motioned me into the inner office and shut the door. "I played you Mickey's—"

"I remember." I hadn't heard so many alien abduction tapes that I was likely to forget one.

I settled into the rattan couch near the picture window. I was getting a bad case of spring fever; I couldn't keep my glance from straying to the view of redwoods in a sunlight-dappled gully. I could have been in Big Sur now.

Fred dropped into his usual chair. "The FBI arrested the father yesterday." He cringed slightly.

That got my attention. "Have you discussed Mickey's tape with them?"

"You don't understand." Fred ran both hands down the back of his head. "The father confessed. They found . . . he had pictures."

We stared at each other a minute.

"So what Mickey said under hypnosis, the aliens and all that . . . they *were* screen memories? His missing time was . . ." Horrible, poor kid, but not otherworldly.

Fred nodded. "Apparently some of it was straight out of an *X-Files* video they saw the night before. But that doesn't say anything one way or the other about Alan Miller's memories."

"Unless he saw the same *X-Files* episode. Which seems a lot more likely than a cruise ship from Zeta Reticuli docking in Davenport three weeks ago." Maybe it was just as well: I was sick of the strain of trying to believe something so unconventional. And maybe I needed reminding that usually, if not always, a nap is just a nap.

"You couldn't have offered testimony from those children anyway," Fred pointed out.

"It doesn't make any difference to my case," I agreed. "But it makes a difference to me, Fred. Me personally. I'm having a crisis of confidence." I shook my head wearily. "Worse yet, a crisis of flakiness."

34

Alan Miller was sitting on Edward's couch. He was scowling, elbows on splayed knees, his fingers laced, his head down. He looked like a kid getting yelled at by his mother. Or, more accurately, by his lawyer.

"Now I can't put you on the witness stand," I complained. "They'll ask you the last time you saw Maria Nanos, and you'll convict yourself right there."

"But all I did was get far enough away with her to give her some money." He looked up, his green eyes beseeching me to understand. "You saw how scared she was. And you said yourself the DA doesn't act like he believes her about her grandparents. I just wanted to help her."

"Money's not going to help her. Living on the street's not going to help her. She's   t even sixteen, she's pregnant; she needs to get all this settled and get on with her life." I was confounded that he didn't see it that way. "Are you telling me everything?"

He sat up. "What do you mean?"

"I mean, you didn't just run after her, you took her hand."

"She was going so slow. I was speeding her up till we got past all those people outside the coffee place."

I continued pacing. Alan claimed he'd returned within half an hour to find me gone. This morning, he'd taken a brief hike, accumulating the mushrooms I'd found on the dresser. Then he'd showered and gone downtown.

He'd seemed surprised I hadn't realized he'd been back. "What about all the extra dishes in the sink? And the mushrooming gear?" He'd pointed to rubber boots, a filthy basket, and a trowel in a corner near the door.

I repeated, "Whatever your reasons, this is a real mess. I think the police spotted Maria coming here; I think that's why they searched the house. I could be disbarred for lying to the assistant DA." Technically, I hadn't lied, but it had been a matter of semantics. And semantics weren't much of a defense. "Now there's no way we can put you on the stand."

His relief showed.

"I realize you don't want to testify, but remember my opening statement? We promised to put your butt up there." With a sigh, I sat beside him. "Your story's most convincing coming from you. You don't seem like a weirdo; that's important to jurors."

He didn't respond.

"Do you know a mycologist named K. L. Korlovatz?"

"Why do you ask?"

"I bought his book today. Was he at your mycology conference? The one in San Francisco?"

"Uh-huh. There were mycologists there from all over the world." Alan watched me blandly. "It's a pretty good field guide; it's small enough to tote around. It's not as good as David Arora's." His tone told me no field guide was.

"What's K. L. Korlovatz like?"

He shrugged. "Loves mushrooms. Takes good pictures." He stood. "Give me five minutes. Nature calls."

I watched him head toward the bathroom.

He hadn't corrected me when I called K. L. Korlovatz a "he." But according to the publisher, Kathleen Korlovatz was definitely a "she."

Alan came out a few minutes later, prattling about Maria. "Whatever the DA says about it, it's his fault. She wouldn't have run away if he didn't threaten to keep her in jail. And if he didn't act like he was going to send her back to her grandparents." He sat beside me again. "I mean, I get your point about how she should straighten her life out. But it's not like I told her to run away; she was already out of here. I just caught up to her and gave her money so she'd have a place to sleep."

"She was going to be a witness against you. Now you've given her money so she can run away and not testify. Don't you see how that looks? This isn't about her, it's about you. It's about blowing a chance for acquittal." Maybe I'd gone too far; he looked stricken. "Not your only one. But damn, I wish I could put you on the witness stand."

He didn't say anything. It was a chance he'd blown willingly. Because he didn't want to testify? Because some other part of his testimony would be perjured?

"Where did you part company with Maria? Where do you think she was going?"

"Maybe Davenport. She said she lived in a tent village there for a while."

"It's not up anymore." Before I left Joseph's, I'd walked up the hill for a quick look. The circles were ragged now, blending back into the meadow. And the tents were gone, every one of them. "Where did you leave her?"

He hesitated. "The Boardwalk area."

I stood, not at all confident he was telling the truth. I was getting angry. If he couldn't see the foolishness of giving money to a pregnant runaway at a time when it could land him in prison; if he couldn't see the wisdom of telling his lawyer everything . . .

"Is the city library open on Saturdays?" I asked him.

He nodded. "It's the one-story building with all the glass walls, a couple of blocks this side of downtown."

I grabbed my handbag and set out.

I got to the library about twenty minutes before closing. In addition to the usual complement of parents with kids, large-print seniors, and high-schoolers laboring miserably over reports, the library seemed to be a dumping ground for street people, their arms flung across tabletops as they slept. Their smell mingled with book dust and Xerox exhaust and the faint breeze of blossoming trees outside. The large room was cool and quiet, reminding me of afternoons I'd escaped the madhouse at my parents' to hide in the library with a yellowed *Scaramouche.*

With the help of a reference librarian, I found the microfilm room.

I typed the name "Korlovatz" into a computer and found a half dozen references, all from the year the mushroom field guide came out. I began looking them up.

Sure enough, one was Leonard Deally's column. It effused about the poetic writing, wittily presented information, and fabulous photographs in a field guide no one should be without. I popped a quarter into the microfilm reader to make a copy.

A later review in the paper's arts supplement agreed that it was a fine field guide, although not on par with that of "mushroom king" David Arora, or as "antic" as the work of "mushroom bishop" Terence McKenna. (Making Alan Miller a mere mushroom pawn?)

In later newspapers, there were brief mentions that the author was signing books at local bookstores.

But the last of the articles, dated six months after the others, announced the engagement of Kathleen Korlovatz. The photograph showed a dark-haired, heavy-chinned woman in logger's flannel holding up a huge mushroom. Seated beside her was Leonard Deally.

At least, that's what the caption read. Leonard Deally, in presumably happier times, hadn't looked much like the priggishly overdressed and balding man he was today. Seated beside his fiancée, a slimmer Deally wore a T-shirt reading "Santa Cruz Fungus Fair."

The headline was *Columnist to Wed Mushroom Queen.* At least the paper didn't mix its metaphors.

I hastily fed in another quarter before the librarian shooed me out.

I sat on a bench in front of the library, smelling the dusty blossoms of nearby trees and watching their pollen catch the sun like drizzle. In the distance, in front of some sidewalk café, a jazz quartet played " 'Round Midnight," heavy on the vibraphone.

I'd found no follow-up article, no Deally-weds-

Korlovatz. Something had gone wrong. And Deally no longer had possession of the field guide inscribed to him by his wife-to-be.

Somehow Alan Miller had ended up with it.

Alan and Kathleen, two pieces in the mushroom chess set; they had plenty in common. Perhaps they'd become romantic. And now, Leonard Deally was getting his revenge.

Or maybe Deally and Alan had been friends once. Maybe Deally had given Alan the book, not wanting to be reminded of a broken engagement.

Hell, for all I knew the book was Edward's.

With the sun in my face, I almost didn't care. I lay on the bench like the hippie I'd once been, and I basked, just basked. I wondered if anyone ever got any work done in this town.

35

On Sunday, I met with Bart Bustamonte to go over his testimony about the hoaxed crop circle.

We were in the hotel cocktail lounge. On the other side of huge windows, kids played volleyball in the sand. Beyond them, the waves crashed in and out, leaving twenty feet of foamy surf. Cliffs mantled in ice plant curved away to a tiny lighthouse.

"You'll be my last witness," I told Bustamonte. The assistant DA planned to question the botany students; I might as well jump the gun. Better to call Bustamonte now than to make him wait around to be a rejoinder witness. "After I put you on the stand, I'm done."

"You're not putting your guy on?" He looked surprised.

"No. He doesn't want to testify."

Bustamonte tapped a copy of the Sunday paper he'd brought to the table. Today, Leonard Deally cited the campus crop circle as proof Miller was a liar and a fraud. "He's embarrassed?"

I shrugged, leaving it at that.

"Yeah, I know the feeling. I once had the Great Debunker himself, Carl Sagan, may he rest in peace, attack me in a national magazine. And you should hear what he said about Fichman." He grinned. "Sagan went, okay, there are a bunch of pyramids on Mars, and they're in an area a lot like

Gizeh in Egypt. But, said Mr. Science Sagan, what's the chance of pharaohs on Mars? This is how deep a thinker Sagan was. Like if you don't have pharaohs, you can't have pyramids." Bustamonte leaned forward. "Here's another example. These two retirees, Doug and Dave, they call the English press corps one day and say, *You know all these crop circles over the last fifteen years? We made them, just to fool everyone.* They offer piddling proof, they don't even *try* to explain the circles in other countries. Colin Andrews confronts them with questions about specific circles, and they say, *Oh, heh heh, no, we didn't mean those circles.* That was in ninety-one; there have been hundreds every summer since. So did Carl Sagan say, *Prove it, Doug and Dave!* Or, *Why didn't you send a registered-mail drawing of a pattern to the press the day* before *a circle appeared?* No, Sagan's last book has a chapter about how easily fooled we were by this crop circle crap, when it was Doug and Dave all along." He grinned. "Hell, I could phone the papers today and say I've been abducting all these thousands of folks. Scientists like Sagan would go, *See, told you it was nothing to worry about.*"

"Well, you've been dealing with this stuff for years; you've developed a sense of humor about it. Alan Miller doesn't even believe it himself. He's really having a hard time."

It wasn't just Alan Miller. I couldn't stop thinking about the vegetation on the verge above the highway. Or the next field south, all traces plowed away. "Me, too. I shouldn't say this, I guess, but I have big-time doubts. I can't prove Miller didn't go off that cliff. And I keep thinking of other equally terrestrial ways the accident could have happened."

"The rowboats," Bustamonte said. "Remember the explorers' rowboats? The Indians weren't able to see the big ships, only the rowboats, because they looked like canoes. That's you. You're looking at something so strange to you that you're having trouble recognizing it. Instead you're seeing what you're used to: a client lying, an accident happening the way accidents usually do, somebody hiding evidence, whatever—things you've seen before. Canoes."

"Maybe."

"You know I'm not a hundred percent on your client. But we should all try to look past our canoes. The more habits of perception you break, the better your chances of seeing that big, important, unfamiliar thing out there."

Bustamonte glanced out the window, where kids were falling over backward to make sand angels.

"There have been a lot of circles on sand, did you know that? And in snow. I've photographed several myself. There were no tracks leading to them. No way Doug and Dave could have made them. Although one guy suggested pogo sticks."

I made a note to ask him a question about this in court.

"Ice, too. Lots of ice circles in Siberia and Greenland. The pattern is melted in."

A beach ball hit the window, and Bustamonte jumped. "I'll be glad to leave here. Too crowded, too hot." He wiped sweat from his cheeks. "Coastal Washington's just right for me—nice and cool."

I guess he didn't mind a little rain. "You must get a lot of mushrooms up there." I'd been reading Kathleen Korlovatz's book; I had mushrooms on my mind.

Bustamonte made a *ffftp* sound, indicating that they certainly did.

"Are you a mushroom hunter?"

He shook his head. "No, but I have friends up there who are into it. Their mushroom god lives in this area somewhere."

I leaned forward. "Kathleen Korlovatz?"

"No, somebody Arora. How do you know Kathleen?" He frowned, lips pursing.

"I'm reading her mushroom book. Do you know her?"

"Unfortunately. We all do. She was at the UFO conference, you know."

"She was? Why?" And why didn't I remember a name like Korlovatz being on the program?

"She calls herself Ninti, after the Sumerian extraterrestrial who gave birth to the first test-tube baby, Adam. Ninti!" He snorted. "The rest of us call her Ninny."

"Adam? Of Adam and Eve?"

He nodded. "You get a lot of nuts at these things. Part of the package," he sighed.

"And Kathleen Korlovatz is one of them?"

"A big one of them."

"What does she believe?"

"That ETs called the Annunaki came to earth four hundred and fifty thousand years ago. They mined gold so they could suspend particles as a radiation shield around their own planet. But a hundred thousand years later, their workers revolted—formed Earth's first labor union. Management decided to go for indigenous labor, but the only thing running around back then was *Homo erectus,* barely smarter than an ape. So they did some genetic engineering. They took an egg from a *Homo erectus* female and fertilized it in vitro with Annunaki sperm. Then Ninti, their chief medical officer, destined to live in legend as a fertility goddess, had the egg implanted into her womb. Ten months later, she gave birth to the first of a slave race they called Adamu. They gave Ninti the nickname Mammi, the root of the universal 'mama.' This is from six-thousand-year-old cuneiform tablets. The story, the names, even an illustration of the lab setup were supposedly handed down to the Sumerians through the generations."

"Kathleen Korlovatz believes a Sumerian creation myth? That humans were genetically engineered to be a slave race?"

" 'With sweat on your brow shall you eat your bread,' just like it says in Genesis. Actually, the Sumerian word for 'life' was the same as their word for 'rib,' as in Adam's rib. And the text says the Annunaki lived in E.Din." He shrugged. "You get your same basic spacemen in Mayan and Hopi stories. I'm not saying it's all crap; myths can be based on history. And the Sumerians did know a thing or two. They left tablets with depictions of our solar system. The planets are shown revolving around the sun—about four thousand years before Galileo got the idea. And they're the right sizes in relation to each other. Plus—here's the kicker—Pluto, Neptune, and Uranus are on the tablet. We didn't discover those planets till this century. Here's an ancient culture with no telescopes, supposedly. How did they know?"

I waited for an answer.

He continued, "When anthropologists and archaeologists vouch for this stuff, you think, Well, maybe." He shook his head. "But then you get Kathleen-Ninti and her airy-fairy overlay about 'positive' ETs and 'negative' ETs, channeling the mushroom, spore vibrations . . . it just about makes you want to turn your back on the whole thing and become an accountant."

"Channeling mushrooms?" Kathleen Korlovatz reborn as a Sumerian goddess; I was still trying to master my shock.

"According to her, when the Annunaki waved good-bye to Earth, they left behind mushrooms to guide the Adamu. Psilocybin's found in cow dung, and that encouraged the Adamu to follow cattle around, eventually domesticating them and using them for farming. Plus, the mushroom-alien talked to them through it, helped them evolve." He scrutinized me. "You're about my age. You know what it reminds me of?"

"What?"

"The sixties, all the psychedelic talk back then."

"Korlovatz's mushroom book seems so normal."

"She was still normal when she wrote it. Now she's part Annunaki—maybe they have more attractive last names." He snickered. "You should hear her story. First she becomes persuaded mushrooms are ETs. Then she decides to let the mushroom-ETs speak through her. She starts scarfing psilocybin—magic mushrooms—and pretty soon she's channeling Ninti, diva from another planet!"

"Alan Miller did his Ph.D. thesis on spores drifting here from other planets."

"There you go," he said. *"Spore Trek."*

"I wonder if that's when she met Alan." I glanced at Bustamonte's newspaper. "I wonder if Alan consulted her about his theory, explained it to her."

And got her started on a line of research that ended up taking her away from a mere earthling like Leonard Deally.

"If he did," Bustamonte said, "it would explain why he's so embarrassed. If I helped create Ninti Korlovatz, I'd go join the Foreign Legion."

36

Bustamonte asked to see the fenced facility I'd stumbled upon yesterday. "If Lockheed took its shingle off the door, it could mean something."

I wasn't thrilled about going back; I dreaded encountering the unmarked helicopters again. But Bustamonte pooh-poohed my fears.

"If they wanted to get you, they'd wait till after the trial —less noticeable. Next month sometime, a thug in an alley . . ." Seeing my face, he burst out laughing. "Kidding, just kidding. Come on, show me this place."

I was glad to leave the hotel, to be out of its air-conditioned, sound-muffled, beach-behind-glass environment. It was around seventy-five degrees with an ocean breeze; no one thinner than Bustamonte would have considered it too hot.

But anyone would have agreed it was too crowded. The beach and wharf area looked like a giant hand had picked up a dozen high schools, some in Mexico, and emptied them within sight of the hotel.

After helping Bustamonte into my Honda—not an easy fit, though he was too polite to complain—we drove up Highway 1. Even in Sunday traffic, it was less than twenty minutes to Davenport.

The winding road up the mountain took longer. And despite the forest shade, it grew hotter. Bustamonte turned his face to the open window like a dog panting for air. I wondered how he'd survived his jaunts to air force bases in Nevada and New Mexico. It said something about the strength of his convictions and his curiosity.

"Wait, wait, wait," he said. "What the hell is that?"

I slowed. We were winding through a fringe of thick forest, with small oaks and knobcone pines beside the road and redwoods rising high behind them. I couldn't see anything but trees and scrub. A red-tailed hawk circled overhead.

"Stop. Back up." He was trying to twist and look over his shoulder.

I shifted into reverse, breaking into a sweat as we rolled backward on the hairpin turn. This was my first car, and I'd owned it only a few years. I bought it when I worked for an L.A. firm, using it to create a slow lane for one.

"Right here!"

I stopped, not bothering to park on the shoulder. We'd seen no traffic since leaving the larger road.

"Here?" I still couldn't see anything but forest.

"Well, I'll be damned!" Bustamonte flung open the passenger door. "I didn't know anybody was still doing this!"

I got out, too. I reached his side of the car as he hoisted himself to his feet, bracing one hand on the seat and the other on the door frame.

"Doing what? What are we looking at?"

"You don't see it?" His face lit up. "Right over there." He nodded ahead into the woods.

I saw splotches of shadow, trees, bushes, birds, light through fluttering leaves . . . ordinary sights, except that one of the shadows—

"Oh, wow!" A pattern of shadow and light suddenly resolved itself into a huge cistern. But it wasn't camouflaged in any way I'd ever seen before. It wasn't splotched beige, green, and black like camouflage fatigues. It was a wild abstract of curves and angles and slashes. "It looks like Sister Corinna on acid. Or Peter Max with a boring palette. I can't believe I didn't see it."

"It's called dazzle camouflage. They were big on it during and after World War One. They'd take a huge ship and they'd paint it in the most way-out patterns you could dream of. Looked like you'd be able to see it a hundred miles away. But you know"—he started walking toward the cistern—"German subs couldn't spot them from the water, and planes couldn't map their velocity. The crazy patterns masked the shape, just like the angles on this thing made it look like shadows and trees and shafts of light. I think the basic principle is that if it's too weird and unexpected, your brain turns it into something familiar, part of the background."

We picked our way over vines—I hoped not poison oak —to get closer. The water tank was twice my height, as long as a limo.

"For fire department use?" I guessed. "It must get dry up here."

"They probably have a mostly volunteer fire department. Why the hell would they want to camouflage a water tank?"

"Maybe they have a problem with siphoning."

"Water's a very damn heavy thing to steal. No." He shook his head. "You might be right about it being for fire protection. But it's privately owned. It belongs to the thing at the end of the road, Lockheed or whatever it is."

I was getting the creeps. "What do you mean, whatever it is?"

"Well, they've got a good supply of extra water. It's possible they've got unmarked helicopters to chase folks away." I'd told Bustamonte about seeing helicopters here yesterday. "And they know their camouflage."

But if he expected something dramatic at the front gate, he must have been disappointed. (I, on the other hand, was relieved.) We encountered no vehicles of any kind, and no people, military or otherwise, armed or not. We simply drove up to the fence labeled "Absolutely No Trespassing or Loitering; Forbidden by Law." We stared at the guard station. We read the warnings and statute numbers.

"This isn't Lockheed," Bustamonte said. "It's on the wrong road, it doesn't have Lockheed written on it. It's just mimicking Lockheed. It's camouflaged, every bit as much as the water tank."

Then we walked into the woods far enough to be convinced the fence didn't just end.

Returning to the entrance, Bustamonte continued to look excited. "The whole setup—the warnings, the guardhouse, those whatever-the-hell barracks things . . . it's supposed to look like Lockheed, only more military. It's like a Potemkin village. You know, like the facades General Potemkin built to fool Catherine the Great into thinking she was riding through villages." He rubbed his neck as if his collar were burning him. "It's a Potemkin Lockheed. It's supposed to look scary, a place with armed guards ready to radio for troops to take you away!"

The place had certainly spooked me yesterday. I'd driven away in a lather of fear that black helicopters, that the shadow government—of this planet or some other—would come and get me . . . for nothing more than driving (and napping) on a public road.

Back at the front gate, Bustamonte stared through the chain-link. "It's just like a movie set, isn't it? Twelve-foot fence with barbed wire on the top, guardhouse, barracks. The road going off into the woods so you wonder what kind of big creepy building they've got tucked away in there—does it look like the Borg ship?" He made a voilà gesture. "The whole thing says, *Stay out.*"

"Of what?"

"Couldn't begin to guess," he admitted.

As we drove back down the mountain, Bustamonte seemed lost in thought.

Suddenly he exclaimed, "This is where your client came! The Potemkin Lockheed, it's where Miller came after he dropped off that teenager. Betcha anything!"

I swerved slightly. "You don't have any reason to believe that."

"Think about it: He was missing all night; that's mystery number one. This unmarked thing is sitting at the end of a lonely road not so far from his house; that's mystery number two. You've got helicopters hovering as subtly as pterodactyls outside the hotel rooms of your expert witnesses, and then you see the same helicopters here." He tapped his head. "It doesn't take a genius. Somebody at Potemkin Lockheed hired the helicopters to excite and titillate your UFO experts. Ergo, this is not about UFOs at all—they're just dazzle camouflage. And if this isn't about UFOs, then your client is lying. That puts him in cahoots with whoever hired the helicopters. And since they parked here, probably he did, too."

My luck: I take my witness for a drive and he becomes convinced of my client's guilt.

37

The next morning, Bustamonte proved to be an ideal witness. He was smart, sure, and quick to contradict unspoken assumptions in the assistant DA's questions. By the time he was dismissed, I wasn't as worried about Toben's botany students. I hoped we'd neutralized their testimony.

I announced that I had no further witnesses and I took my seat beside Alan Miller. The hound-faced judge asked Patrick Toben to begin his rebuttal case.

I caught Bustamonte's eye as he lumbered out of the courtroom. He looked boyishly eager. My detective, Carl Shaduff, waited for him in the hall. They were going back up to the facility Bustamonte persisted in calling Potemkin Lockheed.

Shaduff had looked up title to the land. It was owned by a corporation whose name suggested nothing in particular and whose business was unspecified. To Bustamonte, this meant intrigue.

I hoped their visit would lay Bustamonte's suspicions to rest. But if there was evidence Miller had hidden out up there, I wanted it now. I wanted no last-minute surprises.

The assistant DA didn't begin his rebuttal with the crop circle forgers. He was probably giving the jury time to forget Bustamonte's testimony.

He started with two doctors willing, for a fee, to interpret

Miller's medical chart in a way that proved he'd been in an auto accident.

On cross, I asked each of them how they explained the lack of compression injuries to the spine. Both cited the cushion effect of landing on a car roof. I asked how they accounted for the absence of lacerations. They replied, tautologically, that Miller hadn't been cut. I asked them how blood might have appeared in Miller's urine. They answered, stress.

I took them phrase by phrase through the findings and testimony of examining physicians. I asked if, in general, the observations of attending doctors would be more reliable than later conclusions based only on reading a patient's chart. They said, not necessarily.

I couldn't resist asking, "How do you account for the double puncture wound in Mr. Miller's thumb?"

One of them said, "Bee stings, perhaps."

The other said, "Any heavy-duty staple could leave such a mark."

I had no idea if they'd done us damage.

I sat with Alan during the lunch break. The judge, hoping to wind up quickly, had lengthened the court day and shortened the lunch hour. So we'd taken our places in a cafeteria line crowded with county-building workers.

A group of laughing women clicked by in their high heels. At metal tables, well-groomed men puzzled over sports scores. Secretaries with good haircuts nibbled salads. A hundred people talked at once, gossip ringing through the big basement room. It was crowded enough to offer privacy.

We had a small table to ourselves. I couldn't resist asking Alan, "Have you ever been up to a fenced facility at the top of the mountain? It's unmarked except for No Trespassing signs."

"Lockheed? On Empire Grade?"

"No." I verbally retraced my route. "It's closer to Davenport."

Alan unwrapped his cafeteria sandwich as if it were a complicated and delicate task. Finally, he said, "I've seen it."

"Have you been there lately?"

He bit into the sandwich, shaking his head.

I stared down at my square of white bread fringed with wilted romaine. It would have been hard enough to summon an appetite for it. Right now, I couldn't have eaten anything.

Right now, I was struggling with an occupational hazard. I believed my client was lying.

I just wondered how much he was lying about. All of it?

I was startled to hear him saying, "Willa? Willa?"

I turned to him. "Yes?"

"What is it?"

A practical lawyer would have said, *Nothing.* The trial was almost over; what was the point?

I said, "You didn't tell me about Kathleen Korlovatz, for starters."

"What about her?" His tone was guarded, his sandwich arrested a few inches from his lips.

"Didn't you talk to her about your doctoral thesis?"

He put the sandwich down. "I guess you spoke with her?"

I didn't reply.

"She was at the university as a guest lecturer. She mentioned she'd done some research in spore mutation. And since my thesis was on the effects of cosmic radiation . . . She was really helpful." He sighed. "And then . . ."

"She got more involved in the theory than you expected?"

"She got into mushrooms being alien, yeah." He slumped, straining the seams of his borrowed suit. "I'm interested in the idea theoretically, but, man, she really took off on it."

"Beyond the point where you shared her beliefs?"

"See, I'm in love with fungus; my object was to show one more remarkable thing about it. This culture's so misinformed about mushrooms—afraid to let their kids near them, afraid the least bit of contact will poison them." He ran his hand over his dark hair. "That's what all these years of teaching classes at the museum have been about. Showing people how diverse they are—how much you can do with them. How much fun they are. But at least a dozen times a season, some freaked-out mom comes into the museum with something from her backyard, going, 'Oh my God, Johnny touched this; what should I do?' Like just touching a mushroom's going to—Anyway, you see what I'm saying?"

"I'm not sure." I suspected he was changing the subject.

"People who make a lot of noise about the psychedelic mushrooms just make my job harder. They just make little Johnny's mom more paranoid. They keep mushrooms bad rapped."

"And Kathleen Korlovatz focuses on psychedelic mushrooms?"

He nodded.

"I thought she did something with Sumerian mythology."

"Maybe. I mean, I know she's supposed to be channeling or something. She uses a different name now, Nitsy or something. But it's her thing about *Stropharia cubensis*—a kind of psilocybin—having an alien voice, that you can talk to an alien if you eat magic mushrooms—that's the stuff I hate."

"Why didn't you tell me any of this when I asked you about her?"

"Because I hate it! I hate what happened." He pushed his sandwich away. "She was a good scientist. She was a good thesis advisor. Now she's on mushroom trips talking to alien spore men!"

"You blame yourself?"

He looked surprised. "Blame myself? Why would I?"

"For suggesting to her that spores came from outer space."

He shook his head. "It was a book about *Stropharia cubensis* that did that—an interesting book; a lot of good research by an ethnomycologist. It's just that Kathleen went overboard with it. Changed her name and started coming to conferences in robes and stuff. Got very weird about the mushroom, made it her whole life."

"Is it addictive?"

"Psilocybin? No. But it makes you feel like you're com-

muning with something—not an alien spore creature, but
something spiritual. I think what hooked her was the mind
expansion or the spiritualism or whatever you want to call it.
It's the New Age stuff that's addictive, not the mushroom."

"But you weren't the one that got her into it?"

He shook his head.

"Leonard Deally thinks you were."

"He does?"

"Doesn't he?"

"I don't know. I've never talked to him."

"Even when he was engaged to Kathleen?"

"I knew they were dating—she gave me a book because
she didn't like her inscription to him. But I didn't really
socialize with her. The time I spent with her, we were in the
labs or in her office up on campus."

I looked at the handsome, green-eyed man filling out
Edward's borrowed suit better than Edward ever had.

"You seem to feel so guilty about Leonard Deally's col-
umns, almost like you have his cruelty coming." I rubbed
the spot between my brows, hoping to stave off a headache.
"I thought you must feel responsible for Kathleen breaking
up with him. I thought her mushroom-goddess stuff must
have come from you."

His brows rose. "I feel guilty because Francis Addenaur's
dead. And his widow's gone crazy. And it was my car that
killed him."

"You don't believe your own alibi, do you?"

He winced. "No. I don't."

38

The botany graduate students were on and off the witness
stand in an hour. They admitted getting the idea to make
crop circles from last month's visiting expert. They described how easy it had been to make the campus crop
circle: how few implements they'd needed, how quickly
they'd finished. But they didn't claim to have made the
circles near Joseph Huizen's house. And I'd already rebutted
(prebutted?) their testimony with Bustamonte's.

The assistant DA then called the administrator of the
Bonny Doon airport, which was, apparently, not far from
Potemkin Lockheed.

He testified that a helicopter could easily hover above a
house like Donna Nelson's and shine a searchlight into a
window. And that, in fact, there had been many complaints
about helicopter fly-overs in the mountains these last months.

I felt a pang for the medic who'd been forced to admit
stopping to gawk. Deally's vitriolic editorial claimed he'd
hallucinated a spaceship. Now everyone would laugh that
he'd misidentified a helicopter.

On cross, I asked the witness what kind of helicopters the
majority of complaints involved.

He admitted that virtually all were attributable to the federal Campaign Against Marijuana Planting program that
searched for hidden pot fields.

253

I asked if he'd ever heard of CAMP helicopters hovering over houses at night, aiming their high beams into windows.

He said no.

But the witness left me more shaken than I'd left him.

I imagined a black helicopter would be invisible in the unlighted countryside at night. It would be inaudible over an ambulance siren. Its light would appear to be shining down from nowhere, from space, from an unseen alien craft.

But why would it be shooting a light into Miller's neighbor's house? Mistaken address?

Had it come to pick Miller up? Had it flown him away before the sheriff could find him?

Patrick Toben's final rebuttal witness was one of the deputies who'd examined the crime scene. He went back over details of the accident, deriding the "supernatural" explanations our witnesses attached to it.

He made a point of explaining why the Sheriff's Department hadn't investigated the Brussels sprouts field until 5:43 P.M. "We took a quick look right after the accident in case there was anybody hurt up there. Or anything, you know, important. But we didn't bother checking for tracks then because it was absolutely positively clear the car couldn't have come from any other location. It had to come off the cliff directly above the highway where it landed, no question." He stated that Fiat tire prints were of a size to be wholly obscured by truck tracks. "And at least four sets of truck tire tracks postdated the accident due to the landowner driving back and forth across his field to look down at the site."

And, to my chagrin, he explained why field-edge vegetation needn't have been crushed.

On cross, I hammered him hard for waiting fifteen hours to examine the field for tracks. I suggested that, because of it, his evidence and conclusions were mere guesses. I asked if he had any proof beyond his own supposition that truck tires had obscured preexisting tracks. We went round and round about what "proof" meant.

I asked him if he had any proof beyond his own supposition that Miller was driving the Fiat. We went around about how much information it takes to "know" something.

The deputy held his own.

When I was done, the prosecution rested.

I had one rejoinder witness.

Joseph Huizen, glowing with the thrill of equations that still worked out, took the stand.

If Patrick Toben objected to my line of questions, I could only call it a day. Joseph's testimony had nothing to do with the Miller case, not strictly speaking. But Toben was looking cocky after a good witness.

I gave it a shot. I asked Joseph if Reginald Fulmer's testimony about the crop circle had surprised him. I asked him what he'd done since learning Fulmer's theory that the circle pictogram represented a glucose molecule. Joseph could barely contain his excitement over his mathematical breakthrough. I let him ramble on about it.

At first, Toben didn't object. I caught a glimpse of him out of the corner of my eye; he didn't look concerned.

But as Joseph continued, I could hear Toben's chair scrape, almost feel him realizing it was too late.

Joseph said, "I am now convinced that something not of this world spoke to me the night the crop circle appeared. I am convinced that viewing the crop circle, believing it must relate to my need for glucose that night . . . I'm certain these things triggered my insight. I feel deeply that this breakthrough was a gift to me. That it was a communication from another place, perhaps another world."

He looked so much younger and stronger and happier today. The jurors must see that *something* had happened to him. I just hoped they wouldn't believe, as I did, that the something had been Joseph's doing, that the communication had come from an inner galaxy.

I said, "No further questions, Your Honor."

Toben had Joseph reiterate that he'd been in a state of organic hallucination when he'd received his so-called communication. He asked Joseph whether any two-dimensional rendition of a molecule could really be said to represent it, except by previous agreement between scientists. He asked if glucose was ever represented as swirled circles within circles in the scientific world.

Joseph admitted that it wasn't.

When Toben concluded, I said, "The defense rests."

Toben rose. "As you know, Your Honor, we have been unable to locate one of our witnesses, Maria Nanos. We have no further witnesses at this time. But we would ask that court be adjourned for the day so that we might continue in our attempts to locate her."

The judge called us over to sidebar. He asked Toben, "How likely are you to find this witness tonight?"

"I don't know, Your Honor. We have deputies and city police searching."

"Searching specific locations?"

"No." The assistant DA looked chagrined.

As much as I hated to launch into my closing statement, it was to Miller's advantage to wind this up before Maria was found.

"Your Honor, basically Mr. Toben is hoping the witness will walk right out in front of a police car. He has no reason to believe she's even in this state any longer."

"Well?" The judge regarded Toben over the tops of his reading lenses.

"We were able to locate her previously," Toben pointed out.

"And they lost her previously. Last time they found her in Big Sur. So it's likely she's left the county again." I tried to look impatient. "I would like to get on with the trial. I don't think the People have any reasonable expectation of producing this witness tomorrow."

"I agree." The judge checked his Rolex. "Let's get this trial over with. You've got three hours to finish up your closing statements. Let's try to keep them short and free this courtroom up, Counsel."

Toben watched me through narrowed eyes. Considering Alan Miller gave Maria Nanos her running-away money, I could hardly blame him for being suspicious.

Within moments, I stood before my comfortable-shoes-and-no-hair-spray jurors.

"Ladies and gentlemen of the jury," I said, "during my opening statement and during the assistant district attorney's, we spent quite a while discussing the meaning of the term 'circumstantial evidence.' We explained to you that it referred to what may be deduced from the circumstances surrounding the crime.

"The assistant district attorney is going to tell you in his closing statement that he's presented you with enough circumstantial evidence to convict Alan Miller. Circumstantial evidence . . . from a crime scene that has no tire prints where they should be, no broken vegetation where you would expect to find it, no witnesses, and . . . nothing else at all—nothing!—to prove my client was driving his car at the time. The assistant district attorney calls this 'circumstantial evidence' that Alan Miller committed vehicular manslaughter.

"Well, you don't have to accept that.

"You've heard from a psychiatrist who has testified for the prosecution in dozens of previous cases. He testified here that Alan Miller has absolutely no memory, conscious or unconscious, of having been inside his car when the accident happened.

"If Alan Miller wasn't in his car, it really doesn't matter where he was. If he wasn't in the car, you cannot convict him of this crime. It's that cut-and-dried.

"But the defense has, at great embarrassment to Mr. Miller, tried to explain the terrible thing that happened to him that night.

"You don't have to have an opinion or take a position about any of the information we've presented to you. We presented it because we felt you had a right to know where he was. But for the purposes of this inquiry, you do not have to believe anything except that the prosecution did *not* prove Alan Miller was in his car at the moment the accident occurred.

"That's the only question before you. Not whether or not we are alone in the universe. You've heard that many thousands of people have grown to believe we are not. You've learned that many of them are credentialed and credible people. You've seen photographs and video clips of some of the objects they've sighted.

"But these were shown to you so that you would not dismiss as lies or delusions the statements made by Alan Miller under hypnosis. They provide a context for a horribly traumatic experience that is, unfortunately, not an uncommon one.

"But you are not being asked to decide what you think about it or where you stand on this issue."

And, God, did the jurors look relieved to hear me say so.

"You are only being asked to decide whether the prosecution has proved—*proved* beyond a reasonable doubt—that Mr. Miller was driving his car at approximately two-thirty that morning.

"The prosecution has *supposed* it, and they have reconstructed where the hard evidence *should have been* if the accident had happened the way they claim it did. But they *did not* find that evidence. They did not prove anything except that Alan Miller's car landed on top of Francis Addenaur's. That's because, from the actual evidence in this case, no one could prove any more than that.

"So don't be distracted by the bigger debate about our place in the universe. We promised to provide you with an explanation of where Mr. Miller was that night, regardless of the derision that would be heaped on him because of it."

The DA could certainly have objected to that one. The jurors had avoided reading about the trial, had ignored Leonard Deally's scathing articles—in theory.

"But all of this is, in a sense, irrelevant. The prosecution has not proved Alan Miller was driving his car. It has not proved his injuries that night were consistent with a car accident. It has not even bothered, as we have, to present you with a scenario of where Mr. Miller was after the accident.

"How can there be no reasonable doubt that Mr. Miller was driving his car? Where are his tire tracks? What are the odds of them being obliterated in this convenient way? Where are his accident injuries—the lacerations, the compression injuries, the bruises? You saw photographs of the

258

cars. Do you believe Mr. Miller could have jumped out of that car without a nick? Do you believe he could have jumped out of that car and run so far neither the Highway Patrol nor the Sheriff's Department could find any trace of him for seven hours? And if so, why have they offered no evidence about where Mr. Miller supposedly hid himself?

"They haven't proved a thing, ladies and gentlemen. They don't have a single piece of evidence. They don't have a single explanation that isn't an outright guess. And it would be wrong to convict a man based on guesses.

"So you have to acquit Alan Miller. Because all explanations and theories aside, no one has proved to you that he was inside his car when the accident happened."

I looked at them, wishing some dramatic ending would occur to me.

It didn't. I said, "Thank you."

I returned to the table to sit beside Alan. He stared straight ahead, the corners of his lips turned down, tears gleaming in his eyes.

The assistant DA stood up and gave a stock speech about how important a part of our system the jurors were and how much the People depended upon and appreciated them.

Then he scoffed, "No circumstantial evidence in this case? Is that what the defense is asking you to believe? Why, they might as well be asking you to believe in ... flying saucers!"

I gave him points for that one.

Unfortunately, he didn't lose speed. He ran through every bit of evidence they'd presented, contrasting it with what we were asking the jury to believe instead.

"They tell you that in a field where a farmer routinely drives a big truck, you couldn't reasonably conclude that the farmer might have driven over a single set of tire tracks. They ask you instead to believe that the defendant's car was dropped out of the sky by a flying saucer.

"They quibble about the exact nature of injuries to the defendant. They tell you the injuries aren't consistent with a car accident, though we've presented abundant medical testimony that they are. They ask you instead to believe the injuries were caused by spacemen doing sexual experiments.''

And so on. By the time he finished his list, it was all I could do not to slink from the courtroom in shame.

I certainly had asked the jury to swallow a mountain of weirdness.

As the assistant DA walked back to his table, I noticed several jurors glancing into the pews.

I was afraid to turn my head. I was afraid I'd catch sight of Leonard Deally, bristling with indignation.

We sat through twenty minutes of the judge instructing the jury, his tone ponderous and pompous.

At four-forty, the jury was dismissed to begin its deliberations. The judge was obviously not one to sanction an early dinner.

He instructed the assistant DA and me to remain available from nine to six each day of deliberations, ready to return within an hour of being summoned.

But Toben had another trial coming up and asked for four hours' notice on certain days. I said I needed to return to San Francisco, and asked for a full day's notice. Behind us, spectators murmured. Some could be heard shuffling their way to the aisle. The noise level rose as the courtroom doors opened to let them out.

Toben and I wrangled with the judge for quite a while, trying to reach an accommodation. The judge, as cranky as an importuned parent, was determined to work out a varying schedule, depending on the day. I ended up agreeing to be in court by five-fifteen any day I was notified by eleven. I could return to San Francisco.

Then the bailiff cried, "All rise," and we watched the judge whoosh off to his robing room.

I gave Alan's arm a squeeze. His muscles were knotted so tight it felt like he was flexing. I tried to think of something uplifting to say, but I had so little practice.

With a sigh, I began stuffing my briefcase. Behind me, lingering spectators chatted, others hurried down the aisle. The open doors brought in waves of excited talk and laughter.

I tried again to console Alan. "It went okay. It'll be over soon."

He was sitting as still as a wax statue, staring at the empty jury box. I took my time putting away my notes; no use rushing into the hallway throng. At the prosecution table, Toben smiled at something a woman with a file folder was saying to him.

As we stood to leave, I noticed the bailiff returning to the courtroom, which seemed a little odd. He approached me, blinking like he had dust in his eyes.

He said, "Jury's reached a verdict."

"What?"

"The judge wants to reconvene now to hear it read." He didn't sound convinced it would be worth reading. "You're available now, right?"

"Yes."

I couldn't look at Alan. Instead, I watched the bailiff approach Toben, lean close, and speak to him.

Patrick Toben flashed me a wild look. We were probably mirror images of dread.

Behind me in the courtroom, I could hear rushing footsteps, voices in the hall. I heard spectators hurriedly returning to their seats.

Five minutes later, the bailiff announced that court was back in session. I watched the judge billow in and sit at the bench. It took him a few minutes to quiet everyone down and order that the jury be brought in. My heart was beating so fast it seemed to have forgotten how to pump blood to my brain.

In a daze, I watched the jury file in and take their seats. They didn't look at us.

Beside me, Alan visibly trembled. I wanted to apologize to him. My defense was so stupid, so crazy, that the jury rejected it within half an hour, out of hand, with hardly any deliberation at all.

The judge asked the foreman if the jury had reached a verdict on both charges.

The foreman said, "Yes, Your Honor, we have."

I noticed that her clothes didn't match; I'd chosen her for

that reason, among others. I'd hoped it meant she was no slave to the common view. Maybe she was just clueless.

I wasn't sure which would work most to my advantage.

The judge asked defendant and counsel to rise. We did.

The bailiff collected the verdict and handed it to the judge. The judge looked it over it and handed it back.

Finally, the foreman read it aloud.

"On the charge of vehicular manslaughter, we, the jury, find the defendant, Alan Miller, not guilty."

I grabbed Alan's arm. There was a roar of disapproval in the pews behind us. The judge rapped his gavel.

Startled, the foreman took a moment to continue. "On the charge of felony hit-and-run, we, the jury, find the defendant, Alan Miller, not guilty."

Leonard Deally shouted, "No!"

The judge rapped his gavel again, threatening to cite anyone else who spoke.

Alan Miller dropped into his chair, covering his face with his hands. He began shaking with sobs. I squeezed his shoulder. I found myself wondering if he wept with relief or guilt.

The judge told us to be seated. He polled the jurors, then thanked them at some length. He commented that they had witnessed one of the more unusual cases to be tried in his courtroom. Several of them laughed. A few nodded.

When he dismissed the jurors, I watched them file out. I still couldn't believe it. I was afraid one of them would turn around at the jury room door and shout, *No! What was I thinking?*

For a moment, the judge peered sourly over the tops of his reading glasses. Then he said, "The defendant, Alan Miller, having been acquitted of all charges against him, is hereby remanded to his own custody. And court is hereby adjourned."

The bailiff cried, "All rise," and again the judge departed.

I began congratulating Alan—or, more accurately, consoling him as he wept away the stress of the trial.

The assistant DA came and offered me a manly handshake, quipping, *"Klatu barada nikto."* When I looked bewildered, he explained, "It's what the spaceman says in *The Day the Earth Stood Still*." He tried to smile, but couldn't quite manage it. He lowered his voice. "You know what's really too bad? I think you believe your client. And I think you're going to go home and realize it couldn't possibly have happened the way he said it did. It couldn't possibly have happened any way except how the People presented it."

Spectators buzzed around us, saying something or other, trying to interpose themselves between me and Toben. I did my best to block their view of Alan until he could pull himself together. I lost sight of Patrick Toben.

Joseph Huizen stood on the other side of me. He began diverting people from our table, saying, "Not now, please; not now."

Alan finally got a grip, apologizing for the outburst.

I tried to soothe him, but I could barely keep still. It was finally sinking in: damn, I'd won. Against all rational prediction, I'd won this weird case. I wanted to jump on the table and dance, high-five everyone, phone Curtis & Huston and invite them to choke on it.

I noticed Joseph turning hastily. I thought perhaps he was leaving. I wheeled around, starting to thank him for his testimony and his support.

But he wasn't moving. He was standing very straight, elbows slightly bent as if about to engage in battle. His posture was so militant, so protective, it startled me into silence.

Leonard Deally faced Joseph as if in a showdown. The two stood frozen—Deally leaning forward to spray us with verbal acid, and Joseph apparently determined to shield us from it.

I caught my breath. Joseph was a sixtyish man, overweight and diabetic, standing before a priggish younger man with a bone to pick. That's all; nothing grander.

But they seemed to eclipse the battle between the People and Alan Miller. They were the true faces of this strange coin: Joseph had been given something, and Deally had had something taken from him.

In tomorrow's papers, Deally would write the story the way it was likely to be remembered: as an embarrassment to the legal system and an insult to science. But Joseph's work might eventually nudge the boundaries of orthodoxy. Watching Joseph hold his ground—and ours, too—I almost enjoyed a moment of optimism.

Good thing I'd built up my resistance.

The bailiff moseyed over then, expressing his preference for getting the courtroom cleared out so he could go home to dinner.

Deally flashed Alan a look, then turned and strode away.

The bailiff commenced shooing out other bystanders. On his way back past us, he patted Joseph on the arm and smiled.

"I saw the jurors looking at you in the pews during closing," he told Joseph. "You won this case for them!"

To me, he said, "But of course they'll say the deputy lost it by not looking in the field before the tracks got covered." He seemed to take satisfaction from the thought. "Come on, Judge says to let you out through chambers."

I gave Joseph a hasty hug, and turned back to Alan. He stared at the spot where Deally had been standing, stared as if the gorgon reporter had turned him to stone.

Or maybe he felt too guilty to leave the defendant's table.

I gave him a shove, forcing him to follow the bailiff. Guilty or not, he was a free man.

39

We left through the judge's chambers, where the judge indiscreetly agreed that the sheriff lost the case by letting the tire tracks get obliterated. Obviously our UFO evidence hadn't made a believer out of him.

But he complimented my closing statement. "The prosecution just didn't put your client in the car. They didn't have any of it—tracks, injuries, witnesses. And you didn't let them get away with it." He shook his head. "It's good you didn't close with that outer space stuff, though . . . that was a big waste of the court's time."

I smiled politely. Better to waste the court's time than Miller's life.

To avoid the press, we took a circuitous route out the back of the building. On our way, Alan grew progressively cheerier. He seemed to be realizing, at last, that he didn't have to worry about prison, that, except for a burnt house and a ruined reputation, he'd averted disaster.

Almost.

Ten paces into the back lot where I was parked, we saw Betty Addenaur. At first, I didn't recognize her. She looked frailer than I recalled, her shiny black blouse hanging loose, its flounced collar gaping over gaunt bones and wrinkled skin. Dark roots showed through her badly ratted hair.

She just stood there, ten feet from us, arms dangling.

Behind her in a nearby lot, sheriff's deputies parked their cruisers, perhaps preparing for a change of shift.

She said, "Ain't this always the way." One of her hands fluttered at her side like a drunk bird. "You kill my poor Francis and get away with it. And I have to hide so's they don't arrest me."

I took a step toward her. "Come in with us now. There's a good chance they'll drop the charges. We'll try to persuade them. The district attorney understands your grief."

I considered telling her Alan had already tried to cover for her. And I wasn't above changing my story and lying for her. Because I didn't want her to be right: I didn't want this to always be the way.

She made an angry chopping motion. "Just stop that, stop it! You'd like me to be arrested. But I got it covered this time." She squinted. "You don't want me out free. 'Cause I remind you of the real truth without any of the crap. I scare you, don't I?"

She would have, if she'd been armed. But she didn't have a handbag. She didn't even have a jacket.

"Francis used to say lawyers could get away with anything, but I never ever dreamed you'd get away with this. No, I really didn't think you would." She had the earnest voice of a drunk person who thinks she's fooling everyone. "I lost one good husband already. I used to promise myself I wouldn't lose another one and end up crying every night like my mama." Tears began to slide down her cheeks, taking her mascara with them. "I had the surgeries and I watched my figure. I watched what I said, and I did my very best with Francis. And ain't this always the way?"

Behind her, only a few parking spaces away, I noticed a white van. The one parked near Miller's house before the fire?

I extended my arm like a barrier in front of Alan. I took a backward step, trying to push him back with me. If the white van belonged to Betty Addenaur, we might be in trouble. I'd seen two men inside it before the fire.

It was dawning on me that Betty might not be alone

today. Her handbag and jacket might be in the van. With her accomplices.

I murmured to Alan, "Get back inside!"

Instead, he gushed, "Oh God, I'm so sorry, really." He slapped my arm away impatiently. "I'll do anything I—"

"Alan! She's not alone!" I could see movement in the van now. Someone was in there.

"Not alone? How could I be *more* alone?" She came flying at me, her hands knotted into fists.

Alan jumped in front of me, taking her pummeling.

"Alone, alone!" She kept sobbing the word. "Alone."

I could see bleeding gashes on Alan's neck. She was clawing him and he was letting her.

I got behind her, pulling her by the shoulders, trying to yank her away from Alan, detach her claws from his flesh.

She was so small boned it felt like I was grabbing a bird. She stank of cigarettes, booze, and body odor. I pivoted, hoping to keep my eyes on the van. But for a critical second, I had a face full of bleached, ratted hair.

Alan was still pleading with her. "Come in with us. We'll do everything we—"

"Watch out!" I screamed.

A passenger had leaped from the van, a man with a sandy crew cut. I recognized him from the day of Miller's fire.

He was Betty's minion, I was sure.

At the hospital, I'd stopped Betty Addenaur from taking "justice" into her own hands. But she'd gotten no satisfaction through the courts. She had only managed, with the help of the men in the van, to burn Alan's belongings. That couldn't compensate for the loss of a beloved husband.

So she'd come here to finish what she'd started. Her friends—employees?—would either use or hand her a gun. And she would kill Alan Miller just as (she thought) he'd killed Francis Addenaur.

I let go of Betty and began pushing Alan back. I waited for the sound of a gunshot, my dread half convincing me I'd already heard it.

I pushed Alan with all my might to force him back, to get

us both inside the building. I despaired of making it, but it wouldn't be for lack of trying.

I pressed the crown of my head and both hands against Alan's chest and I gave it everything I had. Despite his resistance, we almost reached the door.

That's when I heard the shots. There were two of them, rapid-fire. They sounded like caps or small firecrackers. But a breeze blew acrid smoke our way; there was no mistaking the smell.

I would have kept pushing till Alan went right through the side of the building, my adrenaline was so high. Fear had turned me into superchicken.

But Alan started pushing back hard, scooting me forward. I couldn't figure it out. Why would he run toward people who were shooting at him? It didn't make sense. And it pissed me off.

Finally, Alan grabbed my shoulders and flung me away like a doll. I ended up on my butt in the parking lot, making freaked-out hooting noises and scrambling to get on all fours so I could scurry to safety. My only consolation was that, so far, only my dignity had been wounded.

I'd finally won a case, and I was about to get murdered for it.

Goddam Betty Addenaur! I was shaking with rage as I struggled to my feet. I was ready to tear the head off the first person who didn't shoot me first.

But the men were kneeling in the parking lot, their backs to me, obscuring Betty Addenaur from my view.

I wasn't sure whether to run inside the building and hide or try to help Alan. From the rear, he seemed all right. The other men appeared busy at something, weren't noticeably threatening him.

Unsure and unsteady, I shuffled a little closer. That's when I saw the blood. There was blood all over the pavement.

I wanted to run away. Whatever the situation—and I was hard pressed to guess, at this point—I wanted to ignore it. I wanted to celebrate my victory and then go home. Back to

ny own little cocoon to deal with my own problems, which
were not seeming so bad anymore, not by comparison.

But I moved closer.

Alan was holding Betty Addenaur's shoulders, and the
two men, far from threatening him, seemed to be begging him.

"Please, you've got to lay her down. Let us look at her,"
the man with the crew cut urged. "Lay her down gently."
He was hunched close to her, his hands cupped as if prepared to hold her head.

But Alan seemed determined to keep Betty upright, to
lean her against him. He was muttering, "You're going to
be okay, you're going to be okay."

I could see that her black blouse was wet and sticking to
her scrawny chest. At least one of the two shots had hit her.

The other man, obscured from my view by Alan, was
saying something. I thought I heard my name, but I was too
aghast to understand or respond.

Alan was crooning, "Nobody's going to charge you with
anything. And you won't be alone; you can live with me, if
you like." His voice was so low it sounded like he was in a
barrel. "You're going to be all right."

The other man was definitely calling my name. He was
saying, "Ms. Jansson! Call nine-one-one! Hurry!"

I watched Betty Addenaur's eyes roll back in her head. A
bloody froth spilled from her mouth down her front, all over
the sleeve of Edward's jacket.

The man with the crew cut pried her out of Alan's grip,
laying her down.

Suddenly, behind us, there were repeated high-pitched
screams; they almost sounded like a car alarm.

I turned. A group of county workers had come out the
back door.

The man who knew my name yelled, "Call an ambulance.
Call nine-one-one right away!"

The flock disappeared inside.

The other man lamented, "I wish we had an ambu bag
out here!" He squeezed between Alan and the now-supine
Betty.

"I always meant to stick one in the van. Just in case."

Alan had been knocked out of his kneeling position. He
sat on the pavement in Edward's ruined suit, crying as if
he'd known Betty Addenaur his whole life.

I stared beyond him, over the shoulder of the crew-cut
man. I could see Betty's mascara-streaked face. Her eyes
and mouth were wide open. She didn't move at all.

And I could see the man who knew my name. It was John
Bivens, the paramedic who'd testified for us. He was ripping
open Betty's blouse. The man with the crew cut pulled off
his sweatshirt. He held it against a wound above her shriv-
eled breast.

There was some kind of leather strap and bag on her
chest. A holster?

The men exchanged pessimistic looks.

I backed away, pressing my knuckles to my lips. I could
see a gun lying in a pool of blood close by.

Betty Addenaur had had a gun, after all. But she hadn't
turned it on us, she'd used it on herself.

Alan was whispering something about the charges being
dropped even if he had to serve her sentence himself; that
she wouldn't always feel so alone, if she'd just hang on a
little longer.

But it was easy to see she was already gone.

Paramedic John Bivens and his partner, Barry Burns, did
what they could until an ambulance pulled up. By then
sheriff's deputies had sprinted out of the county building.

The deputies greeted the medics by name and they pushed
away a photographer who'd happened to come around to
the back of the building. They pulled me and Alan out of
the way. And after Betty was placed in the ambulance, they
herded the rest of us inside to take our statements.

John Bivens walked beside me into a basement foyer. "I
know this is a hard sight for a layperson. Are you doing
okay?"

I felt boggled, blown away, numb. "Yes." The deputies
unlocked a massive door and motioned us into a corridor.
"Why were you here?"

"My partner and I just came to tell you we were glad for

you. I wanted to wish you luck the other day, after I testified, but you were talking to someone in the parking lot. We just wanted to say that we know a lot of people are laughing at you and hassling you. You and Mr. Miller." He seemed embarrassed just mentioning it. "But we saw that light the night we picked up Dr. Huizen, so we know it's for real. And we just wanted you to know not everybody thinks you're . . . you know."

"That was your van in the parking lot the other day?"

He nodded. "That's how I knew which car was yours today. So I could wait for you."

"And on San Vittorio Road a couple of weeks ago?"

"You saw us?" He blinked as if his eye itched, then trapped his hands beneath his armpits. He obviously knew better than to rub his eyes with bloody hands.

His partner was up ahead in the hallway, talking to the deputies, saying, "She just reached into her blouse and pulled it out. We couldn't believe it! She was probably aiming for her heart—got it, too. We get a lot of suicides where a partner's died or run off and the survivor shoots herself in the heart. We had two last Valentine's Day."

Alan shuffled beside them as if he were a zombie.

John Bivens sounded embarrassed. "We sat out in front of Donna Nelson's house three or four times. I guess to see if anything like that was going to happen again, or if there was something different about the house—I don't know. We were just so tripped, we didn't know what else to do."

"I'm sorry everyone had to find out. Where you work, I mean. You must have taken a lot of teasing. I hope your boss wasn't too hard on you?"

Bivens stopped walking. He lowered his voice. "Actually, the insurance company, our employer's malpractice insurance, it freaked out. Especially after what the newspaper said about us having hallucinations. Insurance was afraid the company would get sued if it let us run any more calls. Because we'd been delusional while on the job; that's how they put it."

"What are you saying?" I looked at the fit young man. He seemed so straightforward and practical, and I'd just

271

seen how good he was in a pinch. How could an insurer conclude he'd been delusional?

"Well, to be fair to my bosses, the insurance company threatened to raise the rates big time if they didn't get rid of me and Barry. They said any call we went on from now on, the company could get sued for sending medics with a public history of hallucinations on the job." He shrugged. "Maybe it was the kick in the butt I needed to move on."

"I used to be a labor lawyer," I said. "I'll do anything I can to get you reinstated, both of you. No charge. Okay?"

His brows rose. Despite his brave front, he looked grateful. "If you really think . . ."

"Give me your phone number. We'll get right on this."

"God, that'd be great! Especially for Barry—he's got a mortgage and kids."

He glanced up the hall, at Alan trotting beside the sheriff. Farther ahead, a deputy inserted a key into an elevator lock. I'd be glad to leave the harsh fluorescence of the basement.

"If you're sure you're okay . . . ?" Bivens waited for my nod. "I'm just going to go talk to Miller for a minute. The way he's draggin'; just make sure he's not going into shock or anything."

He strode forward, catching up to Alan at the elevator door. "How you doin'?" I heard him ask.

Of all the people to be fired as a medic . . . Betty Addenaur's words rang in my ears: *Ain't it always the way?*

40

Fred Hershey came to the courthouse to find me after his last appointment of the day. He'd heard the closing statements, then he went out for a few minutes to answer a beeper call. In that short time, he missed the verdict. And when he got back to the courtroom, Alan and I were already gone.

While Betty Addenaur shot herself in front of us, Fred was having dinner downtown with Joseph Huizen. When he dropped Joseph in the parking lot to pick up his car, he noticed the crime scene tape. News reporters and photographers were swarming by then, as they would be for days. Worry made Fred hop out of his car and ask what was going on. It didn't take him long to track us to the Sheriff's Department.

We'd given our statements by then, and were sitting in a drab waiting room while the deputies did some last-minute paper shuffling.

A few of them knew Fred; they let him in to sit with us.

He spent most of that time talking to Alan Miller. I could tell by his soothing tone that he was worried about Alan, about his reaction to both the verdict and the shooting.

By the time Fred turned back to me, his manner was deeply clinical. But I couldn't afford to start expressing my feelings; right now, I'd drown in them.

273

I cut him off quickly. "Did Bustamonte and Shaduff get back?"

For a therapist, Fred sure could look avoidant. "Let's get you guys home and give you some dinner," he suggested.

"What's up? What did they say?" My God, they hadn't found evidence of Miller's guilt inside the mountain facility? They hadn't found evidence he'd fled behind its fence after the accident?

I could still see Betty Addenaur's slack, dead face. If Miller was guilty and I'd won him an acquittal, I'd helped pull the trigger.

"Or isn't this the place to discuss it?"

The main workroom of the Sheriff's Department, visible through the open door, was bustling; Friday night was apparently prime time.

Fred followed both my glance and my train of thought. "It's not that." His voice was quiet; he shifted a little closer. "They left a message at about two." He scowled, his thick brows shading his eyes in the overlighted room. "Shaduff was calling from his cell phone. He said they found something." He averted his gaze.

"What? Just tell me." I'd had too trying a day to mess around with the amenities, to wait for the right moment.

"I don't know." He gave me one of those really-look-at-you looks. "Before Shaduff hung up, as an aside, he said he hoped they hadn't been found, as well."

"What were his exact words?"

"I believe they were, 'We've definitely got something,' or maybe it was 'some activity.' Then he said, 'I hope it doesn't have us, too.' That was at two o'clock. I checked my machine again before and after dinner. Half an hour ago."

"Could you check it now?" It sounded like Shaduff was warning us they might get—what?—detained, attacked? It sounded like they might need help.

Fred stopped to soothe Alan again first. I tried not to be a jerk about rushing him. But Bustamonte and Shaduff had left for the Potemkin Lockheed at around noon. By two o'clock, they'd found something. It was now past six-thirty. They should have returned. They should have phoned back.

In the few minutes Fred was gone, we were brought statements to sign. We were given deputies' business cards (for my collection).

The party was escorted through the main room and out into the hall. I jotted down John's and Barry's phone numbers and promised to call them in the morning. I'd get started hassling their employer and their union rep. I'd get them reinstated if I had to wage a one-woman guerrilla war.

They left.

While waiting for Fred to return, I yanked a red garbage bag out of Alan's hand and threw it in a trash can. The deputies had asked him to remove his bloody jacket and place it inside. They were fussy about their furniture.

We owed Edward a suit.

The deputies also had Alan scrub his hands with Hexol, which was a good thing, since he kept rubbing his eyes.

Finally Fred walked toward us. He was shaking his head. "No message."

"Take me up there?" I didn't trust myself to drive; I felt dazed and foolish. I wasn't unaccustomed to the feeling, but I get tired of being flipped off and passed on the right. "Will you? I'll show you the way."

"Do you think we should spend a little time making sure Alan's . . . ?" There was no tactful way to finish the sentence, I guess.

"I'm okay," Alan said. "I'm just . . . I mean, God, poor lady."

I had to agree with Fred that Alan didn't look okay. But I didn't want to go up the mountain alone, not with only an hour of daylight left. I looked at Alan. "You want to come?"

"He's not up to it," Fred murmured.

Alan surprised me by saying, "You're going up Pine Flat and Bonny Doon Road, up to that area?"

Had I mentioned where we were going? "Uh-huh." I'd asked him about the place over lunch, but had I mentioned sending Shaduff and Bustamonte there?

"I should go with you." Alan waved away the objection

he could see Fred about to make. "I know the mountain. You can get into a lot of trouble up there. You better take me."

Fred was asking, "What kind of trouble?"

But I didn't want to waste time arguing. I started for the exit.

We stopped just long enough for Fred to pop the trunk of his Lexus and pull out his gym bag. He wasn't about to let Alan climb in with a spattered shirt and pants with bloody knees. He tossed Alan some sweat clothes. Using the car as a screen, Alan changed right there.

On our way out of the parking lot, we pulled behind an exiting news van.

I made a mental note not to watch the news tonight. The chances were slim to nil that we'd be congratulated for going out on a limb with the only defense that fit the facts. And juries were rarely praised for reaching difficult, unpopular verdicts.

The judge was right. The jury's quick verdict could only reflect reasonable doubt that Miller was in his car when it landed on Addenaur. The sheriff had failed to collect the necessary evidence and the prosecution had failed to prove it by other means.

It had probably been wise to introduce Miller's alibi, however strange—to offer no explanation would have damned him in the jurors' eyes. But no jury could have endorsed alien abduction so quickly and decisively. The verdict had certainly been rendered on the narrowest possible grounds.

That wouldn't matter to the press. The jurors would be excoriated and ridiculed for accepting the "spaceman defense." Reporters wouldn't bother being analytical when they could be sensational.

Betty Addenaur's suicide in front of the defendant and his lawyer, that would be the lead: a miscarriage of justice with tragic consequences. There would be only one side to the news coverage, the easy side. The monster of orthodoxy liked its food predigested.

We cruised past Shaduff's office, making sure he hadn't returned.

Then I told Fred how to get where we were going. Alan, in the back, suggested a quicker route.

I could see Alan's reflection in the rearview mirror mounted outside the door. He stared through the window, cloud shadows racing across his face. Only when we got near Davenport did he sit up a little. When we turned and started up the mountain, he leaned close to the car window as if inhaling the scenery.

He'd expected a guilty verdict. I could see it in his reverence.

I relaxed into my seat. Thank God Miller wasn't in jail tonight. At least I didn't have to live with that, didn't have to relive my own jail time.

The evening sun bathed fields in golden light. We sped around curves lined with horsetails in the shade and wild irises in the sun, past redwood thickets and Maxfield Parrish meadows, past tangles of wild roses and fields with grazing horses, past dark gullies and feathery meadows buzzing with mosquitoes and sprinkled with purple vetch. Here and there, odd rock formations rose like badly drawn castles.

Alan told Fred where to turn.

Ten minutes later, we spotted the dazzle-camouflaged water tank. Carl Shaduff's Range Rover was parked a little farther up the road, under an overhang of live oaks. The fenced facility wasn't in view; it was another quarter mile or so up the mountain. This was a less conspicuous place to park, but I doubted Bustamonte had appreciated the hike.

There was barely room for Fred to pull over.

I walked around the Range Rover, peering into the windows. I didn't see anything revealing inside. Two jackets lay across the backseat. Foil wrappers from two film rolls littered the passenger seat.

I looked up to find Alan walking toward the water tank, frowning as if he were seeing through it. He went behind it.

I hurried to catch up.

Alan was walking as fast as the wooded, viney terrain allowed.

"Alan!"

He didn't turn.

I didn't want to lose him, too, add him to the list that already included Shaduff and Bustamonte. And Maria Nanos.

"Alan," I called again.

He turned, looking bigger than usual in Fred's too-small gray sweats. Even in the shade of mixed forest, I could see his face was contorted.

"Maria," he said. "I wanted to tell you. She's not . . ."

"Not what?"

Fred was charging forward, in full doctor mode, ready to tone-of-voice us some more.

"What about Maria?"

"In Half Moon Bay, at the Denny's—"

"Alan?" Fred was looking seriously kindly. "Maybe this isn't the best time for you to be—"

I grabbed Fred's arm to shush him. "In Half Moon Bay?"

Alan knotted his fists, crossing them over his chest self-protectively. A response to having a psychiatrist freaking out about him?

"What about Maria?" I prompted.

"She's not the hitchhiker."

"What do you mean, she's not . . ." There was only one thing he could mean. "She's not the girl you picked up in Half Moon Bay?"

"No."

"But you said she was! You saw her picture in the paper, a picture of her at the crop circle, and you said she was your hitchhiker." I was too surprised to do anything but state the obvious.

"I recognized the picture, that's true," he admitted. "And we were looking for the hitchhiker, so I thought that's who was in the picture."

"But she said she was the hitchhiker." And besides, "When she came to Shaduff's office the night the police picked her up, you guys recognized each other."

"I recognized her from someplace else. But she wasn't the hitchhiker."

"Then who is she? How could you get confused about something like that?"

I glanced at Fred, half expecting him to offer a theory. But his lips were pressed into a resolute line, as if he resisted feeding Alan psychiatric terms and jargon.

"I dropped off the hitchhiker, another girl; I have no idea who. Brown haired and young like Maria. I dropped her off just like I said. I guess her face wasn't that clear in my head; I was mostly looking at the road." He put a hand over his brow as if checking to see if he was overheating. "When I saw the picture in the paper and recognized the face, I assumed it was her. Right then, I didn't remember anything besides what I told Fred."

I repeated, "But Maria said she was your hitchhiker. Why would she do that?"

"When she came to Carl Shaduff's and I saw her in person, I remembered. When she walked in, it came to me. I dropped off the hitchhiker—the real one—then I took the turn into Davenport to go home. And Maria, she flagged down my car. She pounded on my window. She begged me to help her."

"Under hypnosis, you didn't say anything about this." Fred sounded too calm.

"I didn't remember it."

"That's the function of hypnosis, to bring out what you don't remember."

No wonder Alan doubted the contents of the tape. He knew at least part of it was a lie. He knew something had happened in addition; he knew it as soon as he saw and recognized Maria.

If he was telling the truth now.

"You must have been very determined to keep this encounter buried," Fred continued. "Do you know why? Do you recall what else happened?"

"Like I said, she pounded on my car window. She kept saying a helicopter was chasing her. She said she was trying to camp up on the mountain, but a helicopter chased her away." He started rubbing his chest. "I know there are helicopters up here. Lockheed's building stealth bombers, and CAMP's looking for pot fields, and there's fire and medical helicopters, and military ones from Monterey and Travis. But I'd never seen a helicopter at night. And I couldn't imagine one chasing her—I thought she might be on drugs or something. I was going to take her home, let her sleep on my couch. She looked so scared; she was so young."

"And what happened?"

"I have no idea. As far as I know, we went to my house and I went to bed." He buried his fists in his armpits. "Except, obviously we didn't. Maybe the helicopter took us somewhere; maybe I mixed up a helicopter with a—That's why I ran after her the other day, when she came and asked for money. That's why I chased her; I couldn't stand not knowing. I couldn't stand wondering and wondering what happened, why this didn't come out when I was hypnotized. If maybe it was a helicopter that took us . . . I went after her to ask her, just ask where we went, what we did there."

"You didn't believe her story that she was abducted by aliens with you."

"I wasn't abducted by aliens!" He scowled at us. "My hypnosis was wrong—it left out the part about Maria, didn't it? Why should I trust any of the rest of it? It was all wrong!" He took a few gasping breaths. "I was a liar and a jerk for not saying so during the trial. And now Betty Addenaur's dead."

"Alan, don't you see?" Fred's tone was gentle. "You're looking for ways to deny what you heard yourself say on the tape. Especially now that you're safe, now that the trial's over. And after what you witnessed in the parking lot."

Man, was I confused. Did Fred think Alan was delusional about Maria *not* being the hitchhiker?

I tried to steer us back to the tangible. "Last Friday, what did Maria say when you caught up with her?"

Fred flashed me a look: Don't interfere with the Doctor-King.

"She looked at me like I was crazy. She might have even called me crazy."

"Alan," Fred began.

"Please, Fred! I need to hear this." I'd just watched Betty Addenaur shoot herself; I needed facts, not psychology.

"I asked Maria where we went after I picked her up in Davenport. She said, God, maybe I really did believe in flying saucers; maybe I really was mental. And she wiggled free of me. I ended up running after her, not running with her." He still looked shaken by her accusation. "I lost her in the crowd at The Boardwalk." He drooped, looking discouraged.

"Why didn't you tell me this before? I'm your lawyer— you're supposed to talk to me."

"She told everyone she was the hitchhiker. I couldn't contradict her. Especially after someone shot through the window. I mean, what if they were shooting at her? What if she had some good reason for saying that?" His expression begged forgiveness. "I didn't want to lie to you. Fred, I'm sorry—you spent all that money on expert witnesses and I didn't want to lie to you. Willa, you spent all this time." He closed his eyes tight. "I didn't want to lie about being abducted."

Fred and I exchanged glances. He was right about Alan; I understood that now.

There was no possible reason for Maria to claim to be Miller's hitchhiker if she wasn't. It only embroiled her in a court case, landed her in custody, and set the police looking for her. If she'd denied it, she'd have been just one more runaway, eventually falling through the cracks.

So Alan had lied, all right—to himself. He'd lied about Maria not being the hitchhiker. He'd intertwined memories of meeting her with prosecution testimony about helicopters. He'd rearranged his actual recollections so he could use them to negate the ones he'd repressed.

The trial was over now, and he was left to face the petrifying story he'd committed to tape under hypnosis. Alan Miller didn't need a lawyer anymore, he needed a psychiatrist.

Fred put his arm around him. "This acquittal was very much to be desired, Alan. For you to lose your freedom would have been a tragedy; you have every right to be happy with this result. As for me paying the expert witnesses, that was my choice. And you had no control over Mrs. Adde-naur. Her reactions and actions were her responsibility, not yours."

I smelled the cool pine of the forest and looked around at the dappled golden light on the duff. Throughout the trial, I had nursed every suspicion of Alan Miller, refusing to be-lieve he told the whole truth.

I still didn't know what the truth was. Patrick Toben might be right. It might have happened exactly as he'd pre-sented it: Alan Miller had gotten to Davenport later than he admitted. He'd been sleepy or drunk, and he'd taken a wrong turn, bouncing across a field and over a cliff, his Fiat tracks later obscured by the farmer's truck. He'd wandered from the accident, roaming the night away in a state of delusion and distress. And as he lay beside some road or in some field, he'd had nightmares based on an *X-Files* episode or a television movie.

I hadn't proved otherwise. I hadn't demonstrated it in court, though I'd won the case. And I certainly hadn't con-vinced myself.

But right now, watching Miller try so hard to fool himself about Maria, try so hard to discount the experiences he'd relived under hypnosis, I was sure of one thing: However much he wanted to doubt it, however hard he worked to deny it, Alan Miller absolutely believed the story he'd re-cited into Fred's tape recorder.

I'd preferred, at times, to hope he was lying. I didn't think so anymore.

It didn't necessarily mean it had happened that way. But I was finally persuaded he thought so. On the deepest possible level, despite all his protestations to the contrary, Alan Miller believed his horror story.

Maybe someday, safe in bed, I'd try to decide what I thought that meant. What thousands of stories just like it meant.

"We've got to find Bustamonte and Shaduff," I urged. "We don't have much light."

Alan turned away from Fred.

Fred said, "Alan, please. Try to forgive yourself for doing nothing more than allowing yourself to be hypnotized. And for being unable to censor yourself under hypnosis."

Alan, his voice husky, said, "The fenced-off area's up ahead. We can reach it faster through here than up the road."

"Let's go," I beseeched Fred. "While we have the light."

Fred's lips were parted as if he had plenty more to say. But when Alan started walking, he followed.

It would have been easy for us to stroll abreast, but I suppose none of us felt like chatting.

We were soon on uneven terrain, pine and oak forest with occasional stands of redwoods and open patches of duff. Within minutes, we reached a spot where a twelve-foot Cyclone fence, topped with barbed wire, turned a corner.

"The Potemkin Lockheed?" I asked.

"The—? Oh, yeah, I guess it does look like Lockheed," Alan agreed. "From where you stop your car and look in through the gate, it's a hike to get to this spot." Alan pointed back behind us. "But from the water tank, if you know where you're going, it's pretty close. Farther on, the fence turns a corner and stops at a gorge. For all intents and purposes, the mountain ends at this facility."

"Have you ever tried to get in?"

"Some parts of the mountain, I don't worry too much about fences. It's just folks wanting privacy or keeping their horses corralled. But up here, you've got Lockheed building missiles and bombers, pot farmers guarding their crops, local militia on makeshift shooting ranges. This far off the beaten path, you've got to take fences seriously. There's plenty of unfenced mountain—it's no use asking to be shot at or have dogs sicced on you."

"Do you have any idea what this place is?"

"No. I always assumed the government owned it; all those signs out front."

"Bustamonte thinks the military/Lockheed-looking stuff is just for show."

"Why does he think that? It sure looks real."

"I guess he thinks it looks *too* real." But Bustamonte was predisposed to look for the circle beneath the square.

Fred said, "If I could make a suggestion . . . let's go back to the car the other way, the long way, keeping to the fence. It's getting dark fast. We've got just enough light to try and spot Shaduff and Bustamonte through the chain-links."

As much as I didn't relish the hike, I had to agree.

We walked in silence, listening to the rustle of duff, the creak of tree limbs, the scramble of small animals. Through the wire mesh, I saw nothing but trees, vines, pecking jays. I saw no buildings, no vehicles, no helicopters, no goons. And no detectives.

It was fully dark by the time we reached the front entrance. But floodlights blazed above the gate, around the guard station, and along the road that curved behind the trees.

The front gate was unchained and open wide enough for a truck to roll through. A uniformed man stood just outside the station. A rifle was slung across his back. He spoke into a radio.

Tonight the place looked like Lockheed on steroids.

Two men trotted toward us. "Please identify yourselves and state your purpose," one of them barked.

He wore a security guard's uniform, not a military one.

I hurried forward. "My name is Willa Jansson. I'm looking for two men, Carl Shaduff and Bart Bustamonte."

No use being coy. If they had Bustamonte and Shaduff, I wanted to know right now.

One of the guards held up a hand, keeping us from coming closer. The other put his radio to his lips and walked away, speaking quietly into it.

Headlights in the parking lot popped on. A doorless Jeep sped toward the gate. Two more security guards jumped out.

One of them, craggy and overweight, approached. "You're looking for a Carl Shaduff and a Bart Bustamonte?" As if there were several.

"Yes. Are they here?"

He said nothing until he was close enough for me to smell the onions he'd had for dinner. He loomed for a moment. Was he going to try to detain us? We hadn't breached the fence.

"What's your business with these men?" He watched us suspiciously.

"They phoned and said they were at the water tank down the road. That's the last we heard from them."

"What was their purpose in coming here?"

"I don't know. I just know they're late and we're looking for them."

"Why?"

"We're going dancing. Do you know where they are or not?"

"A Carl Shaduff and a Bart Bustamonte were placed under citizen's arrest for trespassing at fourteen-forty this afternoon. They were later transported by Sheriff's Department personnel to the County Jail in Santa Cruz. You might try looking for them there."

"They were booked for trespassing? They weren't given citations and released?"

"No ma'am," the guard said. "The statute numbers are clearly posted on the fence; trespassing at this location is a criminal offense. Photography is strictly prohibited. Refusal to turn over photographic equipment and/or failure to leave when requested to do so will result in arrest and prosecution."

Jesus, the guy talked like a penal code.

I wanted to sit down in the duff, just sit there until some semblance of energy and stamina returned to my weary limbs and overtaxed brain.

While we'd hightailed it to their rescue, Bustamonte and Shaduff were being shuffled around the County Jail, right across the street from the courthouse.

They'd probably posted bail by now—probably not much more than a simple citation would have cost, just more of a hassle. More of a message.

"Did you come here in a vehicle?" the Stepford guard demanded.

"It's down the road."

He motioned to someone behind him, saying, "Escort these people to their vehicle."

We could have refused the escort. But a ride was a ride.

We barreled down the hill in the windy, doorless Jeep. The console had a radio with lots of buttons.

"So is this a military base?" I asked the driver.

He didn't say anything.

"Part of Lockheed?" Still nothing. "A dude ranch? A detox center?"

Fred put his hand on my arm to shut me up.

When we got out, I tried again. I asked the driver, "Is that place part of Lockheed?"

He replied, "It's private property."

Gee, no kidding.

But the tight security told me one thing. Bart Bustamonte was wrong about Alan Miller having hidden out there.

The guard waited for us to get into Fred's Lexus. Then he drove behind us all the way to the main road.

It was a step down from a helicopter escort, but just as effective.

41

I hoped Fred continued to feel good about the verdict after assessing the publicity's effect on his practice—and writing all the necessary checks.

Right now, he seemed a trifle annoyed with Bustamonte for reminding him to include the cost of bail.

We were sitting around Shaduff's office, behind his new, shuttered windows. Alan had excused himself, leaving to go back to Edward's. He'd declined Fred's repeated offers of company, saying he wanted to be alone. I knew the feeling.

"I would have left you guys another message," Shaduff complained, "but those dickheads kept us waiting for the sheriff almost two hours, just sitting in the parking lot on the ground. Wouldn't let me near my cell phone."

"Searching us, taking the film out of our cameras—can you imagine?" Bustamonte looked scorched. He'd have sunburn blisters on his rain-coast Washington forehead tomorrow. But he didn't seem disappointed in the outcome of the trip. "There's definitely something up there!"

"No shit, Sherlock." Carl Shaduff looked like he'd had enough of Bustamonte and then some. "I kinda got the hint from the half dozen burly guys ripping film out of our cameras and getting us arrested!" To me, he said, "It's obviously some kind of government-contract facility. It's no eccentric recluse with a tall fence, not with that kind of security. It's a branch office of Lockheed or some other military subcontractor. Probably quite a few of them in odd nooks around the state." Another fed-up glance at Bustamonte. "Nothing sinister about that."

"Uh-uh," Bustamonte disagreed. "They've got serious shit up there—maybe even alien spacecraft. Did you see how many guards came at us from every which way when we jumped that fence? They've got cameras in the woods. They knew where we were parked. They are hiding something big up there," he repeated. "They're as well guarded, if not better, than Lockheed. And they're more remote, better hidden, and nobody knows about them, not even our people." He nodded with satisfaction. "That will soon change! I'll be making some phone calls and getting people down here ASAP."

Shaduff looked beleaguered. Fred looked alarmed.

"You'll be staying in Santa Cruz?"

"On my own dime, of course. You know, it's not really well known that Lockheed operates here, at the end of a mountain road, miles from any convenience." He raised his brows. "And now here's this other place, practically its twin, but unmarked!"

"Granted—they're doing some kind of top-secret research work; you can tell by the setup. But that's not a crime. They don't want protesters and mobs of job applicants up there, so what?" Shaduff demanded.

"So they've been brilliant about keeping a low profile, keeping tucked away, keeping the spotlight on other locations. That tells you something right there. It tells you they're doing something important."

"Every research and development place thinks it's doing something important," Shaduff pointed out.

"This is exactly where you get UFO sightings. Over air force bases, nuclear test sights, NASA research facilities, Lockheed Space and Missile—and spooky places with no name on the gate."

He looked at us, then grinned. "You think I don't know it sounds crazy? You think I have no perspective how this strikes people who haven't put ten years into researching it? But do me a favor before you write me off as a nut."

Fred obliged him by asking, "What?" He handed Bustamonte a check for his days of testimony and, presumably, his bail.

"Just keep your ears open. See if you don't start hearing more and more astronauts admitting what they saw in outer space, NASA workers breaking their silence about what they know, military pilots speaking up. See if you don't hear more and more nice people like Alan Miller telling weird stories." He looked over Fred's check, then he tucked it into his pocket. "There's going to be plenty of discussion here in Santa Cruz about these issues!" he predicted. He smiled at me. "I'm so glad you invited me down."

I'd helped make Santa Cruz a flakier place. I guessed the downtown merchants would be coming around soon to measure me for a statue.

42

By morning, the police confirmed that the bullets from the gun that killed Betty Addenaur matched the ones fired through Carl Shaduff's window and into Colonel Kraduck's vest.

Her grief had made her eclectic as well as crazy. She'd tried to shoot Miller (or perhaps herself) at the hospital. Then she'd tried, with partial success, to burn down his house. Then she'd tried to shoot him (or perhaps me) through a window after following us to Shaduff's office.

Later, her fury over Fred's testimony led her to sneak in through his window and throw things around his condo. I don't know why she chose more drastic measures for Colonel Kraduck. Maybe, like later commentators, she found him to be my most impressively "American" and unassailably "sane" expert; maybe his credibility had infuriated her. She probably tracked him by following me or Carl Shaduff to the hotel. She saw Kraduck alone in the parking lot and fired at him from a borrowed car. The bullet casings (and half a jug of kerosene from setting Miller's fire) were found right on the passenger seat.

The colonel, ironically, owed his life to my mother. Two nights before encountering Mother in the courthouse corridor, he'd seen the helicopters hovering outside his hotel window.

Then, an unstable-looking woman (his description) accosted him in the courthouse and began besieging him about his years at Travis Air Force Base. He decided the two events, taken together, could be interpreted as a threat. He was being told to shut up, and he didn't like it.

So he put on his bulletproof vest, and he let Bustamonte know he was on his way to Travis. He was prepared to have a shouting match with former colleagues who seemed to think they could make him stop speaking the truth.

My mother saved the life of someone who, years ago, had had her arrested. There was a kind of beauty in it, not quite on par with Joseph Huizen's crop circle resembling a glucose molecule.

I phoned her with the news.

She mulled it over for a minute. "Maybe he'll place a higher value on pacifists now."

"Or on bulletproof vests."

"You know who we're having for dinner, Willa? Speaking of all this UFO business? He knows you, he says."

"Who?"

"Reggie Fulmer."

"What? Why? Why are you having that ass over to dinner?"

I could tell by the brief silence that she didn't agree with my assessment of him.

"When WILPF held that meeting down there, remember? To organize a teach-in about how this UFO nonsense is being used by the Republicans as an excuse to raise the defense budget—"

"Mother, I don't want to get into all that. Just tell me why Fulmer's coming to dinner."

"This *is* why. I *am* telling you. He's going to be one of our featured speakers."

"Fulmer thinks the UFO threat is being used to beef up military spending?" Maybe she was kidding. Maybe she'd developed a sense of humor in her old age. "A guy who believes crop circles are subliminal messages from Merlin?"

"He doesn't say he believes that! Just that they're a pictographic phenomenon." She continued hastily, "But what he absolutely doesn't believe is that they have anything to do with UFOs!"

"And that's enough to get him on your debunkers faculty?"

"Well, we were going to invite some scientists. But they believe two men made all the crop circles in England just because the men said so—we want someone more analytical than that. Reggie says scientists are too easily taken in by publicity hounds."

She was always good for a straight line.

I hung up. Reginald Fulmer at my parents' dinner table. I looked out the window of Fred's condo. The sky was blue with feathery trails of cirrus clouds. A breeze played through the open window, carrying the scent of mowed lawn and jasmine.

I tried to think of a reason not to keep seventy-five miles between me and my wonderful but highly exasperating kin.

My second call was to Cary Curtis. If I still had a job waiting, that would be reason enough. But it proved to be a quick conversation.

Cary wasn't impressed that I'd won Miller's case. "What do you expect from a Santa Cruz jury?"

He asked me when I'd be cleaning out my office.

I phoned John Bivens, the paramedic who'd been fired for telling the truth under oath on the witness stand.

"I still want your case," I told him. "You might be my first clients"—albeit pro bono—"in a new practice. I'm thinking about moving down here."

"You'll like it," he assured me. "Except during tourist season. And weekends when the students are in rut."

I packed my bag and went downstairs to thank Fred for his hospitality. If I'd been shanghaied, at least it had been to a tree-lined beach town. And the favor I'd repaid had been a huge one.

I found Fred at his kitchen table, slumped over a cup of coffee. I'd never seen him look so tired. But then, I'd never seen him unshaven, either. I'd never seen his hair uncombed, much less ungelled.

The sight stopped me short. I dropped my suitcase in the doorway and walked slowly toward him.

"Fred? Are you okay?"

I prayed he wasn't going to tell me the thing I most dreaded hearing—that Alan Miller was indeed guilty, that Fred had, during hypnosis, implanted the memories of his wild alibi.

Fred's behavior had certainly been odd: getting the DA's permission to hypnotize Miller, calling in a business lawyer to represent him, breaking the doctor-patient privilege to play Mickey's tape for me, disappearing for two hours in the middle of our witness prep. Now that I'd done all he'd hoped—or, judging from his downcast face, more than he'd hoped—would he confess to me that my client was guilty, after all? In helping to free Miller, had I also helped delude him?

"Fred!" I repeated. "What's up?"

He looked at me, his eyes red rimmed. "I wish I knew. It happened again, just now. I came downstairs to make some coffee. I was going to go back up and change into my running clothes, take a run. Coffee'd be ready when I got back. Then I'd set out some breakfast, have a shower."

I noticed for the first time that Fred was in plain cotton pajamas resembling hospital scrubs.

I walked to the table, squatting beside him. "So what happened?" Close up, he looked ill. I was getting spooked.

"Nothing. Nothing at all happened, except that it's almost two hours later. Two hours later and here I still am in the kitchen. I don't have my running clothes on. I haven't been back upstairs. I haven't been anywhere or done anything, not that I'm aware of. And yet"—his eyes widened—"all that time passed."

He'd lost two hours this morning. As he'd lost them the night I was preparing his testimony? The morning he'd set out to go running but, when I saw him later beside my car, hadn't broken a sweat?

"What are you saying, Fred?" I knew what he was saying. That he'd experienced "missing time."

"You asked me the real reason I brought you down here,

Willa." He sounded bone weary. "This is it. What Alan Miller described, I'm afraid . . ."

"That it's been happening to you, too?" I didn't know how to respond. "Have you been hypnotized?"

He shook his head. "I didn't want to taint my testimony for Miller. In case the DA asked if I'd ever experienced anything like it myself, I didn't want to have to answer yes. I didn't want to undercut my credibility."

"You've been getting up too early, that's all." All I could make myself believe. "You've been under stress and you've been driving yourself too hard. The most likely explanation is that you've been dozing off, catching up on your sleep. You're exhausted—your body's just forcing you to slow down."

"Maybe," Fred agreed.

"Weird ideas are contagious, Fred. I've seen it with my parents a hundred times. Some conspiracy theory starts out seeming too far-fetched, even for them. But the more they hear about it, the more normal and plausible it begins to sound. And next thing I know, they've bought in. It makes perfect sense to them and they revise their version of reality to accommodate it. That's what this UFO stuff is doing to you. If you'd never heard all this from Miller, from the UFOlogists, you'd be fine with the idea of nodding off now and then."

I wondered if he'd risk going to a hypnotist. If I were him, I wouldn't tempt fate. I wouldn't jeopardize a relatively comfortable worldview.

He leaned forward and embraced me. In a brisker tone, he said, "Thank you, Willa."

I knew he wasn't endorsing my advice. He was thanking me for taking Miller's case. I understood now the secret worry that had fueled his request.

I hugged him back. Whatever else might need to be re-solved, we'd done it. We'd won.

43

I wanted to say good-bye to Alan Miller. I wanted to make sure he was okay. I knew today's paper would be especially brutal.

I knocked at the door of Edward's little house. Edward would be home from Panama in a week or so. But Alan's place would be fit to rehabitate before then.

We'd added the final piece to the arson investigator's report: Betty Addenaur had kerosened the area around Alan's heater, then clicked on the *high* button and left. It had probably taken hours to ignite. The damage had mostly been confined to the front corner of the house. Alan's landlord had already contracted out the repairs. Alan agreed to do the finishing work himself so he could return sooner.

I knocked again. It was ten-thirty on a gorgeous Tuesday morning. Maybe Alan was out mushroom hunting, enjoying the freedom he'd almost lost. I was turning to leave when I thought I heard a sound inside.

I hesitated. Maybe Alan heard the knock but wasn't answering. The man was entitled to his solitude. He'd been through enough to make anyone become a hermit for a while. And he'd certainly seen enough of me lately.

I knocked again. Again, I thought I heard a stirring.

I tried the door, finding it unlocked. I pushed it open

slowly, hating to invade his privacy, afraid I might catch him in a depressive's dishabille.

I found him semiconscious on the floor. His face was battered and bleeding. One of Edward's wooden chairs had been shattered against a wall. A leg of it, splintered and with nails protruding, lay covered in blood beside Alan.

"Alan!" I bent over him. The blood on his face was still sticky.

Alan opened his eyes. One was swollen half shut from a scratch across the lid, perhaps from a sliver of the chair leg. Blood soaked his T-shirt. His sweatpants were ripped and bloody at the thigh.

"Alan?" My voice was squeaky with worry. "What happened? Oh my God."

I flung my arm back as if the phone would rush to meet my hand. I scooted backward to grab it. I dialed 911.

"We need an ambulance," I told the operator.

"No. Wait." Alan's voice was woozy. "How long—Oh, shit." He sat up, holding his head.

I gave 911 Edward's address.

"No, no, let me talk." He reached for the phone.

"I don't know what happened," I told the emergency operator. "He's been beaten."

"Let me talk!"

I handed him the phone.

"I'm okay; don't send an ambulance. But you've got to get the police after an old couple with a teenage girl." He was curled over his knees, he could barely keep upright. "They're going to kill her."

"Oh, Jesus," I said to him. "Maria?"

"Maria Nanos is her name. Tell the police her name. They know about her already. Her grandparents went crazy. They're going to kill her. Tell them." He repeated Edward's address. "I think they're on foot, maybe still in the neighborhood."

He hung up, getting to his feet and staggering into the bathroom. I followed.

He splashed water on his face. "She came here for money again. For help. This morning. They were right behind her."

He winced. "They must have been watching the house. Followed us here from court or something." He gripped the sink with both hands. Blood dripped onto the wet porcelain. "They smashed things. They screamed I was her boyfriend and they'd kill me."

He grabbed my arm, pulling me toward the back door. "Come on," he said.

"You're in no shape—Lie down." He looked a little better without the dried blood, but his nose appeared broken, his cheek and eye were hugely swollen.

"I'm okay—just had to clear my head." He continued pulling me toward the kitchen. "They're going to kill her, come on."

"Come where?"

"They dragged her out the back. It wasn't that long ago. They can't have gotten far, not if they're on foot." He bent forward so that momentum carried his shuffling body along.

In the kitchen, he made an effort to straighten. He grabbed his torso, crying out. But he stayed upright. He picked up speed, going out the back door.

There were drag marks and scuffed areas all across the dirt. Alan stopped and braced himself on Edward's kayak so he wouldn't fall. I passed him on my way out the gate.

I looked up and down the tranquil alley. "Maria!" I screamed. "Mariiiiia!" I put as much noise as I could into it, but there was no response.

I ran left toward the coffee shop and tried again, still getting no response.

Not knowing what else to do, I doubled back to the other end. I noticed trash cans tipped over in the next alleyway, their contents spilled.

I dashed across the street. I raced past the downed cans. I could hear Alan's footsteps, in ragged groupings, behind me.

When I got to the end of the second alley, I called out again.

This time, I thought I heard something in reply. A faint, high-pitched cry.

Up ahead, the alley became little more than a gravel path

flanked by huge tangles of wild roses and ivy-covered sheds behind crumbling Victorians.

"Maria?"

I heard a thin whistle, the kind of scream you force out of your lungs during a paralytic nightmare.

Alan caught up to me, running past me like he'd pitched himself down a hill, his gait uneven and staggering.

We could see them now. They were in a bower of ivy and weeds, an overgrown portion of a half-collapsed garbage enclave.

Maria was on the ground, arms raised to protect her head. Her grandparents were stooped over her in their elegant suits, attacking her with the ferocity of tigers.

Alan reached them a few seconds before me. He grabbed a garbage pail lid as the grandfather was about to smash it back down onto Maria. I could hear Alan grunt as the grandfather turned to attack him.

The grandmother was using her fists and feet, kicking Maria's legs over and over and screaming something in another language. I ran up behind her and tried to pull her away, to pull her farther down the alley.

It was like taking hold of a huge wild dog. She was strong and crazy, clubbing my head with her fists, shouting shrill epithets I didn't understand.

"Run, Maria," I called to her.

But she just sat there trembling, forearms crossed over her head.

As Alan and I struggled with her grandparents, she curled into a fetal position and began sobbing. I thought I heard her calling for her mother.

A police siren screamed in my ear. Pivoting and staggering with Maria's grandmother, I hadn't noticed the car racing down the alley toward us.

It took the cop, me, and Alan to get Maria's grandparents into the back of the police car.

Alan turned his attention to Maria. The cop phoned for an ambulance. And I watched the old couple in the backseat of the police car collapse into convulsive sobs.

When the ambulance came for Maria, the paramedics

insisted on taking Alan, too. One of the medics, despite his haste, was good enough to tell me he didn't see anything drastic or permanent in their injuries. But they would definitely need stitches and painkillers and X rays.

As the ambulance pulled out of the alley, the grandparents extended their arms toward it as if to hold on to their wounded child. I saw the stricken looks on their faces, the anguish, the sorrow; they loved Maria. She'd told me they did, but until now, I hadn't believed her.

I'd been scared many times these last few weeks, but this moment was the worst. No alien being could be as frightening as someone truly crazy who truly loves you. Mickey and Joey proved it to Fred, and Maria had just proven it to me.

The policeman took notes while I described what I'd seen. Then he gave me his card, yet another one for the stack. I gave him my phone number and promised to make myself available to the district attorney, if necessary. He drove away.

I walked the few blocks back to Edward's, trying to smell the flowers and catalog the profusion of plants poking through back fences.

I tried not to think about things that could reach out of the sky and pluck people away. I tried even harder not to think about things that could reach out of people's own homes to do much worse.

I walked back into Edward's yard, closing the gate behind me. I went into the kitchen and locked the back door.

The living room was a mess. The wall was damaged where the chair had splintered, and there was blood on the floor.

I swept the mess away and mopped the hardwood with peroxide.

I was sitting on the couch wondering what to do next, whether to stop at the hospital, go back to Fred's, or just drive on home.

I looked up to find Edward Hershey himself standing in his doorway, obviously very surprised to see me there. His hair was long and wild, the tips of his windblown curls bleached golden. He sported a medium-length beard, and his face was tanned a deep clay. He looked like someone who'd just sailed through the Panama Canal.

He dropped his duffel bag, mouth gaping.

"Willa!" He looked alarmed. "What are you doing in my house? What are you doing in Santa Cruz?"

"The short answer?" I smiled. "I moved here."

bibliography

Andrews, Colin, and Pat Delgado. *Circular Evidence*.
  Phanes Press, 1989.
Blum, Howard. *Out There*. Simon & Schuster, 1990.
Bova, Ben, and Byron Preiss, eds. *First Contact*. Plume,
  1990.
Brookesmith, Peter. *UFO: The Complete Sightings*.
  Barnes & Noble, 1995.
Bryan, C. D. B. *Close Encounters of the Fourth Kind*.
  Knopf, 1995.
Cousineau, Phil. *UFOs: A Manual for the Millennium*.
  HarperCollins West, 1995.
Drake, Frank, and Dava Sobel. *Is Anyone Out There?*
  Delta, 1994.
Fiore, Edith. *Encounters*. Ballantine Books, 1989.
Good, Timothy. *Alien Contact*. William Morrow, 1991.
Grossinger, Richard, ed. *Planetary Mysteries*. North
  Atlantic Books, 1986.
Hancock, Graham. *Fingerprints of the Gods*. Crown, 1995.
Hopkins, Budd. *Missing Time*. Richard Merck, 1981.
Horn, Arthur. *Humanity's Extraterrestrial Origins*. A. & L.
  Horn, 1994.
Jacobs, David M. *Secret Life*. Fireside, 1992.
Korff, Kal K. *Spaceships of the Pleiades*. Prometheus
  Books, 1995.

Bibliography

Lindemann, Michael, ed. *UFOs and the Alien Presence.* The 2020 Group, 1991.

Mack, John E. *Abduction.* Ballantine Books, 1994.

McKenna, Terence. *Food of the Gods.* Bantam Books, 1992.

Mouton Howe, Linda. *Glimpses of Other Realities.* Vol. 1. LMH Productions, 1993.

Randles, Jenny. *UFOs and How to See Them.* Sterling Publishing, 1992.

Sagan, Carl. *The Demon-Haunted World.* Random House, 1995.

Sitchin, Jecharia. *Genesis Revisited.* Avon, 1990.

Strieber, Whitley. *Breakthrough.* HarperCollins, 1995.

———. *Communion,* Century Hutchison, 1987.

Terr, Lenore. *Unchained Memories,* Basic Books, 1994.

Thompson, Keith. *Angels and Aliens.* Fawcett, 1991.

Thompson, Richard L. *Alien Identities.* 2nd ed. Govardhan Hill Publishing, 1995.

Vallee, Jacques. *Revelations: Alien Contact and Deception.* Ballantine Books, 1991.

———. *Passport to Magonia.* Contemporary Books, 1993.

Videos

Above Top Secret
Alien Archaeology (with David Childress)
The Alien Autopsy
Aliens Among Us (with Bill Hamilton)
Are We Alone? (with Jecharia Sitchin)
Arthur Horn; Need to Know (with Arthur Horn)
Beamship Trilogy (with Billy Meier)
Bob Lazar; Excerpts from the Government Bible
Countdown to Alien Nation (with Michael Lindemann)
Crop Circle Update (with Colin Andrews)
Cropcircle Communiqué
Dulce Update (with Sean Morton)

Bibliography

Farewell Good Brothers

Flying Saucers Are Real, Vol. I (with Stanton Friedman)

Flying Saucers: The Government Coverup (with John Lear)

From Legend to Reality

Geometric Metaphors of Life (The Meru Foundation with Stan Tennan)

The Grand Deception: UFOs, Area 51 & the U.S. Government (with Norio Hayakawa)

Hidden Memories: Are You a UFO Abductee? (with Budd Hopkins)

Hoagland's Mars I: The NASA-Cydonia Briefings (with Richard Hoagland)

Hoagland's Mars II: The UN Briefing (with Richard Hoagland)

Hoagland's Mars III: The Moon/Mars Connection (with Richard Hoagland)

John Mack; Human Encounters with Aliens (Thinking Allowed Productions)

Lost Was the Key (with Leah Haley)

Masters of the Stars (with Britt and Lee Elders)

Messengers of Destiny (with Britt and Lee Elders)

The Mystery of the Crop Circles (with Michael Hesemann)

One on One: Alien Abductions

One on One: Phenomenon of the Crop Circles

The Pleiadian Connection (with J. Randolph Winters)

Roswell Revisited

The Secret of the UFOs (with Marc Davenport)

A Strange Harvest (with Linda Moulton Howe)

UFO Cover-up: Down in Roswell (with Paul Davids)

UFO Diaries, vols. 1–6

UFO Secret: The Roswell Crash

UFO Sightings (with Michael Lindemann)

UFOs: A Need to Know

UFOs & the Alien Presence (with Michael Lindemann)

UFOs and the New World Order (with Michael Lindemann)

UFOs & Underground Bases (with Bill Hamilton)

Bibliography

UFOs: Secrets of the Black World (with Michael Hesemann)
UFO's . . . The Hidden Truth
UFOs: The Secret Evidence (with Michael Hesemann)
Undeniable Evidence (with Colin Andrews)
Visitors from Space: Films of the Nations

These videos are available from
Lightworks Audio & Video, 1-800-795-TAPE,
and UFO Central, 1-800-350-4639.

LIA MATERA

HAVANA TWIST

A WILLA JANSSON MYSTERY

Attorney Willa Jansson's mother has never balked at breaking the law, especially not for a good cause. So when Willa learns her mother has flouted federal regulations and gone off to Cuba, she figures it's just a harmless pilgrimage to lefty Graceland. But when her mother doesn't return with the rest of her peacenik tour group, Willa fears the feds might consider the trip "trading with the enemy"— with a penalty of ten years in prison and a $100,000 fine. Worse, her mother's bleeding heart may finally have gotten her into more trouble than she can get herself out of.

> "Willa Jansson is among the most articulate and surely the wittiest of women sleuths at large in the genre."
>
> —Marilyn Stasio,
> *The New York Times Book Review*

Now available from Simon & Schuster

LIA MATERA